Praise for
*The Professors' Wi*ves' Club

"As an NYU alum, I enjoyed the behind-the-scenes escapades at the fictional Manhattan U in *The Professors' Wives' Club*. Joanne Rendell has created a quick, fun read about a wonderful group of friends."
—Kate Jacobs, #1 *New York Times* bestselling author of *The Friday Night Knitting Club*

"The four women in *The Professors' Wives' Club* who risk it all in pursuit of life, love, and green space in New York City are smart, funny, and real—friends you'd want for life. Rendell doesn't shy away from tough issues, but her light touch and readable prose make this charming first novel a delight."
—Christina Baker Kline, author of *The Way Life Should Be*

"Alternately amusing and serious, with a little literary mystery thrown in for good measure, Rendell's smart and pleasing tale of friendship and self-actualization has broad appeal."
—*Booklist*

"Joanne Rendell's irresistible debut novel is a captivating look at an ivory tower Peyton Place filled with intrigue, heartbreak, and hope."
—Michelle Yu and Blossom Kan, authors of *China Dolls*

continued . . .

Written by today's freshest new talents and selected by New American Library, NAL Accent novels touch on subjects close to a woman's heart, from friendship to family to finding our place in the world. The Conversation Guides included in each book are intended to enrich the individual reading experience, as well as encourage us to explore these topics together—because books, and life, are meant for sharing.

Visit us online at www.penguin.com.

"As a self-absorbed undergrad, I never realized that the really juicy stuff was going on outside of the frat parties and late nights at the library! The women of *The Professors' Wives' Club* are a force with which to be reckoned. Joanne Rendell's debut novel is smart and suspenseful with an intriguing Edgar Allan Poe backstory. I cannot wait for Joanne's second novel."

—Robin Kall, host of *Reading with Robin*,
a WHJJ Providence radio show

"Joanne Rendell has created characters who will inspire, entertain, and keep you hooked from the very first moment you meet them. I loved spending time with these ladies and only wish *The Professors' Wives' Club* were a bit longer so I could have more time with these wonderful women."

—Yvette Corporon, senior producer for *Extra*
and author of *Peeing in Peace: Tales & Tips for Type A Moms*

Also by Joanne Rendell
The Professors' Wives' Club

CROSSING WASHINGTON SQUARE

Joanne Rendell

NAL Accent
Published by New American Library, a division of
Penguin Group (USA) Inc., 375 Hudson Street,
New York, New York 10014, USA
Penguin Group (Canada), 90 Eglinton Avenue East, Suite 700, Toronto,
Ontario M4P 2Y3, Canada (a division of Pearson Penguin Canada Inc.)
Penguin Books Ltd., 80 Strand, London WC2R 0RL, England
Penguin Ireland, 25 St. Stephen's Green, Dublin 2,
Ireland (a division of Penguin Books Ltd.)
Penguin Group (Australia), 250 Camberwell Road, Camberwell, Victoria 3124,
Australia (a division of Pearson Australia Group Pty. Ltd.)
Penguin Books India Pvt. Ltd., 11 Community Centre, Panchsheel Park,
New Delhi - 110 017, India
Penguin Group (NZ), 67 Apollo Drive, Rosedale, North Shore 0632,
New Zealand (a division of Pearson New Zealand Ltd.)
Penguin Books (South Africa) (Pty.) Ltd., 24 Sturdee Avenue,
Rosebank, Johannesburg 2196, South Africa

Penguin Books Ltd., Registered Offices:
80 Strand, London WC2R 0RL, England

First published by NAL Accent, an imprint of New American Library,
a division of Penguin Group (USA) Inc.

First Printing, September 2009
10 9 8 7 6 5 4 3 2 1

 REGISTERED TRADEMARK—MARCA REGISTRADA

LIBRARY OF CONGRESS CATALOGING-IN-PUBLICATION DATA:
Rendell, Joanne.
Crossing Washington Square / Joanne Rendell.
p. cm.—(The Professors' Wives' Club)
ISBN 978-0-451-22784-3
1. Women college teachers—Fiction. 2. College teachers—Fiction.
3. Triangles (Interpersonal relations)—Fiction. 4. Manhattan (New York, N.Y.)—Fiction. I. Title.
PS3618.E5747C76 2009
813'.6—dc22   2009016562

Set in Fairfield
Designed by Alissa Amell

Printed in the United States of America

For Benny

Acknowledgments

To my editors, Anne Bohner and Kara Cesare. I am so lucky to have worked with *two* such incredible—and fun—people. Anne believed in *Crossing Washington Square* and nurtured it with enthusiasm and a keen eye. Kara then eagerly embraced the book and with astute editing, she added a whole new and fabulous twist. My smart, kind, and hardworking agent, Claudia Cross, cheered and fostered the project from the start. She's a perceptive reader and a great hand holder when I need it.

To my first readers, particularly Yvette Manessis Corporon who is always with me every step of the way and is the best critique partner a writer could ask for. Also, Dina Jordan, Jean Railla, and my mother-in-law, Jana Lewis (whose gusto for getting the word out about *The Professors' Wives' Club* was also staggering—and hugely appreciated).

To those writers whose work inspired many of the themes in *Crossing Washington Square*. Lauren Baratz Logsted for her insightful introduction to the short story collection *This Is Chick Lit*. Janice Radway for her important work, *Reading the Romance*. Elaine Showalter, whose book *A Literature of Their Own* inspired my passion for women's fiction back when I was an English literature undergrad. Bestselling romance author Jennifer Crusie, who has written many great essays about the unfair maligning of the romance genre. All the contributors to the book *Chick Lit: The New Women's Fiction* (edited by Suzanne Ferris and Mallory Young), in particular Alison Umminger, who let me use ideas and some words from her chapter "Supersizing Bridget Jones." Jennifer Weiner, whose books I love and who writes some kick-ass pieces in defense of women's fiction. Scholars such as Stuart Hall, Judith Butler, and the late Michel Foucault, whose works have always inspired me—not just in my writing, but in my life too. The members of the Romance Writers of America, many of whom I met for the first time at the annual convention in San Francisco (your professionalism and success, your support networks and open arms, are truly amazing and should be an example for all writers). Finally, Richard Canning, my PhD supervisor, who taught me that books by white, straight, and elite guys are not the *only* valuable subjects of academic study!

To Melanie Feakins, who lives too far away but is still the greatest friend. As a smart, young (not to mention well-dressed) professor, she was a big source of inspiration for the characters in this book.

To all those who helped me bring *The Professors' Wives' Club* into the world, sending postcards, filming and producing my book trailer, writing reviews, endorsing the book, helping me throw parties, or just being incredibly supportive friends along the way. Susan Basalla, Bonnie Bernstein (thanks for helping me send my little book to the stars!), Judy Bodor, Jessica Brody, Christine Baker Kline, Corey Fabian Borenstein, Lisa Coulthard, Amanda Darrach (your copyediting eye was invaluable), Dominique DeLeon, Heidi Ford, Kate Jacobs, Robin Kall, Blossom Kan, Luke LaCroix, Irene Levine, Sabrina McIntyre, Haleh Nazeri, David Pattillo, Mia Pearlman, Marisa Polvino, Benny Rietveld, Emma Robertson, Lauren Smythe, Phil Treble (your designs rock), Don Troop, Scott Von, Julianna Von, Kathryn Walton, Michelle Yu, and Mary Ann Zissimos. Also, thanks to the Girlfriend's Cyber Circuit and all the other bloggers who toured and reviewed my book.

To all those who read *The Professors' Wives' Club*. How gratifying it was to hear from so many of you and to learn which characters you liked best and whom you most identified with. It seems there are many Hannahs out there! Your kind and appreciative words make novel writing worth every minute.

To all those friends who make my other life, my mum life, so fun and rewarding. Leslie Kauffman, Lenora Todaro, and Jaclyn Schulton, in particular. I will never forget how you stood by me (as I supervised your tunneling children)! Thanks also to my fabulous Benny-sitters, Nikki D'Errico and Holly Ponticello.

To all my family, especially my mum, Kate Matthews. Even though I'm supposed to be old enough to stand on my own two feet, she manages to be the mum I clearly still need. She's the first person I call with good or bad news, she sews the holes in my trousers, she weeds the borders, and she's a wonderful grandmother to boot.

Finally, to Brad and Benny. You two make me laugh and smile every single day. Brad, you inspire me, love me, support me without question, and make me thank my lucky stars I made the long trip to middle-of-nowhere Canada to meet you. Benny, this book is for you because you're a reader now—and because I love what a sweet, funny, sensitive, and clever person you're turning out to be.

"Elinor, this eldest daughter . . . had an excellent heart;—her disposition was affectionate, and her feelings were strong; but she knew how to govern them: it was a knowledge her mother had yet to learn: and which one of her sisters had resolved never to be taught.

Marianne's abilities were in many respects quite equal to Elinor's. She was sensible and clever; but eager in everything: her sorrows, her joys, could have no moderation. She was generous, amiable, interesting: she was everything but prudent."

—Jane Austen, *Sense and Sensibility*

CROSSING
WASHINGTON
SQUARE

One

Rules of the Classroom

Down in the basement of Manhattan University, Professor Rachel Grey was about to speak when the whiteboard behind her gave a violent shudder. Rachel instantly snapped her mouth shut and glanced around the dingy room. Amid the thirty students slumped on chairs in front of her, one or two rolled their eyes and a few more sighed. The seminar rooms in Manhattan U's basement sat only a few feet above New York's busy subway tracks, and since class started an hour ago, at least nine trains had clattered by. Each time the room would be filled with a deafening roar, desks would tremble, and the air vents just below the cracked ceiling would clang and shake. Each time, Rachel would wait impatiently for the subway to rumble past.

Rachel stood up when the train moved on. Her left hand slipped over her amber blouse, checking that all the buttons across her chest were secure, and downward, trying to smooth the stubborn wrinkles that always plagued her black pants. Meanwhile, her right hand picked up her battered copy of *Sense and Sensibility* from the desk. Finally, she moved around her desk and pushed an unruly honey curl off her face.

"Okay, so we've talked about Elinor Dashwood," she said with an eager smile. "What about her sister Marianne?" Rachel paused and looked around the room. Her expectant gaze was met with a sea of glazed eyes and absently doodling pens.

"As we discussed," Rachel went on, her voice a little trill as she tried to motivate the unresponsive class, "Elinor Dashwood is the prudent and reserved sister who in the end embraces romance and emotion and marries her true love, Edward Ferrars." Rachel looked up but still her thirty undergraduates didn't stir. Again, she persisted. "How does Marianne's character develop and change through the novel?"

The room was silent—hot, airless, and silent. The doodling pens had stopped scratching across notepads, and even thundering Broadway, just a few feet above, had ground to an eerie halt. Rachel could have sworn she heard a wristwatch ticking.

After a minute of agonizing silence, Rachel waved her hand toward the class. "Anyone?" she asked, a pleading tone beginning to creep into her voice.

Still nothing.

Disappointment kicked in Rachel's gut, and the smile on her face began to fade. When she started this job at Manhattan U just over six weeks ago and moved to New York, she'd left a lot behind her. She'd quit the University of North Carolina, where she'd been for the past six years, five of those years as a grad student and then the past year as an assistant professor. She'd said good-bye to colleagues and students whom she loved. She'd parted with her rickety but cozy house with its rambling yard and picket fence. And for the first time ever, she moved to a place a long, long way from her parents. In Chapel Hill, Rachel was only a couple hours from their small house in Virginia, and every month or so she'd drive home to enjoy a weekend of her mother's cooking and warm smiles and some unadulterated spoiling from her dad.

Rachel had taken all these good-byes and separations in her stride, however. New York and her job at Manhattan U were going to be the start of a new and exciting life—or so she'd thought when she first arrived. She'd always dreamed of living in New York, and Manhattan U was one of the most prestigious schools in the country. Not only that, Rachel needed a fresh start. She was happy back in North Carolina; mostly she was happy, anyway. But memories of Justin continued to rattle around in the house they'd shared together for a few years. She saw him around town sometimes too, still driving the same red '95 Corolla with its dented bumper. They would wave awkwardly to each other, but that was all. He never stopped; she never tried to flag him down. He'd put his foot on the gas and continue onward to the high school where he taught history and coached the baseball team. Rachel would watch him disappear, sad but also relieved.

In bustling and teeming Manhattan, there would be no chance of running into Justin. More than that, the big city and the new job were going to consume and excite Rachel in a million different ways. There wouldn't be a spare moment even to think about Justin, let alone dwell over what had gone wrong between them. And when she first arrived in the city, all these aspirations for her new life seemed set to come true. She'd landed herself a great, if tiny, apartment in faculty housing on Bleecker Street. Her office had a window, which was a big deal at Manhattan U, apparently. The English department was full of big-name scholars who, up until now, were just names on her bookshelf. Best of all, her fall classes filled up immediately. In fact, for this very seminar, the one she was teaching today, she was allowed to admit only thirty students, but over sixty students had applied to get in.

After the initial high of the first few weeks, things had started to shift—to slide, in fact. Rachel couldn't put her finger on why or how. All she knew was that interacting with her colleagues was proving tough. Many of them seemed uninterested and aloof, and it left her feeling uncomfortable, inferior, and rather lonely. Her teaching, which back in North Carolina had always come so naturally to her, was proving even harder. Rachel was perplexed about what she was doing so wrong. But what was clear was that as each week passed she seemed to be losing her confidence and her ability to engage her students. As this happened, the students would sit in front of her looking more uninterested, more bored, and increasingly resentful. It hadn't helped when, after a few weeks teaching in a breezy, light-filled seminar room on the twelfth floor, her classes had suddenly been moved to this stuffy, clanking, and vibrating basement. A time-tabling error was the excuse she was given for the change. But whatever the reason, the move to the basement only made the stultifying atmosphere in her class even worse.

Today things seemed to be hitting an all-time low.

"Come on, guys," she said with a tight, beseeching smile. "Somebody must have something to say."

Rachel looked around the room, trying to catch her students' eyes and willing them to talk. Even though most of these students were only a decade younger than thirty-one-year-old Rachel, she felt like a very old schoolteacher looking out at a class of stupefied fifth graders. And this prompted in Rachel a flicker of frustration. Why were they such hard work? she wondered. It wasn't as if she were asking them difficult questions. Indeed, fifth graders could probably answer tougher questions than the ones she was currently posing. And why weren't they itching to talk about the book? How could they have nothing to say about Austen? They'd all wanted to be in this class, hadn't they? There was a long waiting list, and each of them had had to fight for a spot. Yet now they looked like they'd rather be pulling out their own toenails than sitting here in Rachel's class discussing *Sense and Sensibility*.

Still eyeing her students, Rachel contemplated, not for the first time, whether it really was her own semicelebrity that had brought these students to her class, rather than the content of the course. Last year, Rachel's first book had been published. *Reading for Love and Friendship* was based on her PhD dissertation and looked at popular women's fiction and the phenomenon of women's book groups. Surprising both herself and her publisher, the book did remarkably well. It received some great reviews in academic journals, followed by a small but glowing review in *The New York Times*. Then, when a researcher at *Oprah* saw the *Times* review, the woman contacted her and invited her onto the show. Rachel spent an exciting yet surreal day in a television studio in Chicago, and for a full five minutes she found herself sitting opposite Oprah Winfrey—*the* Oprah Winfrey—talking about book groups. Oprah had smiled and asked questions, the audience had clapped, and the cameras and studio lights (so many of them) had caught Rachel looking slightly awkward, but nevertheless delighted. After the show aired, Rachel's book even sneaked onto the *New York Times* bestseller list for a couple of weeks.

It all seemed like a dream now, those exciting times that had happened nearly a year ago (and which had served as a much-needed pick-me-up when she was still licking her post-Justin wounds). But it had happened, and it was thanks to the buzz around her book, the *New York Times* review, and the appearance on *Oprah* that she'd been offered the job at Manhattan U. The dean of arts and humanities had contacted Rachel personally and made the offer.

Rachel couldn't help wondering now, however, whether her fleeting time in the limelight was going to be her undoing. She thought back to the posts she'd read on the Web site Rate-My-Professor.com a few days ago. It was a self-destructive thing to do, reading these anonymous reviews by her students, but she couldn't help herself. She was desperate to know why her classes were bombing. The comment had read: *I saw Professor Grey on* Oprah. *That's why I took her course, Popular Women's Fiction. I thought it would be a breeze reading all those easy books like* Bridget Jones's Diary *and* The Nanny Diaries. *But it isn't. She's making us read all this old stuff and lots of dull theory.*

Rachel's course definitely wasn't a breeze. Sure, there were some fun, contemporary novels to read, but there was also Jane Austen, the Brontës, and Edith Wharton too. There was feminist theory to grapple with and cultural studies to understand. Even so, Rachel thought the students would enjoy it all. She thought they would come to class animated and engaged and willing to take up the challenge. How mistaken she was turning out to be.

"Greg?" Rachel said finally, nodding at a student in the front row. Rachel hated to pick on students, but today they were giving her no option. Besides, Greg's long, jeaned legs, sprawled out in front of him, were beginning to annoy her. She'd nearly tripped on them twice since class began.

Greg Shapiro shifted uncomfortably in his seat and then, looking up from under his fraying baseball cap, he glared at Rachel. "I didn't make it to the end of the book," he muttered.

"You didn't finish—" Rachel began, her hazel-green eyes wide and disbelieving.

She was cut short, however, when a female voice piped up. "Marianne starts off romantic and, you know, passionate and all that. And she ends up all, like, sensible and marrying the old captain guy."

Rachel turned and looked over at Heather Glades, a petite girl in a sparkling DANGER: HOT T-shirt.

"Colonel Brandon, Heather, *not* Captain," Rachel corrected. But, instantly feeling guilty for her snappish tone, Rachel softened her voice and added, "But, yes, you're exactly right."

Heather gave a small grin and a wiggle of satisfaction. With a student showing interest, Rachel felt a buzz of excitement. She paced toward Heather and asked with a fresh smile, "And do you find Marianne's arc satisfactory?"

Heather's eyebrows furrowed together and her mouth dropped open. "Huh?"

Rachel kept smiling. "Did you find it satisfying that, as you said, Marianne ends up *sensible* and married to Colonel Brandon?"

Shaking her head, Heather spat out, "Nah, not really." But then, after pausing for a second, she added with a blink, "Well, maybe. I mean, he's kind of hot, in that smart-older-guy kind of way."

A small ripple of laughter traversed the room, and Rachel looked quickly, excitedly around, hoping a discussion might at last ignite.

"Anyone else want to add their thoughts?" she asked, feeling her chest beginning to bubble with anticipation.

The group lapsed into inert silence once again. The excitement in Rachel's chest waned and she felt anger suddenly flickering inside her. She took a deep breath and tried to calm herself. Rachel didn't lose her temper often, but she did have a nasty habit of letting her feelings show too much, of telling people exactly what she thought and how she felt, of wearing her "big ol' heart" on her sleeve, as her grandmother used to say.

Rachel's emotions were never far from the surface. That fact had gotten her into trouble in the past. Like the time she'd sobbed wretchedly to a librarian back at UNC when the computer she was working on crashed and she lost the assignment she'd been toiling over all day. The librarian—a wiry, rigid man with oversize glasses—was clearly not used to such displays of emotion and asked security to remove her from the library. Rachel's sensibility, as her beloved Austen would have called it, had also cost her Justin, of course. "Overemotional," "oversensitive," "overreacting." These were some of the words he'd thrown at Rachel when they fought and, near the end, they'd fought a lot. It so annoyed her that Justin described her in this way, but she knew deep down that he was probably right.

Rachel also knew that, of all places, she must keep composed and cool in her classroom. She knew she must quell any fury or emotion bubbling inside her when teaching. But today it was proving difficult. The apathy of her students was aggravating her beyond words. Luckily, though, as the silence continued and Rachel could feel her anger beginning to rise up to her chest, she was saved by the door clattering open. Peter Zadikian, the chair of the English department, paced into the room. Rachel twirled around, surprised by his sudden and unannounced entrance, but Peter didn't see her. He was too busy studying the open book in his hands.

As Peter continued into the room, still with his head down and his thoughts on the fluttering pages in front of him, Rachel asked, "Can I help you, Peter?"

Peter's gaze jerked up to meet Rachel's. His forehead immediately crumpled and then, as he turned his eyes from Rachel to the class in front of her, his wide, pale eyes shot open even wider.

"I'm so sorry," he stammered, snapping his book shut and pushing a hand through his rumpled salt-and-pepper hair. "So sorry, Rachel. Wrong room. I'm in the wrong room."

A few students tittered and whispered. Rachel ignored them and offered Peter a supportive smile. "No problem. I get the wrong room all the time down here. This basement is a maze."

But Peter wasn't listening. He was already backing out the doorway. As he grabbed the silver handle and began pulling the door closed, Rachel noticed a pinkness tinting his otherwise noble cheekbones. Something about his flush of embarrassment made her think of the emperor with no clothes finally recognizing his nakedness. It was a sad but sweetly human sight.

When the door banged shut and Peter was gone, Rachel turned back to the students. She was surprised and relieved to find her earlier sparks of anger had been extinguished. The interruption had given her a moment to regroup and she was ready to try again.

"Come on," she said, smiling once more, "any other comments on Marianne and her marriage to Brandon?"

It seemed like the class was gearing up for another stubborn silence until Zach Gerritsen, a broad-shouldered student who sat behind Greg Shapiro, muttered something long and inaudible under his breath. Even though Rachel didn't catch his words, the students around him clearly did. They giggled, shoulders heaving, into the backs of their hands.

Straightaway, Rachel's fury reignited, this time with more force. She moved toward Zach and said, with her face deadly serious, "What did you say?"

Zach lolled back in his seat and gave an innocent smile. "Nothing."

Rachel leaned in and laid an open palm on his desk. With her cheeks blooming with anger, she repeated, "What did you say?"

Zach continued to smile, but there was a small flinch of panic on his lips, and his eyes darted left, then right—he was looking to his neighbors for help.

"What did you say?" Rachel asked one more time. Her cheeks were now on fire.

Zach was beginning to look genuinely scared. He opened his mouth to speak but was halted by Greg Shapiro's languid baritone.

"He said," Greg retorted with a gruff laugh, "that Marianne hooking up with the colonel dude is about as barf-making as a hot prof like you hooking up with Professor Zadikian."

The class unleashed a chorus of laughter, and Zach's mouth instantly fell open; he was clearly horrified by the treachery of his classmate. Meanwhile, Rachel whirled around and glared at Greg. Greg, unfazed, pushed back his cap and leveled his gaze with hers. This was his revenge for being picked on earlier; Rachel could see it in his mocking eyes and the defiant curl of his upper lip. She was now livid—unquestionably, uncontrollably livid. She could feel anger pulsing in every vein of her body.

Rachel eyeballed Greg, on the cusp of telling him exactly what she thought of him and his lifeless, uninterested classmates, when the whiteboard gave out a loud thud and began its trembling and unstoppable crescendo. Within seconds, the room was roaring, rumbling, and clanging as the six train stormed by once again. The din made Rachel even more infuriated, and then, spotting a flicker of amusement rippling across Greg's small, deep-set eyes, Rachel flinched. She was overwhelmed with an urge to slap him, but she managed to stop herself. She'd never hit anyone in her life, and she certainly couldn't start with one of her undergraduates.

She felt ashamed that the thought of slapping Greg had even crossed her mind, yet her rage and her disappointment at how badly the class was going didn't abate. Finally she recognized that it was time to remove herself from this situation. There was still an hour of class to go, but she knew she had to leave. If she didn't leave she might lash out or cry or do something equally embarrassing. And so, while the vibrations and shudders began to ease and the subway rumbled onward on its journey downtown, Rachel glared at Greg one last time and then pushed past him toward the front of the room. There, she scooped a pile of books into one arm and threw her old leather backpack over the other. She took three long strides toward the door and, with one hand on the handle, Rachel turned back to the class, her chin raised in defiance, and barked out with her voice slightly strained, "I will see you next week, and next week I expect you to have finished the book *and* have something interesting and intelligent to say."

With that, Rachel opened the door, stepped into the hallway, and, without turning around, let the door thud shut behind her.

At the same moment, twelve floors above, Professor Diana Monroe looked around at her seven postgraduate students sitting at the wide oak table. Seven faces looked back at Diana, each one eager and expectant.

"Let's look at stanza fifteen more closely for a minute," Diana instructed, pushing herself back in her chair.

The students bowed their heads and, with their eyes flitting across the books in front of them, they urgently counted the stanzas of Sylvia Plath's "Daddy." Leaving her own copy of the poem on the table, Diana stood and walked behind her class and around the seminar room. She passed the wide window facing south, and as the morning sun peeked through Manhattan's twinkling, towering downtown buildings, it glinted and flashed on Diana's neat rimless glasses. Amid her coal black hair, which was pulled back into an unfussy barrette at the nape of her neck, a few silver strands—the almost imperceptible testimony to her forty-one years—glistened too.

The room was silent except for the distant hum and buzz of a bustling, late-morning Manhattan. As Diana neared the back of the room, she stopped and, with her back straight and her hands clasped tidily in front of her, she recited the five lines of "Daddy" she'd instructed her students to look at. Her voice was slow yet strong. She gave each word the time, breadth, and power she felt it deserved.

When she was finished, Diana said nothing for a few moments and peered out of the window toward the ornate cornices of the neighboring Manhattan U building. Reciting Plath always left her breathless. It also seemed wrong to Diana to clutter her own words too closely with Plath's. Plath's poetry needed space—immense space. While she stood quietly granting this space, her small group of graduate students shifted their eyes from the poem up to their professor. As ever, their gazes were focused and attentive. Diana had masterful control over her classrooms. She had the grace and flair of a world-class conductor; even her silences were watched, understood, and revered by her obedient orchestra of students.

"Responses?" Diana asked finally, her piercing blue eyes scanning the class.

As always, Charlie Hern was first to speak. He leaned his slight frame forward and scratched his wiry red beard. "The vampire imagery in the stanza is intriguing," he began. "The Daddy figure has morphed through the poem from Nazi to devil, but now Plath is figuring him as a vampire." Charlie paused and pushed his spectacles up his nose. "It is an interesting tweak, with possible homoerotic implications."

The student opposite Charlie sighed. Diana shifted her gaze across to Greta McClean, a willowy student with heavy blond bangs. Diana said nothing but raised her right eyebrow: a small gesture that gave Greta permission to speak.

"The vampire is Ted Hughes," Greta said, with a sullen flick of her bangs, "*not* Daddy. This stanza is all about how Hughes left Plath for another woman. It's about him sucking her dry and then abandoning their marriage."

Greta's words jabbed at Diana's chest and she flinched. Her flinch was small, though—infinitesimal. Not one of her students saw. Diana was used to hearing words like these, after all, and she was used to covering up the pain they wrought. It had been five years now since Graham had left, five years since the day he'd walked out on their marriage for another woman—just as Ted Hughes had done to Sylvia. And over the last five years, while Diana repeatedly taught Plath's poetry and listened time after time to students' simplistic readings of Plath's sorrow, Diana had become a master of disguise. The sorrow of her own abandonment was searing, but she cloaked it well.

"Greta." Diana spoke, her voice as calm as ice. "Remember, the text is our focus. Biographical details must not interfere with our readings."

She paused briefly, as she circled back around the room. When she arrived at the front of the class, she leaned over and prodded the book on the table.

"Let's come back to Charlie's point," she said with a nod. "What is the significance of the vampire metaphor at this point in the poem? What is Plath trying to achieve by using it?"

A lengthy discussion began to unfold. Diana slipped into her chair and, from the head of the table where she sat, nodded, prompted, cautioned, and encouraged her students onward. In no time at all, the earlier pain in her chest had subsided to a dull and distant ache, an ache she was used to, and an ache she'd carried with her for five long years.

Two

Office Hours

Back in her office in the English department, Rachel pounded her fists on her desk. Pens shook in the chipped University of North Carolina mug to her right, and to her left three sheets of paper, which had been teetering on the edge of the desk for nearly a week, finally billowed to the floor. Even the heavy silver photo frame holding the picture of her mom and dad wobbled back and forth. Beating her cluttered desk seemed the only way to deal with the waves of rage, followed by panic, tossing and rolling in Rachel's chest.

"Goddamn it," she cried out, as she continued to pound.

Rachel was infuriated with her students and even more infuriated with herself. Getting so riled up and then storming out of her classroom was completely unprofessional—and utterly perilous. Students had a lot of power these days. One stupid move by a professor could lead to bad student evaluations at the end of the semester, and even just a couple of poor evaluations could put Rachel's hopes of getting tenure in jeopardy. Manhattan U often boasted about their excellent teaching standards, and for any professor wanting a lifetime job here, it was essential to maintain consistently good student evaluations.

Also, if a student were to complain about Rachel to their parents— to their parents who paid a lot of money for their son or daughter to be here and who might even be potential donors to the university—the consequences could be even more immediate. *Will I get a warning?* Rachel wondered, as panic squeezed in her chest. *Perhaps I might even get fired on the spot?* She may have been head-hunted by the dean for this job, but that did not make up for the fact that she was still junior here—and thus easily disposable. Rachel, her one successful book, and her appearance on *Oprah* were just small potatoes compared to the colleagues who surrounded her, with their numerous books, prestigious grants, and their years of teaching experience. Unlike them, Rachel could be easily ejected from the university.

The thought of her colleagues sent another wave of infuriation and panic rippling through Rachel. No doubt if she got fired for what she'd just done, her new colleagues wouldn't be too sad to see her go. They might even be glad of it. Not that she thought they hated her; they just seemed so indifferent, so unforthcoming. Before arriving in September, she'd dreamed of befriending her new superstar colleagues, going for coffees with them, sharing research ideas, going for dinner in their cool, book-lined Manhattan apartments. But these fantasies fizzled fast. With the exception of Peter, the department chair, and a few other junior faculty, most of the other professors in Rachel's department could barely remember her name, let alone spend any time talking to her. On a good day, Rachel put her colleagues' aloofness down to their hectic lives teaching, writing reviews for *The Nation*, lunching with their editors, or retreating to their Catskills country homes. On bad days, however, Rachel couldn't help thinking it was more personal. She had a sneaking suspicion that, unlike her students, her colleagues were unimpressed by her sojourn on *Oprah*. She also suspected they didn't approve of her book and her scholarship.

Rachel sensed in her new colleagues the kind of disapproval that her beloved mentor back at UNC had always cautioned her about. "Be warned, Rachel," Professor Tally McGuiness would say, shaking her head and gesticulating with her long, elegant hands. "At other universities, especially the more traditional ones, you'll find people aren't so accepting of the kind of work we do; in fact, sometimes they are downright hostile." Professor McGuiness had been Rachel's PhD adviser. She was the one who supported Rachel's interest in women's book groups and encouraged her to take seriously the popular fiction these book groups often chose to read. Professor McGuiness also happened to be a big name in the academic world, and her ground-breaking book about romance novels, which she wrote in the seventies, was an international success and had been reprinted numerous times.

"Some of our colleagues in the world of English literature think that studying books that are popular is beneath them," she would go on to say. "They think popular fiction is fluff and that only *serious* or old literature is worthy of academic investigation. You should have heard the grief and ridicule I received when I first started my research on Harlequin novels!" Tally would then wave her fingers and say with a smile, "But you and I know, don't we, Rachel, that popular culture influences who we are, what we think, and what's going to happen in our world and in our lives. It is vital then that we study what is popular, including commercial fiction."

Thinking about Professor McGuiness brought Rachel and her pounding fists to a sudden halt. In the glow of her desk lamp, she sat motionless, staring at the wall in front of her. She started to imagine how Tally would wrinkle her nose if she heard about Rachel's behavior in class. Even though she warned Rachel of academic snobberies, Tally also warned Rachel repeatedly about keeping her cool; about not letting people—colleagues or students—get to her. "Good professors believe in their studies and themselves," she'd once said to Rachel. "A good professor doesn't allow other people's judgments or hostilities or indifference to get under her skin."

Remembering these words, Rachel suddenly realized that today she hadn't been a good professor, and this thought made her raise her fists to start pounding once again. A knock at her door, however, stopped her short. She whirled around in her chair and muttered a gruff, "Come in." She didn't want to talk to anyone, but she had no choice. Right now, it was her office hours and she had to make herself available to any student who needed her. Rachel frowned as the knocking at the door sounded again.

"Come in," she repeated, this time more loudly.

The handle dipped, the door opened, and soon Peter Zadikian stood before Rachel, his lanky frame dwarfing her tiny and jumbled office. Rachel's heart skipped and then volleyed to her throat; her cheeks instantly flushed. Peter had heard what happened in her tutorial, Rachel speculated in silent panic, and now he was here to demand an explanation.

Rachel opened her mouth to speak, although she wasn't sure yet what she was going to say, but Peter spoke first.

"Rachel," he said, flashing a paradoxically boyish smile that deepened the smooth, arcing laugh lines around his light green eyes. "I just came by to apologize." He pushed his hand through his hair, the way he'd done earlier, and looked at Rachel. She stared back, saying nothing, her heart still hammering in her chest.

Evidently bemused by her silence, Peter spoke again. "I want to apologize about barging into your class earlier. I can be so foolish at times," he added with a quick laugh.

Rachel could feel the heat in her cheeks slowly beginning to drain away and her heartbeat beginning to ease. "Please, Peter," she said with a wave, "don't worry about it. Like I said, that basement is a rabbit warren."

Peter grinned. Then, with a conspiratorial wink, he whispered, "I wasn't even supposed to be in the basement. My tutorial was in two-oh-six. I got out of the elevator on the wrong floor!"

Panic still gurgled in Rachel's stomach, but she couldn't help laughing and saying, "Of course. The basement is only for tenure-track professors, after all. Not chairs of the department."

As soon as the words left Rachel's mouth, she regretted them. She knew Peter only slightly. He'd met her last winter when she came to visit the department and talk about the job offer with the dean. He'd welcomed her to the department at the beginning of the semester. And now, of course, he chaired the department's weekly faculty meetings, which Rachel dutifully attended. Other than that, she'd had little to do with her head of department. Making jokes like the one she'd just made was far too familiar, if not downright disrespectful.

Before Rachel's panic could escalate, however, Peter let out a long, low laugh. "Exactly," he said with a twinkle. "When you're granted tenure, Rachel, you will be set free from the cavernous dungeons of Manhattan U."

"Thank God," Rachel puffed out, unsure whether this was an expression of relief that she hadn't caused offense or simply a response to Peter's own joke.

As Peter continued to stand in front of Rachel, still smiling, she noticed for the first time the incongruity of his black-and-silver running shoes against the drab green carpeting in her office. Peter was a tall, lithe man, clearly a runner, and always wore running shoes like these, even to faculty meetings. But this was the first time the sleekness and expense of his shoes struck Rachel as odd and out of place in the world of academe. For a moment, she wanted to remark on it but caught herself just in time.

"*Sense and Sensibility*," Peter said, breaking their brief silence. He was gazing down at the battered copy on the floor by Rachel's desk. She'd thrown it there in rage and disgust after class. "My favorite." He then paused and held a long finger to his lips. "Although, is it? Perhaps *Pride and Prejudice* is my favorite. I can never decide," he said, shaking his head and smiling.

"You like Austen?" Rachel asked, surprised. She hadn't read Peter's books, but she knew they were about Steinbeck and the Great Depression. A far cry from Austen, in other words.

"I *love* Austen." He beamed, his green eyes dancing. "When I started out in grad school, I wanted to write my dissertation about Austen. Somehow I allowed a pigheaded professor to persuade me it wasn't what I should do. The professor didn't think Austen was manly enough." He laughed and then quickly frowned. "I was young and stupid enough to listen to him."

Rachel chuckled. "Mr. Darcy probably wouldn't be too pleased to hear that the book he appears in isn't very manly."

"I doubt he would." Peter chuckled too. Then, after a short, slightly awkward silence that preceded their mutual laughter, Peter slapped his hand on his forehead and said to Rachel, "Oh, yes, yes, I nearly forgot. The other thing I came to say is that the faculty meeting this afternoon will start at four thirty, not four."

Rachel nodded and smiled, but, as Peter turned toward the door, her smile quickly began to fade. Her earlier panic was beginning to resurface, and she wondered whether, by the time today's faculty meeting rolled around, Peter would know about what she'd done in class this morning. His smiles and jokes, if he knew, would surely be gone.

"Diana!"

Peter's shout cut through Rachel's thoughts. She glanced up to see, beyond Peter, Professor Diana Monroe in the hallway. Wearing a pristine suit, with her back ramrod straight, Diana was clutching two heavy hardback books. Her raven hair gleamed under the fluorescent lights.

"Faculty meeting is going to be at four thirty, Di," Peter was saying, standing in Rachel's doorway, grasping the door frame with his long fingers. "Did you get the e-mail?"

Rachel squirmed and sank into her chair as Peter and Diana talked. Rachel lived in dread of this woman and was praying she wouldn't be drawn into a conversation. Not that Diana would initiate any such conversation, of course. If most of Rachel's new colleagues were indifferent, Diana Monroe was the queen of indifference; she was the princess of aloofness. For six weeks, since Rachel had started at Manhattan U, Diana Monroe hadn't uttered one single word to her, not even a "Nice to meet you" pleasantry. Instead, Diana had shown Rachel only coldness. In faculty meetings, her gaze would skim across Rachel's like a pond skater gliding on water. In the hallway, if they ever passed, Diana would always become engrossed by her trim silver watch, or with the paperwork in her hand, or by an old and curling poster on the wall. Rachel could not think of one single time when their eyes had actually met.

Today was no different. Although on the brink of Rachel's office and just feet from Rachel herself, Diana kept her gaze fixed and un-wavering on Peter. It was as if, for Diana, everything behind Peter was a dark, uninteresting void. In spite of her fear, Rachel studied her and listened to the long British vowels that rolled from Diana's wide, elegant mouth as she spoke. As an undergraduate Rachel had read one of her acclaimed books on Sylvia Plath's poetry. She knew about Diana's two PhDs: one from Oxford and one from Harvard. She'd seen pictures of her enigmatic and beautiful face in the *Chronicle of Higher Education* and *The New York Times*, where Diana often wrote book reviews (not the one about Rachel's book, of course). Before Rachel ever came to Manhattan U, she'd revered the eminent Diana Monroe. Rachel had thought she was a role model for young female academics like herself, with her graceful prose, her intelligence, and her effortless beauty.

But now, as Rachel slunk farther down in her office chair, all she felt was terror coupled with a nagging bemusement as to why Diana was so incredibly cold toward her. It was clear that she didn't offer her glacial aloofness to everyone. Rachel often saw Diana having conversations, like the one she was currently having with Peter, with other members of the faculty. Rachel also knew—from her guilty, obsessive, yet illuminating perusals of Rate-My-Professor.com—that Diana's students loved her. Her students were so enamored that they would take time out of their busy days to write long, online rhapso-dies for their adored professor.

"See you later, Rachel."

Rachel flinched in her seat. She hadn't realized that Peter had turned back to look at her. She quickly pulled herself straight, flicked back the ungainly curl that had fallen across her face, and gave Peter an awkward wave. "Yes. See you later."

For a brief second, she thought that Diana was going to look in her direction; but of course she didn't. As Peter stepped out into the corridor, Diana kept her gaze fixed on his. The two of them moved off, and when they were out of sight, just a pair of muffled and receding voices, Rachel shook her head and puffed out her cheeks. Not only couldn't she engage her students, Rachel couldn't engage her idols either.

Today was turning out to be a very bad day.

Diana entered her office first and then held the door open for Peter to follow. After he'd ambled in, with those long and loose strides she'd known for almost ten years now, she shut the door firmly behind him and headed toward her large oak desk. Once there, she lowered herself into her seat and swiveled around to place her two Plath books on a nearby shelf. She lingered for a second, tapping and tweaking them until they stood neat and upright, like all the other thousand or so books that lined every wall of Diana's spacious office.

"You still can't bring yourself to talk to her, then?" Peter asked, his head cocked to one side and a small, quizzical smile across his lips. He was opposite Diana in the velvet reading chair near the window.

"Sorry?" Diana replied, her gaze gliding past his and then fixing on the brilliant blue fall sky outside.

"Rachel," Peter persisted.

"What are you talking about?" Diana said, keeping her tone cool but beginning to feel a pulse of irritation.

Peter sat forward, his elbows propped on his knees and his face resting in his open palms. "Come on, Di," he said. "It might not be obvious to anyone else, but it's obvious to me. You haven't said a word to Rachel since she started."

Diana yanked her gaze from the blueness and leveled it with Peter's. "Don't be absurd," she scoffed. "Of course I have."

Peter let out a small laugh. "Look. I just think you should stop feeling guilty."

"Guilty about what?" Diana snapped.

Peter looked a little taken aback but continued nevertheless. "All I'm saying is, you don't have to feel guilty about not wanting her to be here. You weren't the only one who made it clear to the dean that you thought her appointment was a bad idea."

Diana's back stiffened in her seat. "I *don't* feel guilty," she retorted, her hostility ringing in her ears. "I don't think she's up to the job, and I don't think her area of scholarship is right for this department. Just because she appeared on a television show and her book has sold a few copies and the dean thought her work would sexy up our department a little does not mean she should be a professor at Manhattan U."

Diana did, of course, feel a little guilty for the objections she'd raised about Rachel. She always hated to speak out against hiring people, especially young female academics who were trying so hard to make it. But in this case she really didn't think Rachel deserved the job. But Diana really didn't want to get into this now, and she especially didn't want to get irritated with Peter. Now that Professor Mary Havemeyer had left for the West Coast and her new job at Golden Gate College, Peter was one of her only real friends on faculty. She liked Tom Burgess, another professor in the department, but he was always too busy with his family and his Edgar Allan Poe Research Institute for a real friendship. Peter, on the other hand, had time for Diana, and the two of them had a long and amiable history. Ten years ago, they were hired by Manhattan U at the same time, both of them fresh out of grad school. They first met at a faculty mixer and, wide-eyed and apprehensive, they huddled conspiratorially over the hors d'oeuvres, sharing their fears and hopes and anxieties about their new jobs.

Peter and Diana were both now fully tenured, each of them with a clutch of books to their name and a number of prestigious grants and scholarships under their belts. In the last ten years, they'd taught hundreds of students and flown thousands of miles to give conference papers and keynote addresses. Through it all, their friendship had never waned. Never a day passed when they didn't discuss what they were writing, or gossip about other faculty, or grab a glass of wine together at the end of a long day teaching.

"I don't think that's very fair, Di," Peter said, undeterred by Diana's frosty tone. "It's true that Dean Washington was looking for someone doing exciting and contemporary research to woo prospective students. But Rachel isn't just some airhead celebrity upstart. She's damn smart. She graduated top of her class at UNC, and her book sold more than a *few copies* for a good reason. It's a great read. Her prose is beautiful and the research is rigorous and unique." Peter carried on even though Diana was trying to look away and distract herself with some paperwork in her pending tray. "Furthermore, Rachel knows her feminism, her cultural theory, even her Marx. And its not just contemporary stuff; she has Austen and Wharton on her courses this semester and seems to know them inside out too." He paused and added, "Anyway, this department is way too crusty, old-fashioned, and full of men. You know that. You're always complaining about it."

Although Diana was trying not to rise to the bait, she couldn't help retorting, "I know at least two other female academics who should have been appointed here, both of whom are doing amazing and interesting work on *serious* contemporary writers."

Peter tried to interrupt. "But Rachel's work *is* serious. . . ."

"Two very talented female scholars," Diana blustered on, tapping a pen in her hand, "who deserve the job much more than Rachel does. In my opinion, interviewing a few suburban housewives about the book groups they attend and writing about the books people like reading *on the beach* is not serious scholarship. Plus, if we allow our professors to teach this kind of thing, students will want nothing else. Every senior thesis will be about John Grisham and J. K. Rowling. It's fine for students to read these books during spring break, but do we really want to allow such books"—Diana paused, searched for the right words, and then waved a hand in front of her—"through these doors of learning?"

"'Doors of learning'?" Peter asked, an amused smile twitching at the corners of his mouth.

Diana glared over at him for a second, but then found herself beginning to smile too. She knew it was time to lighten up. "Anyway," she said, now grinning, "Rachel wears an unsavory amount of pink."

Peter's eyebrows arched, but then he chuckled. "Holy cow, you're right." He grinned back. "Let's fire her at once!"

Diana gave a small puff of laughter.

"Perhaps you're feeling guilty because of the room change." Peter was still smiling.

"What are you talking about?" Diana retorted, feeling her hackles rising again.

"I discovered a little earlier that Rachel is now teaching in the very same basement seminar room that you were teaching in until a couple of weeks ago." Peter waggled his eyebrows knowingly. "Until you demanded a room change."

Diana frowned. "Peter, the fluorescent lighting in those rooms gives me migraines, as you know. And as you also know, room changes are arranged by central administration. I had no idea Rachel would end up in the basement." Diana's eyes then flickered and her mouth twitched at the corners. "But I must say, it is much more pleasant on the twelfth floor."

Diana and Peter sat in an easy silence for a few seconds until Peter lowered his voice and asked, "It's not because she reminds you of Annabelle, is it? I mean, you have to admit there is a resemblance."

Diana held up her hand. "Rachel looks nothing like . . . nothing like . . . well, you know who." The iciness had returned to her voice. "Even if she did, that would have nothing to do with it."

"I'm sorry," Peter blurted, his voice meek and whispery. "I shouldn't have brought up Anna—"

"Peter," Diana cut in with a tight smile, "haven't you got a class to teach?"

Peter nodded; he knew this was his cue, and after offering one more apology for bringing up Annabelle, he scooted out of Diana's office. When she was finally alone, Diana slumped her head forward into her waiting hands. She was silent for a few seconds, and then, unaccustomed to screaming or sobbing, she did what she always did: She let out a long, mournful groan.

Every time Diana heard Annabelle's name, for a second she

thought she'd respond better. She thought the pain of hearing the name of the woman who'd taken away her husband would one day be less. She hoped that one day she wouldn't be filled with anger and hurt and bitterness. But even now, five years after Graham left, the name would still tear into her like a knife.

Falling in love had never been high in Diana's priorities. Not until she met Graham, that was. As she'd spent most of her childhood and teenage years in strict all-girls boarding schools in England, the opposite sex might as well have been a lost tribe, an alien species. During her undergraduate years at Oxford, she had a few insignificant flings and one boyfriend for a whole three months. But then she went on to grad school, which took her from Oxford to Harvard, and her work became her love; books became her passion. Relationships weren't something she looked for, let alone yearned for.

Then she met Graham just a month after moving to New York. Perhaps the excitement of the new city and her new job relaxed her a little and let her scholar blinkers drop for a while. Maybe it was the beautiful fall weather. Whatever it was, for the first time ever, when she ran into Graham Cartwright in a busy coffee shop on Bleecker Street, she found herself enthralled with a man. She couldn't stop staring at his dark blue eyes, his rich auburn hair, and when she found out he was a classics professor at Manhattan U, she was hooked.

After just a few dates, she fell deliriously in love with him and married him after only three months. Until the last moment, the moment she found his letter on the dining table, she lived their four years of marriage in blissful ignorance. Meanwhile, over in the university's classics department, everyone knew about the handsome Professor Graham Cartwright and his many affairs. Apparently, the winsome young grad student Annabelle Smith was just one in a long line.

Knowing everyone knew and she didn't was terrible. Knowing she'd let herself be suckered in by Graham was even worse. She let down her guard just one time, fell in love just one time, and then ended up being made a complete fool of. She couldn't stand it. And that was why Diana had resolved never to let it happen again: never to let her guard down for *any* man. Books and classes and Sylvia Plath's poetry, that was her life now—pure and simple.

Remembering this resolution to herself, Diana raised her head from her hands and felt the sadness beginning to subside. She looked around her book-lined office. These books, these thousands of books, all of which she had read, protected her now, and it felt good to be cocooned by them. She twirled a little in her seat and ran her finger over the books on the closest shelf. They felt cool under her touch and, as her fingertips traced their embossed, familiar titles—*Ariel*, *The Bell Jar*, *The Colossus and Other Poems*—she smiled. This was a good way to live, she thought, safe amongst her books.

Diana was about to turn back to her desk and start sorting through the day's mail when a quiet rapping came at the door. She prayed it wasn't Peter, back for another round of apologies for mentioning Annabelle. It would be like him to be so insistent about his remorse. But Diana just wanted to put the whole conversation behind her. Peter had been a great friend over the years, particularly when Graham left, but she'd always been a little uncomfortable with his candor, his "let's talk about it" American-ness.

The person outside the door rapped again. Diana sighed and finally called out, "Come in."

The door opened and Mikey O'Brien stepped in. He was smiling and holding a computer keyboard under his arm.

"Hey," he whispered, his impossibly wide shoulders leaning against the door frame.

"Hi," Diana replied, smiling at first, but then her face snapped into a worried frown.

One glimpse of Mikey, the English department's computer technician, and Diana's calm of a minute ago evaporated. His presence was a brutal reminder that the monastic life Diana thought—and hoped— she was living was a sham, a figment of her own imagination.

Diana was sleeping with Mikey and had been for the past two months.

"Yes?" she snapped.

Unperturbed by her enmity, Mikey continued to smile and paced toward her desk. His Johnny Cash T-shirt, rumpled above his fraying black jeans, moved across his broad chest as he walked. "I'm dropping off your new keyboard," he explained.

Diana nodded, muttered, "Thanks," but kept frowning as Mikey placed the keyboard on her desk and dropped to the floor to hook it up to her PC.

The L key on her keyboard had been sticking for weeks, so Mikey's visit was legitimate. Nevertheless, Diana was angry at his being here. She was furious because his visit reminded her of their secret affair and what an idiot she was being, allowing herself to get involved with this man: a man with whom she had so little in common. Moreover, she was furious that the nearness of his soft, wild curls, his open face, and his lopsided smile made her yearn to wrap herself around him and lose herself in the sweet smell of his skin.

Diana had told herself many times in the last few weeks that it was just sex between her and Mikey, nothing more, and it was definitely not love. She'd tried to reassure herself that she wasn't compromising her vows of purity and scholastic simplicity. But seeing Mikey always shattered those tenuous reassurances.

"Here you go," Mikey said, as he scrabbled around under her desk. "That should do it." Then, peering up at her from his hands and knees, he grinned and asked, "Shall I call back this evening?" After a pause, he added, "Trixie is at her mom's tonight."

Trixie was Mikey's daughter. Diana had never met her, but she'd seen the dog-eared pictures Mikey kept in his wallet. She'd seen the twinkle in his eyes when Mikey looked at those photos and talked about his little girl: a four-year-old with her white blond pigtails, rosy cheeks, and a wide smile that was the image of her dad's. Diana had seen the sadness flicker in Mikey's eyes too when he talked about how he and his wife had divorced when Trixie turned one, and how much he hated the fact that his daughter spent her young life shuttling between her parents' apartments. His devotion to his little girl was so apparent and palpable. It was one of the things Diana found appealing—frustratingly appealing—about Mikey.

"Are you busy tonight?" Mikey asked as he cocked his head, clearly trying to read Diana's momentary silence.

"Yes," she lied. But then she looked down at him again and she thought about kissing his wide lips, feeling his thick curls in her hands, and gliding her fingers over his warm chest. "I mean, no," she found herself saying in a flustered whisper. "I'm not busy. Come by tonight."

As the words escaped her, she felt jittery, guilty, ashamed of herself, and so she jumped up from her seat and walked toward the door.

"Six o'clock?" Mikey asked, as he got to his feet and followed her.

"Faculty meeting's been rescheduled," Diana said, pulling at the handle and opening the door for Mikey. "We'll probably finish at six thirty."

"See you at six thirty-five, then." He winked as he skirted by her and out into the hallway.

She pushed the door closed behind him and then pressed herself up against an adjacent bookshelf. "Tonight," she muttered. "Tonight will be the last time."

Three

Faculty Meeting

Diana whisked down the hallway toward the faculty lounge, her low square heels *click-clack*ing on the polished tiles. A rainbow of posters and flyers stuck to nearby pin boards fluttered as she passed. As she moved onward, Diana smiled to herself. She was feeling much better. Thoughts of Mikey had receded to a distant murmur, and after a quick lunch at her desk of take-out sushi and green tea, followed by a perfectly ripe pear, she'd managed to write four pages on Plath's *The Bell Jar* for her new manuscript. Diana's previous three books had focused solely on Plath's poetry, and this was the first time she'd written anything sustained about Plath's only novel. But she was enjoying the new challenge, and it made her feel good when her writing went well.

As she rounded the corner, Diana saw that the door to the faculty lounge was open and could hear the rumble of voices and the clink of coffee mugs from within. The faculty were already assembling for this afternoon's meeting, and Diana, even though she was still a few feet off, could already feel the buzz of excitement, anxiety, and irritation that always accompanied faculty gatherings. Academics were solitary creatures—so often studying alone, teaching alone, and thinking alone. When they were forced together in meetings such as these, they were both pleased to have their isolation interrupted and annoyed by it too. Being pressed up, cheek by jowl, with other colleagues bred a paradoxical mix of aggravation and jumpy exhilaration. Diana knew, because she felt it all too keenly.

Diana was about to turn into the room when a voice behind her called out, "Professor Monroe!"

She turned to see Rebecca Nilsen tottering toward her in a pair of four-inch heels and a white leather dress coat. At least, Diana *thought* it was Rebecca. Under her flowing and intricately highlighted hair, a pair of huge shimmering sunglasses obscured most of the young woman's elfin face and thus it made it hard to tell whether it was Rebecca or her identical twin sister, Veronica. The sisters were both registered for Diana's undergraduate course, Intro to American Poetry, but Rebecca was the one who showed up to class regularly. The Nilsens were the daughters of Lamont Nilsen: Hollywood director, multimillionaire, and potential benefactor, who, it was rumored, would donate twenty million dollars to Manhattan U when his girls graduated. All faculty had been warned by the powers above about the importance of being attentive to these two students. Most of all, they were told to be meticulous in distinguishing the twins apart. Apparently, the Nilsens hated nothing more than being confused for each other—in spite of the fact that their wardrobes and choice of hair coloring were as identical as their genomic sequence.

Luckily for Diana, as the Nilsen sister drew closer, she pushed the sunglasses up onto her head and Diana knew at once it was Rebecca. When she'd first met the twins, Diana had taken the time to commit their faint, almost infinitesimal differences to memory. Rebecca had a tiny fleck of brown in her otherwise blue eyes; Veronica did not. Veronica's delicate nose tipped a little higher than Rebecca's, and there was something about Rebecca's countenance, the slightly softer arc of her cheekbones perhaps, that spoke of her more open and kinder demeanor. The few times Veronica attended Diana's class, she'd sat morosely at the back of the room, letting out the occasional rude sigh, and looking utterly uninterested. Diana had spotted headlines on glossy magazines at cash registers that claimed that the Nilsen girls were spoiled, bad-mannered, and vacuous. Of course, Diana didn't trust such trashy publications. Nonetheless, everything about Veronica seemed to confirm what the headlines said.

However, the accusations of arrogance and inanity were misplaced when it came to Rebecca. As far as Diana was concerned, Rebecca was bright, engaged, and self-effacing. Moreover, she was always impeccably polite. Diana enjoyed having her in class, and she was pleased to see her now.

"Hello, Rebecca," she said with a warm smile.

Rebecca's eyes twinkled. "I don't want to hold you up, Professor Monroe," she began, "but I just wanted to tell you that I've been accepted for the study-abroad program." She paused and then added, "The Literary London trip this winter? You wrote a reference for me. Do you remember?"

"I do," Diana replied with a nod. "That's wonderful, Rebecca; congratulations."

Diana wasn't at all surprised by Rebecca's news, of course. She'd written Rebecca a reference, but she knew it was a matter of rubber-stamping. A Nilsen sister would never be turned down for something she applied for—not if the rumor was true and Manhattan U wanted their twenty-million-dollar donation from her father. That Diana had written such a sterling recommendation didn't matter. The fact that Rebecca was a freshman, when usually only juniors and seniors were allowed to go on study-abroad programs, didn't matter either. Rebecca Nilsen would always be going on the Literary London program, if that was what she wanted.

"I'm so excited. Seeing all those plays and the British Library and everything." Rebecca was still beaming.

Diana couldn't help letting out a chuckle. Rebecca's excitement was endearing—if a little baffling. This was a young woman whose father owned numerous private jets, had a mansion in every cosmopolitan capital across the globe, and bought his daughters two penthouse apartments on Fifth Avenue just for their years at Manhattan U. If Mr. Nilsen's daughter wanted to see a play in London, he might very well fund it, produce it, and employ a star-studded cast all by himself. Diana knew of Lamont Nilsen's fortune and excesses from Peter. Diana herself had never picked up one of those glossy magazines at the cash register. She had no television and discarded the *Times'* Style section without even opening it. When it came to the Nilsens, though, she'd open her ear and indulge Peter's peculiar love of celebrity gossip. After all, they were her students.

"I'm sure you'll have a superb time, Rebecca," Diana said, and then with a wink added, "Make sure to visit the house where Plath and Ted Hughes lived."

Rebecca's fine, meticulously plucked eyebrows shot up. "Really? I can go see it?"

Diana nodded. "Of course. It's in Primrose Hill, near Camden Town."

After writing down the exact address, Diana pointed toward the faculty lounge. "I must get going," she explained with a kind smile.

"Of course, yes, see you in class, Professor Monroe."

Diana watched as Rebecca tottered off down the corridor. She then tried once again to head into the faculty meeting. This time, though, it was Peter who stopped her.

"You know," he said, sidling up close to Diana and flashing her a playful smile, "you really should volunteer for the Literary London program. Especially now that one of our star students will be going." He nodded toward Rebecca's receding figure.

Diana nudged Peter and rolled her eyes. "Don't you ever give up?" She laughed.

"Nope." He grinned and then bounced off toward the faculty lounge.

Peter had been trying to persuade Diana to go on the study-abroad program for the past couple of weeks. Two faculty members who used to accompany the students to London every year had unexpectedly dropped out, and Peter was scrabbling around trying to find replacements. A trip to Europe would usually have faculty vying to go. But the Literary London program took place, for some inexplicable and insanely bureaucratic reason, in the last ten days of November— which, of course, ruled out anyone with Thanksgiving plans, and thus ruled out pretty much every member of the department. Even Peter was obliged to spend Thanksgiving with his aging father in Oregon every year. But it didn't rule out Diana, not since she and Graham had divorced and she no longer had his sprawling New England family to share the holiday with. Diana refused to volunteer for the London program, though. Admitting she had no Thanksgiving plans would be giving away too much about her solitary life and would prompt all kinds of unwelcome and pitying social invitations.

But, as Diana paced into the meeting and headed for her favored seat next to Peter, she started to wonder whether a trip to England might be what she needed. It would offer a chance to get away from New York, perhaps see her parents, and an opportunity to escape the mess she'd gotten herself into with Mikey. Thanksgiving was still over a month away, of course, and she'd already decided she must end things with Mikey tonight. However, just to be sure, it might be wise to get out of the city for a while.

"I'll do it," she blurted, as she plopped down in her seat.

The words shocked her as much as they did Peter.

"Sorry?" he replied, looking up with his forehead crinkling.

Diana gazed straight at her friend. "I'll go to London."

Peter was speechless for a second. Then, as he realized she was serious, a grin crept across his face. "Great." He laughed. "Great!"

"You owe me, though," she said with a wink.

Peter chuckled. He was about to say something else but the buzz and chatter that had filled the room suddenly ceased. Peter looked around, and, sensing that the faculty were ready to get on with the meeting, he welcomed everyone and promptly started handing out copies of the agenda.

While the papers were shuffled around the room and a couple of sighs and grumbles were let slip as the faculty began skimming the proceedings, Peter turned back to Diana.

"There's one thing you should know," he whispered. Diana arched an inquisitive eyebrow and Peter went on: "Rachel has volunteered for Literary London too." Then, with a small, uncertain smile, he added, "I'm sure you two will make a great team."

Before Diana could respond, Peter shifted his eyes to the front, cleared his throat, and began reading aloud point one on the meeting's agenda.

The faculty lounge was muggy. The windows were closed, the heating was high, and Rachel was beginning to feel the trickle of sweat behind her knees and in the crook of her elbows. She fidgeted from left to right on her hard wooden seat and then smoothed her hot hands across the notebook resting on her knees. It was particularly airless in this back corner where she'd chosen to sit, and every few minutes she found herself stifling a yawn. She couldn't stop thinking back to this morning's class. She was still worried that what she'd done earlier was going to get her in trouble (although so far she'd heard nothing). But she was also feeling a momentary pang of sympathy for her students. *Perhaps,* she wondered, *it was the stuffy basement that had made her students so sluggish and seemingly uninterested. Not her teaching.*

The meeting had been in session for thirty minutes, and they had made it through only three points on the sixteen-point agenda. Rachel hoped that the meeting wasn't going to run too late. Not that she had anywhere exciting to go, of course. Her dreams of a vibrant New York social life were evaporating as fast as her dreams of being Manhattan U's new teaching sensation. Since the semester began six weeks ago, Rachel had discovered that preparing for class, trying to work on her new book, and grading papers sucked up nearly every minute of her time. On top of that, social invitations were about as infrequent as her free nights. Rachel knew only a few people in the city—friends she'd graduated with in North Carolina who were now jet-setting lawyers or stockbrokers who had even less time than she did. As yet, she'd socialized little with her colleagues at Manhattan U, except for a couple of awkward faculty mixers at the start of the semester.

Rachel did have a date with her futon and television tonight, however. *Access Hollywood*—Rachel's secret, guilty obsession and her daily half-hour escape from the scholarly grind—started at seven and she wanted to be home in time.

"Okay," Peter was saying somewhere at the front of the room, "let's move on to point four."

There was a rustle of papers and a number of quiet groans. Someone mumbled, "Oh, Jesus," rather too loudly. Meanwhile, Peter read point four aloud.

"'Finalize syllabus for American Lit 101.'" Then, scanning the room and seeing the frowning faces in front of him, he smiled a meek smile and added, "I know, I know: We've discussed this to death, and *I know* it's a matter of some contention. But it's really time we pinned the reading list down. Next year's course handbook needs to go to the printers by the end of the semester."

There were some more groans and then Bill Roberts, one of the longest-serving members on the faculty, leaned forward and boomed, "As I said, last week, and the week before, *and the week before that*, I think the current reading list is just fine. I don't know what all the fuss is about." With that, he slumped back in his chair, stroked his snow-white beard, and glared through his wire-rimmed specs at his colleagues, daring them to contradict him.

"I agree," George Kramer said, nodding with vigor. "The American Lit syllabus does *not* need to change. It has been working perfectly fine for years. Why meddle with it now?"

Rachel peered over to see baldheaded George and white-haired Bill exchanging conspiratorial nods. She couldn't help sighing. Before she'd started at Manhattan U, she imagined faculty meetings here as one of the best parts of her new job. She couldn't think of anything more inspiring than sitting in a room full of big-name academics, sharing thoughts on department policy and brainstorming new ideas for courses.

The reality was very different. Faculty meetings were tense yet simultaneously very dull affairs. Hours were often spent quibbling over the wording of a prospectus, arguing about what constituted an A grade, or deciding whether a student's behavior was troublesome or simply a manifestation of his or her "atypical personality type." These endless discussions were sometimes punctuated with startling and spiteful jabs, jousts, and even name-calling among tenured members of faculty. Junior faculty, Rachel had quickly learned, were expected to keep their mouths shut and their heads down. At least, if they wanted to increase their odds of one day getting tenure—and thus lifetime employment at the university—they had to keep a very low profile at these meetings.

Today's meeting looked like it was going to follow the usual path: nit-picking, browbeating, the odd insult thrown, and Peter—always remarkably cool under the collar—trying to keep things moving. Just as he was doing now.

"Come on," he was saying with a chuckle. "No other university in this country has an Intro to American Lit course that hasn't changed in twenty years. We have to move with the times, don't we?"

"Peter, the last thing this department wants to do," Bill barked out, still stroking his beard, "is to emulate the goings-on in the Hicksville, no-name, good-for-nothing universities across this country. Our department is one of the highest-ranked in the country *precisely because* we do not adhere to every new fad in the teaching of literature."

A silence followed and then some mutterings. Rachel's gaze darted around the room, scanning over the assembled faculty. She took in the sea of corduroy jackets, white hair, and wire-rimmed spectacles and wondered, not for the first time, what she was doing here. So many of the department's old guard, like Bill and George, who'd been around for decades, were unabashed and outspoken traditionalists who thought anything written after *Moby-Dick* wasn't worth looking at. It was remarkable that she'd been offered a job here. The department needed more women, there was no doubt—including Rachel, there were still only four women on faculty. They also needed more scholars doing contemporary work. Even so, Rachel still couldn't believe that she, with her book on book groups and popular fiction for women, had really been invited to teach in this male-dominated and old-fashioned department.

Rachel awoke from her reflections when Diana's voice cut across the room.

"Oh, for God's sake," Diana interjected with her usual determination, "don't be ridiculous, Bill. You know full well that we need to update the syllabus." She paused for a second and then, holding a piece of paper above her head, she glared around at the faculty. "Two books by women? One novel by an African-American writer? Please. This reading list is archaic."

"Diana," George said, waving a hand, "we know—"

But Diana didn't let him finish.

"George," she retorted, giving him an icy stare, "if we are to remain one of the top-ranking English departments in the country, we need to step up to the plate. Our freshmen need to be introduced to the rich and diverse literature that has been produced in the United States. Not *just* the works of Melville, Twain, and a revered group of dead white men."

Rachel started to smile. Diana might be frosty to her, but Rachel admired the way she faced off with the old guard like this. She did it, as far as Rachel could tell, in every department meeting. Peter and some other faculty would always back her up, although it was Diana who got the ball rolling.

Today, Diana's display prompted a sudden surge of energy in Rachel. The room didn't feel so stuffy anymore, and her desire to yawn or to sneak a look at her watch fizzled away. Rachel felt a desire to say something welling up in her chest. She knew that she should really keep her mouth shut, just like the other junior faculty. But Rachel was beginning to fidget in her seat, and the itch to speak was becoming irrepressible.

"I think," Rachel blurted out when a break in the conversation finally came, "I think maybe we could do both." Then, as every head in the room swiveled and a swath of surprised faces stared over at her, Rachel began to redden. "I mean, well, perhaps we could consider keeping many of the classics," she went on, her voice beginning to quaver a little, "but we could update the syllabus by adding other works by women, minorities, and genre fiction writers."

Every one of her colleagues continued to stare, and she could feel her heart tripping and skipping with panic. Nonetheless, she continued. "Students would still be introduced to the literary heavyweights, like Melville and his dead white boy friends." Rachel laughed, but she was met with blank and stony faces, so she quickly cleared her smile and kept talking. "But they would read these alongside other, um, well, other noncanonical texts. This would give students the chance to explore how modern writers, or female writers, or minority writers, work in . . ." She paused, searching for the right words. "How they work in conversation or opposition with texts like *Moby-Dick*."

Her words were still being met with grave stares. Peter was smiling, though.

"Great," he chimed in, "I like it. So, which noncanonical authors and texts would you suggest, Rachel?"

"Oh," she began, thankful to Peter for his support but alarmed that she must go on talking. "That's tough. I wouldn't want to dictate those kinds of choices. In fact, it might be a good idea for everyone who teaches Intro to American Lit to choose their own."

Peter was nodding encouragingly, so, feeling buoyed, Rachel went on. "Personally, I would include some popular women's fiction, the kind I have written about in my book. I would use such novels, as I do in my classes already, to discuss the very meaning of the canon and to explore why certain writers are deemed heavyweights and others aren't." Rachel's hands started to wave as she began to find her stride: the same stride that had been strangely missing since she'd started at Manhattan U. "Plus, studying these books alongside the classics can open up a whole host of interesting questions about wealth and social class across time, as well as love and sexuality and identity. . . ." Rachel sensed she was beginning to ramble and so quickly concluded: "Anyway, to answer your question, I might choose an author like Emily Giffin. As well as being extremely popular, she's an interesting writer. Her premises are always distinctive and even make some readers uncomfortable, yet her books strike a chord with many, many women."

Rachel stopped there and a deathly silence ensued, until someone muttered, "Emily, who?"

Rachel was about to explain when Jackie Rawlings cleared her throat. Jackie was a renowned Shakespeare scholar with graying hair that hung like indolent curtains on either side of her long, angular face. A pair of tiny silver reading glasses always teetered on the end of her nose. She was one of the department's old guard, and like Bill and George she had been around for years.

"This is a literature department," Jackie drawled, waving over at Rachel. "We are not a *popular fiction* department. We study and teach *literature*, not mysteries or sci-fi or chick lit or thrillers or romance." She puckered her lips and spat out, "Or any such lightweight books."

Rachel was stunned. "But—"

"As Diana has said many times in the past," Jackie interrupted, pointing a long finger in Diana's direction, "if we allow too much of this kind of"—her mouth puckered again—"this kind of fiction, the students are going to want nothing else. We all know how students like an easy ride."

"I—" Rachel tried to speak up again, but Jackie kept talking.

"If our introductory American Lit course is going to include women writers, which I agree it most certainly should, we must include serious contemporary women's writing, such as Danzy Senna's *Caucasia* or Marilynne Robinson's *Gilead* or Lahiri's *Interpreter of Maladies*."

Rachel's skin was now prickling with fury. For the second time today, she was on the brink of an explosion. But just as she was about to speak, she caught a quick yet meaningful glance from Tom Burgess, a colleague sitting nearby. She'd met Tom a few times and liked him. He was one of the few friendly ones in the department. He was also junior faculty, just like Rachel. The last time they'd spoken, Tom had told her, with irony and chuckles, about the pitfalls and politics of life on tenure track at Manhattan U. He was going up for tenure this year. The look he was giving Rachel now was deadly serious. He was on Rachel's side, but he was also warning her. *This could be one of those pitfalls*, his pale blue eyes advised.

Although it was hard, Rachel took Tom's cue, held her tongue, and said nothing. Inside, however, she fumed. She glared across the room at Jackie. *Why are you so mean?* Rachel wanted to scream. *And why don't you realize that knocking popular fiction is just plain elitist? And why didn't you listen to a word I said? The whole point of looking at popular and supposedly* lightweight *novels with students would be to explore the very literary elitism you are guilty of!*

Jackie didn't return Rachel's heated gaze, however. She'd already lost interest in the topic and was back to peering at her agenda through her minuscule specs. Frustrated, Rachel shifted in her seat and then redirected her glaring gaze to Diana, who, as always, was sitting upright in her seat, not a hair out of place, not a wrinkle in her suit. *So that is why you don't like me*, Rachel simmered, thinking about what Jackie had just said. *You think the books I teach are easy. Not just that, you think every lazy, lackluster student will sign up for my courses just so they can get credits for reading easy books.*

As Rachel scanned her colleague, Diana's eyes met Rachel's. But there was no flinch, no twitch of embarrassment about what Jackie had just revealed about her disapproval of the kind of books Rachel taught and wrote about. Diana didn't even look away. Instead, Diana gazed back at Rachel, her eyes flat and cold and unreadable like a frozen lake. It was Rachel who found herself looking away first. The woman unnerved Rachel like no one ever had before.

The faculty meeting went on for another hour. Rachel brooded the whole time, not listening to what was being said. She was vaguely aware that at six twenty-five Peter started wrapping up the meeting and asking for any final comments. But it was only when the door to the stuffy faculty lounge banged open that Rachel was fully woken from her angry trance. Together with the rest of the faculty, Rachel lifted her head, and her previously languid gaze flitted toward the open doorway.

Rachel noticed his deep navy cashmere sweater first, followed by the white shirt opened lazily at the neck. Finally, her gaze moved up to the dark stubble, the sleepy chestnut eyes, and the thatch of deep brown and slightly ruffled hair. Rachel swallowed hard, blinked, and scanned the apparition once again. For a second, she thought she might be dreaming. But then he moved into the room, bringing with him a gust of cooler air, and Rachel realized she was completely awake.

As the man waltzed forward toward Peter, he smiled a wry but confident smile and appeared unfazed by the roomful of eyes upon him. Meanwhile, Rachel clutched hard at her chair, trying to stop herself from swaying in shock. Never, ever in her years holed up in the world of academe had she seen a man so beautiful, so stylish, so easy in his skin.

"Aha!" Peter exclaimed, as he stood to shake hands with the stranger. "Perfect timing." Then, gripping the man's shoulder, he turned to the rest of the faculty and said with a smile, "Everyone, this is Carson McEvoy, our visiting professor from Harvard."

Rachel's jaw dropped—literally and unflatteringly dropped. She was astonished, bewildered. *This* was Carson McEvoy? *The* Carson McEvoy? She simply couldn't believe it. In grad school, she'd read Carson McEvoy's highly acclaimed books on contemporary American literature and had always imagined him as some intense little man with smudged specs, frayed shirts, and bad breath—much like all the other brilliant men she'd known in academia. She would never have imagined *this* in a million years.

"Hi." Carson waved to the room. "Sorry to interrupt the meeting like this."

His voice was low and strong, just as Rachel had always imagined Heathcliff's or Darcy's or Rochester's to be. Rachel's mouth went suddenly dry.

Next to Carson, Peter was smiling. "As most of you know, Carson was supposed to join us at the beginning of the semester but he was held up on a research trip." Peter then turned to Carson, patted him on the back, and laughed. "Better late than never, though!"

Carson laughed a gravelly yet lilting laugh. "I'm glad to be here at last, and I'm really looking forward to meeting you all," Carson said, scanning the room.

Rachel's heart thumped to a halt as his languorous eyes stopped on hers and he gave her the briefest of smiles. Her whole body seemed to turn liquid. But before she could do anything, before she could rearrange her stupefied face into something more normal, perhaps even alluring, Carson's gaze had left her. It was now upon Diana, and he was grinning a broad, flirtatious grin.

"Diana!" Rachel heard him saying. "So good to see you."

The rest of what Carson said was lost amid a cloud of chatter and squeaking chairs. Peter had announced the end of the meeting, and the rest of the faculty were trampling impatiently from the room. Rachel remained frozen in her seat, however. Through the exiting crowd, she stared at Carson and Diana as they talked and laughed and sparkled at each other. Rachel gripped her middle as her stomach kicked with a fierce and unannounced envy.

After a minute or so, Rachel finally dragged her gaze from Diana and Carson, and in one quick, jumpy move she gathered her things and bolted toward the door. In the hallway, tramping back toward her office, she cringed and shook her head. She'd reacted to Carson like some love-struck teenager. She was ridiculous—lonely and ridiculous. Since Justin, there had been no one else. Her friends back in North Carolina had nagged her to go out and start dating again, but then her book, the *Oprah* thing, the job offer at Manhattan U had all happened, and life just seemed too hectic. Plus, if she was honest, she hadn't felt ready. Those last months living with Justin—the fights, the tears, the sad realization they were going to break up—had drained her of so much emotional energy. After that difficult time, she wasn't sure her heart could cope with the ups and downs of another relationship anytime soon. Perhaps it never would again.

"Locked yourself out?"

Rachel was standing in front of her office when Carson's voice rang out and nearly caused her to drop every paper she was holding.

She turned to see him sauntering toward her, a teasing smile crinkling his handsome features.

"No," Rachel replied, her tone terser than she meant. "Just looking for my key." As she spoke, her fingers trembled a little, but eventually she found her key chain, held it up, and exclaimed, "Here it is."

Carson grinned as he leaned on the wall close to her door. "Rachel Grey, isn't it?"

Rachel's head snapped around and she stared at him. "H-how," she stammered, "how did you know?"

"I saw you on *Oprah*." He smirked, his eyes moving slowly over Rachel's hot face. "Any self-respecting professor of literature watches *Oprah*."

Rachel knew he was teasing, but couldn't find any words to respond. It was Carson who filled the silence.

"*Reading for Love and Friendship*. A pretty remarkable book, I have to say."

Rachel, who'd still been floundering with her key, trying to get it into the lock, almost dropped her whole key chain. He knew the name of her book? Carson McEvoy knew the name of her book! Could this really be true? But then she caught herself. Of course he hadn't read it. He'd just heard of it, possibly seen her on *Oprah*, and now he was just continuing to tease her.

She turned to face him, expecting to see his impish smirk. Instead, she was met with a dark and intensely serious gaze.

"The chapter where you use the circuit-of-culture model is quite brilliant."

Rachel was speechless again, but after a couple of seconds she managed to squeak out a pathetic, "Thanks."

Carson scraped a hand through his thick hair and then nodded. His expression was still deadly serious. "Did you see that Gerard Goggin also used the model in his book on cell phone culture?"

"I did!" Rachel laughed, surprised and amused that both she and Carson had read a book that had nothing to do with either of their fields of scholarship.

This kick-started Rachel into conversation. Her earlier embarrassment faded and the two of them slipped into easy academic talk about Goggin's book. They were cut off only when Carson's cell phone rang.

"Talk about cell phone culture." She grinned while he reached into his pocket for his phone.

He grinned too. "We've all been sucked in. There's nothing we can do. We are slaves to the cell."

Carson didn't answer his phone, though. Instead he peeked at the screen and then turned the phone off. Rachel thought—hoped—their conversation might resume, but once he'd tucked his cell back in his pocket, Carson looked at his watch.

"I must get going," he said.

He then looked over at Rachel. The mischievous grin had returned to his face; all traces of the earlier serious scholar had gone. He pushed himself away from the wall and, in one swift move, he reached up, tweaked one of Rachel's wayward curls, and whispered close to her ear, "See you around, Rachel Grey."

Then, with an audacious wink, he moved off down the hallway. Rachel was left, key in hand, with her mind spinning and her cheeks flushing once again.

Four

Once Upon a Time in Grad School

It was Saturday morning, and although the trees were shedding their leaves, the city was basking under a warm sun and a cloudless azure sky. Rachel couldn't stay in her tiny apartment on such a day. She wanted to be outside. She wanted to brunch on a terrace someplace, feeling the sun on her face and watching New Yorkers in shirtsleeves and linen dresses ambling by. Of course, she had a pile of grading to do, and her editor was itching to see a draft of her second book, but this might be Rachel's last chance to enjoy an alfresco brunch before New York's tenacious winter set in.

And so, weaving through SoHo just blocks from her apartment in Manhattan U's faculty housing, Rachel was heading for a place to eat. The sidewalks were bustling with tourists and shoppers and street traders. As Rachel bobbed among them, she peered at the tables strewn with handcrafted jewelry and stopped in front of shopwindows, eyeing the beautiful clothes and purses she could never afford on her professor's salary. Once or twice, as she stared into the glass, she caught a glimpse of her own smiling reflection.

Rachel's week at work hadn't been a good one. She'd stormed out of class on Wednesday and, even though she'd kept her cool in Thursday's and Friday's classes, her students were similarly and painfully apathetic. Extracting responses from them was like trying to extract teeth from a stubborn, frightened, mouth-clenched child. However, the weekend had come and the weather was breezy and warm and perfect and Rachel felt happy. Nothing had been said about her walking out of Wednesday's seminar—at least, she'd heard of no complaints or rumors, and Peter hadn't summoned her to his office. She knew it was wishful thinking, but she hoped that her class had been shamed into silence. They wouldn't complain, she tried to convince herself, because they knew it was their laziness and uninterest that had provoked her anger.

This morning's cheerfulness was also linked to Carson, of course. Rachel had seen him just one other time since Wednesday, the day he tweaked her hair and whispered good-bye. She'd spotted him going into the department office yesterday afternoon, and even though she had no real reason to visit the office, she hurried along the hallway and followed him inside. He didn't notice her at first, because he'd immediately struck up conversation with one of Rachel's colleagues who was standing by the copy machine. While the two men chatted, Rachel busied herself with the mail stacked inside her department mailbox. Every now and then, she sneaked a quick look at Carson. *Here he is again*, she thought, *just as rumpled, handsome, and dangerously alluring as before*. Rachel couldn't help grinning as she looked back down at the mail in her hands and sorted through the array of envelopes, postcards, journals, and memos.

"Good afternoon, Rachel Grey."

Rachel jumped at the sound of Carson's voice. She hadn't noticed that his conversation had ended or that he'd moved a few paces toward her. For the second time this week, Carson McEvoy was whispering close to her ear, and even though Rachel had been telling herself she should be more composed in his presence, she immediately blushed.

"Good afternoon," she murmured.

"I'm glad to see you keep your pigeonhole shipshape." His eyes flashed.

Rachel was still blushing, but she laughed too. "Of course."

Carson then grinned at her for a few seconds, his dark eyes gleaming and dancing. Then his gaze moved downward to Rachel's mail.

"*Differences*," he said, reading the title of the journal that was on top of the pile in her hands. "I always love it when that one arrives in my mailbox."

Without thinking, Rachel rolled her eyes. "Oh, right, and you subscribe to this feminist journal, do you?" She gave a disbelieving chuckle.

Carson's gaze was now sober. "I do subscribe. And . . ." he added, taking the journal from her hands and turning to the contents page, "I contribute too."

He turned the journal around and passed it back to Rachel. Her eyes swiftly moved to where his long finger was now pointing. There was his name, right there, second on the list of contributors. Carson McEvoy had an article in the current issue of *Differences*, a prestigious journal that Rachel dreamed of getting into.

"You? O-oh," she stammered. "Wow."

"It's an analysis of Salman Rushdie's latest novel using some of Spivak's recent theories. . . ."

Carson went on to explain his article further. Meanwhile, Rachel looked up at him baffled, amazed, and in growing awe.

When he was finished, Rachel asked, "Have you thought of doing a similar analysis with Chitra Divakaruni's latest novel?"

Carson raised his eyebrows. "No, I hadn't." Then he waved a finger, his silver watch glinting and jangling on his wrist. "But that's a great idea."

He was silent for a few beats and then his expression morphed into a wide grin. His eyes slid downward. "Nice blouse," he whispered.

Rachel immediately looked down at the white blouse she was wearing and noticed it was straining a little over her chest. Her cheeks burst into flame again, but she told herself to remain calm. She then forced herself to look back at Carson, and as she did so, she noticed for the first time the jacket he was wearing.

"Nice herringbone blazer." She smiled.

Carson gave out a loud laugh. "Too dorky?" he inquired.

She nodded. "A little. Yes."

It was dorky, but somehow Carson could pull it off. His wide shoulders and his smooth olive skin had something to do with it. But he'd also coupled the blazer with a crisp black shirt open at the collar. He made a herringbone sports coat look like one of the sexiest clothing items Rachel had ever seen.

Carson was laughing again. "I admire your honesty, Rachel Grey." He then inched closer and added, "I have a meeting with the dean later. I hear that deans take herringbone more seriously than other fabrics."

It was now Rachel's turn to laugh aloud. But she caught herself as she noticed the department secretary eyeing her suspiciously over the top of her computer monitor.

"Oh, yes," Rachel then whispered back to Carson, finally composing herself. "Herringbone is definitely the way to win the dean's approval."

Carson grinned. He then did the same hair tweak thing again, whispered good-bye, and was on his way. Rachel was left breathless. She felt like she'd just ridden a dizzying and looping roller coaster. One moment Carson was a handsome and flirtatious frat boy making her blush; the next he was a serious scholar who contributed to her favorite academic journal and wowed her with his incredible literary analyses. She just couldn't pin him down. Was he a sexy womanizer or a scholar of distinction? Could he really be both? One thing was for sure: Carson had Rachel utterly intrigued—and more than a little love-struck.

Since their exchange yesterday, Carson was all that Rachel could think about, and now as she bounced along Spring Street with her cotton skirt fluttering around her knees and her leather flip-flops slapping the sidewalks, she remained in a hazy bubble of longing. Images kept flashing into her mind: Carson's ruffled hair, his melancholy eyes, his rumbling voice, and him laughing that full-bodied laugh of his. Then she would imagine the two of them holding hands, Carson's head close to hers and the heat of his laughter on her cheek, her tiptoed feet as she bobbed up to kiss his warm lips. She also imagined the two of them sitting on some park bench or other, their ankles entwined as they leaned together reading a book or discussing a paper they'd both just read. As a couple, she and Carson would have it all: sexual chemistry and the meeting of scholarly minds.

These daydreams left Rachel flushed and beaming—but also frightened. Deep down she knew she shouldn't be having such thoughts about Carson. She didn't know him, after all. The man was a mystery. He was an unfathomable mix of brains and sexiness. Moreover, she had no clue if he was married or taken or even gay. She had no idea if he was a pathological flirt or whether he tweaked the hair of every woman he met. Furthermore, when Rachel got obsessed like this, when she let herself get passionate, intense, and overexcited about a man, that was when things got messed up. At least, that was how they got messed up with Justin.

Justin had been romantic, attentive, and irresistibly charming in the early days when they first got together in their senior year at college. He'd wooed her with roses, his twinkling hazel eyes, wavy dark bangs, and silly jokes. But then, over the next six years of their relationship, his efforts at romance and charm fizzled and he grew tired of Rachel's "mushiness," as he called it. Her displays of affection and her need to talk about their relationship, about life, about what they were thinking, were just "too intense." Justin wanted a quiet life: teaching his kids at school, coaching the baseball team, and then coming home for a beer and to watch the game. He couldn't understand the passions that bubbled in Rachel; he didn't really want to hear about them either. Some days, after Rachel excitedly chattered on to him about a book she was reading or a page she'd just written for her dissertation or when she simply wanted to snuggle up to him and ask about his day, he'd nod toward the TV and say, "Rach, hon, let's just watch the game and relax."

Up until the day Justin moved out, there was still a lot of love between them. He could still make her laugh with his silly jokes. She could make him smile, in return, with her loud, full-bellied laugh. He could still make her feel weak with a flash of his hazel eyes from under his bangs, and she knew he would miss burying his face into her curls and pulling her back against his naked chest in the middle of a dark night. But in the end they just couldn't go on living together. They fought every other day, with Rachel always wanting more—more conversation, more love, more intimacy—and Justin just wanting "a little peace and quiet" after another long day in the schoolroom.

These difficult memories about Justin darkened Rachel's earlier bright mood. They'd also, she suddenly realized, taken her off course in SoHo. She had wanted to try a place on Greene Street for brunch, but in her daze she'd kept on walking and was now three or four blocks east. However, her belly gave out a growl as if pleading with her not to turn back, so she settled for a large, busy restaurant on the corner of Lafayette and Spring. To her disappointment, it looked like she was going to have to eat inside. Every one of the silvery bistro tables on the sidewalk was taken. But just as she approached the restaurant's door, she passed a couple who, amid their empty plates, were slapping down some dollar bills and gathering the shopping bags nestled at their feet. With a questioning nod to a nearby waiter, Rachel established that there was no line and so hovered rather too conspicuously by the couple's table. When they finally moved off, she plopped herself onto one rickety slatted chair.

"Perfect," she muttered to herself as she pushed her sunglasses up her nose and sat, eyes closed, face toward the sun. Trucks and taxis roared by only a few feet away, but her little spot on the sidewalk felt almost tranquil, and thoughts of Justin began to evaporate into the warmth of the bright day.

After her table was cleared and she'd ordered, following some deliberation, French toast and an Americano, Rachel slipped her hand into her cavernous purse and pulled out her aging copy of *The House of Mirth*. She'd read the Edith Wharton classic countless times, but she needed a quick refresher before next week's classes, when she'd be teaching the book. Now, as she enjoyed her brunch amid buzzing New York City, it seemed the perfect time. But, as she flicked to the first page and carefully bent back the book's ancient spine, something made her look up. And as she looked up she found herself face-to-face, eyeball-to-eyeball, with Diana Monroe.

Both women flinched at the sight of each other. But, caught as they were in each other's gaze, there was no escape. They were just feet from each other, and Diana was about to enter the same restaurant where Rachel currently sat. They had to acknowledge each other; they had to say hello.

"Hi, Diana." Rachel went first, her throat suddenly as parched as the autumn leaves on the sidewalk around her.

Diana nodded, her expression somber. "Hello, Rachel."

"Lovely day," Rachel squawked, feeling her cheeks glow. But as she looked up at Diana, whose elegant hand clasped the door to the restaurant, she realized with a kick of surprise that she wasn't the only one who was feeling uncomfortable—nervous even. It was barely visible, but Rachel caught a small flicker of panic in Diana's otherwise steely eyes.

"Isn't it?" Diana nodded again. Then, with her gaze darting from Rachel to the street and then into the large windows of the restaurant, Diana added, "Well, have a nice brunch, Rachel."

Without waiting for Rachel's good-bye, Diana swung the door open and stepped inside. Rachel let out a small sigh. She and Diana might be dining at the same place, but at least they weren't sitting at neighboring tables. At least, that was what she thought until she happened to look through the window beside her and notice that Diana was being shown to a table just a few feet away. In horror, she realized that she and Diana were going to be side by side, separated by only one large polished pane of glass.

Diana had clearly noticed the uncomfortable proximity too and was now in animated conversation with the waiter. The waiter was gesturing around the room and shrugging. Rachel didn't need to lip-read to know he was telling Diana that the restaurant was full and this was his only free table. As she watched Diana shake her head and move reluctantly toward her seat, Rachel snapped her gaze back to the book in her hands. Her pulse skipped and quickened and she repeated in silence to herself, *Don't look. Don't look. Don't look at her.*

Rachel managed not to look for a few minutes. But sensing Diana beside her, she couldn't concentrate either. Her eyes skimmed the pages of Wharton's novel, but she took in nothing, and her preoccupied mind raced with questions about Diana. Rachel wondered, as always, why Diana was so aloof. She also wondered why Diana had gone through with this strangely intimate seating arrangement when it was clear that she felt awkward in Rachel's presence. In other words, why hadn't Diana hotfooted it to some other brunch spot? After all, there were plenty of others in the neighborhood.

Mostly, Rachel wondered how she was going to survive ten days with Diana on the Literary London trip next month. Peter had come to Rachel's office just yesterday and told her that Diana had volunteered for the program. The news horrified Rachel, but, as a new and eager colleague in the department, she knew she couldn't back out. In the end, Rachel had reassured herself that she would be too busy sightseeing and dealing with students to worry about Diana's indifference.

However, as she sat now with Diana just inches away, Rachel's fear returned, and as her food arrived and she was shaking her napkin over her knees, she stole a worried sideways glance through the glass. Diana was clutching a book too, she noticed. Like Rachel, though, Diana wasn't reading either. With her book in her right hand, Diana was checking the watch on her left. Scared that Diana would catch her, Rachel looked away, but not before it occurred to her that Diana was waiting for someone. The way she checked her watch seemed expectant, anticipatory, rather than simply curious.

Rachel started carving into the French toast that was steaming on her plate, but she stopped short of eating her first mouthful when another thought occurred to her. Perhaps it was Carson. Perhaps Diana was waiting for Carson. The very idea made Rachel flush and look, with darting eyes, up and down the sidewalk. Would she soon be sitting just inches from Diana *and* Carson? Would she have an unhindered view of their brunch date?

After seeing Carson for the first time on Wednesday, Rachel had Googled him—of course. She'd trawled through many sites related to his books, his journal articles, and his reviews in national newspapers. She'd mooned over a couple of photographs from his department's Web page. And when she stumbled across an old alumni newsletter, she discovered that Carson had attended grad school at Harvard at the same time as Diana. They were both in the English department and they graduated just a year apart. Carson and Diana must have known each other, and perhaps were even friends. Rachel couldn't help wondering with a twang of jealousy whether they had been lovers too, once upon a time. It would explain the smiles and twinkles with which they greeted each other back in Wednesday's faculty meeting.

Rachel felt instantly nauseous. She did not want confirmation of their past—perhaps even present—love affair, and she definitely didn't want a ringside seat at Carson and Diana's brunch date. At the same time, a paradoxical excitement bubbled in Rachel's chest at the thought of seeing Carson again. *Would he spot her here?* she wondered. *Would he smile and acknowledge her?* Carson's smiles and his whispered, "Rachel Grey," kept running through her mind, and before Rachel knew what was happening the hand that held her fork was trembling. Rachel quickly slapped the fork back down on her plate, aware that at any moment Diana might spot her jitters.

As Rachel sat in awkward anticipation, unable to eat or concentrate on her book, her gaze occasionally flitting up and down the nearby sidewalk, she heard the familiar trill of her cell phone. Without even thinking about how she might annoy her dining neighbors, Rachel snatched the small phone out of her purse and jabbed at the answer button. She didn't even stop to see whose number glowed on the small blue screen.

"Hello?" she said, her voice sounding decidedly jumpy.

"Honey pie!" was the response. "What's up? You sound anxious."

Rachel let out a small sigh and smiled. It was Kat, Rachel's best friend from grad school and the very person, Rachel suddenly realized, she wanted to talk to at that moment.

"Hey!" Rachel replied. Then, taking a small glance around at Diana, who was back to reading her book, Rachel swiveled away from the window and whispered, "Jeez, Kat. You won't believe this."

The day Rachel first met Carson she'd called Kat and told her everything. Kat had laughed and squeaked excitedly, but she also kept asking, "Are you making this up?" Kat understood better than anyone the dearth of good-looking men in academia and could not fathom a man as delicious as Rachel was describing walking the halls of Manhattan U. Furthermore, like Rachel, Kat had read Carson McEvoy's work and was having a hard time marrying her own image of the esteemed scholar with the Adonis Rachel was convinced she'd met. Only when Rachel made Kat Google the pictures of Carson did she believe her friend.

"And he's sitting right there?!" Kat squawked, after Rachel had filled her in on today's embarrassing brunch situation.

Rachel clutched her phone and shook her head. "No, no. He's not here . . . yet. I just think he might be coming."

Rachel heard Kat making a clicking noise close to the phone. She knew straightaway that Kat was thinking. She always clicked the glinting bolt in her tongue against her top teeth when she thought hard. It used to drive Rachel mad when they'd study together in UNC's library. But now, far away from North Carolina and her old life, Rachel missed that sound. She missed even more her friend's bright green eyes and her sprouting, knotted dreadlocks that tumbled down her back. There was something so alive and playful about Kat, so unlike Rachel's new colleagues at Manhattan U.

"So what's the eminent Professor Diana Monroe like?" Kat asked. "I know you said she's got a stick up her ass, but what does she look like?"

Rachel shifted a little in her seat and took another surreptitious glance at Diana. This time, to Rachel's horror, Diana was looking her way. Her gaze, which seemed fixed on Rachel's phone, was steely and one eyebrow was slightly raised. Rachel swiveled away again and instantly repositioned her cell under her curls, buried her chin toward her chest, and whispered, "She's looking at me."

"What?" Kat barked.

"I said," Rachel whispered, more loudly this time, "I said she's looking at me. I can't talk. She clearly thinks I'm one of those annoying brunch-time cell phoners."

Kat made a loud tutting noise. "Rach, honey pie, you need to get over your fear of this woman. She's just a woman, you know. Like you and me."

"I don't know," Rachel interrupted. "She's so brilliant and beautiful and . . ." She searched for the right words. "She's like an android. You know, perfectly created but with no emotion."

Kat let out one of her raspy laughs—another thing that Rachel missed. "Android, I love it." She chortled. Then, after clicking her tongue a few more times, Kat added in a more serious tone, "Listen to me, Rachel: Carson ain't gonna choose an android over you."

"I don't—" Rachel tried to cut in again.

"You're a babe," Kat pressed on. "Beautiful curls. Beautiful curves. Why would he want Professor Android Monroe?" *Click, click* went Kat's tongue again. "Anyway, it's time you, my dear, got yourself some action. You've moped after dull-boy Justin long enough."

"He wasn't dull," Rachel cut in.

"Rachel, he *was* dull," Kat said, her tone matter-of-fact.

"He could be so funny sometimes," Rachel responded in a weak whisper.

"*Sometimes*," Kat huffed. "Exactly. *Sometimes* he could be very funny and charming. But only when he wanted to be," she added. "Most of the time, all that guy wanted to do was sit on his behind, drink a Bud, and watch men on TV hitting tiny balls with wooden sticks."

"He wasn't that bad. . . ."

Kat simply ignored Rachel. "You know what we're going to do?"

Rachel felt herself sighing. She knew what was coming: one of Kat's great plans. In other words, some crazy idea Kat would cook up and would insist on carrying out to the very end with dogged determination. "Uh-huh?" Rachel prompted, reluctant but resigned.

"We're going to make Carson yours. All yours!"

Rachel made a harrumphing noise.

Kat ignored her and carried on. "First off, you need to throw a little party."

"What?" Rachel squeaked.

"Yep, a little party at your place." Kat was excited now, and Rachel could just imagine her big eyes darting and flashing.

"My place?" Rachel said. "My place is the size of a postage stamp. I can't open a bottle of wine for myself without cracking an elbow on some wall or other. It's hardly the venue for a soiree."

"The more intimate the better," Kat responded, undeterred. "Okay, so, you are going to throw a little party and invite all your new colleagues."

Rachel barked out a laugh that was so loud a couple of her dining neighbors turned to look. Guiltily, she buried her chin again and whispered, "I'm *not* inviting all my new colleagues."

"Yes, you are," Kat insisted. "It's about time you improved your social life up there in the big city. You've been whining for too long about how lonely you are. This is your chance to change all that." She let out an evil giggle. "And it's a chance to get Carson into your home and tasting some of your fine Southern cookin'."

Rachel couldn't help smiling as she was reminded of the parties Kat used to throw back in North Carolina. Packed with all their grad school friends, and any other waifs and strays Kat had picked up, these parties would be loud and lively and would go on into the night. Rachel loved to cook and would always help out preparing the food for the party. Kat's messy and tiny kitchen was always a welcome refuge for Rachel, especially when she and Justin fought more and more. Rachel loved those afternoons before Kat's parties when she'd spend hours preparing a vast table of interesting dips, fragrant rice dishes, and homemade breads. As she chopped, blanched, sautéed, and baked, she would chatter with Kat about all those things she rarely got to talk about with Justin: all her dreams, all her thoughts, all her excitement about her work, her books, and her future.

Rachel enjoyed the parties that followed these afternoons in the kitchen. She particularly loved the tipsy dancing and the animated debates on the front porch that would always end the evenings. But these parties were Kat's parties. They were always her idea and she was always the bubbly, raucous, fun-loving host (it was Kat's love of partying, in fact, that had kept Kat from finishing grad school and that meant that even though she'd started her PhD a year before Rachel, she was still only on the third chapter of her dissertation). Rachel wasn't Kat. She enjoyed a party, but she'd never thought to throw one herself. She was always too preoccupied with her work, her books, and her struggling relationship with Justin.

"Even if I did decide to throw a party, no one would come," Rachel said finally.

"Of course they would," snapped Kat. "Who can resist a party?"

Rachel wasn't so sure. It might be true in sleepy small-town North Carolina, but here in New York everyone had busy, frantic, and exciting lives. Why would they come to some little party in Rachel's three-hundred-square-foot studio apartment when they could be going to a soiree at the Met or an opening at a Chelsea gallery or a dinner party with the editor of *The New Yorker*? But perhaps she was just making excuses. Perhaps Kat was right: A party might be a good idea. Who knew, maybe she'd finally get to know some of her colleagues, and there was a chance, just a chance, that Carson might come too.

As Rachel pondered this and began to flush at the thought of Carson in her apartment, she found herself looking up. To her surprise, she discovered that someone standing by the restaurant door was waving and smiling at her. She shook her curls from her face, refocused, and realized it was Mikey, the English department's computer guy. Returning his wave, she called out, "Hey, Mikey!"

"Who's Mikey?" Kat was asking in Rachel's ear.

Rachel ignored her as Mikey stepped toward her saying, "Hi, Rachel. How are you?" Then, noticing her phone, he said, "Oh, sorry."

Rachel dropped the phone away from her mouth and waved her hand, signaling that it was fine to talk. "Great, thanks," she then replied with a smile. "You?"

He nodded, and Rachel remembered how much she liked Mikey. He was just about the nicest person she'd met since she'd started at Manhattan U. He didn't care that she was a complete Luddite when it came to computers, and one afternoon, at the start of the semester, he had spent over two hours in her office setting up her new computer, hooking it to her printer, and answering her dumb questions about the Manhattan U network. She knew it was his job, but unlike other techies she'd known at UNC, he wasn't condescending. He was sweet and amiable and eminently patient.

Still standing in front of her, Mikey looked like he was going to say something else when his eyes moved suddenly toward the window. Rachel followed his gaze, forgetting for a second who was sitting beyond the glass, but remembering very fast as her eyes landed on Diana. Diana didn't see Rachel; she was too busy glaring at Mikey.

"Rach?" Kat was shouting now. "Are you still there? What's going on?"

Rachel turned back toward Mikey while whispering, "Just a minute," to Kat.

But Mikey was backing up. "Nice to see you, Rachel," he stammered, a flicker of panic crossing his face.

Rachel allowed herself a brief smile and thought to herself, *So I'm not the only person who's afraid of Diana Monroe. Computer techies live in fear of her too.*

But then, as she said her good-bye to Mikey and was about get back to her conversation with Kat, she noticed that instead of heading off down the street, as she'd expected him to do, Mikey was disappearing inside the restaurant.

"What the hell?" she said aloud, unable to believe that he was going to go in there when it was clear that Diana could break him out in a cold sweat of fear and panic.

"Rachel, if you don't tell me what's going on, I'm hanging up," Kat grumbled, sounding genuinely exasperated.

"Sorry, Kat," Rachel said. But she was silenced again when, sensing movement in the window beside her, she glanced around to see Mikey sitting down opposite Diana. "What the hell?" she couldn't help saying aloud again.

She quickly snapped her mouth closed as Diana turned around and with cool, hard eyes stared at Rachel. A lump formed in Rachel's throat, and she instantly remembered something a student had written on one of Diana's Rate-My-Professor.com reviews: *You know what Professor Monroe wants from you by just the flick of her eyes.* The look that Diana was now giving Rachel spoke volumes. *Mind your own business*, it warned Rachel, *or you'll be sorry.*

Rachel looked away and muttered into her phone, "Kat, sorry, I need to get out of here. I'll call you back in a few minutes." Then, unable to stop herself from smiling, she added, "It looks like Carson isn't coming for brunch. Perhaps I will be throwing that party, after all."

"What?" Kat said, but Rachel was already snapping her phone shut and waving at the waiter for her check.

Diana opened her eyes and immediately squinted them shut again. A ray of golden evening sunlight streamed in through her bedroom window and onto the spot where she lay, with her long black hair fanned out on the plump white pillows. One of Mikey's big arms rested across her narrow waist, and she could feel the rise and fall of his gentle, sleepy breaths against her naked back. For a short while, with her eyes closed again, she felt utterly serene, utterly happy. Mikey's warmth radiated around her; it encased her and protected her. *How was he always so warm?* she wondered as she found herself snuggling back against his chest.

A second later, however, a car honking in the street below roused Diana from her nestled stupor, and immediately her body stiffened and began to prickle with panic. *This wasn't supposed to happen,* she thought to herself. She wasn't supposed to be lying in her bed with Mikey while, outside, the sun dipped behind the West Village and the city geared up for another bustling Saturday night. Diana had arranged to have brunch with Mikey today with the sole purpose of telling him it was over; telling him whatever it was that was happening between them had to stop. She'd meant to do it earlier in the week, the night they met in her office after the faculty meeting. But then, just like today, she couldn't bring herself to tell him. On both occasions, Diana looked into Mikey's face and scanned his dark eyes, which were somehow both lost and puppylike yet also reassuring and fearless, and couldn't bring herself to say the words. Each time, her desire took over. Her body yearned to be close to his, and inside she ached to have his soft voice near her ear and his lilting laugh in her bed. The "we must end it" speech, the one she'd rehearsed over and over, would simply evaporate.

But, as Diana forced her eyes open and made them adjust to the piercing sun, her desire for Mikey was trickling away and was now being replaced with a simmering anger and aversion. She often felt like this after they'd made love. But today, her disgust and fury were even stronger. Of course, she knew why this was so. It had everything to do with Rachel. Seeing her young colleague at brunch earlier made Diana agitated from the moment she spotted her outside the restaurant. For one, Rachel's presence reminded Diana about the damned Literary London program she'd volunteered for in a moment of haste. When Peter had told Diana that Rachel was going too, Diana felt she couldn't just back out. After all, it would prove to Peter that she had an issue with Rachel. So it looked like she had to go, but she certainly wasn't happy about it.

However, Rachel's presence at the restaurant was discomforting mostly because she'd witnessed Diana and Mikey's meeting. Diana should have left as soon as she spotted Rachel, but she couldn't. Mikey was already on his way to the restaurant, and so she was forced to sit in fear, silently praying that Rachel would disappear be-

fore Mikey arrived, or that Mikey might be held up on his train from
Jersey City. But to her horror, not only was Mikey on time, but Rachel was still at her table when he arrived. With her heart pounding,
Diana watched as the two smiled and greeted each other outside,
and she then felt Rachel's eyes upon them as Mikey came in and sat
down. While Mikey threw his napkin over his knees and picked up
his menu, Diana found herself turning to the window and looking out
at Rachel. She couldn't help it: She implored with her eyes, begging
Rachel to be kind enough, discreet enough, to keep quiet about what
she was witnessing.

Now, as she peeled Mikey's heavy arm off her naked body and
quietly pushed herself up to sit, Diana frowned at how stupid she'd
been. Of course Rachel wouldn't be discreet. Why would she? Jackie
Rawlings had made it pretty clear in last week's faculty meeting that
Diana wasn't a big fan of Rachel's scholarship. No doubt Rachel was
now nurturing a deep resentment toward Diana, and seeing Diana
and Mikey together today at brunch would have been a gift from the
gods. Rachel would have the perfect weapon to appease her bitterness. By Monday morning, Diana was now convincing herself, most
of her colleagues would know about her affair with Mikey. Rachel
would make sure of it.

And that, Diana thought, as she stood up and pulled her white
bathrobe tight around her, was why she must end it today. When
Mikey woke up, she would tell him he had to leave and he couldn't
come back again—ever. Even if Rachel did keep quiet about what
she'd seen, Diana's affair with Mikey was ludicrous and it was time to
put an end to it. They had absolutely nothing in common. He was a
computer tech, she a tenured professor. She lived alone with her cat
and her books; he lived somewhere in Jersey City with a four-year-old
daughter who spent three nights out of every week staying with him.
Diana coveted her season ticket to the Metropolitan Opera; he, apparently, had a roomful of Johnny Cash memorabilia. They were oil
and water. Chalk and cheese, as they said back in England, where
Diana spent the first half of her life.

Staring out of the window, Diana hugged her arms to her chest and sighed. She'd asked herself this a million times, but she couldn't help asking one more time: Why had she gotten involved with this man anyhow? There was the old "opposites attract" adage, but Diana wasn't the kind of woman who yearned for something opposite. She'd never desired the excitement and danger and uncertainty of a Heathcliff or a Darcy. She'd never even wanted, like her beloved Sylvia Plath, a charismatic and brooding Ted Hughes. Her ex-husband, Graham, had had his charms, but even he was familiar and recognizable to Diana. Behind his good looks and sweet tongue, he was as nerdy and bookish as she was.

Mikey, however, was altogether different. He wasn't dangerous or brooding, but he was utterly unfamiliar to Diana. He talked about things she didn't understand, places she'd never been to, people she'd never heard of. And when she spoke, he often had no idea what she was talking about, and it wasn't uncommon for him to stop her mid-sentence and ask her, with no discernible embarrassment, to explain a word she'd just used. Indeed, he seemed to enjoy having these things explained. *How could she have been naked so many times with this man?* she wondered. *How could they have done the things—those very intimate things—they had done in the past few months?* The same things they had done this very afternoon in this very room.

Diana turned, glanced over at her bed, and studied Mikey's peaceful, sleeping face. Straightaway, desire rippled down her neck to her thighs and undermined everything she'd just been thinking. *Of course* she'd slept with this man. How could she not? The chemistry between them was impossible to deny, and it had been there from the very start.

A couple of months ago, just before the semester began and not long after Mikey had joined the English department, they'd found themselves alone in her office—he was there to fix Diana's printer—and a strange and completely unexpected spark sizzled between them. Not long after, Mikey started calling by her office every other day, then every day, all the while making up lame computer-related excuses to be there. Then, one sultry late-August night, when they were both sitting close at Diana's desk peering at her monitor, both of them pretending to be deeply interested in the virus software Mikey was downloading, Mikey turned and kissed Diana. Even though her mind raced and told her not to kiss him back, Diana couldn't stop her hands from moving up to hold his broad neck and her lips from finding his lips with a deep and needy passion.

From that moment onward their lovemaking was intense and exhilarating. They made love on Diana's desk countless times; they sneaked to his tiny cluttered office and had sex amongst discarded monitors and keyboards; and one time, late at night, they stripped each other naked in the darkness of the faculty lounge and made love on the coarse green carpeting. Their risqué sex surprised Diana. Yet, at the same time, there was always a real tenderness in their lovemaking that made it feel far from slutty or depraved. Mikey had a way of holding Diana's face and staring deep into her eyes with a look of such openness and sincerity, and she never felt used or cheap. In those moments, she knew he wanted her in an all-encompassing way, and she wanted him just the same.

But now, even though she longed to get back into bed and squeeze herself against his warm body, Diana was still simmering with thoughts of Rachel and the likelihood of her affair with Mikey being discovered. She clenched her fists into determined balls and forced herself to move backward toward the bathroom and away from Mikey. When she'd showered off, Diana told herself, closing the bathroom door behind her, she'd feel ready. She would go out, sit on the edge of the bed, wake Mikey, and then tell him, as kindly as she could, that it was over. No excuses this time; she would definitely do it.

An hour later Mikey was gone and Diana sat nursing a glass of red wine in her living room. It was dark outside, and from where she was sitting on her long velvet couch she could see the glow from the lamps in Washington Square Park. Although she was surrounded with books, a swarm of handcrafted furniture, and a scattering of ragged toys for Diana's cat, Sylvia, the apartment felt empty and cold. It had felt that way since Graham left five years ago.

The apartment used to be Graham's, of course. On Diana's salary, she could never have afforded such a place—a large one-bedroom apartment in an old town house on Washington Square. Graham inherited it from one of his many wealthy relatives years ago, and, if he had had his way, it would still be his. He fought hard for the apartment during their divorce, but Diana fought harder. Not because she wanted to keep living here, particularly. She did it purely for revenge. Stripping him of his precious apartment was the only way she could think to hurt him like he'd hurt her.

An emptiness and sadness always followed Diana when she was in the apartment. But now, as she sat on the couch clutching her wine, it was even more distinct. The hollow feeling in Diana's gut echoed this emptiness. Just a short while ago she'd managed to say the words to Mikey. She'd told him she could not see him again and that their affair was done. He'd taken it graciously, with no tears or pleas, but his eyes were sad and glassy with confusion. He'd always known she wanted their affair to be kept quiet, and he'd never disputed it. He'd seemed happy to carry on in the secretive manner that Diana insisted on. Nonetheless, her decision today to end it clearly baffled him. After her speech, he'd gotten dressed very quietly and then, before heading out the door, he turned back and looked with his unnervingly candid eyes at Diana and said, "You deserve to be happy, Diana. I'm sorry I didn't give you that." Before she could say anything in response, he slipped out the door and disappeared down the three flights of stairs to the street. As she listened to his retreat, Diana winced with each of his heavy footfalls.

Once he'd left the building, she'd tried to read for a few minutes with no success. Then she opened her laptop and tried to write, but that didn't work either. Finally, she poured herself a large glass of Syrah, plopped down on the couch, and that was where she'd stayed for the last twenty minutes, clutching her glass and staring into space. Diana knew she'd done the right thing by Mikey, yet she couldn't understand why she felt so emptied out and sad. *You have to pull yourself together and do something*, she scolded herself now and again. But still she remained frozen to her seat, unable to snap out of her hollow daze.

It was the phone, in the end, that roused Diana. Its warbling ring startled her so much, in fact, that she slopped a glob of wine on the couch and rug. Flustered, Diana grabbed with one hand for a Kleenex and with the other for the phone.

"Yes?" she barked, as she hurriedly dabbed at the wine stain.

"Austere as ever," came the laughing reply.

It was a long time since Diana had spoken on the phone with Carson, but she recognized his deep drawl straightaway. She stopped dabbing and sank back down on the couch. For the first time in the last hour, a smile crept over her face.

"My austerity," Diana quipped, "is saved only for the wickedest of people."

Carson chortled. "Oh, believe me. I'm very wicked."

"So I hear," Diana responded, flicking back her hair and draping it over the back of the couch.

Before the faculty meeting the other day, Diana and Carson hadn't seen each other in a few years. In spite of this, they'd quickly slipped back into their old flirtatious banter: the same banter that had started twelve years ago, when they were grad students at Harvard. Carson was probably the only person on earth whom Diana bantered with in this way. Nothing had ever happened between her and Carson, of course, but she always enjoyed their flirtations, and only now realized how much she'd missed them.

Carson was laughing again. "So what are you up to, Professor Monroe?"

"Working very hard, Professor McEvoy," Diana drawled, imitating Carson.

Then, switching effortlessly into more serious tones, Diana and Carson talked for a while about their respective book projects and upcoming conference papers. They also traded "have you heard what happened to?" gossip about other Harvard alumni. Finally, they talked about Carson's visiting professorship at Manhattan U, and Diana painted a quick sketch of her department and its faculty.

"So, nothing new then." Carson laughed when Diana was finished. "Your English department has the usual grab bag of neurotics, backbiters, sticks-in-the-mud, and has-beens."

"Uh-huh." Diana nodded with a smile. "Just like every English department."

There was a pause, and after a couple of clicking noises on the line, Carson said, "Listen, someone's calling me. I have to go." He then switched back into his earlier playful drawl and asked, "So, are you working too hard to accompany me to my father's book-launch party next Saturday?"

Diana grinned and, in that moment, realized that the hollowness in her belly had vanished. "I may be able to squeeze in a book-launch party," she said.

Five

Research

Rachel really should have been preparing for class, skimming over *The House of Mirth* one more time, and jotting down some last-minute questions to ask the students. Her Popular Women's Fiction class started in just under an hour, and she knew that, after her performance last week when she fled from the seminar room, she had to do a better job this afternoon. So far, not one student had made a complaint about her behavior, and she wanted to keep it that way. Furthermore, Rachel suspected that the class would have struggled with Wharton's novel. Therefore, she was going to have all her wits about to fight their despondency and to show them exactly why the book was such an important precursor to and point of reference for the contemporary novels, like *Bergdorf Blondes*, that they would study later in the semester. In short, Rachel needed to be much more prepared than she currently felt.

However, her copy of Wharton's novel remained closed, and Rachel sat in front of her glowing laptop, flitting between various food blogs and chefs' Web sites. Having tapped the word "meze" into Google, she was now comparing the various recipes that the search had conjured up. "Pan-fried olives with oregano," "Zucchini fritters with garlic dipping sauce," "Feta saganaki"—the descriptions were as mouthwatering as the soft-focus photographs that accompanied them.

It wasn't unusual for Rachel to waste time hopping between food Web sites like this. She loved food, loved cooking, and often filled

many an hour exploring new recipes. It was the perfect procrastina-
tion activity, especially when she was tired of working on her new
book or when she was numbed by a vast pile of student papers that
needed grading. Today, though, Rachel had a legitimate reason for her
research. She had decided to take Kat's advice. This coming Saturday
night she was going to throw a party for her colleagues. Rachel had
convinced herself that Kat was right: It was definitely time to improve
her social life in New York, and if Carson happened to come to the
party too, well, that would just be the icing on the cake.

Now that she'd made the decision, Rachel was surprisingly excited. She'd already decided on a Middle Eastern theme for her buffet, and last night she'd loaded up her rickety shopping cart with
affordable but carefully selected bottles of wine from the wine store
on Union Square. She'd spent far too many hours daydreaming about
being caught in a corner of her crowded apartment with Carson, the
two of them fuzzy on wine and Carson staring down with his chestnut
eyes into her hazel-green ones. And when she realized what she was
doing and told herself to stop with these daydreams, she was having
long phone conversations with Kat discussing, among other things,
the issue of invitations. Rachel wanted to simply send an e-mail to
the English department's faculty list, but Kat persuaded her that she'd
have more success if she invited each of her colleagues in person.

"They can just ignore an e-mail, pretend they never got it," Kat
had said, "but they can't ignore you in the flesh, all smiling and
beautiful!"

Rachel gulped and asked, "Does that mean I have to personally
invite Carson?" she paused. "And Diana too?"

"Yep," was Kat's succinct reply.

So far, inviting her colleagues had gone surprisingly well. Over
the past two days, nearly everyone she'd spoken to smiled and said
something along the lines of, "How lovely. Thank you, Rachel. I'll try
to make it." Indeed, she'd been so efficient with her invitations that
she had only two left to go, and it was her mission today to issue these
last invites: one to Carson and the other, of course, to Diana. The

thought of inviting both of them sent Rachel's stomach vaulting and somersaulting, but she knew it had to be done.

And so, as soon as Rachel had printed out some particularly appealing meze recipes, she opened one of her desk drawers and pulled out her makeup bag. Holding up a small mirror that she retrieved from the tatty old bag, Rachel teased her curls with her fingers and then checked for mascara clumps and wayward hairs between her eyebrows. She then swiped some clear gloss over her lips, puckered her mouth, and threw the whole makeup bag back into the drawer. Finally, she stood up and wiggled her pencil skirt so it was straight on her hips and smoothed down her linen blouse.

"Here I go," she muttered, before taking a deep breath and walking out of her office and along the hallway.

Carson would be first, she'd already decided. Rachel still had no idea if he was single and whether he would come to her party on his own (if he came to her party at all). But a couple of things did give her hope—he wore no wedding band, and he wasn't dating Diana. After her awkward meeting with Diana on Saturday, it was clear to Rachel that Diana was dating Mikey. Why else would a professor and a computer technician be meeting for brunch during the weekend? And the way Mikey looked at Diana when he sat down at their table spoke volumes. He was completely in love with her; it was so obvious. Diana didn't return his look of love, of course. Rachel doubted whether Diana the ice queen could ever offer someone such an adoring gaze.

Rachel was now nearing Carson's office, but the bounce in her stride was starting to wane. Just because he wasn't dating Diana didn't mean he wasn't dating anybody else. A man like Carson probably had a swarm of women knocking at his door asking him to parties all the time. Rachel kept walking nevertheless. She'd come this far, and it would look bad now if she didn't invite Carson when the rest of the faculty had already received their invitations. Plus, she hadn't set eyes on Carson since Friday, and she had to admit she was missing the delicious sight of him.

Carson's door was shut when Rachel reached it, so she knocked gently. At first there was no reply, and immediately Rachel's spirits sank. After all her planning and fretting, he wasn't even in. However, just as she was about to knock a second time, she heard Carson's low voice calling, "Come in." Rachel swiftly reached for the door handle but found that it dipped down out of her reach, and she was left grasping air as the door swung open. Instead of Carson standing before her, as she'd expected, Rachel found herself face-to-face with one of the Nilsen twins.

Without hesitation, Rachel's gaze moved down to the young woman's purse. It was a bright red, extra-large Goyard bag with racing stripes, which meant this was Veronica. Her sister, Rebecca, Rachel had observed, always carried a more conservative Tod's tote in soft camel-colored leather. The difference in their choice of purse was the only way Rachel could tell apart the two sisters, who were both in her freshman seminar, Introduction to Literary and Cultural Studies. Rachel was no designer-clothes junkie—she couldn't afford to be—but she read *Us* magazine obsessively enough at the gym to know which purses were hot and which were not and which, if she did have any money, she would buy.

"Hello, Veronica," Rachel said with a smile, as her eyes snapped back up to the girl's face.

Veronica's big blue eyes looked glassy and distant as she huffed a brief, "Hello." She then turned back to Carson, whom Rachel could now see lounging in his office chair in front of a vast oak desk, and rearranged her delicate features and lips into a sparkling, camera-ready smile. "See you soon, Professor McEvoy," she purred.

Veronica then moved out of Carson's office. As she passed Rachel, she threw her floaty cashmere shawl over her shoulder and in doing so swiped Rachel's face. Without acknowledging or apologizing for what she'd done, Veronica strode off down the hallway. Meanwhile, Rachel stood in the doorway feeling humiliated, angry, and decidedly unglamorous. Carson was grinning up at her and looking more gorgeous than ever in a soft blue shirt and a pair of fashionably distressed indigo jeans—which served only to make Rachel feel even more ridiculous and agitated.

"These starlet students," Carson whispered, still grinning and with an exaggerated shake of his head that sent his dark rumpled hair flopping into his eyes. "They can be such hard work."

Rachel let out a relieved laugh and said, also in a whisper, "Luckily, that one"—she jerked a thumb over her shoulder—"never shows up for my class."

Carson beckoned Rachel into his office, waved toward the chair opposite him, and asked, "She doesn't?"

"Well, occasionally she does. When she hasn't got a fashion shoot, or an audition, or a hangover, or anything else more pressing to do," Rachel went on, as she seated herself and looked around Carson's large, white, and elegantly sparse office. "Although if I had to choose between a fashion shoot or my class on literary and cultural studies, I'd probably choose to play hooky too," she added with a chuckle.

When Rachel was finished, she looked over and realized Carson's sleepy eyes were staring at her with a curious twinkle. Straightaway, heat flashed across her cheeks, and she realized she'd been burbling on like some banal, excited teenager.

"I-I'm sorry," she stammered, pushing herself out of her seat. "You're probably very busy and . . ."

Carson silenced Rachel as he reached across, gently touched her forearm, and said, "Please sit. I have plenty of time for Rachel Grey." He paused, flashed a grin that made Rachel's heart stop, and then asked, "What can I help you with?"

Rachel's cheeks burned once more. "I'm having a small party at my place this Saturday," she muttered, feeling more adolescent and absurd with every word. "Eight o'clock. It will start at eight." She looked up and Carson's eyes were still twinkling. "But you must have plans."

She began to push herself out of her seat and once again Carson reached over and touched her arm. This time his hand lingered for a second or two. The heat from his fingers shot up Rachel's arm and tingled at the nape of her neck. "Of course I'd love to come," Carson said with a gentle smile.

"Great," Rachel squeaked out.

Carson continued to smile. Rachel pulled her eyes away from his. If she didn't look at him, she wouldn't feel so flustered, so love-struck, so impossibly happy that he'd just agreed to come to her party. Instead, her gaze meandered to his desk, where a myriad of books and papers were stacked up.

"I read your article in *Differences*," she blurted out, remembering his piece in the journal.

"You did? And what did you think?"

"Interesting," she said, finally looking back at Carson.

"Just *interesting*?" His eyes were wide with surprise.

"No, it was *very* interesting. It's just . . ." Rachel then stopped herself.

Should she tell Carson what she really thought? She had a pretty big crush on this guy. The last thing she should do was critique his work.

"It's just what?" Carson prompted. He was now leaning forward on his desk. His dark eyes bored into hers. He'd morphed once again into the intense scholar.

"Well, I . . ."

She paused for a second, but then thought, *Darn it, just tell him.* Rachel had never been very good at holding back, and she couldn't do it now either.

"Well, I think you overlooked some important gender issues when it came to Rushdie's novel."

"It was a postcolonial reading of Rushdie, not a gender one," Carson shot back.

"But aren't those things always, necessarily, entwined? The postcolonial identity is always a gendered identity too."

Rachel then explained her reading of the novel and where she thought Carson's paper had fallen short. Carson looked at her, his gaze intent and unflinching. At one point, he even picked up his pen and made some notes.

When she was finished, Carson simply nodded and said, "You may have a point, Rachel Grey. You may have a point."

He was then silent for a good few beats, and Rachel found herself fidgeting a little in her seat. *Had she upset him?* she wondered. He didn't seem upset, though. He just seemed deep in thought. She studied him for a few seconds and once again realized that Carson baffled her. She really could not pin this guy down. He was such a blend of scholarliness and sexiness. It was quite unnerving, and also incredibly appealing.

"I should leave you to it," she said finally.

Carson nodded. "I have a class to get to."

"But I'll see you Saturday, then?"

Carson looked confused.

"At my party," Rachel reminded him.

"Oh, yes, of course." Carson then clapped his hand to his forehead. "Oh, no, I just remembered my father's book party is on Saturday night."

A wave of disappointment rolled in Rachel's chest. "Oh, right, of course," was all she could say in response.

"But perhaps I can stop by your party afterward?" Carson asked, and before she could answer, the twinkling, flirtatious face was back. "I'm sure Rachel Grey's parties go on into the night, don't they?"

She had no idea what Carson meant by that, or what kind of person he thought "Rachel Grey" was, but she didn't care. He was going to stop by her party, which was all that mattered.

"Sure," she said as she beamed over at Carson. "Sure they do." Then, feeling her confidence growing, she added, "Like any diligent young professor at Manhattan U, I have wild late-night parties *all* the time."

"Wild, eh? I see." Carson's eyes sparkled. "Well, definitely count me in then."

Down the hallway, Diana was alone in her office. Her laptop was open on her desk and she was studying the screen. Ten minutes ago, she'd remembered her plans for Saturday night and found herself getting curious about Carson's father. Although Fergus McEvoy was a National Book Award winner and a darling of the literary elite, Diana had never read one of his books. From reviews she'd read in the *Times* and author profiles in *The New Yorker*, she'd formed the impression that Fergus and his writing were rather grandiose and macho and thus something she wouldn't particularly care for. However, if Diana was going to his book party this weekend, it seemed she must learn a little more, and so, with the aid of Google, she was now doing a crash course on Fergus McEvoy and his oeuvre.

Just a minute ago, she'd stumbled across a Web site that showed an old black-and-white photograph of Fergus standing with a young boy who, although the caption didn't state it, was clearly Carson. The picture was titled, "Fishing in Maine, 1975," and showed Fergus and Carson standing on some windswept rocks, fishing rods in hand, with a frothy ocean squalling behind them. Their smiles were wide, their hair was ruffled by the wind, and their cable-knit sweaters were matching. Diana's gaze settled on the older McEvoy. It was uncanny how much he looked like the Carson she knew now. He had the same playful grin, the same rumpled dark hair, and same chocolate eyes. Even his laugh lines were identical to the ones Carson had sprouted since the last time she saw him, nearly five years ago.

After studying the photograph for some time, Diana tapped the down arrow on her laptop's keyboard and came across another photograph taken on the same trip. "Islesboro, Maine, Summer Vacation, 1975," read the title. In front of a vast and rambling cape cottage stood a group of perhaps fifteen people, with Fergus at their center. This was clearly the extended McEvoy family. As Diana scanned the picture, she noticed that every person—every child and adult and grandparent, every boy and girl, man and woman—was unmistakably attractive. Their smiles were brilliant white, their hair was rich and healthy, their shoulders were wide, and their legs were long. Everything about them spoke of beauty and comfort—and mostly wealth.

So unlike Diana's own family, in other words. Even though Diana had been educated at boarding schools and then Oxford and Harvard universities, there was definitely no blue blood in Diana's veins and certainly no windswept, idyllic vacation homes to inherit. Before he'd retired, Diana's father was a machinist at a shoe factory in the small, run-down town where they lived just outside of London. Meanwhile, her mother worked the early shift at a local bakery, and not once in her working life had she slept later than four a.m. The small town house where they lived, which was packed into an endless row of other similar houses, had just one bedroom, which her parents slept in. Diana, their only child, had to make do with the old couch in the living room. The only picture Diana remembered that could be called a family vacation photograph was taken when she was about seven. It showed Diana and her parents sitting on a bench with fish and chips unwrapped in their laps and scrappy seagulls encircling their feet. They were on the pier at Southend-on-Sea, a seaside resort just twenty miles from their home. The photograph wasn't flattering. Her mother looked dumpy, dressed in an unflattering and unseasonal raincoat. Her dad was grinning with his crooked teeth and squinting into the sun. Diana herself looked sullen and uncomfortable, her eyes underlined by two dark circles and her black hair pulled back into a sloppy ponytail.

Not long after this photo was taken, Diana was singled out as an extraordinarily bright child by a teacher at her local school. Grants and scholarships followed, and soon Diana left to go to expensive private schools (whose gardens alone were bigger than her hometown) and university colleges (which were wealthier than all the shoe and bakery businesses in England put together). Once she'd left and the years passed, Diana's trips home got more and more infrequent. She missed her parents, and she missed belonging to a family, but when she returned to her mother and father's tiny house they would fuss around her as if she were the queen, offering tea in their finest china and feeding her scones specially baked for the occasion. Their conversations would be polite and strained and would always return to the weather. On these visits, Diana felt removed, different, and awkward, like a tourist in a foreign land.

When Diana moved to the States, she continued to send Christmas cards, birthday gifts, and money, which she was pretty sure her parents never spent, but her visits home stopped. When she married Graham she'd invited them to the wedding, but they didn't come because, according to her mother's letter, her father's arthritic knee was "playing up." Though Diana would never have admitted it, she was pleased they didn't make it. Graham's family were New England WASPs much like the McEvoys. Just the thought of her own dowdy, uneducated, and bewildered parents standing for the obligatory family pictures among the Cartwrights, a vast and handsome family of doctors and lawyers, made Diana cringe.

Still looking at the picture of the McEvoys, but thinking now about her ex-husband's family and her own, Diana found that she was frowning. She hated herself for being so ashamed of her parents back then, especially since Graham had gone and left her anyway. Plus, she now understood that her parents' decision not to come was because of their own shame. They'd known, as she had, how much they wouldn't have fit in. In the end, they'd decided it was better not to come. They didn't want to embarrass their beautiful and successful daughter.

What she hated more than her parents' and her own shame, however, was the fact that she still hadn't told them about her divorce. For the last five years, her parents continued to send Christmas cards addressed to the two of them, and every year her mother would ask, in her neat, tiny handwriting, if Graham was well, and would instruct Diana to pass on her best wishes. Each year, Diana would keep up the lie as she held her breath and signed Graham's name on her own Christmas card to her parents.

She hated the lie, of course, but the thought of telling the truth was much worse. Diana's parents were so proud of her. They owned copies of all her books, they framed copies of every certificate she'd

ever received, they compiled a scrapbook of all her newspaper clip-
pings (even the foreign ones, which they had to send off for in the
mail), and pictures of Diana in graduation gowns adorned their cluttered mantelpiece. As far as Diana could tell, she embodied the life
and the chances her parents never had, and she gave meaning to
their efforts and their hardships. A divorced daughter, a daughter
left by her husband for another woman, didn't fit into their dreams
and aspirations for their only child. The news would devastate them
and would prompt worry and heartache they really didn't need. Or so
Diana thought.

Realizing her mood had turned sour, Diana closed the Web site
and the photo of the McEvoys and busied herself with the pile of mail
in her in-tray. Since Saturday, the day she'd broken up with Mikey,
her spirits had ebbed and flowed. One minute she'd be fine, looking
forward to her newly focused life, cleansed of Mikey and filled with
books and writing. The next minute she'd be feeling empty and angry
and sour. Just like she was feeling now.

As Diana prodded her silver letter opener into the first envelope,
there was a knock at the door. Immediately her mood volleyed up-
ward as it occurred to her it might be Carson. All week he'd been
paying her daily visits and, over steaming cappuccinos, which Carson
would bring from the Italian café on Bleecker Street, they'd flirt and
grin and talk about the old times. They understood each other's need
to work, though, and Carson always returned to his office after half
an hour or so.

It wasn't Carson now, however. Instead, after Diana's shout of,
"Come in," it was Rachel's head that peeked around her office door.
Diana stiffened at the sight of Rachel's wide smile and bobbing curls.
The letter opener remained poised and frozen in her hand. Peter had
been right, of course: Rachel did look like Annabelle—Graham's,
her ex's, Annabelle. They shared the same bouncing hair, the same
girlish face; even their eyes were similar. The only difference was
their frames. Rachel was curvier, more womanly, more wholesome.
Whereas Annabelle, who was just twenty-three when Graham ran off

with her, was waifish, coltish, and clearly living on an early-twenties diet of cigarettes and late nights.

"Hello, Diana," Rachel said, as she stepped into the room. But before Diana could respond, Rachel gabbled on, still smiling: "Sorry to disturb you. It's just, well, on Saturday I'm hosting a small party at my place." Rachel paused, and Diana watched as a flush of pink dotted each of her pretty cheeks, "Anyway, I wondered if you'd like to come."

A tightness gathered in Diana's chest that, within a second, moved up to form a lump in her throat. She felt strangled, gagged; she felt like it would take every last ounce of her energy to speak. Finally, though, as the dots on Rachel's cheeks turned an even deeper crimson, Diana found her voice.

"Thank you, Rachel." Diana sounded a little strained. "Unfortunately, I have plans for Saturday night, but it was kind of you to think of me."

Diana spotted a small sigh heaving in Rachel's chest and escaping with an almost infinitesimal puff out of her nose. Once again, Diana was reminded of Rachel's fear: the fear that Diana managed to instill and that secretly pleased Diana, because it meant Rachel remained at a distance. But, if Diana was honest with herself, the fear wasn't all on Rachel's side now. As far as she knew, Rachel hadn't gossiped about seeing Diana and Mikey together last weekend. But fearful people were capable of doing bitter, cowardly things, and who knew what Rachel's fear might stir her to do? Diana was afraid that Rachel would not hold her silence.

"Too bad," Rachel was now saying as she shuffled backward through the door. "Okay, well, I'll leave you—"

But Rachel didn't finish because, just as she took her final backward step out of the open doorway, she collided with Peter, who, by the looks of things, had been idling along the corridor with a file propped in his hands and his thoughts elsewhere. As the two made contact, papers popped from his orange file and cascaded to the floor.

"Shit, sorry, sorry," Rachel muttered, as she swooped down and bustled around retrieving the paperwork.

"No, no." Peter waved his hands. "My fault entirely. Sorry, Rachel." He bent down to help Rachel but ended up bumping her forehead with his own as he reached for the last sheaf of paper.

"Ouch," the two of them cried out.

Still on their knees, they rubbed their heads and chuckled shyly together. Peter then stood and put out his hand for Rachel. Once she was standing and they had done a clumsy dance of hands as Rachel returned his papers, Peter looked at Rachel and asked with a grin, "Are you sure you want a group of ham-fisted academics in your house on Saturday night? We might wreak havoc with your fine china."

Rachel threw back her head and laughed. "I'll be locking up the china. Strictly paper cups and plastic utensils for the scholarly herds." Rachel paused and her eyes darted in Diana's direction; she then said in a more subdued tone, "Hope to see you on Saturday, Peter."

"I'll be there," chimed Peter, before the two of them maneuvered around each other and headed in opposite directions, away from Diana's doorway.

Diana watched the whole thing from behind her desk as an uneasy feeling churned and grew in her stomach. As her two colleagues disappeared from sight, Diana realized in a flash what had unsettled her. It was Rachel and the effect she had on men. Even Peter—solid, dependable, cerebral Peter—was not immune. No doubt Annabelle was the same. A disconcerting image flickered through Diana's mind in which Rachel and Peter were now Annabelle and Graham. *Perhaps this was how they met?* Diana wondered. Perhaps they had collided in the hallways of the classics department, and as Annabelle had fussed around picking up his papers Graham had found himself captivated and love-struck at the sight of her.

A chill swooped up and down Diana's spine, and so she got out of her chair and strode toward the doorway. Once there, she pushed the door shut and stood with her back against the adjacent wall, taking deep breaths.

"Stop," she ordered herself, her forehead furrowed and her jaw set. "Stop this."

Fortunately, she was saved from more painful thoughts about Graham and Annabelle by yet another knock at the door. She was tempted to ignore whoever it was. But she needed the distraction of a needy student or an irate colleague, so she pulled down the handle and opened the door. Behind two cups of coffee stood a grinning Carson. Without saying a word, Diana waved Carson into her office and plucked a hot coffee from his hand as he passed. She pulled off the lid, took a quick sip, and felt her frown evaporating into the steam.

Six

Wine Studies 101

It was a little before eight on Saturday night and Rachel stood in front of the window in her studio apartment. Just a second ago, she'd been flitting around straightening the bowls and dishes crowded onto her small dining table, shuffling the warmed pita in the bread basket, and taking tiny mouthfuls of her homemade hummus and feta saganaki to see if their balance of flavors was just right. She'd fluffed the woven cushions on her futon (now folded for more room), shaken and straightened her small Persian rug, and twirled around the bottles of red wine so their labels were facing front. Finally, after what seemed an eternity of fussing and tweaking, she opened a bottle of white wine from the fridge and poured herself a large glass. Her party was due to start in a few minutes and she needed some wine and a small breather to calm her jittery nerves.

Staring out at the Manhattan skyline, Rachel took a small sip of the crisp, cold wine and smiled. She still couldn't believe this was the view from her window. It was too incredible. Elsewhere in the city, people were paying thousands—millions, even—for this kind of view, and Rachel was paying only eight hundred bucks a month. Thanks, she was sure, to some blip in the system or some strange fold in the universe, Rachel had wound up getting a twentieth-floor apartment in Manhattan U's faculty housing. The place was small, of course. Indeed, it was a struggle to squeeze her futon, small table, tiny dresser, and desk into the space. But none of this mattered. She didn't care that she had to hurdle her futon every morning just to make a cup of coffee, or that her summer clothes were stored in the oven. This apartment, with its wide picture window, was all her dreams come true. Rachel had wanted to live in Manhattan all her life, and now here she was in the heart of Greenwich Village, looking up at the twinkling Empire State and Chrysler buildings. Her parents would no doubt chuckle if they came to visit and saw this view. They'd remember how, as a girl, Rachel used to build New York–style apartment buildings for her Barbie dolls from old shoe boxes. Justin would laugh too. He'd remember the battered poster of the twinkling Manhattan skyline that was tacked, curling and bubbling, to their bathroom wall all the years they lived together. He didn't understand her love for the "big, foul-smelling city," but he let the poster stay on the wall anyway.

Rachel took another sip of wine and made herself smile. Tonight wasn't for thoughts about Justin. Tonight was about her new life, her new colleagues, and perhaps, just perhaps, a new adventure with a new man. Still smiling, Rachel turned back and looked at the buffet on her small table. The party had been a good idea after all, she decided. Her colleagues might be unimpressed by her cramped apartment, but they would enjoy the view and they would enjoy this: the food she'd lovingly prepared. One thing Rachel was confident about was her cooking. Justin, for one, could never resist. Even after their fiercest of rows, he would always want to make up at the sight of Rachel's cranberry-and-white-chocolate cookies or a tray of her perfectly roasted and rosemary-sprinkled potatoes, or at the smell of her freshly baked hazelnut bread.

Today she'd surpassed herself. The zucchinis were crispy, the olives delicately herbed, and the pitas soft and fluffy. Indeed, as she thought about the table stacked with interesting and glistening meze, her stomach growled. Rachel had dipped and pecked as she cooked, but she hadn't eaten a proper meal all day. *You must remember to eat*, she told herself, as she turned back and looked around the room, hunting for any last bowl or cushion that might need tweaking.

At nine thirty, Rachel sat in the office chair by her desk and was

clutching her fourth glass of wine. She still hadn't eaten. Opposite
Rachel sat Peter Zadikian and Mikey O'Brien. The two men, lanky
Peter and wide-shouldered Mikey, dwarfed the low futon on which
they found themselves seated side by side. With empty food plates
by their feet and a glass of wine and a beer in their respective hands,
Peter and Mikey were smiling and laughing. Rachel was doing the
same, although her smiles were wider and her laughs looser and more
giggly. Her cheeks were glowing from the wine.

So far, no one had mentioned the fact that they were the only
three people in the room. No one had mentioned, in other words,
that Mikey and Peter were the only members of Manhattan U's English department who'd turned up for the party. Rachel's disappointment was currently being numbed by her growing wine haze and by
the surprisingly good time she was having with Mikey and Peter. Only
now and again would she sneak a look at the door and wonder whether
Carson might show. His book party would surely still be going on, she
reasoned, so there was a chance he might turn up.

Grabbing his plate and getting up from the futon, Mikey finally
broached the subject they'd all been carefully avoiding.

"Rachel," he said as he moved toward the table, clearly going in
for his third helping, "this food is amazing. I'm sorry none of the other
fuckers in our department turned out to try it. Excuse my language,"
he added with a quick wink.

Rachel laughed, but her laugh was too squeaky and forced, and
she could feel her pink wine flush turning crimson. "It doesn't matter." She waved a hand in the air. "I'm just glad I got to feed you
guys."

Peter leaned forward. "You mustn't take it personally, Rachel," he
said. "People have so many commitments, so many other distractions
in this city."

Peter's soft and serious tone made Rachel's eyes prick with tears,
but she kept smiling.

He went on. "In small university towns in the middle of nowhere
everyone itches for the company of other academics. You remember

what it was like. But here"—Peter waved toward Rachel's window and gave a small smile—"people have friends who are actors and writers and antique dealers and fashion designers. . . ."

"So why would they want to hang out with a bunch of crusty academics, right?" finished Rachel, with another forced laugh.

Mikey waved a pita bread. "Excuse me," he said. "Speak for yourselves. I'm no crusty academic. I'm a very hip and interesting computer technician." He wiggled his jean-clad behind and the three of them laughed again. Then, with plate in hand, Mikey sat back down and said, "But Peter's right, Rachel: Don't sweat it. Some people have all these screwed-up ideas of who it is cool to hang with and who they should be seen with. Often they get so caught up with these ideas, they don't know how to have fun, how to be happy."

As Mikey spoke Rachel was sure she caught a glimmer of bitterness, or perhaps sadness, in his eyes. There was something so kind and open about this guy, but there was also a curious flicker of hurt. She had a sudden tipsy urge to take hold of his cheeks and kiss him gently on the forehead, like a mother would do to a child.

She restrained herself, though, and instead jumped to her feet and said, "Well, *we* know how to have fun."

After pouring herself another glass of wine, Rachel took her iPod from its speaker dock on her desk and started to fiddle with it. Up until now, the iPod had been playing the tracks that she'd painstakingly picked out before the party.

"Aha," she shouted, as she finally found what she was looking for. "Anyone for disco?" she then asked, and, as she hit play on her iPod, she sang, "D-I-S-C-O."

With her wine slopping in her hand, she started to dance. Mikey and Peter were reluctant at first, but before long they pulled their large frames off the futon and joined her. Soon, all three were jiving, flailing, and doing John Travolta—style finger points and thrusts—all within the fifteen square feet of space that Rachel's apartment could offer as a dance floor. As they danced, they laughed and clapped and drank. Rachel drank the most, of course. She was having fun, but she needed the buzz of the wine to stave off the night's disappointments.

An hour or so later, they had danced their way through the whole of the *Saturday Night Fever* sound track and most of a *Best of ABBA* collection. Rachel had drunk another half bottle of white wine and was beginning to stumble and totter. A few times, Mikey or Peter had to stick out a protective arm so she wouldn't clatter into her lovingly made buffet or onto her desk.

"Whoa, there, Dancing Queen," Mikey shouted, as he caught Rachel another time with his wide arm. "Perhaps we should take a breather."

Rachel slumped into her office chair and hitched her tired feet onto the desk. As she did so, she noticed the time—nearly eleven— and a wave of gloom hit her. Carson wasn't going to show. He had better places to be, better friends to hang out with, beautiful friends to hang out with. Why had she even thought for a second that he might want to drop in at her lame party?

Because she was now completely giddy on wine, she couldn't keep her disappointment to herself this time. Looking over at Mikey and Peter, who'd flopped back on the futon, she blurted out, "So, why do you think Carson didn't show? Which cool friends is he hanging out with tonight?" She didn't mean for her tone to sound so bitter. It just came out that way.

Mikey and Peter looked at Rachel, then each other, then back again at Rachel. Mikey spoke first: "You mean that McEvoy guy? That visiting professor dude?"

Rachel lolled her head up and down.

Mikey let out a laugh and slapped one of his thighs. "I knew that one would be a lady-killer." He winked playfully at Rachel. "Do you like him, Rachel?"

Rachel didn't even blush. She was too buzzed to be embarrassed. Lots of wine, in fact, always made Rachel the opposite of coy or self-conscious. It quite often made her stupidly and dangerously unabashed.

"Yes." She flashed Mikey a grin and an exaggerated wink. "I *really* like him."

"Knew it." Mikey chuckled, taking a swig of his beer.

Then, lowering his bottle and looking over at Rachel, he paused for a moment. As she watched him, Rachel realized she wasn't the only one who'd had a lot to drink. Mikey's cheeks had a rosy glow too, and his eyes looked glassy and unfocused. His grin was slightly lopsided.

"I have an idea," Mikey said finally, slapping his leg again. "Let's catch you a Carson."

Rachel, who'd been taking a sip of her drink, spat a mouthful of wine unceremoniously down her black V-neck. Wiping her mouth with the back of her hand and then running her hand over her top (she was too drunk to use a napkin), Rachel demanded, "What?"

"If Carson isn't coming to your party, let's take this party to Carson!" Mikey's eyes flashed and sparkled.

Through the fog of alcohol, which seemed to be getting thicker by the second, Mikey's words made complete sense to Rachel.

"Yes," she shouted. "Let's do it." But as she swung her feet from the desk and leaned forward in her seat, her forehead furrowed. "But how are we going to, you know, Carson me? I mean, catch me a Carson?" She was beginning to slur.

"Easy," Mikey said, taking another slug of his beer. "We'll find out his address and pay him a visit."

"But how . . ." Rachel began, but she was stopped by the sound of Peter clearing his throat.

Rachel and Mikey turned and looked over at him. He'd been so quiet in the last few minutes, Rachel had almost forgotten he was there. Peter was now pushing himself up to standing and smoothing down his black jeans.

"It's getting kind of late," he said quietly, and then, gesturing toward the door, he added, "I should get going."

Rachel said nothing for a second. Their party of three seemed like it would go on all night, and she felt strangely numbed at having Peter suddenly leave like this.

"Really?" she said, as she slouched forward and sloppily touched his arm.

He nodded. "But thank you, Rachel." He smiled as he took her hand in his and squeezed it. "It's been great. The food *and* the disco."

"Oh, please stay," she begged, but his warm hand had already dropped hers and he was moving toward the door.

As he put on his coat, he shook his head. "I should go. I'll see you both on Monday." He then opened the door and slipped outside.

Rachel and Mikey stared at the closed door, both of them squinting a little, thanks to the booze.

"He probably has to run three hundred miles in the morning," Mikey said, breaking the ensuing silence. "I heard he's training for the New York City Marathon. Not to worry. We can still catch you a Carson without Fisherman Zadikian to help us."

Rachel's numb feeling trickled away and she found she was giggling again.

"Aye-aye, Captain," she slurred, and, after taking another big hit of wine, she asked, "So, how do we get Carson's address?"

"He's probably not in the faculty database yet, seeing as he's just visiting. But the department office is sure to have something on him." Mikey then struggled to retrieve something from his jeans pockets.

Finally, he pulled out his key chain and wiggled two keys in front of Rachel. "Not only do I have a key to the office, I have a key to the very, *very* important filing cabinet where they keep the personal records on faculty and students."

Rachel grabbed at the keys but missed. She tried again and caught them. "Ooh," she said, waggling her eyebrows, "this might be fun."

Mikey looked at Rachel. His eyes were still bleary and unfocused, but, like earlier, there was a trace of something sadder and more serious too. "I don't know about you, Rachel," he said with a small smile, "but I could do with some fun right now."

Mikey got to his feet, offered Rachel a hand to help her up, and then the two of them headed out of the apartment, swaying and laughing as they went. Behind them all the lights were left on, the stereo was blaring, and the door was unlocked.

Diana never spoke on her cell phone when at parties or coffee dates or out with friends for dinner. She hated it when others did it, and so she only ever used her phone when she was alone or well away from other listening ears. Tonight, though, amid the hubbub of Fergus McEvoy's book-launch party in the exclusive back room of Nobu Fifty Seven and shielded by the chatter of New York celebrities, *Times* journalists, and big guns of the publishing world, Diana had broken her self-imposed rule. When her phone had buzzed a few minutes ago, she'd peeked into her purse to see her friend Mary's name flashing on the small screen and instantly grabbed the phone. Carson had long since disappeared from Diana's side—he was now milling amongst his father's friends, talking, shaking hands, and laughing his dazzling laugh—and she had been left by herself in a corner, sipping her third glass of wine. Diana was never very good at mingling at these kinds of events. She preferred to stay on the margins, watching and listening.

And so, when Mary's call came, Diana couldn't resist answering. The wine had left her feeling a little giddy and excited and thus eager to share with someone the details of where she was and what she was seeing. Mary Havemeyer was the perfect person. Up until last June, Mary had been a creative writing professor at Manhattan U. She had also been Diana's closest friend in the department. But Mary had moved out west to a new post at Golden Gate College, and these days she and Diana had to make do with a friendship via phone and e-mail.

"Fergus McEvoy, eh?" Mary chuckled down the line, after Diana had filled her in on where she was. "I haven't seen old Fergus in years."

Diana's eyebrows shot up. "You know him?"

"Years ago I did. His first novel came out the same month as mine. We ended up doing a lot of readings in the same towns and bumping into each other at the same parties. But then, I don't know, he kind of disappeared, or maybe I disappeared." Mary laughed again. "Anyhow, I don't think he ever got over *Casey's Echoes* winning the prize."

"The prize," of course, meant the Pulitzer, which Mary had won back in the early seventies for her book *Casey's Echoes*: an accomplishment that she very rarely mentioned. Indeed, Diana was surprised that Mary had mentioned it now. Although, since Mary had moved to San Francisco and escaped the black cloud otherwise known as Dean Jack Havemeyer, her ex-husband, Mary was like a new woman: confident, strong, sparkling, and happy.

The new Mary was laughing now. "And poor Fergus certainly didn't get over the fact that I wouldn't sleep with him."

Diana coughed on the sip of wine she'd just taken. "He tried to sleep with you?"

"That rogue McEvoy tries to sleep with anything in a skirt. I don't flatter myself thinking I was the only one."

"But wasn't he married?" Diana asked, as her eyes roamed the room and finally found Carson's father holding forth amid a gaggle of men in tuxedos and women in subtle yet slick cocktail dresses. Judging by their nodding heads and wide eyes, each one of them was hanging on to every word Fergus was saying.

"Fergus McEvoy wouldn't let a wife stop him," Mary said, followed by an exaggerated tutting sound.

Diana cocked her head to one side and focused more closely on Fergus. He was a very handsome man, just like Carson. Indeed, in twenty-five years this would be Carson: a head of thick silvery-gray hair; tall with just a hint of a stoop; wrinkles that didn't age but rather seasoned an unmistakably attractive face.

"Weren't you ever tempted?" Diana whispered into the phone.

But as the words escaped her, straightaway she felt foolish. She must have had more to drink than she thought to ask such a question of Mary. Mary and she were great friends—they could talk for hours about books and philosophy and writing and politics—but they never talked in girlish ways about men or sex or anything so intimate.

Mary, however, was unfazed by Diana's question. Indeed, she seemed to rather enjoy it.

"Tempted, perhaps." She giggled. "But never enough to act on it. Anyhow, I met Jack around the same time, and the rest, as they say, was history." Mary paused for a moment and then asked in a playful whisper, "Why? Are you tempted by McEvoy Junior?"

Mary knew Carson had invited Diana here tonight. She also knew that the two had been friends in grad school. What Mary didn't know, however, was the flirtatious nature of Diana and Carson's relationship, and Mary's question—her seeming ability to read Diana's mind—made Diana flush. Diana never normally flushed, and the realization that she just had made her flush even harder.

"Never," Diana blurted out, as her cheeks continued their unfamiliar burn.

This was nearly the truth, of course. Even though she and Carson had always had a flirtatious repartee with each other, it had never gone further, and Diana had never wanted it to go further. That was not to say she didn't appreciate Carson's charms. Who wouldn't appreciate his charms, after all? He was brilliant, funny, and articulate, and also happened to be chic and beautiful too. In all the years she'd known him, Carson had never succumbed to tweed jackets or bad facial hair, like so many of his male peers in the academic world. He would always be dressed in soft, sleek, expensive-looking clothes, and his hair and stubble were unkempt, but only in the most strategic and expensive ways. Diana wasn't blind; she saw all this and would often let her eyes and mind wander in admiration over her dashing friend.

But Carson was a womanizer—like father like son, it seemed. Diana had watched Carson flirt and sleep his way through nearly every female member of their graduate class at Harvard. In later years, when she bumped into him at conferences across the country, he would always have some beautiful woman on his arm. Sometimes one on each. Diana suspected they might be his grad students, but some looked so young and coltish, she wondered if they were even his undergraduates. She never committed their names to memory, however, as she knew that by the time the next conference rolled around, they would have been replaced with some other smiling, adoring, slim-hipped youngster.

Although Diana was never really appalled by Carson's gallivanting—even for Diana, Carson was too charming to be appalling—she was never tempted either. When they were grad students, he tried to seduce her many times, but Diana always politely yet firmly declined. She didn't want to be just one of many, and she knew that Carson would always be the type of man who wanted more than just one woman. Furthermore, she enjoyed their banter and didn't want sex and love and Carson's inevitable betrayal to ruin the rapport between them. Even when she'd met Carson at a conference just six months after Graham had left her, and thus at a ripe time for a rebound relationship, she hadn't succumbed. He'd heard about the end of her marriage and suggested, with a playful wink, that he could "help" with the healing process. She'd simply laughed and said, "Good try, Carson, but no, thanks."

However, something strange had happened over the past week. Diana was starting to feel tempted, seriously tempted. Not only was she happy to have Carson visit her office every day for the company, the conversation, and the flirtatious banter. But with each visit she found herself looking at him and wondering: wondering what it would be like to kiss him, sleep with him, even *be* with him in some kind of relationship. Of course, she hadn't forgotten her vow to herself to give up men altogether. After all, it was only a few days since she'd ended everything with Mikey because of her desire for a trouble-free, man-free life. Neither had Diana forgotten all the reasons she'd never been tempted to sleep with Carson in the past. Yet, each time Carson ambled into her office carrying their coffees and wearing a big grin, she couldn't quell the burn of attraction and couldn't stop herself from wondering, *What if?* When he'd rolled up at her apartment tonight, more handsome than ever in his spotless, perfectly tailored tuxedo, she'd nearly grabbed him there and then on the doorstep. It was only Carson's tapping on his watch, telling her that they had to get moving, that stopped her.

Diana wasn't going to tell Mary any of this, however. Admitting this newfound attraction for Carson to someone else would make it all the more real and all the more frightening. Even if she did tell Mary, Mary might disapprove, and right now, with a half bottle of wine inside her and Carson circling nearby, his face striking and sparkling under the light from the iridescent chandeliers, the last thing Diana wanted was a voice of disapproval.

So, with her phone still clasped to her ear, she lied to Mary, telling her that Carson was on his way back over and she had to go. Diana was about to hang up when she was stopped by Mary's parting words.

"Be careful, Di," she warned. "You deserve a good man. Not just a man with a pretty dust jacket and lots of sweet words."

Mary hung up before Diana could even respond, and Diana was left staring down at her phone. Mary hadn't meant to reprimand; indeed, her tone couldn't have been more tender, yet Diana still felt momentarily chastened and exposed by her friend's words. However, as the clinking of crystal, the animated voices, and the melodious notes from the string quartet began to creep back into her consciousness, Diana remembered the party around her and Carson just half a room away. To shut out Mary's words once and for all, she snapped her phone shut and stuffed it back into her purse. Then, noticing her glass was empty, she moved toward the bar. She ordered another sauvignon blanc. Diana never usually drank more than one or two glasses of wine when she went out, but tonight she was in the mood for more. A young man in a bow tie dusted off a glass with a flourish and then poured Diana her wine. She took the shimmering glass and immediately swigged back a large mouthful.

Diana then turned back and scanned the room. Carson was now less than ten feet away, talking and smiling with some petite blonde in a skintight crimson cocktail dress that forced her bosom high up under her chin. The young woman was flicking her luscious hair over her bare shoulder and ogling Carson with big doe eyes. Diana could just about hear her "Ohs" and "Reallys?" interjecting Carson's stream of words. Diana wasn't jealous. Indeed, she couldn't help watching and smiling. Carson was so predictable, honing in on the attractive young women: the attractive women who, at least as far as Diana could tell, could offer him looks but nothing else. They never had minds that could equal his.

Diana took another sip of her wine, but then quickly lowered her glass as her eyes snapped from the young woman to Carson. In that moment, it dawned on Diana that Carson was scared. He was scared of being with a woman whose mind matched his own. It was so clear, yet in all the years she'd known him, it had never occurred to Diana before now. She'd always thought of him as a player, a man who just wanted as many women as he could get. This was probably true, but it wasn't all that Carson was, and didn't speak to what seemed obvious to Diana now: his fear.

Taking another slug of wine and realizing, with a glimmer of surprise, that she'd already drained her glass, Diana set the glass down and folded her arms across her chest. Then she stared harder at Carson. Could she change all that? she wondered. Could she be the one who broke the spell of these brainless, unthreatening young girls in tight dresses? Could she erase his fear? She had no idea. But, as the sauvignon coursed through her veins and up to her tingling head, she decided she wanted to find out. If she could pull it off, Carson was the perfect catch: handsome, smart, and most of all, she thought as she looked around the room, there was all this. His family, their erudite conversations, their interesting friends and careers, their beauty, their vacations in Maine. Graham's family had been the same, and it was only now, as she tasted it again, that she yearned for it once more.

And so, taking a deep breath, Diana moved toward Carson. As she drew close, she flicked back her own raven hair and gently smoothed her vintage Dior dress—a present from Graham's mother years ago—

over her still slim hips. Carson sensed her presence and immediately pulled his gaze from Miss Red Dress over to Diana. His eyes, clearly detecting Diana's prowling mood, widened for a second and then slipped downward over Diana's long, lean body.

"If you'll just excuse me," he said to the youngster as he waved toward Diana.

The woman followed his gaze, and straightaway her delicate features crumpled in disappointment. "Sure," she said, turning on her heel and skulking off.

"Professor Monroe." Carson grinned. "Where have you been?"

Diana returned his grin and winked seductively. "Waiting for you, Professor McEvoy."

Carson's eyes flashed wide again. But even if he was surprised by the ratcheting up of Diana's flirtations, he was dealing with it like a professional.

He cocked his head to one side and whispered, "Waiting for me, eh?"

"Waiting for you to take me to bed," she whispered.

Once again, surprise flickered across Carson's dark eyes, but only for a second.

With a nod, he moved close to Diana, offered his arm, and whispered, "Well, what are we waiting for?"

Seven

Wine Studies 102

Rachel and Mikey weaved their way along West Fourth Street. Having forgotten their coats, they hunkered against the cold, whipping wind. Every now and then, to avoid other late-night revelers, Rachel would stumble this way and that in her two-inch heels. Each time, Mikey would reach out an arm and prevent her from plummeting onto the cracked sidewalk or into the gutters. They were still laughing, still buzzing on the drink, and still on their mission to find Carson's place.

Thanks to Mikey's keys and their bumbling raid on the department office just ten minutes ago, Rachel was now in possession of a piece of paper upon which Carson's address was hastily scribbled. Now all they had to do was weave and bob their way to the apartment on MacDougal Street. Mikey knew which building it was and had offered to escort Rachel there (after that he would jump on the PATH train back to New Jersey and leave Rachel to "catch her fish," as he put it). Carson's building was owned by Manhattan U, he told Rachel as they walked, and he'd been there sometime before the start of the semester to help a senior and rather cantankerous member of the English department hook the man's PC to the Internet. Rachel knew exactly which one of her colleagues he was talking about and shook her head as she imagined poor, kind Mikey receiving orders and booming commands from a short-tempered Bill Roberts.

As they turned the corner onto MacDougal, and Rachel squinted up at a row of town houses where apartment windows glowed in the

Saturday-night gloom, her first pang of doubt hit. The wine buzz had kept her moving up until now; it had made her giggle and laugh and think this was all a great idea. But now that she was on Carson's block, a wave of sobriety and uncertainty grew amid the sea of alcohol and hilarity.

"This is a ridiculous idea," she blurted out, stopping in her tracks and grabbing Mikey's forearm.

He tapped her hand lightly. "Of course it is." He laughed. "But, hey, it might just work." He gently pulled her arm and said, "Come on, don't quit now. We're just two buildings away."

Pulling Rachel along, he pointed up. A Manhattan U flag fluttered above the door of the upcoming building.

"Oh, God," Rachel half cried, half giggled. "What am I supposed to do now?"

They'd reached Carson's building, and Mikey, who was holding a slightly swaying Rachel with one strong hand, pulled at the building's door handle with his other. "I've no idea. Go in there and say, 'Hey, Carson, baby, I was in the neighborhood and . . .' " He laughed.

"And what?" Rachel shrieked, watching Mikey tug at the door.

Of course the door was locked and, for some reason, this made both Rachel and Mikey chuckle and then giggle, and then, pretty soon, they were letting out peals of shoulder-shaking laughter. Rachel laughed so hard she wobbled in her heels and nearly tripped over a pile of garbage bags that were stacked nearby on the sidewalk. Once again, Mikey reached out to save her, but this time he had to use both his arms to stop her from nose-diving into the trash.

Just as Mikey was rebalancing Rachel, using his strong arms to buffer her against any more falls, a taxi pulled up noisily beside them. The screech of wheels and the slam of a door made them both look up, and within a second their laughter and smiles had faded into the night air.

If Diana had any second thoughts, Carson wasn't going to allow them to surface on the taxi ride back to his place. As soon as they got in the cab outside Nobu Fifty Seven and settled themselves side by side on the backseat, Carson pounced. With Midtown whisking by outside, he moved his hand inside Diana's jacket, and his lips followed. Soon, his mouth was tracing the dips and lines of her bare shoulders, and with one hand in her hair, wrapping it around his long fingers, he kissed the nape of her neck and worked around to her collarbone. Eventually, he moved up to her mouth and kissed her lips with firm, probing kisses.

Diana was startled at first, but soon she found she was moving into Carson, giving herself over to his warm lips and exploring touches. But not entirely. She'd thought about this moment all week, hoped and secretly fantasized about it. However, now that it was happening, it seemed unreal, and Diana felt strangely detached. She was enjoying the closeness and the idea of being with Carson; she was enjoying the realization of her week-old fantasies. Yet, at the same time, she was distracted. Something about Carson's touches and kisses didn't feel quite right. They were too polished, too professional, and it felt as if his fingertips and lips were working to a script they'd followed a million times before.

Before Diana knew it, before she could really fathom what she'd gotten herself into, they'd arrived with a juddering, New York taxi–style halt outside Carson's building. Carson quickly threw a twenty at the driver and, as the driver fiddled around for change, took Diana's face and kissed it a few more times. His mouth worked with precision and haste, and Diana, her mind still hovering somewhere above their lovemaking, wondered whether Carson was using his kisses to quash any ambivalence that might be growing inside her.

After he'd received his change, Carson took hold of Diana's hand, opened the door, and pulled her firmly but gently onto the sidewalk. Only when he started to lead her toward his building did Diana spot Rachel and Mikey. Just a few feet away, her ex-lover and her young colleague were clinched in a flushed, giggling embrace. As she spotted them, they spotted her too, and, for a second, it seemed like the entire city froze to a standstill around the four of them. No one spoke until Diana pulled her hand from Carson's grasp, turned on her heel, and began striding away.

"Diana!" two male voices called out.

But she didn't stop. If Diana stopped, her stomach—which suddenly felt as if it had been turned inside out and pummeled with a huge fist—was sure to spill its wine-soaked contents onto the sidewalk. She had to keep walking.

Eight

Academic Allegiances

The reading room in the basement of Manhattan U's library was gloomy. It was lit only by bulbs that seemed on the brink of giving out. The old books packed on shelves in the crowded aisles gave off a musty smell. But for Diana, who was hunched over a small table at the end of an aisle, the smell was familiar and comforting. Manhattan U's library soared twenty floors above where she sat, an edifice of modern New York architecture with its asymmetric roof, huge windows, and shining chrome. Yet, down here in the basement, in the dank and motionless air, Diana felt she could be anywhere: the reading rooms of Oxford's Bodleian Library, the Widener at Harvard, the Bibliothèque de la Sorbonne, which she'd visited one summer when she was a grad student. Old books, their silence and their smells, had a way of erasing the differences of the worlds that surrounded them. The books also shut out those worlds and protected their visitors among their aging spines. It was just what Diana needed.

After her disastrous Saturday night, and the headache-filled Sunday morning that followed, Diana had spent almost every waking hour for the past three days down in this basement. She would surface into the blinding daylight only when she had a class to teach or when she needed to be revived by a cup of steaming coffee. Ostensibly, Diana was here to read some books and articles on electroshock therapy: its history and development, the cultural responses, and its eventual decline in use. *The Bell Jar* dealt, of course, with this rather grisly psychiatric treatment, and so Diana was here to learn what she could for her new book on Plath's novel. Usually Diana didn't allow herself to get so caught up with extratextual details like this. Influenced by her beloved professors at Oxford, then Harvard, Diana believed in the primacy of the text. The words, the imagery, the arcs and flows of a literary work, she believed, were the most important things to be studied. The historical contexts and the biographical details of authors, although important, must always come second to the text itself.

However, after rereading passages from *The Bell Jar* on Sunday morning, as she tried to avoid thoughts of the night before and attempted to fight off her wine hangover, Diana had found herself drawn to the library and to a crash course on shock therapy. The more she read, the more she wanted to know, and now three days had passed and she'd read nearly five books and a whole host of old journal articles. She'd even started reading about lobotomies, which didn't appear in *The Bell Jar*, but nevertheless captured Diana's fascination with their grotesqueness and seeming absurdity.

Today, sitting at the same table where she'd spent the past few days, Diana flicked through a large yellowing book. Her eyes scanned pictures of brains, patients being gazed at by white-coated physicians, photographs of menacing instruments, and worst of all a snapshot of twelve-year-old Howard Dully's bruised and beaten face after his "ice pick" lobotomy. Diana winced and tutted but still kept skimming. Only when a librarian clattered past with a trolley stacked high with books did Diana look up. The clock on the wall in front of her read three. She'd been here since nine this morning and had left her seat only once, to go to the bathroom. As she confirmed the time on her own watch, she realized her back was aching from the hard chair, her eyes were strained, and her stomach was growling.

After stretching, yawning, and then gathering her bag, Diana stood up and started toward the stairs. The thought of coffee and something to eat kept her moving onward, but, as her books and her little table receded behind her, the knot in her chest, which she'd been fighting off all week with her research, began to tighten once again. Diana tramped hard up the library's stairs, but her clattering feet did not stop the constricted feeling under her ribs. Every time she left the library this would happen, and Diana would find herself running around, gathering food and drinks in the blink of an eye, so she could return quickly to her table and her books.

Of course, in the evenings the library would close, and Diana was forced to go home and face the fitful nights where, again and again, she would wake up remembering everything that happened on Saturday. In the darkness, she would cringe at the memory of Carson's proficient kisses and then frown at the image of Rachel and Mikey locked in their playful embrace. Pulling the covers over her head and groaning, she would then remember how she stalked off along Mac-Dougal Street like some petulant teenager.

In the morning light, Diana would usually feel a little better. As she showered and dressed, she would remind herself that everything that happened, happened for the best. Her drunken dalliance with Carson had obliterated all the ridiculous fantasies about him she was entertaining last week. Seeing Mikey with Rachel was good too, Diana would tell herself as she sipped her morning cup of Earl Grey. Mikey had moved on, found someone who better suited him, and now Diana could go on with her industrious and scholarly single life, free of guilt.

As the day wore on, however, Diana's confidence in these convictions would wane, and the only way to stop the strangling feeling that would grow in her chest was to stay in the library, at her secluded table, lost in books that had tenuous relevance to her research. In spite of all these hours tucked away in the library, Diana did not let any of her responsibilities slide. She would arrive to her classes on time, every night she would respond to e-mails, and every day when she passed the department office en route to class she would pick up her mail and sign any forms that needed signing. The only things she wasn't doing was returning Peter's increasingly worried phone messages and replying to Carson's e-mail, which read simply, *What happened, Di?* Books and students and red tape were fine. But facing colleagues, especially those who were friends or almost lovers, felt like too much of a distraction from what she really wanted to be doing, which was losing herself at the library.

On this gloomy November afternoon, however, as Diana left her three-day-old perch in the library in search of food and caffeine, she quickly discovered that avoiding colleagues was no longer possible. Whisking through the library's revolving doors, Diana found herself dumped out onto the sidewalk and straight into the path of a meandering Peter. Thanks to the daylight in Diana's library-deadened eyes and Peter's thoughts being elsewhere, as always, the two collided with a thump, and a stack of papers tumbled from Peter's arms to the ground. Diana's eyes adjusted to the light, and, as she looked from the fluttering papers up at Peter, she was instantly reminded of the scene outside her office, just a week ago, when Peter and Rachel collided in much the same way. At the memory, the knot in Diana's chest gave a quick, breath-grabbing tug.

"Diana!" Peter exclaimed, as the two of them chased his papers across the damp concrete. "You're here. I haven't seen you in days. Is everything okay?"

Diana pulled herself upright, fluttering papers in her hand, and gave Peter a wan smile. "Yes, Peter. Everything's fine."

"I've been trying to get hold of you." Peter pushed back his thick hair and then gave a questioning yet concerned arch of his eyebrows. "Did you get my messages?" he asked.

"I'm sorry. Yes, I did," Diana said, her eyes flicking away from Peter and toward the park. "I've been caught up with a few things."

Peter paused, gave Diana a searching stare, and then, realizing she wasn't going to give a further explanation of what she'd been up to for the past few days, he said, "Oh, right, yes. Well, I just wanted to talk to you about the Literary London trip."

Diana's chest gave another strangling yank. She'd tried not to think about this month's trip to England, and when she had, she'd told herself that she must back out. There was no way she could spend ten days with Rachel—giggling, pink-cheeked Rachel. But now, faced with having to tell Peter of her decision, she felt terrible. Diana was not a flake; she was always diligent and reliable. She hated to do this, but she knew she had to.

"Peter," she said, gathering her face into a look of resolve, "I'm not going to be able to make it."

His eyebrows arched once again. "What do you mean?"

"I can't go on the Literary London trip. Not this year." Diana shook her head.

"What? Why?"

Diana looked away again. She couldn't stand the confused and disappointed look in Peter's wide eyes. "I've realized I have too much work to do here. It just isn't going to work," she said.

Peter's hand was pushing his hair again, this time with more pace and anxiety. "But we've just booked the flights. The students are staying in University of London dorms and I was trying to get hold of you to ask which nearby hotel you'd prefer."

"I'm sorry, Peter, but—" Diana began, but Peter was panicking now and he interrupted her.

"There's no one else who can go. I would go—of course I would. But my dad . . ." His eyes darted as he spoke. "My dad really wants me home for Thanksgiving this year. His bathroom needs fixing and I said I would help."

Diana waved her hand. She wanted Peter to stop. She didn't need this extra guilt. "Do we really need two faculty on the trip?" she asked, changing tack. "There are two student advisers going, aren't there? Plus Rachel. Surely that's enough."

Peter shook his head. "We need you, Di," he pleaded. "We need your experience. Not to mention your intimate knowledge of British culture." He gave a quick, unconvincing laugh.

Diana just shook her head and sighed.

"And"—Peter lowered his voice—"it now looks like *both* the Nilsen sisters will be going."

"What? I thought it was just Rebecca."

"Veronica signed up too," Peter said. "And if Veronica is going, we might be in for some trouble."

"What kind of trouble?" Diana found herself asking, even though the antics of Veronica Nilsen wouldn't ordinarily interest her.

"Veronica loves to party, and the paparazzi love to follow. When she's out on the town, they flock to see whatever stunt she'll pull next."

Diana sighed. "So why are we letting her come on the trip?"

Peter was surprised by Diana's question. "If Veronica wants to come, we have to let her come." He lowered his voice again. "You know what's at stake, Diana."

"I know, I know." Diana sighed again. "The big and *generous* donation from her father."

"Exactly," Peter replied, with a roll of his eyes.

The two of them stood in silence for a few beats. Diana had been backed into a corner, she realized, and the trip was now looking inevitable. Rachel wouldn't be able to cope with Veronica Nilsen and the paparazzi on her own. She was far too young and green. Diana wouldn't even put it past Rachel to go off drinking and partying herself, and the last thing Manhattan U needed was tabloid shots of the Nilsens and their professor parading in the streets of London, drunk and gaily abandoned.

"Okay," Diana said finally, holding up a hand in surrender, "I'll go." As she watched Peter's anxious face sag with relief, she added, "But you'd better make sure I get that sabbatical I've applied for next semester."

Peter grinned. "I'll do everything I can. Hell, I'll even offer to teach your classes so your leave gets approved."

Diana couldn't help returning his smile. "You'd better," she said, patting together some of Peter's papers she was still holding.

Just as she held them out and Peter was about to take them, Diana noticed the title on the top sheet: *Proposed Changes: Introduction to American Literature 101*, it read.

"What's this?" she asked, pulling the clutch of papers back again.

She scanned the page, her eyes roaming over phrases like "conversation with the canon," "augment and enrich the current list," and "introducing a variety of minority, mainstream, and female writers to the syllabus." When she was finished she looked up at Peter and repeated, "What *is* this?"

"This," Peter replied, tapping the sheet with a long finger, "this is the other thing I've been wanting to talk to you about. It's a proposal for Am. Lit 101."

"I can see that," snapped Diana.

Peter looked momentarily baffled by Diana's tone but went on anyway. "A couple of faculty have come to see me since the discussion about 101's reading list. They think Rachel's idea—you know, what she said in the meeting?"

Diana nodded vaguely.

"They think her idea has potential. We're putting together this proposal, and I'm going to pitch it to the faculty in a few weeks."

"I see," was all Diana could say by way of response. Inside, her blood was bubbling, and the knot in her chest seemed to yank so tight she couldn't breathe.

"I wanted to run it by you," Peter added, a twitch of awkwardness flickering on his long face as he sensed Diana's displeasure. "I figured you'd be in agreement. For the most part, anyhow. After all, you've wanted to get the American Lit reading list updated for ages." He gave a brief laugh and tapped the paper again. "Rachel's idea—in other words, using contemporary and previously marginalized texts to speak back to and augment the study of the canon—has a lot of mileage, I think." Peter paused and looked at Diana, waiting for a response. When she offered nothing but stony silence, he added, "Perhaps you want to look more closely at what we've got so far and add suggestions."

Diana ignored this comment and asked only, "Which faculty?"

Peter's eyebrows knit in confusion. "Sorry?"

"Which faculty helped you with this?" Diana's tone was ice-cold.

"Tom Burgess, Richard Kettering," Peter said, "Brian Washington."

"All junior faculty," Diana huffed.

Peter's eyebrows knit even tighter. "True. But I'm not sure that matters. . . ."

"Bill Roberts and the rest of the old guard will veto this." Diana shook the piece of paper in her hands. "Even if they like the proposal, they're not going to okay anything dreamed up by a group of junior faculty."

"Well, that's why I want you on board, Di," Peter said softly, trying hard not to show his confusion at her resistance.

Diana paused for a second and then pulled her bag into her arms and stuffed Peter's proposal inside. Then, handing back the rest of his papers that she'd rescued from the ground earlier, she said, "I'll take a look. In the meantime, I must get going."

Diana and Peter said their good-byes, with Peter looking confused and Diana distracted and harried. Then Diana schlepped her heavy bag onto her shoulder and made off through Washington Square Park. As she strode along toward University Place, her bag banging on her hip, Diana's mind raced and her blood thumped in her veins. All she could think of was Rachel. Rachel and all these men. Mikey and Peter and now her other colleagues—Tom, Brian, and Richard too. All of them had been sucked in by Rachel's pretty face, her bubbly charms. Just as Graham had been sucked in by the sweet, effervescent Annabelle. Rachel's idea for American Lit might be a good one, but when was the last time the faculty had rallied behind one of Diana's good ideas? They never had.

"So predictable," Diana muttered, as she tramped angrily onward.

A few blocks south, Rachel sat on a wooden bench in Manhattan U's faculty garden. It was a dull and gray afternoon, and the heavy clouds had Rachel glancing up at the sky every now and then, checking for imminent showers. No rain had arrived yet, however, so Rachel persisted sitting in her quiet spot, skimming over her well-thumbed copy of Tally McGuiness's famous book about romance novels, *At the Heart of Harlequin.* The trees around her were bare, and she had to keep herself nestled in her winter coat to shut out the cold wind, but she was in no hurry to move. She loved this garden. Even though it was overshadowed by the looming towers of Manhattan U's faculty housing, and busy Houston Street roared just a few blocks away, the garden was peculiarly serene. For Rachel, who'd spent many afternoons here since the start of the semester, it was an inspirational place too. The garden had recently been renamed the Poe Garden, because last summer an archaeological dig at the far end of the garden's long lawn had uncovered the remnants of a tavern where Edgar Allan Poe once drank. On an old wooden beam once part of the tavern's cellar, the archaeologists had found an etching of Poe's name made by the author's own hand.

At the heart of Greenwich Village, then, with the Empire State in the distance and the ghosts of great writers under its lawn, the garden embodied everything Rachel loved about New York. Ever since she was a girl, she'd wanted to be here in Manhattan. The excitement, the bustle, the history, the museums and galleries, the parks, the eclectic, zany, and creative people—it all seemed so impossibly exciting and so different from the small town in Virginia where she grew up.

But over the past few days, since her drunken night on Saturday and her embarrassing encounter with Diana and Carson, Rachel had begun falling out of love. She wanted to be gone. She yearned to be miles away from New York and its crowded, noisy streets and the university that employed her. She wanted the comfort of her quiet life in North Carolina. She wanted her old house, her old friends, and her parents not far away. Right now, sitting on her secondhand couch, drinking a beer with Justin, his arm thrown lazily around her—even this seemed more appealing than trying to carry on with this life in New York.

Nothing had gone right since she'd arrived here, Rachel had realized when she woke up on Sunday morning. Teaching sucked, she'd made no real friends, and now it looked like she'd made her first enemy: Diana. Diana, who not only hated Rachel's scholarship but who now probably thought Rachel was moving in on her ex-boyfriend. After Diana had stalked off on Saturday, Mikey had told Rachel in a whisper that it was over between the two of them. From the melancholy look in his eyes, Rachel knew that he was still nursing some serious wounds over the breakup. And even if it was Diana who'd done the dumping, Rachel could tell that Diana wouldn't be the kind of woman who liked seeing her ex with someone new (not that Rachel was Mikey's "someone new," of course, but Diana hadn't hung around to find that out). Diana was sure to hate Rachel more than ever, and going on the Literary London trip together was going to be insufferable.

And then there was Carson. Thanks to the fiasco outside his place on Saturday night, she hadn't gone through with the drunken plan to seduce him, and therefore, fortunately, hadn't made an utter fool of herself. But over the past few days, she couldn't help feeling a pang of disappointment. Carson had rolled up at his apartment late in the evening with Diana in tow, and that could only mean that something was going on between the two of them. Diana had clearly ditched poor Mikey and moved on fast.

This also meant there was no hope for Rachel having a hot romance with a handsome visiting professor from Harvard. Up against smart and beautiful Diana, she didn't stand a chance. Rachel should have known not even to entertain these thoughts. As she well knew, it was always when she started getting all gooey-eyed and full of romantic fantasies that everything went wrong.

Today, not even the garden could halt the brooding regrets, disappointments, and wincing embarrassments that had plagued Rachel since Saturday. Although lurking out here did have other benefits. All week Rachel had been avoiding her office, the department, and any other destination where she might run into Diana. Rachel was sick of the four walls of her apartment, and the garden offered a convenient hideaway not far from her classes. Rachel didn't really want to see Mikey or Carson or Peter either. She was too mortified by her drunken behavior. The chilly and gloomy garden, where she couldn't imagine any of them wanting to come, was the perfect place to keep a low profile.

Hunkered against the wind on the garden's bench, Rachel finished skimming her book and then started searching for a pen to jot down questions for the class she'd be teaching in an hour. She scrabbled in her coat's deep pockets, unearthing Kleenex and lip balms as she went, and finally found a red pen. Just as she was about to start writing in her notebook, the gate to the garden gave a loud clang. Surprised and alarmed, Rachel snapped her head up. She then glared over at the garden's entrance, her jaw muscle pulsing with annoyance. She really didn't want her tranquil and deserted hideout to be disturbed.

But when she noticed it was Tom Burgess and his family entering the garden, the pulse in her jaw stopped and she immediately smiled. Tom's little girl skipped and ran onto the grass, wearing a bright pink fuzzy coat and bumblebee rain boots. Behind the three-year-old came her parents, Tom pushing a stroller with their bundled-up baby boy, and his wife carrying hot coffees. They saw Rachel on the bench, waved, and walked in her direction. Rachel was genuinely glad to see them. She liked her colleague, and his wife, Sofia, whom Rachel had met just once, seemed witty and warm. She was one of those women, Rachel thought, whom everyone would want to be around. In fact, after she and Sofia met back in September, Rachel hoped they would bump into each other again. But while Rachel always seemed to be running into people she didn't want to see, she'd never run into Sofia again.

"Can we join you?" Tom sang out as they approached. "Or are you having a scholarly moment?"

Rachel laughed. "I haven't had a scholarly moment in months," she said, and then, patting the bench, added, "Please have a seat."

Once they were seated and everyone said their hellos, Tom introduced his kids. "Gracie," he said, waving toward the vision in pink flitting around the garden, and then with a jerk of his thumb, he added, "And fat little Edgar over there."

Sofia was unstrapping the six-month-old from the stroller and pulling him onto her lap, while Tom said to Rachel, "I hear you're signed up for the Literary London trip."

Rachel couldn't help grimacing. "Yes." She sighed. "Although I'd kind of like to get out of it."

"Really?" Tom looked shocked.

"Well . . ." Rachel struggled to think of an excuse. She couldn't tell Tom the real reason she wanted out. "My parents really want me home for Thanksgiving," she lied.

Rachel had already told her parents she wouldn't be home for the holiday this year. They were disappointed, of course. This would be the first time ever that she wouldn't be with them for Thanksgiving. But, true to their loving selves, they understood.

"You've done your duty, Rachie." Her dad had chuckled when she'd called them a few weeks ago to break the news about the up-coming trip to London. "We've had you home for Thanksgiving for the last thirty years!"

"I'm going to miss you, though, Dad," Rachel had replied.

"We'll miss you too, sweetie," he said. "But you go to England and have a wonderful time, and we'll have an extra-special Christmas to make up for it when you come home."

Rachel had hung up and promptly burst into tears. Her parents were so kind and understanding, and she'd realized with a sudden pang how much she missed them. On top of all the other things that were proving tough in New York, it was hard to be so far away from them.

Now, as she sat with Tom and Sofia in the cold garden, she felt the same twinge of homesickness and wished that her parents were the kind of people who would insist their daughter come home for Thanksgiving.

"I'd really think twice about dropping out of the trip, Rachel," Tom was now warning Rachel, as his forehead crumpled with concern. "The old boys in the department *love* anyone who volunteers for the trip because it means they don't have to go. If you want to keep in the tenure good books, I'd say go."

Before Rachel could respond, Sofia playfully punched her husband's arm and then grinned. "Oh, Tom. You and your 'tenure good books' crap." She laughed and turned to Rachel. "He's such a nervous Nellie. He thinks that the only way to get tenure these days is by being the world's biggest sycophant and kissing all the old boys' wrinkly asses."

Everyone laughed, and Sofia went on: "You have to go on that trip, Rachel." She waggled her dark eyebrows and pushed back a lock of curly hair. "You have to go so you can bring us back some juicy Nilsen gossip."

Tom rolled his eyes at his wife. "You and those Nilsens." He gave a long fake sigh. "I don't know why I give you the inside info on them. It just fuels your unhealthy celebrity obsession."

Sofia ignored Tom and carried on speaking to Rachel. "When I was a talent agent in LA, I met Lamont Nilsen a couple of times, and, of course, I met a lot of people who knew him." She shook her head and whistled. "The man's a tyrant. Not just on set, but at home too. Those girls are petrified of him."

"Really?" Rachel exclaimed, her eyes flashing with curiosity.

Just as Sofia was going to speak, Tom laughed and stood up. "I can see my wife has found a soul mate. I'll leave you to it." With that, he trotted off across the grass, swooped up his skipping daughter into his arms, and turned her upside down. Gracie's happy squeals rang out across the garden.

Rachel slid across the bench and took one of the baby's chubby hands in hers, and for the next ten minutes or so, Sofia told her every piece of gossip she had on the Nilsens, from tales of Lamont's bullying tactics on movie sets to a story about the girls, when they were only eight, hiding all night in the family Corvette from their angry father. The girls' mother died when they were three and his overprotective love of his daughters could sometimes tip over into rage. If Veronica and Rebecca were put into danger or hurt or if their privacy was jeopardized, Lamont would lose it. He'd yell, scream, thump tables, and fire child-care staff at the drop of a hat.

"He's never got violent with the girls, though," Sofia pointed out. "He's a good guy deep down, I think. He had to be a mother and a father to the twins and it couldn't have been easy."

Only when Tom jogged back over to the bench with a wiggling Gracie tucked under one of his arms did their conversation falter.

"If I might just interrupt," Tom panted, his hair tousled from chasing his daughter up and down the garden, "there's something I've been meaning to ask you, Rachel."

Rachel smiled. "Shoot."

"I inherited a PhD student last year from a member of the faculty who left the department the summer before. She's great, but I really have no idea why I was asked to supervise her. She's doing work on contemporary adaptations of Austen."

"She is?" Rachel blurted out, shocked that she'd never heard of this student.

Tom sat down and placed Gracie on his lap. "That's the thing. You two would be a great match. You'd be far more useful to her than a Poe geek like myself." He laughed. "Anyway, I spoke to Peter about it, and if you're interested, he agreed you could take over her supervision."

"Palming off your students on poor Rachel." Sofia guffawed as she bounced the baby on her knees.

Rachel was already flushing with excitement. "I'd love to. But . . ." She paused. "I haven't supervised before. I mean, will this student be annoyed to get a newbie?"

"Not at all." Tom waved his hand. "In fact, she was the first to suggest it. She's been over in England for a while doing research at the Austen Institute. She just got back, and as soon as she discovered you'd come to the department, she asked if she could work with you. Although, even if she hadn't said something, I would have suggested it anyway. You're peas in a pod," he added with a smile.

Rachel beamed back at him. "I'd love to do it," she repeated.

"Zadie, the student," Tom went on, "she's volunteered to do the graduate-faculty seminar next week and is going to present some of her recent work. She's excited, but pretty nervous too. You might want to meet with her soon and guide her through it. Here's her e-mail," he said, grabbing Rachel's notebook and pen.

Tom didn't have to explain what "guide her through it" might mean. Rachel had been at Manhattan U only a couple of months, but she already knew what a bear pit the grad-faculty seminar could be. She'd witnessed a number of grad students deliver their papers and then get ceremoniously ripped apart—word by word, idea by idea—by the assembled faculty. One time, a student left the faculty lounge in tears. Rachel just hoped that this student, Zadie, was up to it.

"I'll e-mail her today," Rachel said, taking her notebook back from Tom.

Tom stood and, before chasing Gracie, who was off running around the garden again, he said, "And did you hear about the proposal for 101?"

Rachel looked up. "Hear what?"

"Peter's putting together a proposal based on your idea for Intro to American Lit," Tom said as he backed away. "It looks good. You'll be pleased."

"My idea?"

"The one you came up with at the faculty meeting."

"You're kidding," she said.

Tom was running again. "Nope." He shook his head. "Ask Peter. He'll show you the draft proposal."

Rachel was baffled, but she grinned nonetheless.

"It sounds like things are going well for you," Sofia said after a few beats, and ending Rachel's excited trance. "It can be hard when you start at a new place. I remember what it was like for Tom. But you seem to be cruising." She tapped Rachel's knee and smiled.

Rachel shook her head. "I wouldn't go that far," she scoffed, but then she paused and grinned. "But perhaps things are beginning to look up."

In silence, the two women watched Tom and Gracie weaving around the garden, giggling and squealing together. Rachel continued to grin. For the first time that week, she felt good. In fact, she felt better than good. Her funk, she realized, had finally lifted, and she was ready to come out of hiding. She was a grown woman with a job at a prestigious university. It was time to stop acting like a fourth grader afraid of her teacher. If she were to bump into Diana, then so be it.

"I love this garden," Rachel said, as she felt her chest swell with confidence.

Sofia simply nodded in agreement.

Nine

Advising Grad Students

Another week passed, and Diana was still spending much of her time in the reading room in Manhattan U's library. She'd finally moved on from the books about psychiatric treatments and now took her laptop with her each day and tapped furiously away on her new manuscript. It looked like she was committed to the Literary London trip, and so, during the couple of weeks before they set off, she wanted to get as much writing done as possible. The quiet and solitude of the library's dreary basement offered the perfect place to focus. No disruptions from students, no knocks on the door from colleagues she didn't want to see, no distracted thoughts as she gazed out of some window or other. Indeed, she'd gotten a lot of work done in her nook in the library. And for almost two weeks now, she'd managed to avoid Mikey, Carson, and Rachel—the three people she had no desire to see—and, in the surprisingly small and intimate world of Manhattan U's English department, that was quite an achievement.

However, on this bright, clear Thursday afternoon, Diana was in her office. One of her grad students, Belinda Clair, was here for a supervision. Clutching the teas Diana had just made with the small electric kettle in her office, the two of them sat facing each other on each side of Diana's large desk. The low fall sun shone in the window and reflected in the chunky black glasses that sat under Belinda's straggly bangs and dwarfed her small face. With her one free hand, Belinda scribbled in the notepad balanced on her knees.

"I think you should look again at your reading of 'I Heard a Fly

Buzz,'" Diana was advising, as she tapped a copy of Belinda's work on her desk.

Belinda, a fourth-year PhD student, was deep into her dissertation on Emily Dickinson, and the twenty-page document in front of Diana was a draft of her sixth chapter. Belinda had submitted it to Diana just a few days ago, and already the margins were full with comments made in Diana's small yet precise handwriting.

"You spend a lot of time discussing the second stanza," Diana went on, while Belinda continued to nod and scribble in her notepad. "But I don't think you talk enough about the last two lines." Diana looked out of the window and quoted the lines from Dickinson's poem that she was thinking about: "'For that last Onset, when the King/Be witnessed in his power.'" She then looked back at her student and continued, "You point out the oxymoronic nature of the phrase 'last onset,' but don't flesh out the significance of Dickinson's decision to use this oxymoron."

Diana paused for a second, letting Belinda's scribbling hand catch up. As she waited, she realized how relaxed she felt—the most relaxed she'd felt for quite some time, in fact. Aside from reading and writing about Plath, advising grad students was the best part of her job—especially when the students were keen and bright like Belinda. Diana loved guiding and shaping their dissertations and seeing their work change and grow strong. She enjoyed watching her grad students mature and develop into real scholars who would eventually fly off to universities across the country and take up teaching positions of their own. Under her diligent supervision, most of Diana's grad students finished their PhDs promptly, and their work was always strong enough to secure them appointments in the very tight academic job market. Diana was proud of her students, and proud too of the work she did with them.

"Do you mean its significance in relation to the poem's general theme of death?" Belinda was asking.

Diana leaned forward. "Yes, of course. But also, more specifically, its juxtaposition with the Christian imagery that precedes it."

Belinda scribbled more notes and gave more nods, as Diana continued to talk. Only when a light knock sounded at the office door did Diana stop talking and Belinda halt her furious note taking.

As Diana looked up, she gave Belinda an apologetic nod and shouted toward the door, "Hello?"

The door slowly opened and Mikey's face looked in. Straightaway Diana's chest balled into a fist, and the air seemed to evaporate from her lungs.

Mikey gave an awkward half smile, and his eyes darted from Diana to Belinda and back again. "I'm sorry to interrupt," he said. "I'm just letting everyone know the network is going to be down for the next half hour. Central IT is doing some maintenance," he added.

Diana nodded, and in a flat and strangled voice, she replied, "Thank you, Mikey."

No sooner had he arrived than Mikey was gone, and as the door clicked shut behind him, Diana sucked in a quick breath to try to ease the knot under her ribs. Just seeing Mikey's face, his sweet yet uncomfortable smile, triggered all the guilt and anxieties and loneliness Diana had tried to ignore over the past week or so: the same feelings that she'd tried to shelve away like the books in the library's basement, where she'd been spending most of her time. If Belinda hadn't been in front of her, Diana might have slumped onto her desk and let out a low, guttural moan. But Belinda was there, and so Diana kept her composure. Her face was calm and her eyes steady. Under the desk, however, her fingers gripped and ungripped the edge of her seat.

"Sorry, Belinda," Diana said, finally finding her voice. "Where were we?"

"You were talking about Dickinson's choice to capitalize the words 'Onset' and 'King' "

"Of course, yes," Diana replied.

As Diana picked up where she had left off, her fingers started to relax. Soon she'd let go of the chair and was gesticulating with gentle waves of her right hand, as she often did when she talked about poetry she loved. The tightness in her chest began to ease.

"The 'King,' of course, alludes to God," Diana was saying. "And 'Onset' refers to Christian notions of eternal life. However, Dickinson also seems to be equating the King with death. . . ."

Diana didn't get to finish her point, however, as another knock sounded at the door. Diana sighed. Why hadn't she remembered to post a Do Not Disturb sign? She really had to start doing that when she was conducting grad student supervisions. It seemed as soon as word was out that Diana was in her office, the whole department wanted a piece of her. For the sake of her students, she needed some peace.

"Come in," Diana barked with a grimace.

This time it was Carson who poked his smiling face into the room.

"Here you are!" he exclaimed. "I was beginning to think you'd gone AWOL."

Diana hadn't seen either Mikey or Carson since that awful night nearly two weeks ago. The irony, then, of Carson turning up so quickly after Mikey made Diana feel stunned and discomfited. She also felt a kick of annoyance at Carson's unapologetic entrance.

"I'm rather busy, Carson," Diana said, with a nod toward Belinda. "Is it something important?"

"Oops, sorry," Carson replied with the smirk of a scolded but unrepentant child. "I'd better get on my way then," he added, flashing a playful grin in Belinda's direction.

Carson left as quickly as Mikey had done earlier, and Diana was left apologizing yet again to Belinda. Belinda waved her hand and seemed unbothered by the interruption, but Diana found she couldn't quell her displeasure at Carson's appearance. During the rest of Belinda's supervision, her mind kept wandering back to Carson, his roguish ways and mischievous grins, and her own ridiculous behavior that fateful night. How had she been so stupid? The question had plagued her for way too long now, and still she struggled to answer it.

An hour later, once Belinda had left, Diana turned to her laptop in an effort to distract herself from thoughts of Carson—and Mikey.

The university network seemed to be up and running again, so she decided to check her e-mails. Her in-box, as usual, was overflowing: e-mails from students, messages from the various poetry and Plath Listservs she was a subscriber to, and announcements from the English department's administrator about upcoming meetings and seminars. She flitted through some of these messages, answering some and saving others for later. One e-mail, entitled "This Afternoon," reminded her that the graduate-faculty research seminar started in just five minutes. She'd completely forgotten about the seminar and immediately found her mood souring again at the thought of another hour away from the library and an hour among colleagues she really had no inclination to spend time with.

Diana was about to close up her office and head out toward the faculty lounge when her laptop pinged, announcing a new e-mail. She scrolled back up her in-box and, as her eyes settled on the new message, she gasped. Every muscle and vein in her body froze, and the familiar knot in her chest reemerged with a breathtaking yank.

Hello, read the subject heading, and in the sender column it said, *Graham Cartwright*. Diana read and reread these words. Then she sat, utterly motionless, her finger poised over the mouse pad, staring at her ex-husband's name. How long had it been since she'd seen his name in an e-mail like this? she wondered as her heart pounded. Probably not for over three years. Not since the days of their divorce, when every day Graham would send a flurry of e-mails cataloging his wants and demands and the times of meetings with lawyers. Since then, however, there had been no contact at all—just a wide and painful silence.

Soon after Graham left Diana for Annabelle he also left Manhattan U to take up a new position at Berkeley. Diana was of course relieved that she wouldn't have to bump into Graham around campus or, even worse, bump into him and Annabelle snuggled up on a bench in Washington Square Park. Yet his disappearance from not just her marriage, but also New York and the university too, was oddly hurtful as well. Diana imagined that if he had been around, even if it had been heartbreaking to see him, it would also have been a place to channel her anger and resentment. If she'd spotted him in a restaurant, Diana imagined throwing a glass of water over him. If she'd seen him teaching in some seminar room or other, she could have caused a ruckus outside or handed out flyers telling students about his affairs with grad students. Deep down, of course, she knew she would never have done these things. But she liked the possibility of it. And Graham's move away killed that possibility.

With her temples throbbing and her chest squeezing tighter, Diana was motionless, her finger still frozen above the mouse. Whether to read the message or delete it, this was her conundrum. If she deleted it, Diana would always be curious about what it said. But if she read it, what it said would no doubt hurt her, tie her in knots for weeks, make her feel sad and resentful and rejected all over again. Nevertheless, she had to do it; she had to read it. She couldn't spend the rest of the day, the rest of the month, the rest of her life wondering.

Diana tapped on her laptop with reticence and disgust, as if she were touching a mangy dog or decomposing vegetable. Graham's e-mail popped up to fill the screen. Her eyes skipped, panicked, over his short message and then went back and read it more slowly.

Dear Diana, his words read. *It's been a long time. I hope you are well. I was proud to hear you were awarded tenure, and saw your last book is getting fabulous reviews—of course, your books always do. I'm in the city for a few days and would love to meet for a coffee or dinner. I miss you, Diana. There is so much we need to say. All my love, Graham.*

Diana reread the message more than twenty times. Each time her chest would flinch and tighten, and each time her fury would grow. *How could he be so casual and insensitive and blasé?* she fumed. *"I miss you"? "All my love"?* Graham had clearly forgotten that five years ago he'd cast aside Diana's love and left her for a younger, fresher-faced woman with a cutesy name usually reserved for rag dolls.

"I was proud to hear you were awarded tenure"? When they were married, Graham was too caught up in his own research and his own climb up the academic ladder to show much interest in Diana's work.

He never asked about the publications she was working on to secure tenure, and he rarely mentioned her successful book reviews. Diana always suspected he was threatened by her, and when he left to be with Annabelle, a mere girl who hadn't even finished her doctorate, her suspicions were confirmed.

So what was this e-mail about? Diana wondered, still raging. All this flattery and talk of missing her and having things to say . . . he must want something. Perhaps it was the apartment. He'd hated having to hand it over to her when they divorced—even though he still owned a house upstate and a beach place on Fire Island, thanks to his wealthy family. The apartment had been his favorite, though, and that was why Diana fought tooth and nail to get it. There was no danger he could make a claim on it now; it was all there in their divorce settlement. But maybe he was going to try a new tack. Maybe he was going to switch back to the charming Graham she'd known when they first met and married; no doubt the same charming Graham who wooed his young grad student.

The thought of this made Diana thump her laptop closed. She then slouched back and bounced in agitation in her seat. She stared up at the ceiling and blinked, trying not to let the hot and angry tears that were pricking in her eyes escape and run down her cheeks. She hadn't shed that kind of tears in a long time, and she wouldn't allow Graham to make her cry again. She blinked hard another time and balled her hands into fists. No, she must be strong. She would ignore his message and certainly never reply to it. She would not fall for his charming wiles ever again.

Diana rubbed her face, took a deep breath, and then searched for her bag under the desk. Without another look at the closed laptop, she left her office and headed for the faculty lounge, where the graduate-faculty seminar was about to start. As she walked, she felt shaky—shaky and angry. But anger, she knew, was good. If she could remain furious, then she could keep Graham and his e-mails and his fake flattery at bay. Her anger would be her shield, her suit of armor, and woe betide anyone who got in the way of this reawakened fury.

* * *

"If you remember one thing," Rachel was saying as she and her new grad student, Zadie Browne, strode side by side along the English department's main hallway, "just remember to listen to what you're saying and to enjoy it. If you are enjoying your paper, they will enjoy it too."

By "they," Rachel of course meant the grad students and faculty who would be assembling in the faculty lounge at this very moment to hear Zadie's presentation. Rachel had met Zadie for the first time only a few days ago, but already the two of them had spent a number of hours preparing for the seminar. Rachel wasn't bothered by the extra work. Indeed, it had been the most enjoyable and rewarding experience she'd had since she started the job. Zadie was fun, bright, and engaged, and Rachel loved the research Zadie was doing for her dissertation. "Mimicking Jane: Adapting and Re-creating Austen in Popular Culture" was her working title, and Tom had been correct: It was right up Rachel's alley.

"Oh, no," Zadie exclaimed, coming to a sudden halt. "What about the questions?"

"The questions?" Rachel asked, stopping beside Zadie in front of a crowded notice board just a few feet from the faculty lounge. "What about the questions?"

Zadie's pretty brown eyes flickered in panic and her ebony brow furrowed into three distinct lines. "What if they hate the paper and start asking a bunch of mean and impossible questions?"

"We talked about this." Rachel patted Zadie's arm. "You're going to be just fine. Nobody will be mean. Although they might ask some tough questions. You're up to it, Zadie," Rachel assured her. "I've been asking you some really tough questions over the last few days, and you've answered all of them perfectly. You know your stuff; just relax and let them see that."

The presentation Zadie was about to give looked specifically at the movie *Clueless*, a modern-day *Emma*, and the recent novel *The Jane Austen Book Club*. Zadie and Rachel had spent the last few days going over her main arguments and revisiting the quotations from feminist and cultural studies texts she'd chosen. They also watched and rewatched the movie clips that accompanied the presentation. Furthermore, they had discussed all the usual critiques that would no doubt be lobbed in Zadie's direction—especially those from the old curmudgeons in the department who thought research on anything modern or, even worse, *popular* was a frivolous waste of time.

"Okay, okay," Zadie said, sucking in a big breath of air. "Relax and enjoy it," she added with a grin.

Rachel nodded and smiled back. She then waved toward the open door of the faculty lounge, and the two of them moved off. Once in the room, amid the hustle and bustle of the collected faculty and students, Zadie took her place at the front and Rachel took a seat close by. Rachel would rather have sat at the back in a corner, of course, far away from the likes of Diana and Carson. But she wanted to be near Zadie and lend moral support with her proximity, even though Rachel had no doubt her student would do fine. In spite of the last-minute nerves she had just shown in the hallway, Zadie was confident and strong: definitely not the type to fall apart in front of this crowd.

At the front, Zadie was fiddling with the DVD player and checking the television. Meanwhile, Rachel settled back in her seat and smiled. After all that had happened last week, this week had been a good one. Working with a young and enthusiastic grad student like Zadie, Rachel felt like the professor she'd always dreamed of being, and after two months at Manhattan U, she couldn't help feeling it was about time. The confidence that working with Zadie had given her had rubbed off on her teaching too. The three classes she'd taught this week weren't great, but they were certainly better than any class she'd taught all semester.

Rachel scanned the room. There was no sign of Diana yet. Although Rachel had managed to avoid Diana for over a week now, she was bound to see her today. But this prospect didn't dampen Rachel's spirits. She was too buoyed by her renewed enthusiasm for her job. Not only that, if Zadie was brave enough to stand in front of the de-

partment and talk about her research-in-progress, then Rachel reckoned she should surely be brave enough to sit in the same room as
one of her colleagues. Even if that colleague did hate her guts. Rachel
still felt a small knot of anxiety every time she thought of spending
ten days in London with Diana. But, in her current good mood, she
was choosing to banish worries about the upcoming trip to the back
of her mind.

As Rachel's eyes wandered toward the door, she suddenly found
herself gazing straight at a twinkling, smiling Carson. Before she
could stop herself, she flicked back her curls and grinned. In a black,
heavy-ribbed sweater and snug Diesel jeans, Carson looked hand-
somer than ever, and it was hard not to smile. Since that awful night,
she'd vowed not to entertain any more thoughts about Carson. He
was Diana's now, not hers. But, as Carson clocked Rachel's smile and
mouthed a smiling *Hi*, Rachel was unable to stop a flush of attraction
in her cheeks and the ripple of longing in her chest. *God, he's sexy*,
she thought, her eyes unable to shift from his thick, disheveled hair,
his sleepy dark eyes, and his perfect lips.

Rachel's yearning for Carson was cut short, however, when Diana
appeared behind him in the doorway. Rachel wanted to look away.
She really didn't want to see Diana and Carson together, even though
she'd tried to talk herself out of feeling jealous. She certainly didn't
want to witness those small signs—a smile, a light touch, a whisper—
that signaled an intimacy between them. But Rachel didn't look away.
Diana's expression was too intriguing. Her cheeks were pinched, her
eyes narrowed, and she looked livid enough to slay any mortal who
crossed her path. As she moved into the room, she stomped past
Carson, ignoring him as she went. Then, with a thump, she plonked
herself down in the chair opposite Rachel's and stared, with a stead-
fast and frowning gaze, at the floor.

Watching Diana, Rachel felt a pulse of surprise. She'd never seen
Diana look anything but poised. Rachel's surprise was followed immediately by a pulse of panic. Diana's obvious black mood did not
bode well for Zadie. Diana was sure to give her a tough time. In pre-

vious weeks, Rachel had watched Diana fire a litany of challenging questions at grad students who'd just given their presentations. With the precision of a talented neurosurgeon, Diana would home in on the flaws in their arguments and the weaknesses in their theories. Although Rachel had felt sorry for the students' discomfort, she'd also admired Diana's razor-sharp mind and her impressive ability to hear a paper just once and immediately identify the problems and imperfections. Today, however, Rachel wished Diana weren't quite so smart. Her intelligence, together with her clearly thunderous mood, was a frightening prospect.

Rachel's gaze flicked from Diana toward Zadie. She was standing by the television talking to Peter, who chaired the grad-faculty seminars every week. Zadie was smiling, laughing, and nodding at something Peter was saying. She looked calm, composed, and ready to roll.

"Okay," Rachel whispered under her breath, trying to talk herself out of her growing panic. "She's going to be okay."

Ten

Scholarly Disputes

"In conclusion, *Clueless* and *The Jane Austen Book Club* mimic Austen in order to explore bonds between women, as well as the pressures women face to conform to the expectations of their social milieus." Zadie looked up from her paper and spoke her final sentences by heart: "Amy Heckerling's movie and the recent novel by Karen Joy Fowler do not seek to be *true* to Austen. Instead, they rework, borrow, and imaginatively absorb Austen's novels in order to be truly Austenian."

With her last words done, Zadie sat down and a ripple of applause immediately followed. Rachel clapped extra hard and beamed over at Zadie. She'd done a great job, and Rachel's chest kicked with pride. Throughout the entire paper Zadie was confident and clear, and she even worked the DVD player without fumbling (something unheard-of during most academic talks). If she could just maintain her composure during the Q&A, Rachel thought, it would be a home run.

"Thank you, Zadie," Peter was now saying as he smiled over at her. "Fascinating. Really fascinating," he added with an enthusiastic nod.

Zadie smiled back, but Rachel noticed something flicker across her face. It looked like panic. A faint panic, but panic all the same. Rachel tried to catch Zadie's eye. She wanted to will her with a silent glance to keep calm, but Zadie's gaze was fixed elsewhere.

Meanwhile, Peter asked the assembled faculty and grad students, "Does anyone have any questions or comments?"

Without raising his hand, Bill Roberts boomed out from the back,

"'Truly Austenian'? I don't think so," he scoffed, plucking at his snowy beard. "*Plundering* Austen might be a better way to describe this." He waved toward the television where Zadie had recently screened a clip from *Clueless*. "All these tight clothes, shopping malls, sports cars. They hardly capture the subtleties of Austen's irony and the deftness of her wit, do they?"

Before Zadie could answer, Jackie Rawlings cut in. "I agree. To call them 'Austenian' is rather a grandiose claim, don't you think? I mean," she went on, peering over her tiny reading glasses, "I follow you up to a point. I see that this film and the book are dealing with *some* of the issues we see in Austen's novels. But where Austen's novels are literature, this movie and book are for a popular audience. They are more concerned with entertainment and the dollar than they are with Austen."

Listening to Bill, then Jackie, Rachel felt a familiar pulse of annoyance. It was as if they hadn't listened to a word Zadie had said. One of the main points in Zadie's talk was to discuss these curmudgeonly assessments of Austen adaptations and to try to think beyond the tired old "it's just not true to Austen" critique. Rachel did not speak up, however, because as she looked back toward Zadie, she noticed that the panic of a moment ago was gone and now there was a defiant twinkle in her eyes. Thanks to the hours working with Rachel this week, Zadie was prepared for this response, and it looked like she was gearing up for the fight.

"As I said in my paper," Zadie began, raising her chin and smiling a little, "I acknowledge the obvious differences between Austen's novels and the works I've talked about here today. However, I believe that *Clueless* and Fowler's novel *do* share Austen's concern with representing women and women's issues. I also think they echo Austen's own mimicry—or *plundering*, as you call it, Professor Roberts," she added, nodding at Bill.

"Austen's plundering?" Bill shot back. "What on earth do you mean? I hardly think you can describe Austen as a plunderer," he sneered.

Zadie's eyes twinkled again. "As I am sure you're aware, before Austen wrote her most famous works, she adapted Samuel Richardson's seven-volume novel, *Sir Charles Grandison*, into an eighteen-page playlet to entertain her young niece."

Bill was silent for a second and then said with a dismissive wave, "Of course, of course." Bill was no Austen expert, and it was clear he didn't have a clue.

"As Jocelyn Harris has pointed out," Zadie continued, as she flipped through some pages on the desk in front of her to find a quote, "In the playlet, Jane Austen 'transposes events, characters, and speeches from Richardson's context to her own, she misapplies his tones and registers, she inverts his priorities and she wildly exaggerates his scenes.'" When Zadie was finished reading from her notes, she looked up at Bill and smiled. "I would say she is quite a plunderer."

Rachel wanted to whoop aloud. Zadie had socked it to Bill Roberts. But Rachel knew that whooping wasn't appropriate in faculty-graduate seminars, and so instead she looked over at Zadie, this time catching her eye, and gave her a quick wink. Zadie flashed a small grin back.

For the next ten minutes, Zadie answered questions with unflappable ease. She was on a roll and seemed to be loving every minute. Rachel was enjoying it too and had to sit on her hands a couple of times to stop herself from applauding her student and the smart, insightful answers she was volleying back to the questions being fired at her. Uneasiness flickered in Rachel only once, however, when she caught a glimpse of Diana across the room. So far, Diana had said nothing, which was unusual. But she was clearly following the discussion, because her gaze kept flitting from questioner to Zadie and back again. The look on her face, although keen, was not lighthearted. It was thunderous, in fact, even worse than it had been when she first came into the room. Her violet eyes were brooding, and a heavy crease divided her high and otherwise flawless forehead. As Rachel moved her own gaze away from Diana and back to Zadie, she just hoped and prayed that when Diana did speak, which no doubt she would, Zadie could remain cool.

After a barrage of questions were asked and Zadie had answered them all with aplomb, there was a lull in the conversation, and Peter took it as a cue to start wrapping up the seminar.

"Well, if there are no more questions?" he began, as he scanned the room one last time.

There was a silence, and Rachel felt herself breathe a long silent sigh. They had escaped Diana—or so she thought.

Just as Rachel was gathering her face into a "you did it" smile for Zadie, Diana raised her hand and said in a gruff tone, "I have a question."

Rachel's heart plummeted.

Peter nodded at Diana. "Please," he said with an inviting wave.

Diana turned her ominous eyes onto Zadie. "How does your work add anything to existing scholarship on this topic?"

Zadie, for the first time in a while, looked panicked. Nevertheless, she pushed back one of her long braids and beamed at Diana. "I think my work looks at contemporary adaptations of Austen in a unique way. It doesn't try to re-cover Austen, but instead attempts to understand—"

Zadie didn't get to finish because Diana, while shaking her head vigorously, interrupted and said, "How is this any different from what John Wiltshire has done in his book *Recreating Jane Austen*? For me, it seems like you are saying nothing new from the work he has done."

Zadie's eyes flew open and her jaw dropped. Rachel found that her own face had fallen into the same shocked pose too. How in the hell did Diana know Wiltshire's book? How did she know about a book that had nothing to do with her field and that wasn't exactly a best-seller outside of this specific area of Austen studies? Zadie's work was different from this book, of course. But it just amazed Rachel, and clearly Zadie too, that Diana knew the text in the first place.

"Well," Zadie began, trying to compose herself, "Wiltshire's book is concerned with modern re-creations of Austen. However, as he says himself in his introduction, he is more concerned with the *process* of imitation or re-creation."

Diana folded her arms and leaned back in her chair. Her gaze was still black, and now unsatisfied too. "But correct me if I am wrong, Zadie," Diana said, "Wiltshire's thesis on imitation is built on his readings of *Clueless* and the like. Readings which, I must say, are very similar to your own."

Zadie was now looking flustered. "Of course, I *did* refer to Wiltshire's book when I spoke about *Clueless*," she stammered. Then her hands flew down to the papers in front of her and she started flipping through them to find the section she was thinking about.

"I remember," Diana barked, before Zadie was finished. "I'm just not convinced you've added anything further to Wiltshire's work."

Zadie looked up, and her eyes darted in panic from Diana across to Rachel. She then said in a quavering voice, "Wiltshire's book is concerned with the *process* of adaptation. My work is more concerned with the adaptations themselves and—"

"So you keep saying," snapped Diana.

So far, Rachel had said nothing, even though her whole body was taut with rage and disbelief that Diana was being so mean. It was unheard-of in these seminars for a faculty member to step in and defend her student, as there seemed to be an unspoken policy—which Rachel thought absurd and ruthless—of making the grad students duke it out for themselves. But, glancing over at Zadie, who was now flustered beyond words, Rachel could not keep quiet any longer.

She looked straight at Diana, took a deep breath, and began: "As Zadie pointed out, Wiltshire is primarily concerned with the psychological dimensions of adapting Austen." As she spoke, Rachel's voice was a little loud and awkward.

"That may be so," Diana retorted, stiffening in her seat. "But he is still making many of the same points Zadie made today."

Rachel could feel the heat rising in her cheeks, but she carried on nonetheless. "Zadie's work looks beyond the individual and psychological motivations of authors and screenwriters and explores the political, cultural, and gender dimensions of Austen adaptations. I think this is an important addition to scholarship in this area."

Diana's eyes narrowed and her nostrils flared as she glowered at Rachel. "You seem to know Zadie's work much better than Zadie herself, Professor Grey."

Rachel stared over at Diana for a second, speechless. Part of her mind was chanting, *Keep cool. Don't rise to her bait.* Another part screamed, *The bitch. The complete and utter bitch!*

The angry voice won, and so, with her cheeks now flaming, Rachel spat out, "I know about Zadie's work, Professor Monroe, because I listened to her paper."

"Are you implying I didn't listen?" Diana growled.

You could hear a pin drop in the room. Every pair of eyes was on either Diana or Rachel. Zadie's gaze flitted back and forth, and her brow creased with worry and humiliation.

"I am not implying anything," Rachel responded. "I'm just saying it was all there in Zadie's paper. She made it very clear how her work was furthering recent scholarship."

Diana's eyes sizzled with antipathy. She was silent for a beat, and then, removing her stare from Rachel, she scanned the room. "This has always been my concern with this kind of work," she announced, more to everyone else than to Rachel. "Too many graduate students these days want to look at popular culture, whether it's *Clueless* or, God forbid, *American Pop Idol.* But because of the shallowness of these artifacts"—she sneered just slightly as she said the words— "there is very little to say about them, and people end up saying the same things."

Something snapped inside Rachel and she shouted over at Diana, "Are you saying nobody should study popular culture?"

Diana gave a small, tight smile. It was clear that, with Rachel's outburst, she knew she had the upper hand.

"Of course not," she said in the poised, cool tone that she usually maintained. "I'm saying that there are reasons to be wary of this new fad amongst grad students to look only at popular books or recent blockbuster movies."

"Hasn't over thirty years of cultural studies scholarship taught us the importance of examining popular culture?" Rachel demanded, her chest pounding with rage and incredulity. "Didn't Stuart Hall once say . . ." She thought for a moment, making sure she got the quotation right. "'Popular culture is the arena of consent and resistance. It is partly where hegemony arises, and where it is secured.' In other words"—Rachel then quoted verbatim the words of her mentor, Professor McGuiness—"'Popular culture influences who we are, what we think, and what's going to happen in our world and in our lives.' Isn't it vital then that we study popular culture?"

Diana simply ignored Rachel's question. "I hope you are not taking this personally, Professor Grey," she said quietly, while flashing another small smile. "I know your own work is concerned with contemporary fiction for young women, and I am sure your approach is unique and important."

Rachel opened her mouth to respond, but Peter cut in and stopped her.

"Rachel? Diana?" he said, looking at them both with a flustered smile. "Perhaps we could continue this conversation later. We're already five minutes over time; I think we need to wrap up."

Diana nodded at Peter. "Of course."

As Peter thanked Zadie for her paper and announced next week's seminar, Rachel sat in stony silence. She was on the verge of tears. She was on the verge of crossing the room and slapping Diana. She was on the verge of shouting out to everyone, *Why do you put up with this woman? Can't you see she is a mean-spirited, uptight witch?* Instead of doing any of these things, however, she managed to keep her cool enough to lean forward, grab her heavy bag, and then leave the room without uttering another word.

Hot tears sprang from Rachel's eyes as soon as she was out in the hallway. Before anyone could see, however, she quickly jogged away from the faculty lounge and down the hallway.

Eleven

Visiting Scholars

"Your passion is very rare," Carson said with a small smile.

He was leaning against the door frame of Rachel's office. His dark eyes were twinkling. Standing just a few feet from Carson with her hand on the door handle, Rachel didn't know how to respond.

"Oh, thanks," she finally mumbled with an embarrassed shake of her head.

The graduate-student research seminar had only just ended, and Rachel was still sniffing into a Kleenex and dabbing at her eyes when Carson came knocking at her door. She wasn't going to answer at first. She was too much of a jittery, tearful mess to face anyone. But then it occurred to her it might be Zadie, and Zadie, she figured, might need to talk. So she'd answered the door, only to find Carson in front of her. Of course, there was no way to disguise that she'd been crying, no time to dab concealer under her eyes, or hide the balled-up Kleenexes on her desk. Carson had caught Rachel in all her puffy-faced, red-eyed glory, and Rachel was mortified.

Fortunately, he chose not to remark on her tears and instead launched into a monologue about how impressed he'd been by Zadie's talk and how even more impressed he'd been by Rachel's comments in the Q&A session.

"You don't see it enough in academe," Carson was now saying. "Too many people try to play it cool. You don't see your kind of passion very often. It's very"—he paused, searching for the right word—"very fresh."

"Thanks," Rachel muttered once again, still at a loss for what to say.

During the Q&A, Carson hadn't said a thing. In fact, Rachel had been so involved in the proceedings she'd completely forgotten he was there. But clearly he had been there, and he'd been paying attention.

"Very appealing, too," Carson added, flashing Rachel a wide grin.

Rachel flushed. She was in equal parts embarrassed, flattered, and utterly bemused. She had no idea why Carson was saying all this and why he wasn't currently at Diana's door telling her how clever she was and how her laser-sharp mind was so appealing. After all, weren't they together? Wasn't Diana the person he brought back in late-night cabs to his apartment? Why, then, was he here in Rachel's doorway when he should be at Diana's?

Of course, Diana hadn't gotten as riled as Rachel in the seminar. Indeed, Diana had morphed from the simmering dragon who entered the faculty lounge, back to her familiar steely ice-queen self. Diana's composure at the end of their altercation made Rachel feel angrier—and more idiotic. No doubt Diana wouldn't be in need of any reassuring or supportive words from Carson. She seemed the type that would shun that kind of thing from even her nearest and dearest. Nevertheless, Diana probably would not like the idea of Carson lounging at Rachel's door lavishing her with compliments, either.

This last thought made Rachel feel a little better, and at last she was able to find her tongue and string together a few more words than "oh, thanks."

"I'm not sure if everyone would agree with you," she said, looking Carson properly in the eye for the first time. "I certainly don't think passion gets you tenure these days."

Carson leaned toward Rachel, tapped her arm with a long finger, and then let his finger rest there. "I don't know about that, Rachel Grey," he said in a low whisper. "Your passion would get my tenure vote."

Heat immediately flushed back into Rachel's cheeks. Carson was flirting with her again, just like he had those first few times they met. But this time it wasn't sporadic or fleeting; it wasn't punctuated with more serious academic chitchat. The man was going all out. He was *really* flirting with her. No sooner had this realization sunk in than Rachel found her blush turning into a small smile. If Carson McEvoy was flirting with her, then, hell, she was going to flirt right back. He was too sexy to resist. On top of which, this would be the sweet revenge she was looking for. Diana had been an utter bitch back in the graduate seminar. Rachel's blood pulsed in her veins just thinking about it. And thus, if Diana's man was flirting with Rachel, then Rachel wasn't going to shrink away and close her door. She was going to enjoy herself. In the meantime, Diana would get the justice she deserved.

So, tossing back her curls and looking at Carson from under her long eyelashes, Rachel quickly transformed herself. No longer a puffy-eyed victim, she told herself, from now on she would be a slinky, murmuring sex kitten. A sex kitten that would leave Carson breathless and incapable of ever returning to iron-woman Diana. Of course, she was a little out of practice. The last time she'd turned on her full flirting charms was back in college, before Justin. But it would come back to her—it had to.

"Why don't you come in, Carson?" Rachel purred, flicking back her curls one more time.

Carson's grin widened as he responded, "I'd love to."

As Rachel led them both into the room, Carson's hand grazed the small of her back. In that instant, as lightning sparked at the spot where he'd touched her, Rachel knew the two of them would sleep together.

And it would probably happen tonight.

On the ten-minute walk from the English department to her apartment, Diana's mind swirled and the familiar clenching feeling returned in her chest. She was still angry about Graham's e-mail. But that, she reminded herself, was a good thing. The longer she could remain angry at him the better. If she let her shield of anger fall, if she allowed herself to entertain the idea of meeting him while he was in the city, it would be the end. The fortress she'd built up around her pain over the last five years since Graham left her for Annabelle would crumble, and she would spiral headlong into paralyzing despair.

Deep down, though, Diana also knew her anger wasn't all good. In the graduate-faculty seminar earlier, she'd been tough on Rachel and her student. Their ideas and arguments needed to be challenged, she told herself. Yet, the suspicion that her anger had made her go too far nagged in the back of her mind. Diana never intended to humiliate anyone, and she had a feeling she had done just that today. She'd crossed some invisible line that she'd always believed people in her position should not cross. Professors should be tough and critical and perceptive, but they should never embarrass or upset.

Diana shook her head, sighed a little, and tried to erase the memory of Rachel's flushed cheeks and dismayed wide eyes. She then turned into Washington Square Park from Fourth Street, where she'd been walking, and quickened her pace toward home. A moody evening gloom hung over the city, and the old-fashioned street lamps dotted along the park's wide walkways offered a dim yellow glow. Diana kept her head down as she walked. She really didn't want to run into a colleague or a student, as she so often did in the park. She just wanted to get home, bake herself the fresh salmon she'd bought at Whole Foods this morning, and pour herself a glass of cold white wine. She would then immerse herself in writing next Monday's lecture until it was time for bed.

But just as she reached the other side of the park and was about to cross the road toward the front door of her building, a voice called out to her from the darkness nearby.

"Diana!"

Every muscle, every vein, every pulse in her body froze. It was Graham's voice.

"Diana," he called out again, clearly wondering if she'd heard him the first time.

Slowly, she turned. Amongst the shadows, she saw Graham stand up from a bench where he'd been sitting and move toward her. She couldn't see his face at first, but she could tell from his gait, the small bounce in his step, that he was smiling. She knew he was smiling that smile of his that, from the very first moment she'd set eyes on him all those years ago, had sucked her in.

Before the lamplight could fall across his face, Diana began to move backward and away from Graham. If she could just get away, she told herself with her heart beginning to thump at her ribs, if she could just get away before seeing that smile, she would be safe. But it was too late. Graham moved quickly, and soon he was in front of Diana, the yellow lamplight illuminating his distinguished forehead, his wavy red hair with its speckles of gray, and his broad, handsome smile.

"Diana," he said for the third time, looking down at her with his familiar deep blue eyes, "you're here!"

Before she knew what was happening, Graham swooped in, took her in his arms, and hugged her tight against his chest. She remained motionless throughout the whole thing. Even her mind ground to a halt. She felt nothing but cold, empty shock.

Graham let go of Diana after a few seconds and held her at arm's length.

"As beautiful as ever," he said, scanning her face and still smiling his inimitable, charming smile.

Diana stared for a moment, and then, as a cold wind unexpectedly whipped around them, something kick-started inside her brain. She pulled her elbows out from under his grasp and moved back another step.

"What are you doing here?" she hissed.

Graham's smile faded a little as he realized he was in for a fight. "I wanted to see you, Di," he said in a soft whisper. "I need to see you."

"So you said in your e-mail," she snapped as she hefted her bag on her shoulder and tried to move past him.

Graham reached out, grasping her arm with a soft yet determined grip. "Please, Diana," he begged. "I thought you might not reply to my e-mail. So that's why I came here." He waved to her building across the street. Their old building. "I've been waiting for an hour. Please hear me out," he added.

If Diana had any sense, any courage, she would have moved off and never looked back. But she couldn't. Graham's spell was already working. The only thing she could do, the only weapon she had, was her anger.

Stay mad at him, she reminded herself before she shot an enraged glance up at Graham and barked out, "Why? Why should I hear you out?"

Graham shrank back a little, startled by the venom in her voice.

"I don't blame you, Di," he began. "I don't blame you for not wanting to talk to me. I don't deserve to be heard out." He gave a boyish shrug of his shoulders. "But there's so much I need to say. So much I need to apologize for."

Diana flinched at his words. In all the years she'd known Graham, pretty much all of which she'd been married to him, she had never, ever heard him apologize. Not to her, not to anybody. Graham held unwavering convictions in everything he did and said. There was no need, in his mind, ever to apologize. Even his "Dear John" letter, which he had left for Diana on their dining table, didn't contain the word "sorry." Instead, he laid out his decision to leave and "hoped and trusted" that Diana would understand and not take it personally. Not take it personally? Those words had caused so many tears and so much bitter, hysterical laughter after he'd left as Diana reread the letter a million and one times.

"Apologize?" She suddenly laughed that strangled, bitter laugh once again. "Apologize? Since when does Graham Cartwright apologize?" But before Graham could respond, Diana narrowed her eyes and asked, "You're not in one of those twelve-step programs, are you? One of those where you call up all the people you have wronged in your life and try to make amends?" She shook her head furiously. "If you are, you can forget it. I'm not granting you forgiveness. Never."

Graham ventured a small smile. "Me? In a twelve-step program? Are you kidding?" He puffed out a laugh. "What would I be recovering from?"

"Philandering? Adultery?" Diana shot back.

Graham blinked and held up his hands. "I deserved that." He sighed and then, after a pause, he shook his head. "I'm not in any program, Diana. This is for real."

Through the evening gloom, Diana eyed her ex-husband suspiciously while saying nothing.

"Diana," Graham said, stepping closer.

She backed away. Even though she was unable to cut Graham completely loose, she knew the least she could do was to keep him at arm's length.

Graham studied her face and sighed once again. After a few silent beats, he whispered, "I've left Annabelle."

The name Diana loathed so much reignited her anger. "Wonderful," she spat out, her flinty tone slicing into the night air. "Just wonderful."

She then turned on her heel and tried again to leave. But Graham had preempted her movements and swiftly stepped into Diana's path. He didn't touch her, but he stood just an inch away.

"Please," he begged, his dark blue eyes boring into hers. He was so close she could feel his breath on her cheeks. *"Te careo. Ego amo te."*

With these Latin words, Diana knew she was lost. Her anger, her hatred, the pain in her chest, which had all been so intense just a second ago, instantly began to melt into the darkness. *I miss you. I love you.* She'd heard these words so many times. She remembered every rise and fall, every sound and pause of those phrases that had so often rolled off Graham's proficient Latin tongue. When they were married and found themselves separated by some conference or a lecture trip to some far-off city, Graham would always end their conversations on crackling phone lines by murmuring these words to Diana: *"Te careo. Ego amo te."* At least, in the early days that was what he used to say.

Now, as she heard them again after all these years, Diana's world buckled and collapsed. Every shred of reason or dignity disappeared, and all the ice and steel and flint she'd built up inside her to protect her wounded heart crumbled into dust. All she could do was sigh, "Oh," as Graham swept her up once again into his familiar arms.

Twelve

Academic Passions

Rachel had never had so much sex in her life. For two weeks, since the day of the graduate-faculty seminar and her fight with Diana, she and Carson had spent every night at her apartment, and every night they'd made love at least twice, often three or four times. They'd drunk wine, eaten Rachel's lovingly made suppers, and talked a lot too about their work, books they'd read, and conferences they'd attended. They'd even had one heated debate about literary theory. But mostly they spent their time naked in bed—or on Rachel's desk, or in her shower, or sometimes on the tiny workspace between the stove and the cluttered sink. They'd had sex on every single surface, in fact, and contorted themselves into positions that Rachel, up until now, would never have believed possible.

It had never been like this with Justin—not ever. Sure, there were sparks at the beginning, before they settled down into the quiet, sweet, and routine lovemaking that had marked their living together. But even in those heady days when she and Justin were still college kids with all the time and energy in the world, their more frantic, first-throes sex was nothing like this—nothing like what Carson and Rachel had been up to for the past couple of weeks.

On the fourteenth morning waking up next to a naked, sleeping Carson, Rachel did what she'd done every morning since they'd first hooked up: She smiled a wide, beatific smile and then let her eyes wander over Carson's long back. Only a few hours ago she'd been woken by Carson's kisses on her shoulder, and it wasn't long after that she was holding his back—this beautiful, rangy back—as Carson lifted her onto the tiny dressing table next to her futon and the two made loud and pounding love against Rachel's cold wall mirror.

This morning, like every morning, her body ached from their late-night (and early morning) antics. But Rachel's exhaustion was mixed with the ecstatic realization that, yet again, she'd spent the night with Carson McEvoy. *The* Carson McEvoy. She gazed over at his slumbering body and wondered, not for the first time, how she'd managed it: how she'd snagged such a beautiful, sexy, incredibly smart man and secured him in her bed for two whole weeks. Also, as she woke a little more, she wondered whether it all might continue when she got back from London.

This last thought prompted the smile on Rachel's face to wane a little. She was setting off for London tonight, and not only was she not ready to leave Carson for ten days, she wasn't anywhere near ready for the trip. Since Carson's arrival in her life—and her bed—Rachel had let pretty much everything else slide. She hadn't written one new word for her book. Her preparations for her class were slapdash and thus resulted in some of her worst seminars yet, with her students looking like they wanted to kill themselves from boredom in every session. She still had ten papers to grade from their last assignment, and her pigeonhole in the department office was about to burst with unretrieved mail. She certainly hadn't made any preparations for the Literary London trip. She hadn't even checked to see if her passport was up-to-date.

Every day she'd meant to get organized, to grade some papers, to do a little work on her manuscript, to peek at her passport. But every day she'd find herself shaving her legs instead, or gazing out the window thinking about Carson, or wandering to the farmer's market on Union Square to pick up fresh herbs or interesting cheeses or juicy asparagus. Then every night, when Carson would show up at her door with a bottle of wine in his hand, she'd serve up the food it had taken her hours to prepare. They would eat, drink, and not long after they would strip each other naked and head for the bed—or another interesting new surface.

Deep down, Rachel knew what she was doing was reckless. Not only were her end-of-semester student evaluations destined to be abysmal, but it seemed she was burning bridges with even her more favored colleagues. Peter had tried to pin her down for her first appraisal, but she'd blown him off twice already, claiming she needed more time to prepare. In short, Rachel was making a very poor start on the tenure track. If she kept this up, she'd do a good job of screwing all her chances of a lifetime job at Manhattan U.

In spite of this, she couldn't help letting everything at work fall by the wayside. Carson was too alluring, and her enthusiasm for her teaching, her students, and her research just couldn't compete. The fight with Diana seemed to cement a feeling that had been growing in Rachel's mind for some weeks prior to their fight: Rachel probably would never get tenure, even if she tried. She wasn't respected by Diana, and not by many others in the department either, and her work was a joke to them. With the exception of Zadie, her students were bored and uninterested too. Tenure at Manhattan U was just a pipe dream.

At least, that was what Rachel thought when she allowed herself to contemplate her situation. Most of the time, however, Rachel pushed all these thoughts as far back as she could in her mind and buried herself in Carson. Just as she was doing now, in fact, as she reached across the bed and stroked his neck with her fingertips. It was easier to immerse herself in his delectable body than to contemplate how she was screwing up her career.

Under her touch, Carson finally stirred. "Mmmmm," he sighed, before turning over, blinking open his dark eyes to look at Rachel, and then reaching out for her.

Maybe she wouldn't need the damn job anyway. Maybe she and Carson would carry on this way and she could just spend her days being his girlfriend, mistress, lover, or whatever she was. Okay, it contradicted everything she'd ever thought and stood for about men and relationships and feminism. But who cared when she had Carson at her fingertips and in her bed? He was smart and funny and incredibly sexy. Who could really blame her for losing her bearings over such a guy?

These were Rachel's last dreamy, light-headed thoughts before Carson pulled her on top of his warm, waiting body and they began to make love once again.

Afterward, as they lay panting and sweaty, Rachel's imminent trip and all the things she had to get done that day started creeping back into her mind.

"I have to pack," she found herself saying aloud, although her comment was more for herself than Carson.

"Pack?" Carson muttered.

"For London."

"London?" Carson muttered again.

Rachel propped herself up on her elbow and looked down at him. "I'm going to London today. Remember?"

Carson's eyes were closed and his arm slung lazily over his forehead. "Is that today?"

A jolt of disappointment rippled through Rachel. She'd been talking about her upcoming trip for days. She'd thought and hoped that Carson, like her, would be wondering what it would mean for their affair, perhaps considering how much they would miss each other. But, in fact, he seemed to be having trouble remembering when she was even going.

"Yes, today," she said, her voice a little strangled.

Carson blinked open his eyes. "Of course, yes." He grinned as he reached up and twirled one of her curls around his index finger. "London will rock. You're going to love it."

This wasn't exactly the response Rachel was looking for either. She was hoping for something more like, *Today? Really? Oh, no. I'm really going to miss you, Rachel.* But, as Carson kept on grinning and twirling her hair, she realized such a reply wasn't going to come. Her disappointment shifted to annoyance, and she found herself pulling away from him.

"What's up, babe?" Carson said, noticing the change in Rachel's disposition.

"Nothing," she muttered. "Nothing."

She didn't want to have to explain. If Carson was feeling anything like she was feeling about what was going on between them, he'd just say those things, wouldn't he? He'd miss her like she was going to miss him, right? Rachel looked back down at Carson. His eyes were closed again.

But that was their problem, wasn't it? she thought, her mind continuing to whir, their one little problem. Amid all the sex, they weren't saying much about what was going on. In fact, they weren't saying anything at all. After their first night together, Carson had simply shown up at her apartment every night afterward with his heart-tugging smile and a bottle of wine. And that was that. In two weeks they hadn't been on a real date. They hadn't even been to Carson's apartment. In the English department, if they passed each other in the hallway or caught each other's gaze in a faculty meeting, they simply smiled flirtatious and knowing smiles at each other but said nothing.

Rachel was too scared to ask Carson about what they were doing and what it all meant. He wasn't forthcoming about what he was feeling, and she'd already learned from her experiences with Justin not to push it or probe. She'd shown her heart too clearly to Justin, demanded they talk about their feelings one too many times, and in the end it had just screwed everything up. She wasn't going to make the same mistake with Carson. They were great at the flirtatious banter and they excelled at the academic chat, but Rachel knew she must leave it at that.

There had been one time, however, when she wasn't able to hold back. It was on the second or third night they'd spent together, and she'd tried to bring up Diana. Rachel was still baffled by what had happened between the two of them. But Carson, with an impish grin, just pulled Rachel into him and muttered, "We go back a long way. She's an old friend," before he set about peppering Rachel's neck with kisses. Rachel wasn't particularly satisfied with this response, but she realized fast not to press the issue. She just had to presume that if anything had been going on between Diana and Carson, it must have ended.

"You want me to drive you?"

"Sorry?" Carson's question shook Rachel from her thoughts.

Carson opened his eyes again and propped himself up against the pillows. "You want me to drive you?"

"To London?" Rachel blurted out, not really thinking.

Carson laughed and then leaned over and playfully bit her shoulder. "To the airport, you dummy," he mumbled into her skin.

"Oh." Rachel blushed; then she looked down at Carson nuzzling into her and asked, "You have a car? In the city?"

"Uh-huh," Carson grunted, but he was no longer concentrating. He was busy snaking his arms around Rachel and burying his head in the spot below her chin and above her cleavage. "One more for the road?" he whispered.

Rachel was exhausted. She couldn't believe he wasn't exhausted too. But she found herself succumbing under his kisses to her collarbone. What did it matter if she knew nothing about this guy? she thought. So what if she didn't know he had a car? Or what his apartment looked like inside? Or what he thought about her? He must care something about her, about them, if he was going to drive her to the airport and wave her off on her ten-day trip to London.

But just as Rachel was about to lose herself in Carson all over again, an image crept into her mind. She saw Diana with luggage around her feet, standing at the British Airways terminal and spotting Rachel and Carson kissing each other good-bye. Diana's face was icy and aloof, but there was a hint of anger too. The image caused a strange mix of guilt and smugness to rise up in Rachel's chest. She'd poached Diana's man and that was satisfying. But, in spite of everything, in spite of how mean Diana had been to Rachel, it felt bad too.

Rachel shook her head, banishing the image from her mind, and then looked down at Carson. He was still kissing her collarbone, but for a second he caught her eye and smiled.

"Rachel Grey," he whispered.

In that instant, the image of Diana and all Rachel's worries about Carson and work and her life evaporated.

"I'll be with you before you know it," Graham said, as he reached across the backseat of the cab and squeezed Diana's knee.

It was seven in the evening and they were whizzing over the Williamsburg Bridge. Manhattan receded behind them, and the lights from the bridge flashed monotonously through the window. They were both heading to JFK: Diana for her flight to London, Graham for his much-delayed flight back to Berkeley. He'd only meant to stay in New York for a few days but ended up staying two weeks.

Diana glanced over at Graham, gave a small smile, and nodded. She hadn't been thinking about when they would be together again, even though Graham had read her silence as such. Instead, she'd been thinking about Rachel and how she hoped she would get to the airport before her young colleague and secure herself a seat on the plane between two strangers, or perhaps two students. Anywhere except next to Rachel. Seven hours squashed together in coach class was too horrifying a prospect for Diana.

Since their altercation a couple of weeks ago at the grad-faculty seminar, Diana had successfully avoided all contact with Rachel. Except one time, when they'd nearly collided in the hallway outside the English department office and, upon realizing what was about to happen—and whom they were in danger of running into—they'd both swerved away from each other and averted their eyes in opposite directions. Diana knew she should be more mature about the whole thing and end this game of dodging and avoidance. She was the more seasoned and experienced academic, after all, and should probably take Rachel to one side and attempt to iron out their differences. At the very least, she should try to end the awkwardness that fizzed between the two of them. But as soon as this thought occurred to Diana, her old resentment of Rachel and, by association, of Annabelle would rise up from her belly, and she could not find the will or energy to initiate a reconciliation with Rachel. On top of which, her mind and thoughts were elsewhere at the moment. Since he'd walked back into her life just two weeks ago, Graham was taking up every shred of Diana's emotional energy. She had nothing left for Rachel.

Diana glanced over again at Graham as he stared out the window of the speeding cab. His high cheekbones, his distinguished nose, and his thick auburn hair were all so familiar to her. Yet thanks to the years they'd been apart, Graham's profile also now seemed foreign and unknown to her. The hints of gray at his temples, the deeper lines around his eyes; these things had grown while Graham was in the arms of another woman. A lot had happened in the last two weeks between them, many apologies had been made, but Diana still could not fight the resentment that simmered low down inside her. The resentment that another woman had stolen five years of Graham and five years of their marriage.

But what exactly had happened over the last couple of weeks? Diana still wasn't sure. Even now, sitting in the taxi with Graham's hand perched on her knee, she wasn't clear about how she felt. She knew that something inside her had lifted since Graham had returned and the knot in her chest had finally loosened. After Graham found her in the park, after they'd returned to her apartment for Graham's long explanations and apologies followed by a night of quiet and tentative lovemaking, they'd quickly fallen back into a familiar and comforting routine. Dinners at intimate French restaurants in the West Village. Readings at the Ninety-second Street Y. A Puccini at the Met. A wine tasting at a small wine shop on Elizabeth Street. Diana hadn't done these things for so long and, doing them again, she felt as if she'd been woken from a long, deep sleep.

Yet Diana also felt dazed—rather like she did when she'd been roused from a night of heavy, undisturbed sleep. The old routine felt comforting, but at the same time it felt unreal and shaky and dream-like. Diana couldn't quash the anger at herself for forgiving Graham so easily. She was ashamed at how quickly she'd succumbed to his charms, in spite of all her earlier resolve that she wouldn't. She was so ashamed, in fact, that she hadn't told anyone yet that Graham and she were together again. Not Peter. Not Mary, her friend in California. They would be too shocked and appalled, and Diana could not face it.

Graham, it seemed, had done a quick job of finding his way back into Diana's life with his uncharacteristic apologies, his pleas that he missed Diana's "brilliance and beauty," and his stories of his unsuccessful relationship with Annabelle, who, according to Graham, was more preoccupied with upcoming bachelorette parties in Tahoe than with her flailing PhD on Greek tragedy. They really had nothing to say to each other these days, he claimed.

However, Graham hadn't been wholly successful in worming his way back into Diana's heart. Disbelief, distrust, and anger still bubbled deep down in Diana. She knew that he'd extended his stay in New York just to be with her. She knew he'd missed almost two weeks of his classes at Berkeley to do so. She knew that he'd promised that after returning to Berkeley "to clear up some things," he'd be with her in London for Thanksgiving. But even though she knew all this, she couldn't quite believe or trust it. She couldn't shake the feeling that the bubble Graham and she were living in might burst any minute and she would find herself, once again, alone in her apartment with only her cat and her books for company. Even when they made love, Diana felt she was hovering somewhere above the bed looking down, surveying the pair of them like a disbelieving stranger.

As if reading her bewildered, annoyed, and uncertain mind, Graham squeezed her knee again and whispered, "She won't be there, you know. Annabelle. She's away on one of her *girls-only* trips," he added with a roll of his eyes. "I'm just going to zip into the house, take a few things, and check into a motel for a few nights. I'll be in London for Thanksgiving, I promise."

"Great," Diana responded with a tight smile.

Graham continued to watch her. "You're an incredible woman, Diana."

She swatted away his words like a fly.

"No, I mean it," he insisted.

Diana then shook her head and muttered, "I know, I know."

Unlike the old Graham, the new Graham was full of compliments. Since he'd been back he'd showered Diana with them, and at first she'd been bemused yet pleased all the same. She had no idea what had come over the new Graham, but she couldn't help feeling flattered. But now, after two weeks, the compliments were beginning to grate. Was it that he was trying too hard or that his words didn't quite seem sincere? She wasn't sure. All she knew was that in the last few days, when Graham would whisper his compliments into her ear as they shared a pillow, or when he would squeeze her hand across a candlelit table and tell her she was "exquisite" or the "most articulate woman" he'd ever known, she'd give an involuntary flinch and the hairs on her neck would bristle just a little.

Graham seemed to be reading her mind again. "You're too modest for compliments, I know." He grinned, squeezing her knee one more time before taking his hand away and looking at his watch. "We're making good time," he then said, changing the subject. "Perhaps we can grab a glass of wine before we catch our planes."

"That would be nice," Diana replied.

She was about to turn and look out the window when she felt Graham's hand on her neck.

"I'm going to miss you so much," he murmured, pulling her in for a kiss.

Diana resisted a little but then allowed him to kiss her. Deep, long kisses. She could feel her cheeks burn, though. She wasn't used to doing this kind of thing in public. She felt exposed, caught out—cheap, even. But her unease wasn't just about the lack of privacy or the juvenility of what they were doing (or even how it reminded her of the regrettable night with Carson). It was also about how Diana couldn't help thinking about Mikey every single time Graham kissed her or touched her in an intimate way. Over the past weeks, every time Graham would move close and his lips would touch hers, immediately Mikey's wide face and kind eyes, his broad shoulders and lingering smile, would shimmer into Diana's mind. If she concentrated hard enough, she could shut out the image after a while. But in those first few moments with Graham's lips or hands on her, it was always there. Always.

This time in the cab Diana found she couldn't shake the image of Mikey, and so she ended up pulling away. "Lipstick," she muttered, waving her hand in front of her mouth.

Graham smiled and nodded, seemingly unfazed, and the two of them turned to look out of their respective windows. With the buildings and lights of the city flashing by outside, they rode onward in silence.

Thirteen

Upper Class

Rachel's ride to the airport was an unexpected and hair-raising adventure. It seemed that behind the wheel of his silver-gray 1963 Alfa Romeo, Carson morphed into Steve McQueen in *Bullitt*. They'd left Rachel's apartment in good time and were in no apparent rush, but Carson still took it upon himself to weave, bob, and screech his way through the busy streets of Manhattan. His hand remained permanently on the horn as he hurried along dithering drivers. Out on the expressways of Brooklyn and Queens, he stepped hard on the gas and drove at speeds Rachel didn't know were possible in a forty-six-year-old car. Rachel found herself gripping the door handle as Carson raced onward, and her knuckles turned white on numerous occasions as they skimmed taxis and whizzed past SUVs and overtook gargantuan Mack trucks.

Halfway into their trip, it occurred to Rachel that Carson driving his silver Alfa Romeo was much like Carson making love: slick, beautiful, fast, and adventuresome—but also a little frightening for those who were along for the ride. Rachel was not used to this kind of driving, just as she wasn't really used to Carson's insatiable hunger for sex and the often acrobatic ways he wanted to make love. No doubt about it, she was enjoying the thrill of Carson in her bed every night, as she was enjoying being driven to the airport by a handsome, world-renowned professor in a gleaming vintage sports car. She was also thankful just to be having great and exciting sex, after not having had any for such a long time. But the small-town girl in Rachel couldn't help being a little scared by Carson's lovemaking—and his driving. Her belly flew up and down with the pace, the newness, and the riskiness of it all.

By the time Rachel and Carson reached the ramp to terminal four, however, Rachel had managed to push these fears to the back of her mind and was now peeking out the corner of her eye at Carson, admiring his ruffled hair and his languid brown eyes that she'd come to know so well in the past two weeks. The roller-coaster thrills were worth it, she reckoned, if she got to be with Carson every day—or at least every night.

"Shit!" shouted Carson, as he swerved into the right-hand lane to avoid a car braking in front of them.

Rachel's hand, which had loosened a little on the car handle in the last few minutes, gripped hard, and her knuckles went white again. She then sighed deeply as the Alfa Romeo roared, unscathed, up the ramp toward departures.

"You don't have to park," Rachel insisted, as she found her breath and noticed they were following the signs to parking. "You can just drop me off at the doors. I don't mind."

Carson looked over and grinned. "That wouldn't be very romantic, would it?"

Rachel's heart hiccuped in her chest and a smile inched across her face. He wanted to be romantic. How sweet and unexpected, she thought. Over the past couple of weeks, Carson seemed like he couldn't get enough of Rachel and her body. But what had been happening between them didn't exactly feel romantic. There were no roses or candlelit dinners or walks at sunset along the Hudson River. Not even a newspaper and hot muffins in bed on a Sunday morning. Rachel ached for such romance; she secretly yearned for these kinds of loving gestures, but she knew not to demand them. If she started demanding these things, Carson would probably never arrive, wine in hand, at her door again.

Before she let her mind dally on this, another thought occurred to Rachel.

"There will be students there. At check-in, I mean," she said, her eyebrows knitting with concern.

"If it doesn't bother you, it doesn't bother me," Carson muttered, as he turned sharply into the airport's parking garage. He then reached over, tweaked one of her curls, and said, "But no trying to jump me in front of them, you hear?"

Rachel smiled briefly, but then her forehead gathered back into a frown.

"What is it?" Carson asked, seeing her expression change.

"Diana will be there too."

Carson slammed on the brakes and the whole car lurched and then skidded to a halt. "What?" he blurted out.

Rachel's cheeks flushed. "I thought I told you," she whispered, knowing full well she *had* told him. "Diana's coming on the trip too. Peter said all study-abroad programs need at least one member of tenured faculty. Diana volunteered."

Carson didn't seem to be listening, though. He was moving the car off again, tapping his fingers on the steering wheel, and looking left, then right, clearly scanning for a space. Finally, he said in a distracted and unreadable tone, "Well, I can see Diana off too, then."

Rachel gave out a nervous half chuckle, not knowing whether Carson was joking or not. They hadn't talked about Diana, and Rachel still had no idea what exactly had gone on between them. But it looked like she wasn't going to find out now, either. Carson had already swung into an empty spot, turned off the engine, and jumped out of the car. By the time the two of them met by the trunk, Carson was whistling an airy tune and busying himself with Rachel's luggage. He didn't say another word about Diana as they headed toward the terminal, and Rachel, as ever, was too scared to ask.

Rachel breezed through check-in. Thanks to Carson's rally driving she was one of the first in line and managed to secure herself a window seat near the front of the plane. Rachel was in no hurry to pass through security and leave Carson behind, however, so with nothing else to do in the check-in area, the two of them idled on a bench in the bustling terminal and flipped through *The New York Times Book Review*. As Rachel turned the pages, Carson pointed out authors he knew and books that were on his desk at home, awaiting his reviews for various academic publications.

She liked moments like these, when they would talk about books and their work. Carson would get a serious look on his face, and his brown eyes would take on a passionate gleam. She liked the playful, sparkling, flirtatious Carson too, of course. But in these moments, she felt she saw the real Carson: the Carson she could really imagine herself being with for the long haul. Justin and she had been so different in many ways and certainly never had conversations like this. He'd never read her book—the book that had done so well—and he knew about its content only because he'd watched her on *Oprah*, like everyone else. Carson, on the other hand, had read Rachel's book, and he had astute and interesting things to say about it. When it came to literature and literary theory in general, he had so many thoughtful comments to make and ideas to express. Rachel couldn't help being sucked in by this man who was not only breathtakingly sexy, but who could also talk the kind of literary talk she enjoyed.

When the two of them were finished discussing the latest books in the *Review*, Rachel caught Carson peeking at his watch. Her heart sank a little as she realized he needed to go and she should let him leave.

"You probably need to get back to the city," she said, nudging Carson softly with her elbow and hoping he might insist on staying a little longer.

Instead, he nudged her back, pulled a playful frown, and whispered, "I do." He then grinned and added, "But let's get you through security first."

With Carson holding her hand, they moved across the terminal. The line for security was long, and as they drew close Rachel noticed a group of familiar students gathered at the end of the line. Some of them were wearing Manhattan U sweatshirts or baseball caps, but some she knew from her classes. All the students were clutching their boarding passes and passports and chattering excitedly. She smiled as she approached and said brief hellos to students she knew. She couldn't help feeling a small kick of satisfaction as she saw their surprised gazes shift from her to Carson and down to their clutched hands. Rachel liked the idea of being the subject of their gossip instead of the source of their boredom and frustration, as she suspected she was in her classes.

Rachel joined the line behind the gaggle of students and was just turning to Carson to say her good-byes when over his shoulder she spotted the Nilsen sisters coming toward them. Both girls were wearing vast sunglasses that covered most of their tiny faces, and huge fuzzy winter coats with turned-up collars. Behind them followed a man in a blazer and cap; he was pushing a cart piled high with expensive leather luggage and was clearly their driver. Around them, travelers stopped and stared, either recognizing the sisters or realizing they should know who they were. Veronica and Rebecca, unfazed by this attention, swished on toward Rachel and the rest of the line.

When they were about ten feet away, however, a flashbulb snapped in their faces and caused them to falter a little. A scuffle then broke out between the driver, who'd let go of his cart the minute the bulb flashed, and a man in a leather jacket with a large camera swinging at his chest. Everyone nearby turned to stare. But within seconds the driver, although a slight man, had the photographer's jacket in his hands and was herding him quickly and firmly away from the sisters.

"Are you okay?"

The voice came from somewhere to Rachel's left, and it made her blood instantly turn to ice. It was Diana. She was dashing toward the two sisters, her small hand luggage banging against her thigh, and her face tight and concerned.

"We're fine. We're used to it," Rebecca Nilsen replied.

Rachel knew it was Rebecca from her signature Tod's tote bag dangling at the crook of her arm.

"Good," Diana was now saying as she neared Rebecca and Veronica. "Good. Let's hope we can avoid that kind of thing in London."

Rebecca nodded and said, "I'm sure we will."

Meanwhile, her sister stood beside her, tight-lipped and saying nothing. Although it was hard to tell behind her dark glasses, Veronica seemed to be staring in Rachel's direction, lost in her thoughts.

Diana had also noticed the second sister's silence and asked, "Are you okay, Veronica?"

When Veronica continued to say nothing, Diana looked again at the girl and then turned her head, following Veronica's gaze toward the line and toward Rachel. Diana's mouth puckered ever so slightly as she spotted Rachel, and then, as her gaze drifted toward Carson, Diana's dark eyebrows rose into two small, perfect arches. The arches lasted only a fraction of a second, however, before Diana found her composure and then altered her expression into a tight smile.

"Rachel. Carson." She nodded.

Rachel nodded back, her heart thudding in her chest, while Carson said, "Hi, Diana."

Carson's voice sounded strained, and Rachel turned to look at him. He'd dropped her hand a while ago and was now raking his own fretfully through his thick hair. His eyes had a worried flicker too. Clearly bumping into Diana was proving to be a more uncomfortable experience than he'd expected. Perhaps, Rachel thought, the feelings between them had run deeper than she suspected.

Just as she thought this, Carson returned her gaze and whispered, "Okay, Rachel. I'd better get going." He then pulled her into a quick hug, patted her on the back as he would an old friend, and said, "Have a great trip."

He was then off, hurrying across the shining floor of the concourse and toward the terminal doors. Rachel didn't even get a chance to reply. She just watched him go, her mouth open in shock and her back still tingling from where he'd patted it. *What on earth happened?* she wondered. Carson had seemed so cool about a possible encounter with Diana back in the car. But the moment she showed up he'd lost it and vanished before Rachel even had a chance to kiss him good-bye.

As she considered this, her heart beginning to feel heavy in her chest, Rachel noticed out of the corner of her eye that Diana had moved away from the Nilsens and was now standing with a man Rachel didn't recognize. The two of them were whispering and smiling at each other, and the man's hand was resting on Diana's elbow. Rachel couldn't resist turning to take a better look. The man was very attractive, in his midforties, with graying reddish hair. The aristocratic slope of his nose and his high forehead, coupled with the smart blazer and immaculate wing-tips he was wearing, made him seem like some English lord.

Rachel was trying to work out who this man might be when he and Diana moved close and kissed. After gawping for a millisecond, Rachel snapped her eyes away and swung back around to face the line in front. Her mind instantly began to whir with questions. Diana had another man? First Mikey, then Carson, and now this man? How many men was Rachel going to spot Diana with this semester? How come all these men were flocking to cool and austere Diana in the first place? And why had Carson disappeared so fast if Diana was with another man anyhow? Had he been dumped by Diana and run into Rachel's arms on the rebound?

These questions plagued Rachel all the way through security. She continued to mull them over as she searched for her gate and then waited to board the plane. She glimpsed Diana one time, as she sat brooding on one of the hard plastic chairs at the gate. Diana was no longer with her man friend, but was now talking to a group of students gathered around her. She was smiling and animated, like she never was in Rachel's presence. Rachel's face gathered into a confused frown as she looked over at her colleague and wondered yet again why all the students and all these men seemed to love her so much. This trip, Rachel could already tell, was going to be awful. It was bad enough being in a crowded departure lounge with Diana. Ten days running a study-abroad program in a foreign city with her would be torture.

When they finally boarded the plane, Rachel was still brooding and frowning.

"Are you scared of flying, Professor Grey?"

The question came as Rachel passed through first class on her way back to economy. She looked down to see Rebecca Nilsen staring up at her from one of the wide, plush seats. Her sister was beside her and was staring up at Rachel too. But instead of Rebecca's friendly smile, she wore a frown as deep as Rachel's had been until a second ago.

"Sorry?" Rachel said, flustered at having her thoughts interrupted.

"I wondered if you were scared of flying." Rebecca continued to smile. "You look anxious."

Rachel forced a laugh and waved her hand. "No, no. I'm fine." Then, sensing the clamor of people waiting to get through behind her, she moved off while calling to Rebecca, "See you in London."

As she passed into economy and started to scan for the seat number that matched her boarding pass, she heard two girls behind her whispering. She didn't turn to see, but they were clearly Manhattan U students.

"How come the Nilsens get to come?" the first asked. "I thought study-abroad was only open to juniors and seniors? They're freshmen, aren't they?"

"They are," the second replied. "I'm sure *Daddy* had something to do with it. Probably donated a few squillions so they'd be accepted for the program."

"I bet he did." The first girl snorted and then added, "Well, it looks like they're upperclassmen now."

Both girls hiccoughed with laughter, until one of them said, "Did you hear about Veronica and—"

The rest of their conversation was lost, however, as the plane's intercom pinged and a flight attendant's voice crackled out from nearby speakers.

"Good evening, ladies and gentlemen. We'd like to welcome you aboard British Airways flight six-oh-seven to London's Heathrow Airport."

Rachel didn't listen to the rest of the announcement. She'd found seat nine-A and was just lifting her luggage into the overhead bin when she noticed Diana . . . sitting in seat nine-B.

For the second time that evening, Rachel's blood turned to ice.

Diana held her breath from the moment she saw Rachel emerge from first class into economy. *Please don't let her be next to me*, Diana prayed over and over. *Please*. But then Rachel stopped at the end of Diana's aisle and started manhandling her bulky hand luggage—which looked big enough to hold a small child, Diana noticed—into the overhead locker. In those last seconds, Diana continued to pray, hoping that perhaps Rachel might be in the row in front or behind. But when Rachel finally clapped eyes on Diana and the color drained from her cheeks, Diana knew her worst nightmare was about to come true: seven hours sitting next to the very last person on the plane she wanted to be next to. Diana's chest instantly lurched and tightened.

For the first hour of the flight, as they taxied and took off, Diana and Rachel said very little except to exchange pleasantries about the weather and talk briefly about the trip ahead. Rachel was clearly as tense as Diana felt. But unlike Diana, who remained rigid with apprehension, gripping a heavy book on Plath in her lap, Rachel fidgeted in her seat and flitted between different brightly colored paperbacks pulled from her purse. After she'd tried looking at three of these books, she put them all away and started flipping through the channels on the small television in the seat back in front of her. All the while, she tossed and tweaked her unruly hair and repeatedly smoothed down her blouse and pants.

Diana watched her colleague out of the corner of her eye. At some moments, she felt sorry for her. Diana knew that it was her own presence making Rachel so agitated and unsettled. At other moments, all Diana's antipathies would return. When Rachel would flick back her hair, Diana would be reminded of her likeness to Annabelle, and when Rachel would smooth her hand over her tight-fitting blouse, Diana couldn't help thinking of Carson.

Since Graham had come back into Diana's life, Diana had thought little about Carson and had almost forgotten her stupidity that night, the night of the book launch and the taxi ride home. But when she'd spotted Carson with Rachel at the airport, anger reignited inside her. It wasn't that she wanted Carson anymore—far from it—it was just the predictability of it all that infuriated her. The fact that Carson couldn't keep his hands off a beautiful young thing like Rachel, with her curvy, sexy body and the chest-hugging blouses she wore to reveal it. There was also the fact that Rachel seemed to be able to lure any man she pleased. Even a handsome, blue-blood professor from Harvard who was ten years older than her and a whole lot more successful and established.

Seeing Carson and Rachel together also raised a question that agitated Diana: What about Mikey? The disastrous night when Diana had glimpsed Mikey and Rachel fooling around together outside Carson's place felt like aeons ago, and since that night Diana had tried really hard not to think about what was going on between the two of them. When she did think about it, she tried to convince herself it was all for the best. Mikey had found someone new, and that was a good thing. At least, on her better days she thought it was a good thing. Yet, in spite of the work Diana had done to bury the knowledge of Rachel and Mikey being together, it seemed that Rachel had moved on anyhow. Carson, not Mikey, was the one hugging her good-bye at the airport just now, and it was Carson who was followed by Rachel's gooey, love-struck eyes as he left the terminal. *So what had happened to Mikey?* Diana wondered. *Had his heart been broken yet again?* Diana reluctantly found herself thinking back to the day he'd left her apartment—the day she'd told him they were over. His face was crestfallen yet brave and still kind, forever kind. Diana's chest gave a wrench and a tug just thinking about it.

"Will you see your family when you're in England?"

Rachel's question blasted into Diana's thoughts and caused her to jerk her head back and stare, bewildered, over at Rachel.

"Sorry?" Diana blurted out.

Rachel's cheeks turned pink. "I was just wondering if you plan to see your family when you're back home. In England," she added with a nervous smile.

"Yes, I will," Diana responded with a nod. Then, realizing how curt she sounded, she went on: "My parents live just outside London. I will spend Thanksgiving with them."

"Really?" Rachel cocked her head. "They celebrate Thanksgiving?"

Diana nodded again. "Only since I moved to the States. It's become a tradition for them. I suppose it makes them feel more connected to me."

Rachel studied Diana's face for a second and then said, "They sound lovely."

"They are," was Diana's short reply.

She wasn't going to give away any more to Rachel, to this person she didn't even want to be sitting next to, let alone having anything to do with. Diana wasn't going to tell her that, although her parents were the sweetest and most well-meaning people on earth, she hadn't visited them in over ten years. She wouldn't tell Rachel that her own parents didn't make it to her wedding and had never met Graham. She certainly wouldn't be telling her young colleague—the one who looked so like the woman who'd taken Graham away from her—that for the past five years she'd pretended to them that she and Graham were still married. And there was no way Diana would reveal that she planned to take Graham to her parents' house next week on Thanksgiving.

Taking Graham home was what Diana wanted most from this trip. Of course, when Graham arrived he would insist on treating her to the opera in Covent Garden, or to a new exhibition at the Tate, or to his favorite French restaurant in Islington. But Diana could take or leave all these things. What she wanted above all else was to watch her parents' proud, smiling faces as they finally met the handsome, wealthy, and urbane man who'd married their daughter. That he'd divorced her too would never have to be mentioned. The two people who'd loved Diana all these years, in spite of her absence, in spite of her distance, would never have to know the hurt or sadness she'd endured. They could still be proud and happy for her and never pitying or sad or regretful of the sacrifices they'd made for their daughter. Diana was still ambivalent about Graham and his return into her life, but if taking him to meet her parents could erase the lies she'd told them and the sadness she'd felt without their knowing, then that was what Diana wanted more than anything else.

"Excuse me." It was now a flight attendant's turn to interrupt Diana's thoughts. Diana looked up to see a woman in a blue blazer and with glossy red lips peering down at her.

"Are you the professor supervising the Manhattan U group?" the woman asked.

Diana was about to respond when Rachel's voice chimed in, "Yes." Then, noticing Diana's fleeting glance in her direction, Rachel added, "I mean, we both are." Her cheeks were flushing again as she waved from herself to Diana.

"Great." The attendant smiled. She then lowered her voice. "We have a little problem in first class with one of your students. I wonder if you could come and help us."

Diana's heart sank. The Nilsens were the only students in first class, and the Nilsens were the last students Diana wanted "a little problem" with. Donations like the one their father was offering didn't come by Manhattan U very often, which meant any "little problems" with the Nilsen sisters was going to have to be treated with the utmost sensitivity and diplomacy. Diana wasn't sure she had it in her today to execute any such negotiations with the necessary skill. Nonetheless, she unbuckled her seat belt and started to stand.

She noticed Rachel was doing the same.

"I can handle this, Rachel." She waved.

Something unreadable flickered across Rachel's face. She said nothing for a second and then puffed out, "Okay," and flopped back in her seat with a frown, like a child upset at being scolded.

Diana continued on her way, however. She didn't have time for Rachel and her hurt feelings. She had this problem with the Nilsens to clear up, and she'd prefer to do it without Rachel looking over her shoulder.

"Veronica has locked herself in the bathroom," the flight attendant whispered as they reached first class. "She's been in there for half an hour and won't come out. Her sister"—she waved toward the front of the cabin, where Rebecca stood with her ear pressed against the bathroom door—"her sister thinks she's crying. Other passengers are beginning to complain," she added with an apologetic smile.

Diana nodded and then moved quickly down the aisle toward Rebecca.

"What's going on?" she asked Rebecca gently when she reached the bathroom.

Rebecca shook her head and frowned. "I don't know what's up with her," she hissed. "She's been in there for ages. She's crying and won't tell me what's wrong."

Diana looked from Rebecca to the door. "Has she been drinking?"

It was the first question she had to ask. Looking after a group of students on a trip abroad, especially where the drinking age was younger than in the States, she knew the alcohol issue was a big one. Diana had no doubt that student drinking escapades could start as early as the plane ride out.

Luckily, though, Rebecca gave an emphatic shake of her head. "She hasn't drunk anything," she said. "I've been with her all the time. I would have seen."

"What do you think the matter is then?"

Rebecca shook her head again. "I have no idea. She's been in a foul mood since we got to the airport, and every time I ask what's wrong, she tells me to mind my own business." She jerked her thumb toward the bathroom door. "Like she's doing now. I'm really beginning to lose my patience," she added with a desperate sigh.

Diana looked to the locked door once again and then back at Rebecca. She reached out and touched Rebecca's elbow. "Let's see what I can do," she said. "You go back and sit in your seat."

"Thank you, Professor Monroe." Rebecca half smiled before loping off down the cabin.

Diana turned to the door and knocked. "Veronica," she whispered. There was no reply, so she tried again a little louder. "Veronica."

Only after the fifth or six time of knocking and saying the girl's name did Veronica finally shout out, "What?"

"Are you okay in there?" Diana asked, her heart skipping with relief that she'd gotten an answer, which, of course, ruled out the possibility that Veronica was lying in a wine-induced coma.

"Yes," Veronica hissed through the door.

"Well, why don't you come out?" Diana said in the most coaxing voice she could muster.

There was a silence, followed by Veronica's, "I don't want to," which she said in a strangled, clearly tearful whisper.

Diana stepped back from the door and thought for a second. *Which way should I play this?* she wondered. She'd once heard Peter say something about the Nilsens and their authoritarian father. Apparently he was immensely strict with the girls, and Veronica and Rebecca were terrified of him. It could have all been tabloid gossip, but Diana decided to err on the side of caution. The schoolmarm approach was probably not the way forward. If she barked at Veronica to "Get out now," they might end up with Veronica locked in the bathroom for the whole flight.

So instead Diana softened her voice and whispered, "Veronica, we're worried about you. Rebecca is very worried about you."

Silence followed.

"Why don't you come out and let us see you're okay?" Diana went on. "This is a long flight, Veronica; we don't want you holed up in this tiny bathroom all the way."

Diana's words were met with more silence. But just as she was about to open her mouth and speak again, the door gave a decisive click. Diana stepped back in surprise while the door slid open. Veronica then shuffled out of the bathroom. Her sunglasses were on and covering most of her face, but from the snippet of pink and puffy cheek Diana could see, it was clear she'd been crying. Veronica moved past Diana without saying anything and headed down the aisle. Diana watched her go, shocked that her words had worked, but mostly re-lieved that the whole thing was over.

When Diana finally moved through the cabin and neared the sis-ters, Veronica was already back in her window seat, slumped against the window with a blanket wrapped around her. Rebecca, meanwhile, was looking up at Diana and mouthing, *Thank you.* Diana simply nodded and carried on through to economy class.

"Is everything okay?" Rachel asked, as Diana slipped back into her seat.

"Fine, fine," Diana said with a wave. "It's all taken care of."

Rachel looked at her, clearly expecting further explanation. But Diana suddenly felt tired—overwhelmingly tired. The situation with Veronica had resolved itself remarkably easily, yet Diana had a feel-ing there might be more to come. The next ten days were going to be hard work, and she wasn't entirely sure she had the energy reserves to deal with it. Since Graham had sprung back into her life, her poor mind had been working overtime taking it all in. She had slept badly for almost two weeks. Now she just wanted to sleep. When they ar-rived in London it would be ten a.m., and they had a full day in front of them. She had to get a couple of hours' rest.

No sooner had Diana settled back in her seat and shut her eyes than the flight attendant was calling her name.

"Professor Monroe?"

Diana squinted up. "Yes," she replied, feeling her heart beginning to sink again. *What now?* she thought. *Please, no more trouble.*

The flight attendant was smiling, though. "Rebecca Nilsen won-dered if you'd like to come through to first class."

Diana's eyebrows knitted in confusion.

"She's offering you an upgrade," the flight attendant explained in a whisper.

"Oh, I see," Diana muttered.

She then looked from the flight attendant over at Rachel. Rachel was staring hard at the television screen in front of her. Diana felt a stab of shame. She hadn't engineered this so she would be offered a seat in first class, but that was clearly what Rachel was thinking. She could feel the annoyance oozing from Rachel's rigid body. But, in the next second, another wave of tiredness hit Diana, and she couldn't help thinking about those deliciously wide and reclining seats in the next cabin. Also, the chance to escape the awkward seating arrangement with Rachel was enticing.

"That would be lovely," she found herself whispering as she unbuckled her seat belt yet again. She then reached up into the overhead locker for her bag and, while she swung it down, she said to Rachel, "See you later."

Rachel's eyes didn't move from the screen. "Hmmpphh," was her nearly inaudible reply.

Fourteen

Study Abroad

The first day in London was a rest day for the students. For Rachel and Diana, however, there was no time to recover from the red-eye flight or the five-hour time difference. No sooner had they reached their hotel than they headed back out the door for a meeting with the two student advisers who'd arrived a week ago and were responsible for setting up and administrating Manhattan U's Literary London program. Nadini and Zach had an office in the University College London dorm near Russell Square, where the students were staying, and which was a short walk through Bloomsbury from Rachel and Diana's hotel.

Their office was also where, on this dreary London afternoon, Rachel and Diana had been sitting for the last few hours. The room was tiny and overcrowded with papers, files, and aging computer equipment, and there was barely enough space for Nadini and Zach, let alone two other people. The claustrophobic setting wasn't helped by the old radiator chugging out heat and the small, steamed-up window that refused to open. Rachel spent the better part of the meeting fighting yawns and blinking her heavy, tired eyes, trying to keep them open. Every now and then she'd sneak a look over at Diana and observe how bright and fresh her eyes were and how alert she seemed. If Rachel had spent the night in first class, she couldn't help brooding, no doubt she'd look the same.

But Diana's little sojourn in first class wasn't what Rachel was most irritated about. Rachel was more annoyed by the way Diana had shut her out of the Nilsen incident: the "little problem" on the plane that, up until a few minutes ago, Rachel had been completely in the dark about.

"We'll have to keep a close eye on Veronica," Diana was now saying as she finished explaining what happened on the flight over. She then looked at Nadini, Zach, and, ever so briefly, at Rachel and added, "A very close eye."

Nadini sighed a little, as she shook out her long dark hair. "It's going to be difficult. Veronica and Rebecca aren't staying here." She waved a hand around her. "They're staying over at the Hotel Russell on the other side of the square." Nadini's mouth twisted a little at the corners. "The dorms aren't good enough for the Nilsens."

Zach was shaking his head too. "I knew it was going to be a bad idea having students staying elsewhere," he said, pushing his glasses up his boyish nose. "We should have insisted they be here."

"Let's not dwell on the difficulties and the should-haves," Diana cut in. Her tone was calm and measured, but there was also a commanding and imposing air in what she said. It was clear that even if Nadini and Zach were running and producing this show, Diana had already taken up her role as director. "We just have to find ways to be vigilant and keep watch over Veronica."

Rachel knew that Diana would probably knock back anything she suggested, but she decided to speak nonetheless. At this point, she was too tired to care.

"Perhaps," Rachel said, sitting forward, "we could arrange some sort of daily check-in. The girls will be with us during events and trips, but in the downtimes perhaps we could take turns going over to the Hotel Russell to see how they're doing."

"Good idea," Diana replied, giving Rachel a small, tight smile.

For a second, Rachel was too shocked to speak. But then she found her tongue and said, "I'll go first. I'll run over there when we're finished and see how they're settling in."

Nadini and Zach nodded, and Diana muttered, "Thank you," under her breath.

Zach then tapped on the heavy binder in his lap and said, "This might be a good time to go over emergency procedures and student crisis protocols." He looked at Diana and added with a blush rising to his cheeks, "What do you think?"

Diana nodded. "Of course."

Zach then flipped through some pages in his binder. "Okay. If you turn to page fifty-four . . ." he began. Both Rachel and Diana riffled through the pages in their identical binders to find the right section. When they were there, Zach continued. "We'll go through emergency procedures first, starting with hospitalizations." He grimaced and looked up briefly. "Let's hope we can avoid these at all costs."

Diana, Rachel, and Nadini all agreed with a nod.

"'At least one member of the study-abroad faculty or staff must accompany the student to the hospital,'" Zach read from the sheet in front of him. "'In the event that a student is hospitalized before staff or faculty have been notified, a member of staff or faculty must immediately join him or her at the hospital.'" Zach took a breath and then continued. "'Next of kin—in most cases, the student's parents—must be notified straightaway.'" Zach looked up again and waved toward Nadini. "Nadini and I both have a copy of the contact details for all the students on this trip. Just get in touch with one of us and we can either pass on those details or call the parents ourselves."

As Zach's gaze returned to the binder and he continued to read, Rachel's eyes scanned the page, but she was tired, unable to fully concentrate, and her mind began to wander. The first thing it wandered to, of course, was Carson. On the long flight to London, she'd fidgeted and dozed as Carson's swift departure from the airport replayed over and over in her drowsy thoughts, and once again, in the stuffy London office, the image returned. She still couldn't figure it all out. Had he really been so unnerved by seeing Diana? Only minutes before, he'd been happy to hold Rachel's hand and whisper in her ear, and all the while he knew Diana was likely to show up. But the moment Diana did show, he bolted like a startled deer.

Rachel's mind continued to slip back and forth. One moment

she'd be scribbling down details about upcoming events or discussing the merits and disadvantages of assignments being set for the students. The next moment her thoughts would drift and she'd think about Carson and what had been going on between them. Was Carson in love with Diana? Or just embarrassed about being caught with Rachel? And if he was embarrassed, what did that mean? Rachel's mind flipped and flopped. She knew she was overthinking it all. "You're overthinking everything" had been another complaint of Justin's. She'd fought this portrayal of herself at the time, just as she'd argued that she wasn't as "oversensitive" or "overemotional" as Justin seemed to think she was. But perhaps Justin had been right all along, and perhaps it was time to take what Carson was offering and stop fretting, questioning, and hoping for anything more.

The meeting dragged on for another hour, and when Rachel finally escaped Nadini and Zach's cramped office, she felt much like she had that morning when she'd disembarked the plane: lethargic and fretful. However, as soon as she got out on the wet street, a red London bus swished past through the puddles, and Rachel remembered where she was. Excitement kicked in her belly. Rachel loved London. She'd been several times over the years and never tired of the bright red buses, the chunky black cabs, the bustling streets of the West End, the grand town houses in Bloomsbury where the likes of Virginia Woolf once lived and wrote, the cozy pubs in tiny alleyways, and the interesting bookstores tucked down in old basements. She even loved the rain and the sidewalks full of jostling umbrellas that the downpours would always prompt.

Most of all, she loved the London parks. She'd spent time in most of them: Hyde Park at the center of the city nestled against the grand hotels on Park Lane; St James' Park stretching out at the foot of Buckingham Palace; and Rachel's favorite of all, the vast and undulating Hampstead Heath, with its breathtaking views over the city. But even Russell Square's small park, which Rachel was just about to enter on her way across to see the Nilsens, had a special place in her memories.

A little over ten years ago, Rachel herself had been on a study-abroad program in London at the end of her junior year at college. Like the Manhattan U students, Rachel and her UNC classmates had stayed in University College London dorms, and thus spent their free time wandering the neighboring streets of Bloomsbury. When they felt adventuresome, they would keep going, down to Covent Garden and the excitement of the West End. Unlike the Manhattan U program, however, Rachel's program happened in the summer, which meant that when they were too tired to explore, she and her college friends would stretch out in sunny Russell Square park, reading books, gossiping, napping, or wolfing down "ninety-nines"—those curious ice creams with a stick of chocolate plunged into their middles. For Rachel, the time spent idling in Russell Square had been the best part of the trip.

As Rachel walked through the park today, she found it hard to believe it was the same place. Shrouded in a wintery, late-afternoon gloom, the park was now a collection of bare trees, long shadows, and gleaming puddles. No one was loitering on benches or in the grass. Instead, people were hurrying by, hunched under umbrellas, and weaving around the wettest spots on the gravel pathways. Rachel was similarly hunched under her own umbrella, although she walked a little slower. Every now and again she would peek up and stare through the drizzle and try to make out some spot or other where she'd once spent a happy afternoon. Just as she came to the northwest corner of the park, she realized she was beside the one triangle of grass she remembered vividly from her study-abroad trip. It was the spot where she'd first read *Bridget Jones's Diary*.

Helen Fielding's book had just been released and was causing quite a buzz that summer in London. Rachel had picked up a copy at a vast bookstore on Gower Street, and one warm afternoon, while her classmates played Frisbee nearby, she sat on this very patch of grass, pulled the book from her bag, bent back its spine, and began to read. From the first page she was hooked, and in spite of her friends' pleas to stop being lazy and join in their game, she kept on reading. She even kept reading when, pooped from all the exercise, her classmates flopped down beside her, saw what she was reading, and began their teasing.

"Why are you reading *that* trash, Rach?" someone asked.

Somebody else chimed in, "Just because everyone on the tube is reading it doesn't mean you have to."

"That kind of thing will rot your brain, Rachel," the next person scoffed.

Another friend waved a copy of *Mrs. Dalloway* at her and said, "This is what you should be reading. What will Professor Simpson say!"

Rachel and all her classmates were juniors in UNC's English department. They'd come to London for an intensive summer course on modernist literature—hence the copies of Virginia Woolf's *Mrs. Dalloway* stowed in everyone's backpacks. Rachel was loving every minute of the program. She lapped up the lectures and the tours, and she was devouring the modernist novels they'd been assigned. She'd finished Woolf's novel days before her friends and had already moved on to Joyce's *Ulysses*. Just as she did when she was back at home in North Carolina, however, Rachel made time for all kinds of other books too. She was no snob. She could switch easily from *Ulysses* to a Grisham thriller or a Nora Roberts romance or a vampire tale by Anne Rice. Sometimes she read new books like Fielding's simply to see what all the fuss was about.

Whenever she produced one of these paperbacks from her bag, she would be teased by her friends in the program. But she didn't care. In fact, she enjoyed the ribbing, because it meant she got to fight back. She loved nothing more than fighting back in those days— unlike these days, when she too often let the likes of Diana have the upper hand and the last word. Back when she was a young college student, she was tenacious in her counterattacks and would fight hard to defend the books—*all* the books—she loved.

The day she was teased for reading *Bridget Jones* was no different.

"Have any of you actually read this?" Rachel had demanded, as she sat up on the grass and waved the book in front of her six sweating and smiling friends. A wide grin was inching across her own face. "Anyone?" she demanded again.

They all shook their heads, and a couple of them muttered something along the lines of, "I wouldn't waste my time."

"Well, perhaps you should," she retorted with a playful huff. "That way you'll see that this isn't brain-rotting trash and that it is, in fact, a great read. Plus, it's a witty and playful homage to Jane Austen's *Pride and Prejudice*."

A guy called Kevin snorted. "From what I've heard, it's not exactly Austen. It's a run-of-the-mill romance about a woman trying to get a guy and obsessing about her weight while she's at it."

Rachel leaned forward and tapped the book. "Yes, there's a love story. Just like there's a pretty important love story in *Pride and Prejudice*, as I'm sure you recall." She waggled her eyebrows. "But you wouldn't call Austen trash, would you?"

Kevin opened his mouth to respond, but Rachel cut across him.

"Sure, Bridget obsesses about her weight, but don't a lot of women these days?" Rachel looked over at her female friends in the group. "Admit it," she demanded. "When you were scoffing down those ice creams earlier, don't tell me you didn't think about the calories and the effect they'll have on your butt."

Jenny, a girl with long blond hair and a rail-thin body, raised her hand and nodded her head. "I did," she confessed.

"See," Rachel blurted out with a triumphant grin. "You see—"

But she was cut off by Kevin. "It might be what women do. But who wants to read about it?"

"Women might," snapped Rachel. "They might enjoy reading a story about a woman who's like them, who obsesses in the same way they do, and isn't scared to admit it." As she said the last words, Rachel gave a wink to the two other girls in the group who hadn't admitted to counting the calories in their ice creams. "Not only that," she continued, "the way Bridget obsesses about her weight is self-aware and just plain funny. Why wouldn't someone want to read that?"

"It's not literature, though, is it?" another guy added.

"I'm sure Helen Fielding never wrote this to be literature," Rachel countered, waving the book again. "Not in the way you probably mean 'literature'—in other words, lofty, cerebral, and with elegant and wordy prose. But let me ask you this: How different is her book from Austen's, which I'm sure you would regard as literature?"

There was a silence, probably because no one had read the book and thus had no idea how it might or might not resemble Austen's. But this didn't stop Rachel. She was really beginning to enjoy herself.

"Just as Austen's characters negotiate the social and financial disadvantages of living in a patriarchal world, Fielding is also concerned with modern woman's ability to negotiate the patriarchy in which we still live." Rachel took a breath. She knew she was sounding like a textbook, but she carried on anyway. "Bridget Jones might not be living the confined, eighteenth-century life of Elizabeth Bennet. After all, she has a job, her own apartment, she goes out drinking with friends. But she still has to endure all the pressures on women—to be thin, to get a man, to be financially secure and respected by those around her."

Rachel then riffled through the pages and found a passage she'd read earlier. "Here," she said, pointing to the paper. "Here she talks about being 'traumatized by supermodels.' She's joking, of course. But there's also something compelling and brilliant about this statement. In a way, we're all traumatized by supermodels, or at least we're traumatized by our culture that produces and reveres supermodels. Women can't eat an ice cream without thinking about their asses. Young girls starve themselves to death in their plush, suburban homes just to fit into their size-zero jeans. Even if a guy likes a girl with curves, he can't show up to the prom with one on his arm. . . ."

"Okay, okay, Rach." Kevin waved his hands and laughed. "We get it, and we all promise to go out and buy a copy tomorrow."

"And read it!" Rachel waggled her finger and laughed too.

"Only if you buy me another ice cream," Jenny called out.

Rachel grinned. "My pleasure. But don't come crying to me about your butt later tonight."

"I wouldn't dare!"

After her friends teased Rachel some more about the minilecture she'd just given, they got up to play Frisbee once again. Meanwhile, as the sun began to set over the University of London library to the west, Rachel turned with a smile back to her book and read until she finished. It was a perfect summer afternoon in the park.

Now, as she looked through the rain at the same grassy spot, Rachel thought about herself back then and how spunky she used to be. In those days, it was as if she could take on the world, and no amount of teasing or scoffing at her books and ideas would stop her. She was probably a little overbearing, but her friends never seemed to complain too much. Her passion and tenacity no doubt amused them. In grad school she'd been pretty much the same, although Rachel got a little better at moderating her monologues and sounding less like she'd swallowed the last academic journal she'd read. But it seemed recently that her old feisty flames had dampened somewhat, especially since she'd arrived at Manhattan U. Sure, she'd gotten mad at her students that day she stormed from the classroom, and in the graduate-faculty seminar she'd taken on Diana—at least she'd tried, not very successfully, to take on Diana. On the whole, though, her blood didn't bubble like it used to. Her passion and her gumption seemed to be waning. And she had no idea why.

Rachel buried herself back under her umbrella and continued her walk toward the Hotel Russell, whose majestic windows and ornate cornices towered over the eastern side of the park. Perhaps it was a good thing, she tried to tell herself; perhaps it was good that she wasn't so spunky anymore. It wasn't exactly professional and tenure-savvy to get worked up and excited like she used to as a student. Most of the academics Rachel now worked with, although serious about their scholarship, were composed and unflappable when it came to sharing their work and opinions. Diana was the queen of this kind of equanimity, but most of Rachel's other colleagues were pretty calm and collected too. No one yelled or ranted or flew into rages if their opinions were maligned or dismissed. No one ever left a room in tears.

Carson had said he admired Rachel's passion that day of the seminar, the day she'd left the room and burst into tears, but Rachel was convinced he'd said that to get into her bed. Someone so urbane and poised as Carson wouldn't be attracted to the Rachel of old—the Rachel who'd rant at her friends and badger them into reading *Bridget Jones*. Rachel whose cheeks would burn, whose eyes would flame, and who'd launch into an impassioned monologue if she ever read a snobby or disparaging review in *The New York Times* of a book she loved. Rachel who was needy and mushy and overemotional with her boyfriends. Nope, the old Rachel wouldn't be attractive to someone like Carson. He'd no doubt swat away such a woman like an irritating fly. If she wanted to hang on to Carson, she needed to be more self-possessed and composed, like he was. And like Diana was too.

As Rachel's thoughts turned to Carson and she found herself stopped on the side of the busy street, waiting to cross over to the hotel, she switched her umbrella to her other hand and automatically reached for her cell. Since they'd arrived that morning, she'd been checking the phone every now and then, hoping for a text or message from Carson. So far there had been nothing. Not a peep. Of course, he was five hours behind in New York and had probably only just surfaced from bed, on top of the fact that she'd left only last night. But he had promised he would call or text when she arrived, and so she couldn't help peeking—and praying—that she'd see his name on the small screen. Rachel flipped the phone open and yet again she found no messages. Disappointment rolled fleetingly in her belly until she told herself to stop being so ridiculous and needy. *Of course he hasn't called yet*, she scolded as she trotted across the street and toward the Hotel Russell's grand entrance.

A few minutes later, Rachel stood outside the Nilsens' suite on the tenth floor knocking on an oversize, white-paneled door. She had checked with reception first to make sure the sisters were in and had been told by the clerk, who'd made a brief call to their room, to go on up. But now, after she'd knocked twice, there appeared to be no reply, and Rachel was beginning to wonder if she'd gotten the wrong room. She tried knocking one last time to be sure, and this time was relieved to hear some rustling and movement on the other side of the door. Finally, there was a clicking noise from the lock, the door was nudged open, and Veronica's face appeared in the gap. Her hair was in unusual disarray, and her eyes were heavy with sleep, but Rachel knew it was Veronica. There was something about the slight downcast turn to her otherwise pretty mouth that was different from her sister's.

When Veronica's eyes focused on Rachel, they quickly narrowed, and she rasped out the word, "Yes?"

Rachel was taken aback by the young girl's tone, but remained composed. Composed would be her new modus operandi from now on. With a smile, she said, "I was just swinging by to—"

"Is that Professor Grey?" Rebecca's chiming voice from inside the room cut Rachel off. "Let her in, V," she added.

Veronica was still glowering at Rachel, but she shoved back the door so Rachel could enter and then promptly stalked off across the vast suite without saying another word. Meanwhile, Rebecca was emerging from the bathroom wrapped in a white robe and toweling off her wet hair. She was about to say something to her sister, who was walking in her direction, but Veronica swooshed past Rebecca and into the bathroom, where she slammed the door with a thud.

Rebecca looked over at Rachel and pulled an apologetic frown. "She was taking a nap," she explained. "She's never good at being woken up."

Rachel nodded. "Who is?" She chuckled. She then added, "Sorry to barge in on you guys, but I just wanted to make sure you're settling in okay."

"Everything's fine." Rebecca waved and smiled.

Rachel couldn't help glancing over at the closed bathroom door. "Is Veronica okay? I heard she was little upset on the plane."

Rebecca followed Rachel's gaze and then waved her hand again. "She's fine. She just got worked up about something. But she's refusing to tell me what." She lowered her voice. "She gets worked up about a lot of things, so I'm not too worried. She's fine," she added with a nod. "Really."

"Okay, I'll take your word for it," Rachel responded. "But if she gets upset again, let us know if we can help."

Rebecca nodded. The two of them then went on to talk about the Literary London program, which was kicking off tomorrow with a tour of the British Library.

"I'm so excited," Rebecca said, her big eyes flashing. "Haven't they got all this really old and rare stuff in their vaults, like Shakespeare's original manuscripts?"

"I don't think they have his own manuscripts." Rachel gave a gentle laugh. "Those disappeared long ago. But the library does have a number of really early printed editions of the plays called quartos, some of which were published while Shakespeare was still alive. So, yes, they have some really old and rare stuff." She waggled her head. "I don't think they'll be letting us anywhere near those things, though."

"Not a bunch of rowdy American students, no."

Rachel and Rebecca both giggled, and then Rachel pointed toward the door. "I'll leave you guys to it." But before she turned to go, she had a thought. "Let me give you my cell number. You know, just in case."

Rebecca was back to drying her hair. "Sure," she said from under the towel.

Rachel walked over to the low table in front of an ornate velvet couch at the center of the room and started to scribble her number on the Hotel Russell notepad that was lying there. She wasn't quite finished when a cell phone, also lying on the table, started to vibrate and jingle. Rachel flinched in surprise and then, out of habit, glanced over at the nearby phone. The name Mack glowed on the small screen.

"Is that mine?" Rebecca was muttering, as she bustled over toward the table.

After throwing down her towel, she scooped up the phone, snapped it open, and called, "Hello?" into the sleek silver metal. Rebecca's eyebrows shot up as the person on the other end of the line spoke. She then pulled her phone from her ear and looked at it.

"Um, I'm sorry," she said, replacing the phone. "This is Rebecca. I answered my sister's phone by mistake." She paused while the caller said something else and then replied, "Don't sweat it. I'll go get her."

Rebecca weaved her way around the couch and walked back over to the bathroom.

"V," she shouted through the door, "phone!"

There was some mumbling from inside the bathroom that Rachel couldn't make out, although Rebecca clearly could.

"I answered your phone by mistake," she called.

More mumbling.

"I dunno," Rebecca responded, beginning to sound frustrated. "Whoever he is, he says he's very sorry."

The bathroom door clicked open and a slim arm poked out. Rebecca took her cue and silently dropped the phone into her sister's hand. Then the arm disappeared and the door thudded shut again.

Rebecca turned back to Rachel, and after giving the same apologetic frown she gave earlier, she mouthed, *Guy troubles.*

"I see." Rachel nodded and flashed a sympathetic smile.

Once she'd left the Nilsens' room and was on her way to the elevator, Rachel felt a little agitated and found herself muttering the words "guy troubles" under her breath. Her hand crept down to her purse and delved around for her phone.

"No," she scolded herself in a whisper as she stopped in front of the elevator and snatched her hand out of her purse. "Don't."

She had to stop checking her phone to see if Carson had called. Rachel would not be like Veronica. She would not be reduced to all the classic "guy trouble" behaviors: tears, moody faces, hiding in bathrooms, feverishly waiting for calls. Those behaviors were okay for love-struck nineteen-year-olds like Veronica. But they were at odds with the poised and composed persona that Rachel was determined to maintain from now on.

Yet, when she stepped into the elevator, her cell buzzed in her purse. Without pausing to think, she immediately lunged to retrieve it, and, spotting Carson's name on the screen, Rachel let out a puppy-like yip of delight and punched the air with her free hand.

She then flipped the phone open and placed it to her ear. "Hello," she blurted in a breathy, excited whisper.

When they left their meeting and Rachel headed east to the Hotel Russell, Diana had walked south with no particular destination in mind. It had been a long time since she'd last been in London, and even though it was drizzling, she wanted to be out and about, wandering the streets and seeing how things had changed. She was in good spirits, thanks to her comfortable flight from New York and a pretty hassle-free meeting with the study-abroad staff. Even Rachel hadn't irritated her today. However, Diana was in no rush to get back to the hotel. No doubt the quiet and the solitude of her small hotel room would have her mulling over Graham again. The busy and wet streets of London were a good distraction, and while she dodged puddles, peered in glowing windows of Bloomsbury town houses, and reminisced about past trips to the city, Graham lurked harmlessly at the back of her mind.

Diana had never lived in London. But when she was a student at Oxford, she would come regularly to do research at the British Library or to catch a play in the West End or to meet old school friends for dinner at some new restaurant in Islington or Camden or Fulham. Sometimes she would do all of these things in one breathless, jam-packed day. London was just an hour by train and offered a welcome escape from Oxford. Diana loved her doctoral studies, there was no doubt. She adored looking out of her college window each morning to see the slate gray dome of the Bodleian Library and the twirling peaks of Jesus College Chapel. But life in Oxford often felt insular and claustrophobic for Diana. In London, by contrast, she felt free and soothingly anonymous. No one ever recognized her or called her over to discuss a lecture they'd attended or to quiz her on her latest thesis chapter or journal submission. In London she was a stranger, and being a stranger was how Diana felt most comfortable.

For most of her childhood Diana had been an outsider, of course: someone who didn't quite fit with the world around her. At the expensive boarding schools she attended, she was the poor girl on a scholarship, and unlike her classmates, she had no family coat of arms, no summer house in France, and no vintage Rolls-Royce to pick her up at the end of each semester. Yet when she went home to her parents' tiny house outside London, she was a stranger there too. She lived another life from her parents and their neighbors, who knew nothing of horse riding or archery or choral singing or Latin drills: the pursuits that occupied Diana's every waking hour during term time. Diana even looked and sounded different. Where her mother and father would slouch and shuffle around their tiny Essex home, Diana stood as straight as a pin and walked with her chin held high. All thanks to her headmistress, Madam Bentley, and her lectures about good posture, refinement, and grace. Diana also learned very fast that the queen's English was the only English accepted at Marsha House Girls' School. A dropped H or swallowed G could provoke outrage and disgust. Back at home, however, the clipped and precise pronunciations Diana had learned at school sounded forced and snobby next to the lilting " 'ellos" and "darlin's" that would roll from her parents' Essex tongues.

In both worlds, at home and at school, Diana felt like a stranger, an outsider, and an interloper, and as the years passed it was a feeling she got used to. Indeed, being the stranger felt more comfortable than anything else. Hence her love for the anonymity of London—and New York too. It was no wonder she'd chosen to go so far from home after graduating from Oxford. Setting up a life in Harvard and eventually Manhattan, she could always remain the stranger.

"*L'Étranger*," Diana muttered to herself, as she skipped another puddle and thought of Albert Camus's famous novel about a tragic and estranged man.

She immediately shook her head. This was a good day. Things were going well, she told herself. She couldn't get maudlin. If she did, she'd only start fretting about Graham—whether he was going to show in London, what her parents would think when they met him, what was really going on between the two of them, would Annabelle lure Graham back. She really didn't want to be thinking about all those things right now. She was in London and she had to enjoy it and not spend her whole time worrying.

"Bloody 'ell. They sold 'em all. Every last bleedin' one."

The male voice, thick with the Essex accent she knew so well, broke into Diana's thoughts. She'd been watching the traffic lights and waiting to cross the street, but now she turned, peeked out from under her umbrella, and saw a balding man talking to his wife and teenage daughter. The family all wore thin raincoats over their stocky bodies and held two wind-beaten umbrellas between them. Each face looked wet, pink, and disappointed. They were standing outside a theater, and a neon sign jutting out above their heads read, HAIR-SPRAY: THE MUSICAL.

"What d'ya mean, Dad?" the daughter was now saying. "You said we'd get 'em, no problem."

The father shook his head and frowned. "Gazza said it would be dead easy," he muttered.

"We shoulda booked it on the Internet." The wife was beginning to look angry. "That's what Gail down the shop said we oughta do. I told ya millions of times."

"We ain't got Internet, Mum." The daughter sulked. "Remember?"

Diana's eyes skimmed the family and moved up to the facade of the old theater behind them. She wondered how she'd walked so far without even realizing it. It seemed like only a moment ago she was passing the British Museum with its grand columns and high iron fences. But already she was at Shaftesbury Theatre on High Holborn and thus almost halfway to Covent Garden. London was deceptive like that. Sometimes it felt so large and spread out and so unlike dense and cluttered Manhattan. Yet at the same time, if you weren't careful, London could just flit by you. One mishmash of streets would lead to another, and the next thing you knew you were in the West End or wandering the South Bank or idling across Hyde Park.

Diana's gaze drifted back to the arguing family. At the same moment, the wife had turned to scan the street. Her eyes glided past Diana at first, but then they hopped back and settled on Diana more firmly. As the two women locked gazes, both flinched.

"Oh, my gawd." The woman spoke first, as she slapped her hand to her cheek and continued to stare at Diana.

"What is it, Mum?" her daughter asked.

"I've seen a ghost," she mumbled through her hand.

Her family all turned to see who or what she was staring at. Meanwhile, Diana stared back, her mind doing somersaults. She knew this woman. But where from? How? Who was she?

"A ghost? What ya talkin' about?" the husband said.

But the woman ignored him. "Diana." She gasped. "Diana Monroe. Is that you?"

A split second after the woman said Diana's name, Diana remembered exactly who she was. "Tracey Nicholls." She whispered.

"Oh, my gawd!" the woman exclaimed again. This time she moved toward Diana, and when she was just a few feet away, she said, "It's you, ain't it?"

Diana nodded and smiled, temporarily lost for words.

"Blimey, 'ow many years 'as it been?" Tracey laughed.

"Twenty, perhaps?" Diana said, finally finding her tongue and shaking her head in disbelief.

Tracey Nicholls and her family used to live next door to Diana's parents, and before Diana went off to boarding school, she and Tracey were the best of friends. They had been inseparable, in fact. Only a month apart in age, the two girls spent every summer afternoon in

the tiny yards attached to their neighboring homes, making neck-
laces from sun-dried daisies and lying on their backs watching clouds
shaped like rabbits and horses and dragons float by. Every dreary winter day they would get under their mothers' feet, constructing make-
believe castles under their kitchen tables, and pirate ships on their
living room couches. When they started at the nearby school, they sat
together at adjoining desks. At recess, they held hands and skipped
together in the schoolyard.

Everything changed when Diana left for Marsha House Girls'
School, however. The two girls could see each other only at vacation times, and this, coupled with their increasingly diverging lives,
meant they soon stopped knocking on each other's front doors. Tracey
spent her summer days playing, biking, and eventually hanging out
and smoking with groups of kids from the local school she attended.
Diana, meanwhile, spent most of her time indoors, reading books and
writing letters to her boarding school friends who were off in holiday
houses or hotels scattered across Europe. Sometimes she'd peek out
the window and watch Tracey disappearing with her ragtag gang of
friends. Diana would yearn to run out and join them, but fear and
shyness and a sense of superiority, which her school had instilled in
her, held her back every time.

By the time Diana and Tracey were teenagers, they would see
each other only once a year for a couple of hours. Every Christmas
Eve it was a tradition for the Monroe family to invite the Nicholls
family over for mince pies and sherry, and as an old record player
belted out carols from two crackling speakers, the families would mill
around catching up on local gossip and toasting Christmas when the
clock finally struck twelve. Conversations between Diana and Tracey
on those evenings got shorter, more awkward, and more embarrassed
with every passing year. Soon both girls would lurk behind their parents, Tracey picking at her painted nails and Diana surreptitiously
trying to read a book.

When Diana was fifteen, the Nicholls family moved away. She
was relieved, and no doubt Tracey was too. The family moved only a

few streets, but it was far enough away for the Christmas tradition to fizzle out. Diana ran into Tracey a couple of times after that and they would always say polite hellos, but their interactions were fleeting and superficial. From best friends, they had become strangers.

"Ya know what?" Tracey was now saying, as she beamed over at Diana. "I was just talkin' about you the other day. Me mum saw your mum at Safeways."

Diana asked, "How are your parents?"

"Not so good these days," Tracey said, pulling her face into a frown.

As a child Tracey had had an impish demeanor: pointy chin, sparkling blue eyes, wispy body, and long chestnut hair pulled into two straggly pigtails. These days Tracey's face was round, her hair was short and neat, and her bangs were speckled with gray. Fine lines arched out over her cheekbones. Yet her eyes, Diana noticed, still had the girlish twinkle they'd always had.

"Me dad's lungs are bad," Tracy went on. "Mum's hip is givin' 'er problems."

"I'm sorry," Diana responded. "Please send them my love."

"I will." Tracey was smiling again. She then seemed a little distracted as she studied Diana's face. "Gawd, you're lookin' a lot better than me at forty." She laughed finally. "Or should I say forty-one!"

Although Diana knew Tracey's words were meant to be kind and lighthearted, she was beginning to feel uncomfortable and ready to get away. But as she opened her mouth to try to say she had to run, Tracey's husband appeared at Tracey's side.

"Brian," Tracey said straightaway. "This is Diana. We used to live next door when we woz kids. I ain't seen 'er in donkey's years."

Brian smiled, shook hands with Diana, and then slid an arm around his wife. "You poor thing." He chuckled, jerking Tracey into his wide barrel chest. "I 'eard Trace was a bit of a wild one as a kid."

"Aw, shut up, Bri," Trace said, playfully slapping at her husband. She then nodded over at Diana and spoke as if Diana weren't there. "Don't she look lovely, Bri? And she's brainy too. She went to this posh school and then Oxford. And then didn't ya go study abroad somewhere?" She addressed Diana with her last question.

Diana nodded and gave a tight smile. "Yes, I studied at Harvard. Now I live and work in New York."

"The Big Apple?" Brian raised his eyebrows and then whistled in amazement.

Tracey shook her head. "Ya don't sound like a Yank, though." She chuckled. "You still speak lovely. When you went off to that boarding school, they taught you how to talk all la-di-da. I was always dead jealous."

Diana flushed. "Well—"

But Tracey cut her off. "Where's your other 'alf, Di?" she asked. "I 'eard you married some really rich and clever bloke. Is 'e 'ere with ya?"

"No." Diana shook her head, feeling herself flushing again. "No." She then paused and added, "He's not here yet."

"Is 'e American?"

Diana nodded.

"I bet 'e's so 'andsome." Tracey hooted.

Brian nudged his wife and grinned. "Calm down, darlin'." He then winked at Diana. "Sorry, love, she's been watching too many of them TV shows about American celebrities. She thinks she's gonna run off with Brad Pitt one of these days."

Diana really wanted to go now. She didn't want any more questions to be asked about Graham. She didn't want to watch Tracey and her husband teasing each other with a familiarity and fondness so obvious you could touch it. She had to get away.

Once again, though, she was too late.

"Diana," Tracey was now saying, "this is my daughter, Kelly."

Reluctantly, Diana smiled and said, "Nice to meet you, Kelly," as the girl shuffled forward and stood by her mother's side.

Kelly muttered a shy hello back, as Tracey slid her hand through the crook of her daughter's arm, pulled her close, and launched into the same speech she'd just given her husband about how she knew Diana as a kid. "Isn't she lovely?" Tracey kept repeating.

Every time Tracey would say this, Diana would feel heat bounce up into her cheeks. She hated being talked about and looked at in this way, as if she were some precious ornament on display. But Tracey's compliments also made Diana think of Graham and all the compliments he'd been firing her way recently. Tracey's compliments weren't wordy and articulate like Graham's, of course, yet they seemed so much more heartfelt and genuine. The realization of this made Diana flush even more.

"Kelly's fourteen on Saturday," Tracey was explaining now that she'd finished her introductory monologue about Diana. "We're trying to take 'er to a show as a treat."

Kelly pouted. "But it's all sold out."

Diana looked at the girl. She was a rounder version of Tracey at that age. She had the same soft blue eyes, though. Diana's gaze then shifted back to Tracey. Tracey was looking at her daughter and offering an apologetic frown.

"I'm so sorry, love," she was saying, her own blue eyes glassy with regret.

"Do you 'ave kids?" Brian asked Diana.

But Diana wasn't listening. Her thoughts had skipped elsewhere. Watching Tracey with her daughter, Diana felt something shift inside, and she suddenly found herself wanting to help.

"Would you see another show?" The question escaped her before she could stop it.

Three pairs of eyes turned to stare at Diana.

"What d'ya mean?" asked Kelly.

"If you could get tickets for *Chicago* or another show, would you like to go?"

Kelly's blue eyes glimmered, just like her mother's used to when she was excited as a kid. "Yes!" She nodded, her wavy brown hair flopping up and down.

Diana reached into her purse and pulled out her cell. After a few swift prods of the phone's small buttons and a few seconds' wait, she was on the line with Nadini, the student adviser she'd just had a meeting with. Nadini was helpful and swift, and in no longer than two minutes, she'd confirmed online that there were tickets available for *Chicago*. Diana then rattled off her credit card number, and three tickets were bought for Tracey's family.

"Just give your names at will-call," Diana instructed when she got off the phone.

Tracey, she suddenly noticed, was blushing bright red. "Diana." She waved her hands. "You didn't 'ave to go to all that bother."

"It wasn't any bother," Diana replied, momentarily slipping back into an Essex accent she hadn't used in over thirty years.

Brian stepped forward, his wallet open, and started trying to press crumpled-up ten-pound notes into Diana's hands.

"No, no," she said, pushing away his hand. "It's on me."

"Don't be daft, darlin'." He laughed. " 'Ere, take it."

Diana tried again to push the money away, but with a gentle yet firm grip Brian took her wrist and placed the notes in her palm.

Tracey was still blushing. "That was so kind of ya, Di."

"It was nothing." Diana shook her head.

She was now beginning to feel a little embarrassed herself with all the fuss they were making. She realized it was really time to go.

"I should get going." She waved vaguely in the direction of Covent Garden. "I have to meet a friend," she lied.

As they said their good-byes, Tracey moved forward and drew Diana into a warm, tight hug.

"It was so lovely to see ya, Di. If you make it down our way to see your mum and dad, give us a tinkle," she said, letting go of Diana and making a phone gesture with her right hand. "We'd love to meet that fella of yours too." She then delved into her overstuffed purse and extracted a small white card. " 'Ere's our number. Call us anytime."

And then they were gone, the three of them ambling off toward Monmouth Street and the theater where *Chicago* would soon be playing. Diana watched them leave for a second and then turned on her heel and walked in the opposite direction. She would take Drury Lane toward Covent Garden and there, she decided, she would find a place for a glass of white wine and perhaps a fillet of smoked salmon. As she walked, she fiddled with Tracey's small white card, which she'd placed in her coat pocket. Finally, she pulled it out and studied it more closely. The card was clearly made at home on a personal printer, and among chintzy flowers it read, *Tracey Jones*—Jones was clearly her married name—and underneath her address and telephone number were printed in a flowery font. Tracey still lived, Diana realized, just a few streets from where they'd grown up.

Diana slipped the card back into her pocket. She doubted she would look at it again. Even if she did pass near their house on her way to her parents' next week, she couldn't imagine calling them or dropping in. She and Tracey weren't just continents apart these days; they lived on different planets. What could they possibly have to say to each other? And there was certainly no way Diana would take Graham to meet them. As soon as their backs were turned, he'd no doubt scoff at their stocky bodies, their cheap furniture, and their accents.

But as Diana thought this—as she thought about how Tracey's card would remain in her pocket until it got gnarled and crinkled and she'd finally give in to the guilt and throw it away—the tightness that often gripped her chest was usurped by an aching emptiness. While black cabs honked and double-decker buses whizzed by through the wet streets, a curious and unexpected thought then occurred to Diana: She wanted to run after Tracey and her family and join them for the show. Ordinarily, she hated all-singing, all-dancing, big-budget productions like *Chicago*. But for some inexplicable reason, she suddenly wanted to be there with Tracey and her husband and daughter. She wanted the loudness of the music and the buzz from the excited audience to wash over her. Most of all, she wanted to be encircled by the smiles, the bigheartedness, and the apparent happiness of Tracey's small family.

Diana stopped and looked back along the street where she'd just walked. There was no sign of Tracey. But, she thought, her mind beginning to whir, if she hurried perhaps she might catch up with them. And if she acted quickly, she could secure herself a ticket for the show too. She thrust her hand into her purse to find her phone, but as she pulled it out she froze. The screen winked the words, *Missed Call*, and underneath Graham's Berkeley number glared at her.

It was the reality check Diana needed. She shook her head and turned quickly around. What was she thinking? she scolded herself. *Chicago?* With Tracey? Had she gone mad? Then, instead of scrolling to Nadini's number, as she was going to just a second ago, she jabbed at Graham's number and held the phone to her ear.

She listened as it rang. And rang.

Fifteen

More Scholarly Disputes

Nothing annoyed Diana more than a student's checking his or her cell phone while in one of her classes. Of course, a tour of the British Library wasn't exactly one of her classes, but the fact that Veronica Nilsen had checked her phone every single minute since they'd entered the building half an hour ago was really beginning to test Diana's patience. The small, sparkly-eyed tour guide hadn't noticed Veronica's distracted shufflings with her phone. But Diana, who'd happened to be standing next to Veronica for most of the tour so far, had definitely observed them and was having a hard time not saying anything. If it had been any other student, she probably would have taken the phone from her hand, upbraided her in a furious hissed whisper, and confiscated the cell until the end of the tour. But Lamont Nilsen's vast donation to Manhattan U hung invisibly and ominously over his daughter's head. Snatching Veronica's expensive cell from her hands was definitely not an option.

However, Diana was not in the mood to have her patience tested. She had not slept well last night; in fact, she hadn't slept much at all. It seemed jet lag had hit her really hard this time, which was curious, because Diana rarely suffered from jet lag when she flew across the Atlantic. But last night she'd lain awake until six in the morning, staring up at the shadowy ceiling trying not to think about Graham. But of course, as hard as she tried, her mind continually came back to him. She thought about the big questions: Were they really going to get back together? Had she really forgiven him for all the hurt? Was he really going to leave Annabelle? Then she'd dwell on the small details, like why Graham hadn't left a message earlier when he called, or why she hadn't been able to reach him when she called him back. Occasionally, as she would drift into a semidoze, she'd imagine Graham at Tracey's house. She'd see them drinking tea from chipped mugs and Graham watching Tracey with an amused and patronizing twinkle in his eyes. Only as the birds began to chirp and the first delivery trucks rumbled past on the street outside did Diana's mind begin to fizzle and blur and finally allow her to fall properly asleep.

As a result, Diana was now feeling groggy and peevish, and because of Veronica's fidgeting and phone checking, she was unable to concentrate on the tour. This served only to make her more irritable. She knew the old British Library inside out, but since the library had moved to this new site near King's Cross Station (and she, at the same time, had been living in the U.S.), she wasn't an expert anymore. This tour would be a quick way for Diana to do some much-needed catching up on the library's new layout, collections, and developments. But not if some young, spoiled, and indifferent student was going to distract her continually.

They were just entering the library's main reading room when Veronica pulled out her phone once again and Diana decided it was time to act. She couldn't hold back any longer.

"Veronica," she whispered, trying to keep her tone neutral, "I think it is time to put the phone away." She followed this statement with a meaningful glance at the girl's cell.

Veronica looked down at her hand and then up at Diana. She frowned and muttered, "I'm waiting for a call." Still holding the phone, she showed no signs of putting it away.

Diana was taken aback. Students never disobeyed her. Not ever. Usually one glance or one comment was all it took. Diana's skin prickled with her disbelief and annoyance.

"I'm sure the call can wait a little while," Diana hissed, finding it hard to keep a cool tone. "The tour will be over at four."

"I'm waiting for a call," Veronica repeated. This time, however, she spoke more loudly, and instead of pouting, her mouth had formed a tight, defiant line. Her eyes were bloodshot and there were dark circles underneath them. She looked like she'd had about the same amount of sleep as Diana.

Diana had no time for sympathy, however.

"If you insist on *waiting for this call*," she snapped, causing some other students in the group to turn and stare, "I suggest you and your phone go outside." The words flew from Diana's mouth before she really thought about what she was saying, and she was left feeling a little shocked at her own angered outburst.

"Fine," huffed Veronica, as she turned on her heel, nudged past some of the students still filtering into the reading room, and began to head out.

Diana watched her go for a second, but then, feeling a pulse of panic rise in her chest, she quickly followed after her.

"Stay nearby," she called down the hallway after Veronica. "We'll be heading to the Globe immediately after the tour ends."

Veronica didn't look back or reply. She just tottered onward in her knee-high, four-inch-heel boots. Diana watched her go for a second time and wondered whether she should hurry after her. She had no idea whether Veronica would do what she'd asked and stay near the library. Would she even care about the trip to the Globe Theatre later? Veronica didn't seem the type of student who'd be itching to see a reconstructed Shakespearean theater, so was it even worth worrying whether Veronica stuck around? Diana knew it wasn't really wise to let students wander off by themselves—especially a high-profile student like Veronica. But it wasn't as if she could keep a tight leash on the Nilsen girls. They were staying in their own hotel room. They could do whatever they wanted when they weren't on excursions or trips. It would be delusional to think she could realistically tell Veronica where she should or should not go.

On top of which, Diana did not want to miss the rest of the tour. The guide had made a special exception for their group and was allowing them to peek in at the library's main reading room, even though it was a weekday and there would be people studying and expecting silence. Diana was keen to take a look at these rooms and to hear what the guide had to say. So, deciding once and for all not to chase after Veronica, Diana headed back through the reading room's doors.

When she caught up with the group, they were standing by a set of computer terminals and the guide was explaining how readers searched and called up books or journal articles held in the library.

"When a book or journal order is ready," he whispered, "a light flashes at the desk where the library user is working. They must go to the main desk over there." He waved his hand. "That's where they collect it."

Diana scanned over the room. The building was impressive, with its high modern ceiling and its wide wood desks, low-slung chairs, and soft yellow desk lamps. But it was nothing like the library's reading room when it had been housed at the British Museum. The old reading room was a perfect circle lined with books and topped by an elegant domed roof. Long oak tables radiated out from the center, and high windows shed daylight across the entire room. Oscar Wilde, George Orwell, and Karl Marx had all studied in the old reading room once upon a time, and when Diana used the reading room back in her student days she always felt as if the spirits of the great writers still wandered there.

"Any suggestions for a book or an author to look up?" the guide was now saying. He was about to demonstrate a search and was looking for an example.

The group of students surrounding him looked tired and restless and said nothing. They were probably jet-lagged, as well as suffering from their first night partying in London. Rachel, Diana noticed, was eyeing the students, imploring them to speak. Her gaze was met with yet more silence. Diana decided it was time to turn her own steely gaze upon the group. She would soon get one of them talking.

She was right, of course. As Diana's eyes settled on Rebecca Nilsen, Rebecca instantly spoke up.

"How about Sylvia Plath?" she said, looking at the tour guide and then offering a quick, approval-seeking smile at Diana.

Diana nodded, smiled, and then watched as the tour guide punched Plath's name into the keyboard in front of him. A list of books and periodicals on Plath popped up on the screen, and the guide explained the various codes and abbreviations.

"The library also holds a number of original manuscripts," he said, looking up from the computer. "Typewritten drafts of some of Plath's poems, for example."

"Would it be possible to see one of those today?" asked Diana.

She'd seen these manuscripts before, of course. But she always enjoyed the opportunity to see them again and to look at the very papers that Plath herself had touched, typed, and scribbled on. Diana also thought the drafts might inspire the students out of their current lethargy. Who wouldn't be impressed by a Sylvia Plath original?

The tour guide looked reticent. "I'm not sure," he began. "The Manuscripts Reading Room is open only to scholars with specific research requests and not to the public."

Diana flashed him a smile and said, "Just one?" She then leaned over and pointed to one of the book references on the screen. "That's mine," she added. "*Plath's Poetics*, that's my book, and I really would love for my students to be able to see one of Plath's manuscripts."

The tour guide blushed. It was clear that he was both embarrassed and charmed by Diana's striking face and smile. He didn't doubt her for a second either. Something in Diana's countenance had this compelling effect on people.

"I see," he said, and after thinking for a second, he added, "Perhaps I could ask my manager."

He then scuttled away from the group and toward the doors. Within five minutes, he was bounding back into the room.

"I've been given the go-ahead." He beamed. "Follow me. We need to head up to the Manuscripts Reading Room."

At first, the students were slow to follow after him, and from the rear Diana had to hurry them along. Soon enough, though, they were out of the main reading room and heading toward the stairs. The students chattered and laughed, clearly pleased to be out of the somber and silent reading room, and perhaps, Diana hoped, they were getting a little excited about being allowed into the sacred British Library Manuscripts Reading Room.

As they took the stairs, Diana overheard a snippet of conversation going on in front of her. Rachel was talking with Rebecca Nilsen.

"I've always thought of Sylvia Plath as the foremother of confessional chick lit," Rachel was saying, chuckling lightly. "At least, she was in her *Bell Jar* phase. Perhaps not so much in her heavy and dark 'Daddy' phase."

"Really?" Rebecca responded. "You think so?"

Before Rachel could reply, Diana couldn't help cutting in. "'Foremother of confessional chick lit'?" she said, amid a puff of incredulous laughter.

Rachel turned on the stair, spotted Diana, and flushed a deep crimson. But then, as if pulling together every vertebra in her spine, she stood straight and responded in a cool tone, "I would argue that. Yes," she added with a nod.

"By 'chick lit,' I suppose you mean those commercial, neon pink books that have overtaken bookstores," Diana replied, her voice low and gruff.

"That's one, very pejorative, way to describe chick lit," Rachel shot back. "Other people, myself included, might describe chick lit as popular women's fiction. Or fiction by women, about women, and for women . . ."

Diana wasn't listening. "I think Sylvia Plath and chick lit have very little to do with each other," she interrupted. She then shook her head and tried to continue up the stairs.

Rachel, however, moved a little to the left and prevented Diana from moving any farther.

"I think they have a lot to do with each other," she said, her voice still cool but with an edge of defiance.

The students in the group were filtering past and casting curious glances in Rachel and Diana's direction. Meanwhile, Rebecca Nilsen stood next to Rachel with her eyes darting between her two professors. Her expression was curious but also slightly worried.

"I don't think we have time for this now, Rachel." Diana sighed.

She was both surprised and frustrated that Rachel wanted to have this discussion. Diana really didn't want Rachel getting all riled up and impassioned, like she had in the grad-faculty seminar. Diana was too sleep-deprived to deal with any such histrionics now. Also, she had a date with a Plath manuscript that she was eager to get to. She immediately regretted piping up in the first place.

"I think Plath's *The Bell Jar* and books like *The Devil Wears Prada* or *The Nanny Diaries* or *Bridget Jones* have a lot in common," Rachel said, pulling her spine even straighter and leveling her gaze with Diana's. "For one, they are all memoirs loosely disguised as fiction. They are confessional novels, in other words."

Diana opened her mouth to speak, but Rachel was talking again.

"Second, all these books tell coming-of-age stories about young women in the city."

Diana was getting impatient, so she decided to cut in. "*The Bell Jar*, as I'm sure you're aware, starts with the sentence, 'It was a queer, sultry summer, the summer they electrocuted the Rosenbergs . . .'" She paused and then added, "I hardly think that a book that opens in this way and that deals with the struggles, depression, and despair of an eloquent young woman can really be compared to commercial fiction about women obsessed with fashion, shoes, and how much weight they've gained."

A blush bloomed on Rachel's cheeks and her eyes flickered with anger. Yet, much to Diana's surprise again, Rachel maintained her cool tone as she responded to Diana's barbed comments.

"As I'm sure you're aware," Rachel said with a tight smile, "*The Bell Jar*'s protagonist, Esther Greenwood, wins a summer internship at *Ladies' Day* magazine in New York. During this period, she goes to banquets and functions, worries about what she and her friends are wearing, meets and frets over men." Rachel smiled again. "Not a whole lot different, in other words, from the concerns of heroines in today's 'commercial fiction.'" She flicked her fingers with these last words.

"Esther Greenwood leaves New York, goes home, despairs, has electroshock treatment, and then attempts to commit suicide," Diana shot back. "Not exactly a commercial-style happy ending."

Diana's neck prickled as she spoke. This whole exchange was really beginning to annoy her. She wanted to move on and let this go, and although she was offering decent ripostes to Rachel's ridiculous arguments, Diana didn't feel on her game, and that bothered her more than anything.

"True. *The Bell Jar* deals with weightier emotions and darker events than, say, *The Devil Wears Prada*," Rachel was now saying, her eyes slipping from Diana to Rebecca, who was still standing nearby, listening. "But the first-person narrative and confessional tone of Plath's novel, the kind of woman the story follows, the things that she thinks about, aren't so dissimilar. Also"—she raised a finger—"*The Bell Jar*'s ending is ultimately pretty upbeat. You have the sense Esther Greenwood feels renewed and over the worst of her struggles and sadness."

"The end is very ambiguous," Diana snapped back, her neck prickling even deeper. "Scholars have been talking and writing about its ambiguity for years. It's rather naive to simply categorize it as a happy ending."

Diana glared up at Rachel. There was still a flush of pink on Rachel's cheeks, but other than that her gaze was rock-steady, and she still looked surprisingly unflustered, in spite of Diana's own harsh words. Indeed, it was Diana who seemed more irritated and disconcerted by this conversation, not Rachel. She didn't like how she was beginning to sound: in other words, bitchy and snappish.

Rachel was about to respond when a call came from the top of the stairs.

"Professor Monroe?" It was the tour guide. He was looking down at their small group of three, his eyebrows slightly knitted in confusion. Students milled around behind him, still chattering. "The document is ready for viewing," he said.

Diana, who was peering around Rachel, raised her hand and called back, "We're just coming."

She then moved past Rachel and up the stairs without saying another word. She knew it was rude and unprofessional just to walk off, but she was scared that if she said anything more she would lose her cool—and this was neither the time nor the place. Plus, she didn't want to give Rachel the satisfaction.

A few minutes later, the group was standing in a corner of the silent Manuscripts Reading Room. Diana stood at the center, closest to the guide, and looked down at the typewritten draft of Sylvia Plath's poem "Mushroom," which the guide had placed on a table in front of them. The prickling in her neck brought on by the earlier confrontation finally began to ease as she stared at the aging paper. She breathed deeply and smiled as she read Plath's eerie poem. As her eyes took in every word and the poem sang out in her head, Diana could feel Sylvia's presence—someone she felt she knew and understood—and this soothed her, in spite of the poem's ominous tone. London and Rachel and Graham all seemed to be unraveling her, but at least Plath was a constant: her calming constant.

Sixteen

Literary London

"The Globe Theatre does not put on any productions between November and April."

Rachel, Diana, and their group of twenty or so students stood on a wide stage between two ornate columns looking toward their new tour guide, a woman in her fifties with sparkling white hair and tiny glasses perched on her nose. Three tiers of carved wooden seating circled around above them, and a "pit," which according to the guide was the area for standing members of the audience, splayed out from the foot of the stage. Everything in the theater looked old and hand-crafted and as if it really had been constructed while Shakespeare was still alive—and not ten years ago, when the replica theater was actually built.

"With our rainy British winters, it's just not feasible to run shows." The woman was now chuckling. "Even in the summer months, Hamlet, Romeo, or Lady Macbeth have been known to run for cover."

Rachel smiled at the woman and pretended to laugh along with her, but really her mind was elsewhere and her stomach was in knots. She'd held her own with Diana earlier in the library. She'd remained composed and aloof, like she'd been telling herself she must. Yet she didn't feel triumphant or satisfied. Not even happy. It had been a struggle to keep cool, and the whole exchange had left a bitter taste in her mouth and an entangled feeling in her gut. It bothered her that Diana had rudely walked off, especially as she had so much more to say on the matter. It bothered her that she hadn't felt more satisfied and victorious with her own performance. If she'd managed to pull off her new composed persona, why wasn't she feeling confident and poised and ready to take on the world?

"Today, I'm afraid, you will have to make do with some video clips from last summer's productions," the tour guide said to the group, as Rachel's mind whirred. "I'll take you down to one of our screening rooms. It's not the same as seeing a play live, but it will give you a taste of our fine, fine productions here at the Globe."

She then led the group off the stage and toward their next destination. As they jostled along narrow corridors and downstairs, Rachel was careful to avoid any more close calls with Diana. It looked like Diana was doing the same, as she charged ahead and launched into deep conversation with the theater's guide. Rachel watched Diana for a few seconds, her immaculate black hair swishing as she walked and her strides precise and purposeful. Rachel could not fathom this woman—not at all. During their meeting with the support staff yesterday, Diana seemed in good spirits and amenable to Rachel. Today Diana was back to despising her again. But there had also been a shift. When they'd sparred earlier, for the first time ever Rachel sensed that she'd ruffled Diana's feathers. She'd made the ice queen melt just for a moment or two.

"I just had a text from Veronica."

Rebecca had appeared at Rachel's side and was waving her phone.

"You did?" Rachel shot back.

Rebecca nodded. "Yup."

When they left the library earlier, they found Veronica Nilsen had disappeared. Diana told Rachel in a dismissive whisper that she'd reprimanded the student about her phone and told her to leave, but she also "asked the girl to wait." It seemed Veronica hadn't listened. For a few minutes, Diana and Rachel had discussed what to do and whether one of them should go looking for the wayward student. But in the end they decided they would call Nadini and Zach and get them to start the search. In the meantime, they would head on to the

Globe, and Rebecca would try to call her sister and find out where she'd gone.

"Where is she?" Rachel asked.

"I'm not sure. But she says she's fine and not to worry."

Rachel narrowed her eyes. "Should we be worried?"

Rebecca shrugged. "I'm sure she's fine. I don't think this"—she waved her hand around—"is V's idea of a good time. She's probably shopping at Harrods or something," she added with a light laugh. But then, clearly feeling disloyal to her sister, she said, "Or maybe she was just tired and headed back to the hotel."

Rachel thought for a second and then said, "Okay, well, text her back and tell her we'll want to check in with her tonight."

Rebecca nodded and started tapping at her phone. Rachel walked on and wondered whether she'd done the right thing and whether they were wise in not being more proactive about Veronica's disappearance. They couldn't keep shackles on their students, but they were still their— and ultimately Manhattan U's—responsibility. Daddy Nilsen wouldn't be pleased to hear that the university he might possibly donate a chunk of his money to had let one of his daughters loose in a foreign city.

A little while later, as they sat watching the clips from recent Globe productions, Rachel managed to shake these worries from her head. She stared up at the screen and breathed peacefully in time with Shakespeare's familiar iambic pentameters. Even when an actor playing Hamlet charged onto the screen and, in his dark, brooding, and rumpled glory, reminded Rachel of Carson, she didn't allow her mind to start spinning again. She was excited that Carson had phoned her last night, of course, and brief though his call may have been, it had reassured her that what was happening between them was real and possibly had some future. He'd even told her he missed her. But as she watched Carson's look-alike on the screen, she told herself not to get distracted. Not to get excited or restless or hankering. As she'd decided last night, she must remain unruffled, mature, and serene when it came to Carson.

However, when the *Hamlet* clip ended and a segment from *Mac-*

beth began to roll, Rachel's mind kick-started once again and her thoughts returned to Diana. An actress playing Lady Macbeth filled the screen, and with a scrunched up letter in her hand and her eyes wild and glistening, she was delivering a speech that Rachel knew well from her undergraduate days.

> *Come, you spirits*
> *That tend on mortal thoughts, unsex me here,*
> *And fill me from the crown to the toe top-full*
> *Of direst cruelty! make thick my blood;*
> *Stop up the access and passage to remorse,*
> *That no compunctious visitings of nature*
> *Shake my fell purpose, nor keep peace between*
> *The effect and it! Come to my woman's breasts,*
> *And take my milk for gall, you murdering ministers . . .*

The woman's performance was captivating. She made Lady Macbeth's murderous desire for her husband to become king so palpable and believable. Even the students seated around Rachel, who were fidgety and restless just a while ago, seemed to straighten up and listen more intently as the speech progressed.

Rachel gawked at the screen like everyone else, yet she wasn't really thinking about the woman's talent or the brilliance of her portrayal. Instead, she found herself thinking about Lady Macbeth's passion, her unbounded desires, and how she was the exact opposite of someone like Diana. There wasn't a shred of composure when it came to Macbeth's wife. She couldn't help but let her ardor and deadly ambitions surface. And Rachel found this curiously captivating and enlivening. Lady Macbeth was no role model, of course, and Rachel was not going to summon up "direst cruelty" and murder Diana (although the thought did prompt a wry smile to flicker across Rachel's face). Yet, if you subtracted Lady Macbeth's murderous intentions, she wasn't so different from Shakespeare's Cleopatra or Romeo or Juliet, all of whom were passionate, compelling, and inimitably memorable characters.

As Rachel thought about this, she found herself questioning her vow to be composed and buttoned-down like Diana. The altercation in the library earlier had shown Rachel that she wasn't comfortable in a Diana-like aloof mode. She was proud of how she spoke up and stuck to her guns, but it hadn't felt good being so poker-faced and impassive. It rankled deep, in fact. As Lady Macbeth continued with her speech up on the screen, Rachel then wondered if it wasn't so bad to be unrestrained and passionate. Maybe she'd been wrong last night when she decided the old ardent Rachel was just young and naive. Was it time to stop being anything other than her old self? The feisty undergraduate who'd rant to her friends about *Bridget Jones*, and the tenacious, passionate grad student who let nothing get in her way? What was more, maybe Carson had been telling the truth when he said he was impressed by her passion that day after the grad-faculty research seminar. If she were more like her old self with him and showed him the emotions she'd been holding back for too long, perhaps he'd be the same and offer more than a hurried, "Miss you," at the end of their phone calls.

Rachel was smiling when they left the Globe Theatre and moved out into the dark and drizzling London evening. Ironically, the deadly Lady Macbeth had provided her with a breakthrough, and she felt as if a huge weight had been lifted from her shoulders. After too long cowering and holding back, she was going to be her old self once again. She would act on her impulses, say what she really felt, and start being the real Rachel Grey. In the process, she might even do what Mikey had once drunkenly promised her: She'd catch herself a Carson. But this time she would catch him good and proper by showing him who she really was and thus ensuring he wouldn't wriggle free from her hook.

She looked out over the twinkling Thames and almost giggled to herself as she imagined Carson naked and writhing on the end of a fishing line. She then turned and trotted toward the group, who were busy boarding a small bus that would, in a few minutes, ferry them back to Russell Square and the student dorm. Manhattan U had made the decision this year that, where possible, the students would not take public transportation. They believed it would be safer for the students to ride in hired vehicles. Rachel had thought this decision was overprotective, expensive, and rather shortsighted. After all, students like Veronica could make off through London however they pleased during the rest of their stay.

But now, as she settled into one of the front seats near the driver, Rachel was pleased to have a ride back home. Today had been a long one, lots of standing and waiting during their tours of the library and the theater, and she was glad not to have to battle through the rush-hour commuters on the underground. Besides, she wanted to get home as soon as possible. She wanted to call Carson, she wanted to tell him how she felt and ask him what he was feeling, and she wanted to do all this in the quiet of her hotel room, perhaps with a glass of wine from the minibar in her hand.

"Is that everyone, darlin'?"

The driver had turned to look at Rachel. At first, she said nothing. She'd been lost in her thoughts and didn't realize he was talking to her.

"Is that everyone?" he repeated.

"Oh, right," Rachel said, sitting up straight and pushing back her curls. She stood up, looked down the bus, and started counting heads. Within a minute she was done. Everyone was here, with the exception of Veronica, of course. She turned back to the driver and nodded her head.

"Yep." She smiled, sitting back down. "All here."

But as the driver revved the engine and started to pull out into busy Southwark Street, Rachel realized she'd missed one head: Diana's. Panicked, she looked out the steamed-up window, and twenty or so yards away she could see Diana still in conversation with the theater's guide. She clearly hadn't noticed the bus was moving away without her. Rachel was about to call out to the driver to stop, but then she froze. Gurgling in the pit of her stomach was the mischievous desire just to leave Diana behind. It was a cruel and childish thing to do. Nonetheless, she desperately wanted to do it.

"What would Lady Macbeth do?" she whispered under her breath.

Leave her behind, she thought with a small grin. Meanwhile, the bus picked up speed.

Back in her hotel room an hour later, Rachel felt the guilt that had already begun to kick in, and also a slight panic that any minute Diana would pound furiously on her door. But Rachel was too preoccupied with the call she was about to make to get particularly worked up. She'd poured herself the wine she'd promised herself, kicked off her shoes, and was now busy scrolling down her phone list to Carson's number. As she reached it, however, the phone jumped and jingled in her hand. She almost dropped it with the shock.

When she finally focused on the caller's name, she saw it was Nadini. She opened the phone straightaway.

"Hi, Nadini," she chimed.

Nadini's tone was not so cheery. "Professor Grey?" she said. "I've got bad news. Veronica Nilsen's in the emergency room at University College Hospital. She was found, passed out, in a pub bathroom in the West End. It looks like she got herself completely drunk on vodka."

Rachel's stomach lurched and then sank. She didn't hesitate for a second, though. Standing up, she slipped her shoes back on her feet and said, "I'll be there as soon as I can."

After jotting down the directions to the hospital, Rachel was on her way. She sucked in a breath as she reached Diana's room and knocked on the door. She wasn't prepared for Diana's wrath, but she had no choice. Diana had to be told, and Rachel needed her help dealing with whatever they were met with at the hospital. She knocked a couple of times but there was no answer. She couldn't waste any more time, so she scribbled a note, slid it under the door, and then headed toward the hotel's elevator, where she pulled out her phone on the way and tried to call Diana's number. There was no reply there either.

As her stomach sank for a second time and the elevator doors closed in front of her, Rachel found herself thinking again of Lady Macbeth. What she'd forgotten earlier in her moment of revelation was that unbridled passion like Lady Macbeth's—or Romeo and Juliet's, for that matter—always came at a price. A heavy price. It looked like Rachel was going to have to deal with this Veronica mess on her own, and it was all thanks to letting her gut feelings lead the way, not her head. If Rachel hadn't left Diana on the curbside, Diana would be here now, knowing exactly what to do with a multimillion-dollar, high-profile student who'd been found drunk and passed out on some dirty floor of a pub bathroom.

Diana was disgusted that Rachel allowed the bus to head off without her. She was absolutely positive her young colleague had done it on purpose. But one thing that didn't bother Diana was having to take the underground back to the hotel. She preferred it, in fact. After a day walled up in the library and then the theater, it felt refreshing to be out and about again amid London's hustle and bustle. It felt calming too. After the run-in with Rachel earlier, Diana had been flipping between teeth-grinding agitation to scolding herself for letting the whole silly exchange get to her.

Now, sitting on the underground's hard plastic seat beside a priest in full regalia and opposite two Japanese tourists, Diana breathed with the click and clack of the rumbling Northern Line train. She tried to clear her mind of everything—Rachel, students, Graham, her upcoming visit to her parents—and for a while she was successful. But when the train pulled into a station and the two tourists hopped off and were replaced by a young woman in a neat chocolate pantsuit, Diana's trance was interrupted. The woman was holding a book in her hands, and as she sat down in the vacated seat opposite Diana, she flipped it open and began to read. Diana's eyes automatically drifted down to the book's cover. She always did this on trains, or buses, or planes; she was always curious to see what other people were reading. The woman held her book at an awkward angle, so Diana couldn't quite see the title, nor the author. But from the silhouette of a cocktail glass splashed across the cover and the paperback's neon pink spine, Diana could tell it was some sort of chick lit novel, the kind Rachel had been talking about back in the library.

Diana had never read a chick lit book in her life, and she'd never so much as looked inside a copy of *Bridget Jones*. But she'd read the reviews in publications she trusted, like *The New York Times Book Review*, and she'd seen the tables devoted to these pink and frothy books in Barnes & Noble (no doubt forcing out novels by much more talented women authors). She had a pretty good idea what they were all about, and she knew she wouldn't want to waste her time reading them. What she couldn't understand, however, was why someone like Rachel would feel so passionately about them, and why she would want to base her scholarship on them. After all, weren't these books shoring up every derogatory stereotype about women? Didn't they make women sound like a tribe of flaky, shoe-obsessed, man-obsessed airheads? Diana's jaw pulsed with annoyance as she remembered Rachel comparing Plath's work to these mindless books.

Diana looked again at the woman opposite. The young woman was half smiling as her eyes traced the words in front of her, and she gave out a quiet chuckle as she flipped over a page. As Diana continued to watch the woman, her annoyance turned quite suddenly and unexpectedly to guilt. Did she think women who read these books were as mindless and shallow as the books they chose to read? Perhaps she did. When Diana's gaze skimmed the covers on the bookstore table, she certainly wondered whether these books might dumb down female readers and distract them from reading anything more challenging. But did she really think women who read these books were dumb too? She hated to think she would be judgmental of other women in such a way.

Diana was awoken from these thoughts as the woman opposite got to her feet, tucked her book into her purse, and then headed toward the carriage doors. After the train had stopped, Diana watched from the window and saw the woman exit the train and walk down the platform. Just as she heard the bleeping noise that signaled the doors closing, Diana caught sight of the station sign. They'd arrived at King's Cross and she hadn't even realized it. This was Diana's stop too. She started to grab for her purse and umbrella, but then let them go and sat back against her seat. An idea had occurred to her. Perhaps she would stay on the train for a couple more stops and go to one of her favorite places in London. She hadn't been there for many years, and all of a sudden she felt a strong yearning to go back. It was exactly the place she needed to be right now.

A little while later, Diana stood on a quiet street in London's Primrose Hill and looked up at the elegant town house in front of her. It was dark now, but under the glow of the street lamps she could clearly see the familiar blue plaque—mounted to the right of the front window—that stated that Sylvia Plath lived there from 1960 to 1961. Diana pulled her jacket around her against the cold wind that had suddenly whipped up and stared at the plaque for some time. At first, she smiled. It had been a long time since she'd stood on Chalcot Road, and it was nice to be back. But as the seconds and then the minutes ticked by, her smile disappeared and was replaced by a frown.

Earlier, when she stood in the library scanning Plath's poem, she felt calmed. But outside the poet's old house, Diana wasn't feeling the same soothing vibes. Indeed, she was feeling more agitated and more unsettled than she had all day. If she were a few blocks away on Fitzroy Road—the other London home where Plath once lived—she could have understood such uneasiness. The Fitzroy house was the place where Sylvia had lived alone after her husband had left her, and where she finally killed herself while her young children slept in a bedroom next door. *Who wouldn't feel a little unnerved in front of that house?* thought Diana. But here on Chalcot Road, Sylvia Plath and Ted Hughes had lived together. Sylvia was newly pregnant and the couple was ostensibly happy.

Perhaps the nagging disquiet in Diana's chest had more to do with the fact that Graham still hadn't called her. Perhaps it had nothing to do with Plath's house at all. When Diana walked over to Chalcot Road from the local tube station just ten minutes ago, she'd checked her cell but there were still no messages. It would be morning in California now, and Graham had always been a very early riser. There really was no good explanation for his phone silence. She'd been tempted to call him again, but then her stubborn streak kicked in. She was the last one to leave a message; it was his turn to call.

Looking up at the house again, scanning the elegant sash windows and the white columns on either side of the front door, Diana found herself thinking about Ted and Sylvia and about her and Graham. The Plath-Hughes relationship was one of the great romances of the literary world. It was the meeting of two fine minds and the union of two elegant and evocative poets. But unlike the Barrett-Browning marriage, the other great literary couple, Hughes and Plath's romance was doomed. Only a few years after their wedding, Hughes played around with and eventually left Plath for Assia Wevill, a woman they'd rented their apartment in this very house to. Plath, meanwhile, got sadder and sadder and eventually committed suicide.

Just like when her students would talk about this famous doomed romance, when Diana thought about it, as she was doing now, she'd reluctantly draw similarities to her and Graham's relationship—the meeting of minds, the big romance, the philandering, the disappointments. Their stories were unnervingly similar. Although now hers and Graham's was different, wasn't it? Graham had returned. But as Diana thought this, uncertainty began to throb in her chest. Hughes had returned to Plath a few times too before finally leaving her. Was Graham's return going to be as fleeting and impermanent as Hughes's had been? Diana had wondered this before, of course, but she'd tried to shut it out. Now, in front of 3 Chalcot Road, blocking it out seemed impossible.

Diana pulled her jacket tighter around herself and began to move away from the house. As she did so, she dug in her purse for her cell. The only way to stop thinking these thoughts was to be proactive, she told herself. She'd call him. She'd let Graham reassure her he was back for good. He wasn't Ted Hughes. She wasn't Sylvia Plath. The ending of their story would be a different and happy one. It had to be.

She opened her phone and saw she'd missed a call. But the number wasn't Graham's, so she didn't bother listening to her messages. Instead, she scrolled straight to Graham's name in her phone list.

"Hello?"

The voice that answered Graham's cell was not Graham's. It was a chirpy and young female voice. Diana had never actually spoken to Annabelle, but she knew this was her. She knew it.

"Hello?" Annabelle said again, her tone still upbeat but now a little curious.

A million questions ran through Diana's mind. Why was Annabelle answering Graham's phone? Wasn't she supposed to be away somewhere? Where was Graham? Why did Annabelle sound so chipper? Wasn't Graham supposed to have ended things with her?

In spite of all these questions nagging at her, Diana said nothing.

"Hello?" Annabelle said one more time. "Whoever this is," she added, sounding a little frustrated, "if you're after Gray, he's out in the yard. I'm just going to get him. . . ."

"Don't bother," Diana snarled, before she slammed the phone shut and then hurled it with all her might into the cold London air.

She didn't stick around to see it tumble back to earth, but as she strode off she heard the tinkle and clack of shattering plastic.

Seventeen

University Protocols

"Please don't call him, Professor Grey."

Rebecca Nilsen was standing in front of Rachel with her hands clasped. Her face was pale and her eyes were wide and beseeching. Around the two of them, the hospital waiting room was bustling with people; some were sitting on the rows of plastic benches, others waiting in line to talk to the receptionist or buying snacks and soda at the vending machine. Every now and then a person in scrubs or a white coat with a stethoscope dangling around his or her neck would fly in and out of the squeaking swinging doors beside the receptionist's desk.

"I have to, Rebecc—" Rachel began.

"Veronica's going to be okay. The doctor said that once she sleeps off the alcohol poisoning, she'll be fine." Rebecca went on: "There's no need to worry my dad now, is there?"

Rachel shook her head. "She's not out of the woods yet. She's been through a lot in the last few hours." She frowned. "The doctor said they'd need to do a couple of tests when she wakes up. Plus, there's clearly something going on that made her get so drunk and messed up in the first place. Like you said, she's been upset and tearful since we got here. Your dad would want to know if his daughter is distressed, wouldn't he?"

Rachel felt bad having to repeat all this to Rebecca, who was worried enough already about her sister. At the same time, she had to convince Rebecca that they must call their father. Rachel was sure that Lamont Nilsen would want to know one of his daughters was in the hospital. Besides, it was Manhattan U's study-abroad protocol to contact a student's next of kin if something like this happened.

"But surely I count as next of kin," Rebecca was now saying, refusing to answer the question Rachel had posed.

They'd been over this a few times already. Rachel had told Rebecca about the Manhattan U policy, and Rebecca had jumped on it as a valid excuse not to contact her father.

"Rebecca," Rachel said, as she reached out and touched the girl's clasped hands. "I don't think that's really the point. Your father should know. He'd want to know." She pulled a sympathetic frown. "I'd rather you called him. But if you don't, I'll have to get his number from Nadini and call him myself."

Rebecca stared up at Rachel, her eyes glassy with frustration and worry. She said nothing for a few seconds and then whispered, "Let me think about it." She then jerked her small thumb over her shoulder. "I'm going to go back in there and check on her." By "her," Rebecca meant her sister, who was still sleeping in one of the small ER cubicles beyond the swinging doors. The doctor said they would transfer her to a ward for the rest of the night as soon as a bed became available.

As Rebecca trotted off, Rachel slumped onto one of the seats in the waiting area. Suddenly she felt overwhelmed with tiredness, and she found herself looking at her watch. It was only ten o'clock, but what with the remnants of jet lag and the fact that she'd been in the hospital for nearly three worried hours, it felt much later. She looked up from her watch and scanned the waiting room. There was still no sign of Diana, and Rachel remained baffled as to where her colleague had gone. Surely by now Diana would have gotten the phone messages she'd been leaving? And if there was something wrong with Diana's phone, she must have gotten the message at the hotel. It couldn't have taken Diana all this time just to get back to Russell Square from the Globe, even if she stopped to eat on the way.

The guilt Rachel felt earlier about leaving Diana behind was rap-

idly being replaced with anger and frustration. *Why* wasn't Diana
here? This was surely the lowest, most unprofessional way to get back
at Rachel for what she'd done. One of their students was in trouble,
and Diana should be here helping Rachel deal with the situation. Of
course, Rachel was doing okay without her, and there wasn't much
to deal with, as Veronica was being taken care of wonderfully by the
medical staff. Rachel had even told Nadini to go home earlier, because there was little any of them could do but wait. However, Rachel was struggling with this issue of Lamont Nilsen, and she could
really do with Diana's help and advice on the matter. She couldn't
keep letting the time slip past and not call him.

Rachel's gaze returned to the swinging doors Rebecca had just
left through. She just couldn't figure out why Rebecca was so ada-
mant about not wanting her father to know. The first explanation
Rebecca had given was that her father would overreact in worry and
probably insist on flying out to London. When Rachel pointed out
that this was not necessarily a bad thing, Rebecca faltered for a second and then changed tack, saying her father was extremely busy
and would be annoyed at having to leave his work. This made no
sense to Rachel, of course. Was Lamont Nilsen an overanxious par-
ent willing to fly to London on the next plane or an uncaring father
who would see his daughter's hospitalization as a rude interruption
to his work? Rachel had a suspicion that the latter might be true as
she remembered the conversation she'd had with Tom Burgess's wife
earlier in the semester. According to Sofia, Lamont Nilsen was a tyrant and his girls were afraid of him, just like everyone in the movie
world was. But this was all rumor and hearsay, and just because the
man had a temper did not mean Rachel shouldn't call him. It was
her job to call him, in fact.

While Rachel was still mulling all this over, Rebecca returned.
She plopped down into the seat next to Rachel.

"She's still sleeping," she whispered.

From Rebecca's red cheeks, it was clear she'd been crying, and
Rachel automatically leaned over and took her hand.

"She'll be fine," Rachel said in a soft whisper. "Just like the doctor said."

"I know." Rebecca sniffed. "It's just . . ." She paused as she shook her head. "It's just . . . I feel so bad. I knew she was down over the last few days, but I didn't think she'd go get herself really drunk and then pass out in some grungy bathroom." Her tone was sad but also a little angry. "Not this time, anyway."

Rachel looked over at Rebecca. "What do you mean, 'this time'?"

Rebecca's cheeks flushed and she bit her bottom lip. "I . . . Nothing," she said, shaking her head again.

"Come on," Rachel said, squeezing her hand. "Tell me. You shouldn't have to deal with this all on your own."

Rebecca looked at Rachel, her eyes red and her cheeks blotchy. She searched Rachel's face for a few seconds and then said quietly, "But please don't tell anyone. My dad did a lot to cover up the . . . well, the last incident."

"I swear, anything you tell me won't go any further," Rachel said in a grave whisper.

Rachel turned in her seat. "Over the summer," she began, after taking a big breath, "Veronica split up with her boyfriend. She took it pretty badly. Anyway, one night she ended up like this." Rebecca nodded toward the doors she'd just come through. "She went out, got completely trashed, and was found in the toilets of a skanky bar in Hollywood."

Rachel nodded, encouraging Rebecca to go on.

"Anyway, as soon as she got out of the hospital, Daddy sent her straight to rehab. It was a superexpensive place, of course: a cutting-edge rehab center that does all this scientific research on addiction and the brain. It was totally over-the-top for Veronica," Rebecca continued. "And she was completely miserable there. They kept her in a room on her own for hours; they did a billion tests and MRIs, and gave her a bunch of drugs that made her feel weird and nauseous. When she did get out of her room, there were all these other patients who had nothing in common with V, and all they wanted to do was talk about their serotonin levels and broken synapses and stuff like that." Rebecca paused and shook her head. "She's been so scared of being sent back there, she hasn't done anything like this since. She hasn't touched one drop of alcohol. Not until today, that is."

"What do you think made her do what she did today?"

Rebecca shook her head. "Like I said, she's been down since we came to London, but she won't tell me why." Her cheeks flushed again as she waved a hand. "I just didn't think she was unhappy enough to do something like this."

"You mustn't blame yourself," Rachel replied.

Rebecca didn't seem to hear, though, and carried on. "She got a call last night that really upset her, and when she disappeared today at the library, I should have gone after her. But I was being selfish. I didn't want to miss the tours."

Rachel released Rebecca's hand, which she'd still been holding, and took the young student by both shoulders. "It isn't your fault, Rebecca," she said, her voice firm. "Veronica went out and did this by herself, and you didn't know she was going to do it."

Even as she said this to Rebecca, Rachel felt a stab of her own guilt. If anybody should have been looking out for Veronica, it should have been her—and Diana too, of course. They were the faculty in charge of this trip, and it was up to them to keep a close eye on their students. Diana had seen Veronica's tears on the plane, and Rachel had seen a moody and taciturn Veronica when she'd gone to their hotel room last night. They should have known something like this was going to happen. They should have prevented it.

"It's because of what happened before," Rebecca was now saying. "Rehab and everything. That's why I don't want to call our father. He'll put her on the first plane back to that horrible place."

"Are you sure he would?" Rachel asked, letting her hands drop from Rebecca's shoulders.

"A hundred percent certain," she replied. "My dad is very strict about these things. And now that *The New York Times* and *Newsweek* featured the rehab center as the best in the country, he's definitely going to be sending her back there. He's convinced Veronica's an alcoholic, even though she really isn't."

Rachel raised a questioning eyebrow.

"She really isn't." Rebecca sighed. "Veronica loves to party; it's true. But she hardly ever touches alcohol, and when she has those few times, it's because she's been really upset about something. Her therapist said she uses the alcohol as a cry for help."

"Her therapist?" Rachel asked. "She has a therapist?"

Rebecca nodded. "After Veronica got out of rehab, she was determined never to return. She decided she'd do just about anything rather than be sent back. Veronica's not good at opening up, but someone recommended this great therapist in New York, and when we started at Manhattan U a few months ago, she started seeing her."

"And how's it been going?"

"Veronica really loves Dr. Goldstein—*really* loves her. She looks forward to going to see her. When she gets back from her sessions, she is always much happier and much more talkative."

Rachel looked over at Rebecca and thought for a few seconds. If Rachel was to call up their father, it sounded like he was certain to pack his daughter back off to this rehab place she hated. And how much good was that going to be for Veronica? Or for Rebecca, for that matter, who had to pick up the pieces and deal with the guilt after her sister's incidents. Rachel didn't want to make either of the girls suffer any more than they had to, but she had no idea where to go from here. She had no Diana to consult. Perhaps, she thought, this therapist might be able to help.

"Do you think we could talk to her?" she found herself asking Rebecca. "Her therapist, I mean."

"I don't know." Rebecca frowned. "I could get her number easily enough, but . . ."

"But would her therapist agree to talk to us about Veronica?" Rachel said, preempting Rebecca's next thought. "We need Veronica's permission, I suppose."

Rebecca was silent for a beat but then held up a finger. "Wait a

minute," she said, before she trotted off through the swinging doors
and toward her sleeping sister.

A minute or so later, Rebecca returned holding a small cell phone
in her hand. Without saying a word, she gestured for Rachel to follow her outside. Soon the two of them were standing in the cold, wet
night in front of the ER's waiting area, huddled under a small umbrella. Rebecca was frowning at the phone in her hands and jabbing
at its small silver buttons.

"Did you wake Veronica?" Rachel asked, slightly confused. "Did
she give permission?"

Rebecca continued fiddling with the phone and mumbled, "She's
still out of it in there. I didn't want to wake her. It doesn't matter,
though. She'll want us to do this if it saves her from rehab. . . ."

Rebecca trailed off as she held the cell to her ear. After a few beats,
she said into the phone, "Can I speak to Dr. Goldstein?" And, waiting
another beat, she then added, "It's Veronica. Veronica Nilsen."

As Rebecca waited for Dr. Goldstein to come on the line, she
looked up at Rachel and gave a small shrug. From Rebecca's one
small gesture, Rachel could tell this wasn't the first time she'd pretended to be Veronica. Over the years, there'd no doubt been many
times in which Rebecca had used their identical looks and voices to
help her needier sister get out of trouble. Rachel carefully chose not
to say anything. She knew that, at this moment, she should be calling
Lamont Nilsen and telling him what was going on with his daughter.
That was what university protocol told her she must do. At the same
time, though, she knew there must be a better way of dealing with
this situation, and if the therapist had some answers, she wanted to
hear them.

When the doctor finally came on the line, Rebecca spoke to her
only very briefly. In a fake sickly voice, she said, "Dr. Goldstein? I've
gotten myself into some trouble in London." She waited a second
as the doctor made her reply on the other end of the line and then
added, "I'm feeling too yucky to talk about it at the moment, but
would you speak with my professor?"

Before Rachel really knew what was happening, the phone was thrust into her hands.

"What's going on?" demanded Dr. Goldstein into Rachel's ear.

Rachel quickly introduced herself and explained what had happened to Veronica.

"One thing is for sure, Professor," Dr. Goldstein said when Rachel was finished. "Veronica must not go back to Petersburg Rehab. I think it will do a lot more harm than good if she's readmitted. Furthermore, it will undo all the work Veronica and I have done together trying to get her over her many bad experiences there."

Rachel hadn't gotten around to mentioning the rehab issue yet. It seemed that Dr. Goldstein knew her patient and her patient's fears all too well.

"Rebecca . . ." Rachel began to respond, but then corrected herself: "I mean Veronica . . . Veronica doesn't want to tell her father what has happened. She's positive he will send her back there."

"Of course he will," Dr. Goldstein responded. She had a thick Brooklyn accent that was both determined and authoritative, yet at the same also curiously calming and reassuring. Rachel could feel her anxiety about Veronica waning just at the sound of this woman's voice. "Mr. Nilsen is convinced his daughter is an alcoholic and wants his daughter to have the best care an alcoholic can get."

"But you don't agree?" prompted Rachel.

"Not at all. Veronica is not an alcoholic." Dr. Goldstein made a clicking noise with her tongue. "But she does have many emotional immaturities. She's a lonely young woman who isn't dealing well with the media spotlight she's under. She has many issues, yes. But she does not have an alcohol addiction. Veronica is not an addict, and thus Petersburg Rehab is not the right place for her."

"You really think she's lonely?" Rachel asked, a little surprised. She found it hard to imagine that someone as young and pretty and wealthy as Veronica would be lonely.

Dr. Goldstein made another clicking noise. "Most definitely," she said. "Veronica loves being with people. That's what makes her happy.

But it's hard for her to make friends, being Lamont Nilsen's daughter. It's hard for her to make real friends who really, genuinely care about her. She likes to party because it offers, even if only temporarily, the company she craves so much."

Rachel thought for a second and then asked, "So do you have any suggestions, Dr. Goldstein? Where should we go from here?"

"First, we must avoid rehab," Dr. Goldstein shot back. "And if that means avoiding Mr. Nilsen, then so be it. Second, Veronica needs company and love—and lots of it."

"Company and love? How are we going to do that?" Rachel blurted out.

But even as the questions tumbled out of her, an idea began to form in Rachel's mind. Perhaps it wouldn't be so hard to give Veronica what Dr. Goldstein thought she needed.

"I think—" Dr. Goldstein began.

But Rachel cut her off. "Do you think it would help if we moved her to the dorm with the other students? Perhaps we could get a group of students and her sister to watch over her—as well as the staff and faculty, of course. Would that be a good idea?"

"Professor Grey," the therapist barked out, "that's an excellent idea. The more around-the-clock company she can have, the better. When Veronica is feeling stronger, she should also call me once a day and we can conduct our sessions over the phone. We can work on whatever it is that got her in this mess in the first place." Dr. Goldstein paused for a second, clicked her tongue, and added, "You and I should check in once a day too, and we'll talk about Veronica's progress."

Rachel and Dr. Goldstein talked a little while longer about the logistics of this new plan, and when they were finished, Rachel hung up and looked over at Rebecca, who was still huddled under the umbrella beside her. Rachel gave the young student her sister's phone back and told Rebecca to go back inside, out of the rain.

"I'll be there in a minute. I have one more phone call to make," she explained.

Rebecca looked panicked, clearly thinking that Rachel might still call her father.

"No." Rachel shook her head. "I'm not going to call him."

Rebecca's shoulders slumped with relief.

"I have to talk to one of the student advisers and make some arrangements," she said. Rachel then smiled at Rebecca and said in a whisper, "Veronica is going to be fine. We'll make sure she's fine."

"Thank you, Professor Grey," Rebecca responded, as she ducked out from under the umbrella and scampered through the puddles toward the hospital doors.

When Diana got to the hospital, she found Rachel outside the ER's waiting room standing under an umbrella, talking on her cell phone. Diana's first impulse was to keep on walking past her young colleague and into the hospital. But she knew that would be unprofessional, as well as ridiculous. After all, they were both here for the same reason: Veronica Nilsen.

Rachel spotted Diana when Diana was just a few feet away, and immediately she blanched.

"I'd better go," Rachel said to whomever it was she was speaking to.

Diana suspected it was Carson on the phone, and annoyance kicked in her gut. She'd tried not to think too much about the two of them being together. In fact, she hadn't thought about it at all since they were on the plane. Diana wasn't jealous, but the fact of their union still annoyed her. Especially after what had happened earlier tonight. Peter had always been right: Rachel *did* remind Diana of Annabelle, and tonight Annabelle was the last person on earth Diana wanted to be reminded of.

"How is she?" Diana barked out as soon as Rachel closed her phone.

"If you mean Veronica," Rachel snapped back, "she's doing okay. She's over the worst of it. She's now asleep, and the doctors are going to keep her overnight just to be sure."

Diana nodded. "Good," she said.

Although her tone was cool, inside Diana was fraught and guilty. And now, with the news that Veronica was okay, she felt giddy with relief. After her trip to Plath's house and the dreaded phone call to Graham, she'd spent the last few hours wandering the streets of London. She was hungry but she didn't eat. Her feet were sore but she didn't stop to sit down. She just kept walking. Only when it started to rain and her shoes began to get soaked in the deepening puddles did she finally head back to the hotel. Under the door to her room she'd found the hastily scrawled message from Rachel, and on the hotel phone she had four messages from Nadini. Diana didn't even stop to change her shoes. With her heart pounding, she'd headed straight back out in the direction of the hospital, scolding herself all the way about breaking her phone and not being around earlier to receive the messages about Veronica.

"Where is she?" she now asked Rachel.

"In here," Rachel replied, turning to head back into the hospital, and as Diana followed her, she added, "She's still in an ER cubicle. But the doctor said they'll move her up to a ward as soon as they can."

"She'll get a private room, I presume?"

Rachel looked out the corner of her eye. "This is the British health service, Diana. I don't think they have *private* rooms."

"I know a thing or two about the health care system in this country," Diana shot back, her hackles raised by Rachel's sneering tone. "And I know they do have such things as private rooms." She then added, "Veronica cannot be put on a public ward. The last thing any of us want is the British tabloids finding out she is here."

"I'm sure they won't," Rachel responded. Her tone was still feisty, but Diana could tell from the hint of pink on her cheeks that Rachel wasn't sure at all, and clearly hadn't given any thought to the media or Veronica's need for privacy.

The two of them walked back into the waiting room in silence.

Rachel didn't say anything about the bus incident earlier. Diana didn't give an explanation as to why she was so late. They were at a silent and stubborn impasse, neither of them wanting to be the first to explain, neither wanting to be the first to apologize.

"Are you okay?" was Diana's first question when they reached Rebecca.

Rebecca looked worried and red faced, but she nodded and said, "I'm fine." She then added, "Veronica's going to be okay too."

"Have you called your father?" was Diana's second question.

Rebecca immediately looked over at Rachel, and Rachel glanced from Rebecca to Diana.

"We've decided not to call him," Rachel said.

Diana's eyebrows slammed together. "What?"

Rachel and Rebecca exchanged quick glances, and Rachel whispered to Rebecca, "Can I tell Diana some of what you told me earlier? About Veronica?"

Rebecca thought for a second and then slowly nodded. Rachel then turned to Diana and explained about Veronica, her father, and the rehab center she hated so much.

Diana listened, but wasn't convinced. "This is between Veronica and her father," she said when Rachel was finished. "If Veronica does not want to go back to this rehabilitation center, she must tell her father that. In either case, he must be informed about what's happened tonight."

"But he won't listen," Rebecca pleaded.

"I'm sorry, Rebecca; it's university protocol. We must contact your father."

Rebecca and Rachel exchanged glances once again.

"If neither of you is going to make the call," Diana said, feeling a pulse of frustration rising in her chest, "then I will do it."

She then reached for her cell in her purse, only to quickly recall what had happened to it. She winced as she remembered Annabelle's chirpy voice and then the later sound of shattering plastic. How ridiculous had she been to throw her phone in the air like that? What had she been thinking? Not only had she broken an expensive phone, but she'd also missed important calls.

Rachel seized on Diana's momentary silence and started to speak.

"I've just spoken to Veronica's therapist back in New York," she began. "She agrees that we should avoid calling Mr. Nilsen, if we can. She thinks rehab is completely unsuitable for Veronica."

"Does she now?" Diana barked out, her tone dripping with skepticism. "And *who* is this therapist?"

"Dr. Amanda Goldstein," Rebecca whispered.

Diana flinched. She'd heard of Dr. Goldstein. She'd never been to therapy herself—talking to some stranger about private matters, and paying money to do so, just wasn't Diana's style. But, after Graham left, a few concerned friends had pressed their therapists' cards into her hands and told her how she might benefit from seeing them. She never called any of the numbers, of course. But she did remember that Dr. Goldstein's name came up a few times. People seemed to love and respect her.

"What else did Dr. Goldstein say?" Diana asked finally; her tone was still doubtful but now slightly curious too.

"She thinks Veronica would fare a lot better if she is watched over by her sister and her peers and by us," Rachel responded.

"I don't know—" Diana began.

Rachel cut across her, however. "Dr. Goldstein thinks it would be a good idea if Veronica moved into the dorms with the other students for the rest of the trip. That way everyone will be able to keep a watch on Veronica, not just Rebecca. We can organize regular check-ins and round-the-clock company, just to be sure she's doing okay. Plus, Dr. Goldstein will talk to Veronica every day on the phone."

"Putting Veronica amongst twenty other partying undergrads is hardly a good solution for her drinking problem," Diana said, shaking her head.

"According to her therapist, her drinking is a symptom of her loneliness," Rachel countered.

Diana was about to respond when Rebecca spoke up.

"I like this idea," she said with a small smile. "I really do. Daddy was the one who insisted we stay in the hotel in the first place. Veronica and I would do just fine in the dorms."

Diana looked from Rebecca to Rachel and back again. "Even if we were to do this," she said, her voice still pierced with uncertainty, "what happens when Veronica goes home? She's not going to have a gang of happy students watching over her then."

"Maybe she will," responded Rachel. "Perhaps she'll make some friends while she's here. And even if she doesn't, she'll be able to see Dr. Goldstein every day, and she can work on whatever it was that made her so upset. In any case, she'll be in a stronger, better place to deal with her father by the time she gets home." Rachel flicked a glance at Rebecca. "From what Rebecca has told me about Mr. Nilsen, he can be very insistent."

Rebecca was nodding. "He is. Veronica has no chance against him now. She'll be groggy and weak and he'll ship her right back to that place."

Diana thought for a few minutes. She was beginning to think they might have a point. Perhaps Veronica would be better off without her father's intervention. And if the much respected Dr. Goldstein believed this was a good idea, then perhaps it was. But it seemed a very risky route to take. What if Veronica went out and did this again in a few days? What then? As well as the trauma to Veronica, it wouldn't be good for Diana or Rachel. Manhattan U would come down hard on them for not calling the family in the first place. They might even get fired. They *would* get fired, in fact, and the last thing Diana needed right now was to get fired.

"But it is Manhattan U protocol to call a student's parents. I'm not happy about going against protocol," Diana said finally.

Rachel shook her head. "Protocol says we should call next of kin, which we did," she said, as she waved toward Rebecca.

Diana lifted one eyebrow doubtfully.

"Plus," Rachel continued, "they're going to want to know why we didn't call Lamont Nilsen nearly four hours ago, when Veronica was first brought in."

As she said this, Rachel glared hard at Diana. Diana knew exactly what she was getting at. She was implying that, sooner or later, Manhattan U would want to know where she'd been all the time one of their students was in the emergency room. Diana's excuse of a broken phone and being left behind at a theater by Rachel would no doubt sound lame, whiny, and as if she were trying to pass blame onto a younger and more inexperienced colleague. Diana hadn't been here, no one could reach her, and she didn't really have a decent excuse. Manhattan U would not be happy.

"We won't have to answer those kinds of questions if we stick to our story that we took Rebecca to be Veronica's next of kin," Rachel added. She sounded more pleading now than accusing.

Diana knew she was being forced into a corner. Even if this plan had merits for Veronica, there was no doubt it would land Rachel and herself in a lot of trouble.

Nonetheless, she found herself snapping out, "Fine. Do as you please."

Just as the words flew from her mouth, a young female doctor swished across the waiting room and came to a halt beside the three of them.

"Veronica has just woken up." She smiled. "Would you like to come and see her? She's a little groggy, but physically she's fine."

Rebecca went first, and Diana and Rachel followed wordlessly behind. The three of them moved through the swinging doors and then passed a number of cubicles with their green curtains drawn. Machines bleeped and medical staff clacked about on the polished floors. The mood was serious but calm. Finally they got to the last cubicle, and Rebecca pulled back the curtain and led the way in. Veronica lay against a stack of pillows, her face ashen and her hair a straggly mess.

Before anyone spoke, Rebecca and her sister embraced and both of them then sobbed quietly for a few minutes as they held each other tight. Meanwhile, Diana and Rachel lurked to one side of Veronica's hospital bed with their heads bowed, trying to be as invisible as possible.

"Why did you do it, V?" Rebecca kept asking.

"I'm sorry," Veronica repeatedly replied.

When they were finished hugging and crying, they both dried their eyes. Veronica then looked up at her sister and clasped her hands together.

"Daddy doesn't know, does he?" she whispered.

Rebecca shook her head.

"Please don't call him, Becca," Veronica then pleaded. "I can't go back to that place. He'll want me to go there, won't he?"

Rebecca shook her head again. "We won't let that happen, V," she said. Then, with a wave toward Diana and Rachel, she said, "We're going to make sure he doesn't. We're going to take care of you."

For the first time since they'd arrived in the cubicle, Veronica looked over at Diana and Rachel. Her tired eyes struggled to focus for a few seconds, but when they did, she instantly slapped her hand across her mouth.

"No!" she shouted through her fingers. *"No!"*

Frantic gazes darted between Diana, Rachel, and Rebecca.

"What is it, V?" Rebecca asked her sister as she leaned forward and patted her arm. "What's the matter?"

Veronica dropped her hand from her mouth and said in a groggy but still harsh whisper, "Why did you bring her?" Her eyes burned straight at Rachel. "Why did you bring her? Why now?"

Rebecca looked flummoxed, but she said in a soothing tone, "Professor Grey was worried about you, V. She and Professor Monroe came to see how you were doing."

"She stole him," Veronica replied, a sob catching in her throat. "She stole him from me."

"What?" both Rebecca and Rachel replied in startled unison.

"Carson. She stole Carson." Veronica was now sobbing loudly, her small shoulders heaving up and down.

Diana looked over at Rachel. Her eyebrows were knitted and her high forehead furrowed by two deep lines.

"I stole Carson?" she was saying. "What on earth do you mean?"

Rebecca was shaking her head. "Who's Carson?"

"Carson McEvoy," her sister sobbed out.

"That professor guy you had the hots for?" Rebecca asked.

Veronica looked up through her glassy eyes. "I didn't just have the hots for him. We were dating. I—"

"You were dating him?" Rachel asked. Her voice was strangled and tight.

Diana knew it was time to step in. She had a horrible sinking feeling that what Veronica was saying was true. It certainly wouldn't be unheard-of for Carson to be sleeping with a nineteen-year-old under-grad, especially a pretty, rich one like Veronica. Diana had to break up this confrontation now.

"Rachel," she said, waving her hand toward her colleague, "it's probably time we left. Veronica clearly needs to rest some more."

Veronica shuffled up in the bed. "You don't believe me, do you?" she croaked.

Before anyone could answer, she was grabbing for her purse, which had been put on the cabinet next to her bed. She heaved the gaudy purse onto her lap and rifled frantically inside it.

After a few seconds, she looked up, panicked. "Where's my phone?"

Rebecca pulled the cell from her own pocket. "I, um…" She blushed, clearly scrabbling to think how she was going to explain taking the phone when her sister was sleeping.

But Veronica didn't wait for an explanation. She grabbed the phone from Rebecca's hand and then, after a few jabs and punches with shaky fingers, she turned the open phone toward Rachel.

"See for yourself," she barked.

Although Diana was farther from the small screen than Rachel was, the photograph of Veronica snuggled against Carson McEvoy was abundantly clear. Diana heard Rachel let out a small gasp. She peeked over and saw that every trace of color had left Rachel's pretty face.

"Let's go, Rachel," Diana then said. "It's time we left."

Rachel didn't respond. She was still staring wordlessly at the phone, so Diana turned, hoisted her purse up onto her shoulder, and took hold of Rachel's elbow.

"Come on," she coaxed, as she guided Rachel back through the green curtains and out into the hallway.

Eighteen

Past Examinations

Fifteen minutes later, the two women were sitting on a brick wall just outside the hospital. Diana held an umbrella over them while Rachel sniffed and dabbed her eyes with a sodden Kleenex. Just a short while ago, Diana had tried to coax Rachel back to the hotel, but Rachel had simply shaken her head, sniffed, sighed another time, and then buried her head in her hands for a fresh round of sobs. Clutching the umbrella, Diana's hands were beginning to get cold, and she wasn't sure how much longer she could go on sitting here. But she couldn't leave Rachel either. In spite of everything that had happened earlier, in spite of what Rachel had done, leaving her at the theater, Diana couldn't desert her young colleague. Not when she seemed so distraught.

Although Diana couldn't find it in herself to leave, she didn't really know what to say to Rachel either. The tears, the sighs, the sniffing into the Kleenex made Diana feel bad for Rachel. But they made her uncomfortable too. Such open displays of emotion always made Diana feel awkward. And now, especially now, while she herself felt so freshly hurt and betrayed by Graham, having to witness Rachel's tears and pain was almost unbearable.

"Come on, Rachel. It's time we headed back," she said quietly, trying once again to persuade Rachel to start moving toward the warmth and dryness of the hotel.

Rachel didn't seem to hear. Instead, she looked up and studied Diana with her bleary, puffy eyes. After a pause, she said in a trembling whisper, "I'm so dumb. So, so dumb. Why did I let myself get sucked in by him? Why?"

Diana didn't know how to respond. She was in no place to start sharing Carson stories with Rachel. She didn't want to discuss how she herself had almost succumbed to Carson and his charms. Carson was one of the last people she wanted to be thinking about at the moment, and having some kind of heart-to-heart about him with Rachel was definitely something she didn't want to be doing.

Instead, she offered the following brief response.

"Carson is a very attractive and charismatic man, Rachel. Not many women could avoid being lured by him."

Rachel shook her head, her pretty curls bobbing around her wet cheeks. "But we're supposed to be smart women, Diana. We should be able to see through his charming ways. We're not nineteen and naive, like Veronica."

Diana flinched. What she'd just said about Carson was meant to be a detached, impersonal observation. She hadn't meant to imply she was one of those women who were sucked in by Carson—even though, of course, she was. But Rachel was clearly seeing them both in the same boat: both of them Carson dupes. This thought made Diana flinch for a second time. Before she could say anything, however, before she could try to change the subject and entreat Rachel to come back to the hotel, Rachel was talking again.

"Who am I kidding?" Rachel was now looking into the distance, but still shaking her head. "I was ripe for Carson's picking. Lonely and desperate, that was me. Of course I was going to be suckered in. Since Justin there's been no one. I didn't let anyone close because I didn't want to make the same mistakes again."

In spite of herself, Diana found she was curious. "Who's Justin?"

Rachel flipped her gaze toward Diana. Her expression was surprised and a little embarrassed, as if she'd been talking to herself and just discovered someone was listening. "My ex-boyfriend," she explained, after a moment's hesitation.

"I see." Diana nodded.

"We lived together back in North Carolina," Rachel went on. "But we broke up about a year before I moved to New York."

"Ah." Diana didn't know what else to say.

Rachel turned away and continued to talk. It was as if she were speaking more to herself again than to Diana.

"We weren't right for each other. Or at least, over the years we became not right for each other. We grew into different people." She sighed. "But maybe I was too hard on him. Maybe I could have changed and chilled out a little, given him more space. Maybe I should have shown some interest in baseball or something."

As Rachel continued to talk about her ex-boyfriend, considering what went wrong and what she might have done to change things, Diana couldn't help but think of Graham. The detour to the hospital and dealing with Veronica meant she hadn't had to reflect on the phone conversation earlier. But now she could do nothing else. And the more she thought about Graham and the phone call, the more she thought about him and Annabelle. She imagined them sitting in their Berkeley yard, perhaps drinking iced teas under the warm California sun, laughing happily together, not a care in the world. Annabelle, of course, would know nothing about what had happened between Graham and Diana recently. She might have been a little confused by the phone call Diana had made earlier. But Graham was a master liar. He'd proved that to Diana five years ago, and he'd just proved it to her again. After some slick excuses from Graham, no doubt Annabelle would be happily cooing over her handsome and esteemed professor completely unaware of all his deceptions.

Diana never thought she'd feel sorry for Annabelle, but now, as she sat on the cold stone wall on this drizzling English night, she did. This pity for Annabelle, combined with her own humiliation, disgust, and sadness, made her feel suddenly weak and breathless. The familiar knotting feeling in her stomach had returned with a wrench, and now her chest—her heart?—ached too.

"I'm sorry," Rachel was now saying, having finished her monologue. "I've been blathering on. You don't want to hear all this."

Diana was scared at first to reply. She wasn't sure she had the breath or energy to speak. However, after a pause, she found herself saying, "Don't blame yourself, Rachel. Take it from me: You don't want to add blaming yourself to all the other sadness and pain you feel after a relationship has failed."

Rachel looked up at Diana, her eyebrows gathered in confusion. She then scanned Diana's face again and began to ask, "Was that man at the airport—"

Diana cut her off. "He was my ex-husband. We divorced a while ago."

"Oh," Rachel said. "I'm sorry. I didn't realize. I thought . . ." She then trailed off and turned her gaze back to the street.

Diana let out a small sigh of relief. Perhaps, finally, this whole wet and awkward exchange was about to end. But just as she was pulling herself upright, getting ready to stand, Rachel turned back to her again.

"So what happened with you and Mikey?" she asked, as she dabbed her nose with the Kleenex.

Once again, Diana flinched. Then in a tight voice she replied, "That's all history too."

Rachel shook her head and blurted out, "The way Mikey looked at you . . ." She paused and shook her head again. "I would give anything for a look like that. I certainly never got that look from Carson."

"What are you talking about?" barked Diana. She hadn't meant it to sound so snappish, but it came out that way nonetheless.

Rachel was clearly taken aback. "I'm sorry. I just meant that Mikey looked at you with such love in his eyes, with such adoration and joy at the very sight of you."

Diana let out a snort of laughter. "You *do* read too many romance novels, don't you?"

As soon as the words were out of Diana's mouth she regretted them. This was no time to be getting into one of their academic spats about the kind of books they liked to read—or the books they disparaged. Luckily, though, a smile broke across Rachel's face. The first smile since they'd left the hospital, in fact.

"Unfortunately," Rachel began, "I don't read enough romance novels these days. All the frivolous academic work keeps sucking up my precious romance-reading time."

Diana smiled too. She was relieved that Rachel had taken her comment well and wasn't going to pick a fight.

"But you know what?" Rachel then went on, pushing back her curls and looking Diana straight in the eye. "As a woman and a feminist, you might not want to dismiss romance novels so easily."

Diana felt a deadweight fall upon her. *Here we go*, she thought. It looked like she was going to have to just sit here, in the cold and pouring rain, and listen to Rachel pontificate about the romance genre. She was too tired and deflated to stop her.

"Heroines in romance novels are no trembling wallflowers, you know. They're never needy or clingy or weak. They don't lie unconscious like Sleeping Beauty or Snow White. They don't jump under trains like Anna Karenina, or swallow arsenic like Madame Bovary, or poison themselves with snake venom like Cleopatra. The heroines of romance fiction are passionate, spirited, smart, feisty, and life-loving." Rachel's eyes were sparkling with excitement now, rather than tears. "And, most important, the men they end up with love them for all their gumption, optimism, quirks, and zest. It's *Pride and Prejudice* replayed over and over—handsome, proud, and upstanding Mr. Darcys pursuing and loving their gutsy and intelligent Elizabeth Bennets."

Diana looked at Rachel for a second and then said in a skeptical tone, "Is that so?"

"What am I doing?" Rachel then said, rolling her eyes and giving a small laugh. "Trying to convince you of the merits of romance novels? I must be mad." She smiled and added, "Perhaps all I'm trying to say is that I would give anything for a Mr. Darcy—or a Mikey, for that matter." She flicked another smile at Diana. "A man who would look at me, all of me, with such love and admiration. A Mr. Darcy who would want me and love me for everything I am."

Diana couldn't help grinning. "I fear your romance novels may have given you impossible dreams, Rachel."

"Maybe so," Rachel conceded. Her shoulders then slumped and she looked forlorn all over again. "Maybe so," she repeated, this time with a sigh.

"Come on," Diana said. "It's time to go."

Diana was too cold and tired for another round of Rachel's heartbreak and sobbing. Gripping the umbrella, she stood up and nodded in the direction of the hotel. She didn't want to talk anymore. She wanted to be back in the hotel, in the darkness of her room, under the bedclothes. Rachel paused for a second, looking up at Diana, but then, after stuffing her Kleenexes into her pockets, she stood up too.

Still sharing the umbrella, the two women began to walk slowly through the puddles and dripping rain. They said nothing, but at some point during their silent walk Rachel slipped her hand through the crook of Diana's arm that held the umbrella. Diana stiffened at first. But as they continued to walk she found that the knots in her stomach and the pain in her chest began to ease just a little as the warmth of Rachel's arm radiated against her own.

Nineteen

Women in Academia

The morning sun was bright, and as Rachel stepped out of the front door of the student dorm, she immediately put on her sunglasses. She was pleased to see something other than rain and heavy gray clouds, but her eyes were tired and sensitive. Over the past six nights they'd done too much crying and staring into the darkness of her hotel room to cope with such merry and startling sunlight. Thank God she'd remembered to bring her sunglasses, she thought, as she looked up and down the London street.

It was eight a.m. and the sidewalks were already packed with people in work suits and long winter jackets. The road too was gridlocked with double-deckers and black cabs revving their engines. It felt weird to see all this activity today. Back home in the U.S. it was Thanksgiving, and although New York wouldn't come to any kind of standstill, it would certainly be a lot quieter than this. And back in her parents' town in Virginia, where Rachel was last Thanksgiving, the only cars on the streets would be the ones shuttling loved ones to family dinners or friends to each other's houses to watch the game.

There were no study-abroad excursions today because of the holiday. The students were being given the day off to celebrate Thanksgiving in whatever way they chose, and the only reason Rachel had been to the dorm this morning was to do one of her daily Veronica check-ins. Six days after getting out of the hospital, Veronica was doing surprisingly well. According to Rebecca and a group of girls who'd offered to help watch out for Veronica at the dorm, she seemed happy and she'd spent most of her evenings in: reading, hanging out, and watching TV with other students. Rachel hadn't seen much of this for herself, of course. Although she was going over to the dorm a few times a day to coordinate the "Veronica watch" and taking turns with Diana to call Dr. Goldstein every evening with updates, Rachel stayed away from Veronica herself. She knew Veronica wouldn't want to see her, and Rachel didn't really want any awkward conversations with Veronica either.

They hadn't avoided each other altogether, however. Diana agreed that they would not call Lamont Nilsen so long as Veronica participated fully in the study-abroad program when she was strong enough. So, over the past couple of days, when she'd begun to feel better, Veronica had joined Rachel, Diana, and the rest of the students on two theater trips, a lecture at University College London, and a literary walk near Hampstead Heath. During these excursions, Rachel had kept at a safe distance and let Diana be the one to interact with Veronica. Rachel had observed Veronica from a distance, though. She noticed more color returning to her cheeks as each day passed, and watched as Veronica began to chat more easily, sometimes animatedly, with her classmates.

Rachel was glad to see these improvements. She wished no ill on Veronica. As far as Rachel was concerned, this whole horrible mess was Carson's fault, not Veronica's. What had a forty-year-old man—a distinguished visiting scholar from Harvard, no less—been doing dating a nineteen-year-old student? Had he no brain? No conscience? No ethics? Clearly not. When Rachel first saw the photograph on Veronica's phone, she couldn't believe it. She didn't want to believe it. But then, as the minutes, the hours, and then the days passed by, she started to put pieces of the puzzle together: Carson's reaction to seeing Veronica at the airport (for it must have been Veronica he was running from, not Diana); the phone call Veronica got that night in the hotel from someone called Mack, which must have been a shortening of McEvoy. And then there were the subtler things, like the fact that when Rachel and Carson had been together in New York he'd refused to talk about people he dated, and if she ever tried to find out such details he would cover her in kisses to end her questions. Now Rachel realized why he'd done that. Veronica probably wasn't the first. He no doubt made a habit of running around after pretty young undergraduates, and it made Rachel feel sick to the bottom of her stomach to think she'd slept with such a man.

As she stood on the side of the busy street, Rachel shook her head. She'd been over this so many times in the last week, she was sick to death of thinking about it all. She was tired of flipping from hatred of Carson to anger at herself for ever getting involved with him in the first place. She was irritated by all his calls to her cell phone. Carson knew that she knew about Veronica; Rachel was sure of it. The day after Veronica's hospitalization, he started to phone her constantly and left a barrage of messages. She didn't answer any of his calls, and she deleted his messages as soon as they flashed up on the screen. Fortunately, though, his persistence seemed to be waning. After the initial slew of calls, she'd been hearing less and less from him, and in the last few days he'd called just a couple times. Yesterday only once.

"Typical," Rachel muttered under her breath, as she began to cross the street.

It didn't surprise her that he wouldn't fight hard to keep her. He was probably after his next piece of tail already and thus had other things—pretty, just-out-of-puberty things—on his mind.

Rachel had reached the opposite side of the road and headed right toward the bookstore on the next block. She planned to spend the long and empty day ahead of her holed up in the bookstore's café working on her new book. Her publisher was eagerly awaiting the first complete draft. If she buried herself in this task, she wouldn't have to think about how lonely she felt and how much she wished she were at home with her mom and dad, basking in their love and smiles and tucking into her mother's familiar and delicious pumpkin pie. Most of all, however, she needed to bury herself in work so she wouldn't have to think about Carson and how angry she was at him, how angry she was at herself, and, if she admitted the truth to herself, how hurt and sad she was that their brief and passionate fling had come to this humiliating, abrupt end.

Ten minutes later, Rachel had secured herself a great spot in the bookstore's café beside a wide window overlooking Gower Street. A steaming cup of coffee stood on the table beside her; her laptop was open, but the file for her book manuscript wasn't. When she'd opened her laptop just a minute ago, she'd wavered between opening the file she was meant to be working on or logging into her e-mail. She knew doing the latter wouldn't be wise. She hadn't checked her e-mail for over a week, and no doubt she would get sucked into the vortex of replying to e-mails and fretting about things she hadn't done and needed to do. If she checked her e-mails, in other words, she wouldn't get to her work for another hour, possibly two.

But Rachel just couldn't find the enthusiasm to start writing, and so in the end she couldn't resist checking to see if she had any interesting messages. Of course, as soon as she opened her e-mail account, she immediately wished she hadn't, because Carson's name winked out at her a number of times from her list of messages. It was clear he'd been trying to contact her by e-mail with the same regularity he'd been trying by phone.

With heavy, thumping fingers on her keyboard, she started to delete his e-mails. But as she reached one of the older ones, her finger slipped, and she accidentally opened the message instead of deleting it.

Veronica was a big mistake. A huge mistake, it read, *But, Rachel, please listen to me. I like you. We were having a lot of fun together before you left for London. Please let's put this behind us and have some more fun. Call me. C.*

In one short message, Carson had answered every question that Rachel had mulled endlessly over during the past week. He'd dated Veronica, probably slept with her, and he knew Rachel knew. Also, just as Rachel had suspected in those restless nights in her hotel room as she cried and thrashed in bed and hid under the covers,

Carson didn't regard their brief fling as anything more than that: a brief fling, a bit of "fun." He had never thought about love or relationships or meeting each other's families, as she had secretly been doing. He'd wanted her purely for the good times.

Rachel continued to stare at the e-mail while her stomach rolled and tears pricked in her eyes. She was furious, and at the same time she was overwhelmed with despair and humiliation. She grabbed for her coffee as she tried to stop a sob from rising in her throat, but the coffee was hot and she scalded her tongue.

"Shit," she said, throwing the paper cup back down on the table.

She didn't have a good grasp on the coffee, and it wobbled and slipped in her hands and sent huge globs of steaming liquid over the table and onto her laptop, and some on her knees.

"Shit, shit, shit," Rachel hissed as she grabbed some napkins and furiously started to dab at her laptop and then her clothes.

"Are you okay?" came a voice beside her.

Rachel looked up. An old lady with neatly pinned white hair, small shining glasses, and a flower-speckled scarf draped around her neck was standing over her holding out a wad of fresh napkins.

"Here, take these," she said in a kind whisper.

In silence, Rachel took the napkins and used them to wipe up the rest of the mess.

"I did the very same thing only last week," the woman was now saying, as she sat down in a seat near Rachel's. From the open book and half-drunk cup of tea on the table in front of her, it was clear the woman had been sitting there for a while, but Rachel hadn't even noticed. "I stained my favorite skirt and did untold damage to the carpet in here," she added with a chuckle.

Rachel smiled weakly at the woman. The woman smiled back—a wide, twinkly-eyed, and kind smile—and all of a sudden Rachel found she was crying. She couldn't stop herself. Her shoulders heaved up and down and big tears streamed down her cheeks and plopped onto her pants.

"Oh, dear," she heard the woman saying.

Then, through her bleary eyes, Rachel saw the woman stand up and shuffle her chair closer. As she sat down, she put one small, age-worn hand on Rachel's arm.

"What is it?" she asked in a whisper. "You have a lot on your mind, don't you? When I came in and saw you there, staring so hard at your computer, I just knew you must have a lot on your mind."

The woman's kind tone set off a fresh round of sobs from Rachel. The old woman sat patiently beside her, patting her arm and handing over yet more napkins for Rachel to dab her tears. When it seemed like she'd cried all she could possibly cry, Rachel looked over at the woman.

"I'm sorry," she croaked.

The woman tapped Rachel's arm again. "Don't be."

"It's just . . ." Rachel began, "there's this guy." She then stopped herself. What was she doing? She couldn't pour her heart out to this stranger; this sweet old lady with her snowy white hair and floral scarf.

"Carry on, dear," coaxed the woman. "Get whatever it is off your chest. You've heard the old expression about 'the company of strangers.' Well, you're looking at your stranger, with her sympathetic and listening ear." She smiled again and tapped her ear.

Before she knew it, Rachel was telling the woman everything. She told her about Carson, from the day he first showed up in the faculty meeting to the day he knocked on her office door after her run-in with Diana. She told her about their ensuing affair—leaving out the more intimate details, of course. Finally, she told the woman about Veronica, the night in the hospital, and now this, the awful e-mail. Rachel even turned the laptop toward her new companion so she could read the message for herself.

The woman peered at the screen through her small glasses, and when she was finished reading she shook her head, made a couple of disapproving clicking noises with her tongue, and said, "What a silly, silly man. Fancy letting himself get involved with a girl so young. And a student to boot!" She then turned to look at Rachel and, with a serious and unflinching gaze, she went on: "You are very lucky. You found out in time. You won't end up being hindered by such an ignorant and silly man."

"But he's a professor at Harvard," Rachel found herself blabbing out.

The woman laughed and waved a hand. "Those men are often the silliest of all. They might have all kind of degrees from prominent universities and hundreds of books with their names on them, but it doesn't mean a thing. Professors like this one"—she tapped the computer—"they're often the silliest of men. No common sense, and certainly no decency or morality. Take it from me; I know."

"You do?" Rachel asked, still dabbing at her blotchy cheeks.

"I was a professor at the London School of Economics for forty years," she said.

Rachel's mouth dropped open. "You were?"

She couldn't help being surprised. This woman looked nothing like what she thought a retired professor would look like. There was something so sweet and homely and kind about her. Rachel imagined her working in a tea shop in a quaint English village, or spinning wool on a Scottish Highland, not lecturing to hundreds of students at the prestigious London School of Economics.

The woman was clearly pleased by the surprise she'd caused. "Yes," she went on, "and I was the first female professor in my department. The first one ever," she added with a small wiggle of pride.

"Wow," was all Rachel could say at first. But when she found her tongue, she asked, "Which department?"

"International relations," the woman said. She then nodded at Rachel's laptop and said, "So, yes, I know a thing or two about such characters. Even back in my day, there were too many professors who couldn't keep their you-know-what in their trousers." She grinned at Rachel. "I even got stupidly involved with one or two myself. But I was lucky like you: I realized in time and left the silly gooses behind me and concentrated on my scholarship and teaching instead." She paused for a moment and asked, "What's your name, dear?"

"Rachel," Rachel replied. "Rachel Grey."

"Well, Rachel, my advice to you is to forget this man and thank your lucky stars you're rid of him. Fate will serve up the punishment he deserves, and in the meantime, you can enjoy the bright future in academia that awaits you. And"—she waggled her eyebrows—"along the road I'm sure you'll find yourself a nice, decent, and clever man, just like I eventually did, who appreciates just how smart and wonderful you are."

Rachel was now frowning and shaking her head. "I doubt it," she muttered.

"Doubt what?" the woman demanded.

"For one, I doubt some bright future in academia awaits me. I've had a terrible first semester at Manhattan U. I bore my students. My colleagues don't respect me. I suspect some of them hate me. I can't even seem to get to work on my next book. I'm a hopeless professor," she concluded with a distraught pout. "A failure."

"Stop right there, Rachel," said the woman, raising her hand and staring hard at Rachel. "You are not hopeless or a failure. Never, *ever* underestimate yourself in such a way." Rachel opened her mouth to say something, but the woman went on: "You do realize, don't you, that you're already more successful than nearly everyone else in the world of academe? You are on faculty at Manhattan U, one of the most respected and preeminent universities in the world. It sounds like you've already written a book, is that right?"

Rachel nodded wordlessly.

"On top of that, you are a woman. For a man to get a job at a university like yours, the wind blows favorably behind his sails. But for women, even today, the wind is against you. It batters and tugs at your sails. How many women are there in your department?" she asked.

"Four," Rachel replied.

"And how many men?"

"Over twenty."

"You see," the woman barked out. She then waggled her finger at Rachel and continued, "So don't call yourself a failure, young lady.

You've already succeeded in an extraordinary way where many, *many* people haven't. And I know it isn't going to be easy sailing from here, but I have a feeling you are going to do just fine. More than fine, in fact. I can tell you have passion here." She patted Rachel just below her collarbone with an open palm. "Your passion and your sense will make you a great, wise, and much-loved professor. Mark my words."

Rachel blushed. No one had talked so generously to her in months, perhaps years. "I hope so," she said in a meek whisper.

"And you know what?" the woman added, with a nudge and another grin. "A beautiful girl like you? You'll get yourself a good man one of these days. I just know it."

Rachel was on the verge of tears again. The woman's kindness touched her to the bone. But as she felt her eyes pricking, the woman looked at her watch, frowned, and then scrambled to her feet.

"Oh, bother," she muttered, as she gathered up her purse and book from the nearby table, "I'm late."

"Oh. I'm sorr—" Rachel began to say.

"Not your fault." The woman waved her hand. "I'm always running late these days. I tell you, if you think life as a professor is busy, wait until you retire!" She then pushed her leather purse into the crook of her arm, smiled a last wide smile, and said, "Remember, Rachel: Never underestimate yourself."

With that, she was gone. Rachel didn't even get a chance to say good-bye, let alone ask the woman's name.

For the next five minutes, Rachel stared into space. With the woman gone, she felt even lonelier than she had before. At the same time, though, Rachel felt as if something had shifted inside her; as if the heavy weight she'd been carrying on her shoulders all week had finally lifted a little. Rachel didn't really believe what the woman said, of course. She couldn't see any bright future awaiting her. Nevertheless, the woman had been so sweet and kind and encouraging, Rachel's spirits couldn't help but lift. At least for a while.

Rachel turned back to her laptop and finished deleting Carson's e-mails. The woman was right about one thing: She must just forget

Carson. He *was* a silly, silly man, and if she kept telling herself that, one day she would really believe it. When Rachel deleted every last one of his messages, she scanned the rest of her e-mail list and noticed one from her friend Kat entitled, "New York sucks. This one is for you!" In the body of the message, Kat wrote, *Please apply for this and come back to the place where you belong.* Underneath, she'd pasted a link to *The Chronicle of Higher Education's* Web site.

Rachel immediately clicked on the link and found herself staring at an advertisement for a job at Duke University. The ad read, *The department of English and comparative literature invites applications for a tenure-track appointment as assistant professor.* Rachel kept reading and sucked in a surprised breath when she saw the lines, *The successful applicant will teach seminars in contemporary and popular fiction, as well as gender and feminism. It would be advantageous, although not essential, if applicants could also contribute to teaching in the following areas: women's writing through history, film adaptations, cultural studies.*

In the tight academic job market, Rachel was shocked to see a job that so exactly matched her skills and expertise. They were looking for her, it seemed. How many other people could cover all the bases they were asking for? Popular fiction, cultural studies, women's writing through history? Rachel felt a pulse of anticipation in her chest. Should she apply? Perhaps she should. After all, Manhattan U and her life in New York were turning out to be disasters. It was nothing like how she dreamed it would be when she was back in North Carolina and yearning to get out from under the Justin memories and away from small-town life. She thought New York and a job at one of the country's most esteemed English departments would be everything she ever wanted. But it wasn't, of course. Just as she'd told the woman earlier, her first semester had sucked, and now this whole Carson debacle was just going to make everything even worse and more humiliating.

Applying for the job at Duke wouldn't be underestimating herself, Rachel told herself as the old woman's parting words flashed back into her mind. Duke was a great school, and this job had her name all over it. She could be damned good in this position, instead of crappy, like she was in her current one. Besides, it looked like she'd been hasty in her desire to get to New York. Life in North Carolina wasn't so bad by comparison. If she got this job, she could have a big house and a yard again. She wouldn't be cooped up in a ridiculously small apartment. Her mom and dad would be just a few hours' drive away once again. She wouldn't be friendless either. She'd be near Kat, and perhaps the two of them could even be roommates. They could find a place somewhere between Durham, where Rachel would teach if she got the job, and Chapel Hill, where Kat was still a grad student. They could party like they used to, and Rachel could cook for all their friends. Sure, she might run into Justin from time to time, but would that be so bad? Maybe it would be worth trying to patch things up with him. He was no Carson, after all. He'd never treated her badly or humiliated her.

Rachel started to smile as she looked once more at the job advertisement. Of course, the best thing of all about applying for this job was that she could forget that Carson McEvoy, Veronica Nilsen, and her sea of bored students at Manhattan U ever existed. She was going to apply, she quickly decided. This was what she must do. She needed a new job, but she also needed her old life back—her old life where she felt comfortable and at home and surrounded by people who appreciated her. With this thought in mind, Rachel minimized the ad on the laptop's screen and called up a blank Word file. She titled the file "Duke Job," and then sat back, chewed on a cuticle on her right index finger, and mulled over what her cover letter might say.

After a minute or so, no immediate thoughts came to mind, and so Rachel's eyes drifted from the blank screen up to the bookstore. Since she'd arrived, the place had filled up considerably. Shoppers idled in front of the nearby bookshelves, and a long line of people were waiting to buy their morning coffees. Nearly every table in the bookstore's café was now occupied. Rachel was about to return her gaze to her laptop when she did a small double take. About ten feet away, obscured slightly by a large potted plant, Rachel spotted a jacket and scarf she knew all too well. They were draped on the back of one of the café's wooden chairs. Without really thinking, she leaned out on her own chair to get a better view. She immediately wished she hadn't, because in the next second, she was face-to-face with Diana.

There was no avoiding it. They'd both seen each other, and it would be absurd not to acknowledge each other. Rachel gave an awkward nod and wave, and Diana repeated the gestures. Rachel then noticed Diana blush (something she'd never seen before) and shuffle some books from her table down to the chair beside her. Rachel looked away before Diana could see her watching.

Rachel and Diana, of course, had seen each other every day for the past week. They'd discussed Veronica, talked about the logistics of the study-abroad excursions, and they'd gone to the hospital together again when another student tripped and split her knee. But in spite of these interactions, things still weren't exactly easy between them. They conducted all their exchanges in polite but slightly awkward tones. Rachel had no idea how things stood between them or whether Diana was still angry. Neither of them mentioned the day at the Globe Theatre. Neither of them talked about Diana's lateness that night in the hospital. Neither of them brought up the conversation they'd had under the umbrella, against the cold wall, after leaving Veronica. Rachel cringed a little every time she thought about how she'd babbled on to Diana about Carson and Justin. At the time, she couldn't stop herself. But now Rachel regretted trying to engage Diana in an intimate conversation that she clearly didn't want to have. And why, oh, why had she topped it all off by jabbering on about romance novels and suggesting that Mikey was some modern-day Mr. Darcy? She could be such an idiot at times.

Today, with Diana so close by, Rachel was completely unable to concentrate. To make matters worse, her coffee had run its course and she was now needing to go to the restroom. But going to the restroom meant passing right by Diana, and that was something she definitely wanted to avoid. However, as her bladder began to ache, she shook her head and muttered, "This is ridiculous." It was time to stop being such a coward, she told herself. She had to get over her fear of this woman. Besides, if she applied and got this job at Duke, she'd never have to think about or deal with Diana Monroe ever again.

She took a deep breath, pushed back her chair, and stood up. She then moved in Diana's direction, and as she got close to her colleague's table Rachel gathered her mouth into the polite smile she'd been using all week to greet Diana. As expected, Diana looked up just at the moment Rachel was about to pass.

"Hi," Rachel blurted out.

Diana blushed an even deeper pink than she had earlier and slapped the book she was reading down onto the table.

"Hello, Rachel," she then murmured.

Rachel found herself faltering beside the table and saying, "Happy Thanksgiving, by the way."

"And to you," Diana replied, looking pained. Her hands continued to push down hard on the open book in front of her.

Rachel was about to leave when she caught a glimpse of the books that Diana had placed on the chair beside her. They were all Harlequin romances—all six or seven of them. Rachel's eyes then slipped back to the book on Diana's table, which, now that Rachel thought about it, Diana appeared to be trying to hide. By the size and shape, it looked like another Harlequin. Rachel's eyebrows shot up, and she automatically opened her mouth to say something, but then caught the icy stare Diana was casting her way. *Don't say a word*, Diana's eyes seemed to demand. *Not a word*.

"O-okay, well," Rachel stammered, "see you later."

"Yes," was Diana's curt response.

Perhaps she should escape now, was Diana's first thought as Rachel walked away. It didn't look like Rachel was leaving the bookstore; her coat and computer were still on her table by the window. She'd probably gone to the bathroom or off to find a book. Either way, she'd be back in a few minutes, and no doubt she would pluck up the courage to ask about the books Diana was reading. Diana had managed to head off the questions just a moment ago, but Rachel seemed pluckier these days. At the British Library last week, when they'd sparred over Plath, Rachel had seemed stronger and more resolute than before. Finding Diana reading Harlequin romances would understandably pique Rachel's interest, and she was sure to ask Diana what she was doing.

And what on earth *was* Diana doing? The question would shoot through Diana's mind every time she turned a page of *Love Everlasting*. Although so far she hadn't managed to answer the question, because with each new page her eyes would speed voraciously onward, and her eagerness to know what was going to happen next would overtake any soul-searching about what she was doing with these books in the first place. Diana had been sitting with this book for only an hour, and already she was nearly two-thirds of the way through. She'd always been a fast reader, but this was a record.

Diana had come to the bookstore with the intention of working on her new book. She had her laptop in her bag together with three library books and a clutch of her own typewritten notes. She'd planned to bury herself in her writing. But for some inexplicable reason, on the way into the bookstore today she'd taken a right turn in the fiction section and scooted toward the romance shelves. The conversation she'd had with Rachel the other night, against the cold wet wall, lurked in the back of her mind. But she hadn't really been consciously thinking about Rachel's defense of romance when she shuffled five or six Harlequin classics into her arms. Nonetheless, she'd done it anyway, and now she couldn't put *Love Everlasting* down.

There was one good outcome to all this, at least. Buried in the book, she'd so far managed to avoid thinking about the trip to her parents' house later this afternoon. They'd called her last night at the hotel and told her that all the preparations were in place for the Thanksgiving meal they would be preparing for her. They sounded happy and excited, anticipating their daughter's arrival home. Although her mother was fretting a little too.

"They didn't have any cranberries," she'd said, her voice whispery and anxious. "I went to Pete's fruit and veg shop on the High Street. I even went to the new superstore on Essex Road, but I couldn't find one. Will Thanksgiving dinner be right without fresh cranberry sauce?" she then asked.

"It doesn't matter, Mum," Diana replied. "Remember, Thanksgiving is a pretty new thing for me too. I don't really care."

"But what about Graham?" her mother then asked. "Will he mind? About the cranberry sauce, I mean."

Diana had stiffened at the sound of his name, and then after swallowing hard, she said, "He won't mind."

Of course, she should have told them then and there, on the phone. But she just couldn't, which meant today she would have to endure their disappointed faces as they opened their front door and saw her standing alone on the doorstep. Then she'd have to spin a web of lies about why Graham wasn't with her. Today, she'd already decided, was definitely not the day to tell her parents about the divorce or about Graham's betrayal—his many betrayals. Diana hadn't seen her parents in too many years. Their reunion had to be a happy one and not one filled with her own sad story—and a story that was sure to upset and disappoint them.

Coming to the bookstore this morning to write, Diana planned to shut out these worries. She'd also hoped that working on her manuscript would stop her mind from wandering back to Graham. All week, since making the phone call and hearing Annabelle's chirpy voice on the other end of the line, Diana hadn't stopped. When she wasn't on excursions with the students or checking in to see how Veronica Nilsen was doing, she was pounding away on her laptop or doggedly rereading academic tomes on Plath from cover to cover. She'd kept herself constantly on the go so she wouldn't have to think about Graham. She was successful, for the most part. But she couldn't avoid the messages he was leaving on the hotel phone, which, at the first sound of his voice, she would delete. And at night, alone in the darkness, she'd see his face as he'd waited for her that night outside her apartment—that night she'd stupidly allowed him back into her life. She'd hear his whispered promises as they'd lain in her bed together. She'd remember his hand squeezing her knee in the taxi to the airport when he'd told her he would join her soon in London.

During these moments, Diana didn't really feel sad. She didn't even feel betrayed. Mostly she felt angry—angry at herself. She'd so easily allowed him back into her life, and she was furious with herself for doing so. All those promises about leaving Annabelle and coming to London were empty, of course. He'd never intended to do any of those things, and she'd been idiotic to think, even for a moment, that he would. She had no idea what Graham had wanted, coming back into her life like he had. Perhaps it was the sex (not that they had had a whole lot). Perhaps it was just the perverse pleasure of winning her back after all that had happened. Or perhaps his plan had been more sinister. Had he wanted the apartment back and hoped that wooing Diana again would secure it? Whatever it was, Diana had been a first-class fool to be duped so easily. She might have two PhDs and a tenured professorship at Manhattan U, but she clearly had no sense, no brain, and certainly no dignity.

"You should try this one."

Rachel's voice cut into Diana's thoughts. Diana looked up to see Rachel standing beside her table, holding a fresh cup of coffee in one hand and proffering a book in her other.

"I haven't read it in years, but it was always a favorite of mine," Rachel went on.

The book was another Harlequin, and Diana's eyes immediately narrowed. Rachel was clearly making fun of her. Either that or she was gloating. Rachel had waxed lyrical about romance novels the other night, and no doubt she was assuming her ode to romance had won Diana over. It hadn't. Or at least, Diana didn't think it had.

"I'm serious," Rachel said, giving a defensive wave. "I love this book and thought you might want to try it."

Diana said nothing for a second and studied Rachel's face. There was a hint of pink on Rachel's cheeks and an uncertain tightness in her lips. Yet her gaze was firm. She wasn't trying to make fun of Diana or taunt her; Diana could see that now. Rachel was, in fact, scared—scared but also resolute. She was fearful about what she was doing but she was doing it anyway. Rachel was presenting this book to Diana as a peace offering, as a way to try to move past all that had happened between them, all the arguments they'd had and the resentments that had built up between them. Rachel was holding out an olive branch, and Diana knew she must accept it.

"Thank you, Rachel." Diana smiled as she reached up, took the book, and studied the cover. *Passion Becomes Her*, read the title. "I'll add it to my pile," she said, waving toward the stack of other books on the chair beside her.

Rachel smiled, and a flash of relief streaked its way across her face. As she began to move off, she whispered, "Happy reading, Diana."

Diana watched Rachel head back to her own table. She studied her honey curls, her tall, curvy frame, and her bouncy, vivacious stride. For the first time Diana realized how shortsighted she'd been to compare Rachel to Annabelle. There were resemblances, of course—the hair, the eyes, the youthful faces—yet there was something much more powerful and beautiful in Rachel, something much feistier and stronger. Rachel had proved her strength this week in the way she'd dealt with Veronica. Although news of Veronica's affair with Carson had clearly crushed her, Rachel hadn't let it get in the way of her job or her desire to help Veronica. Rachel worked hard with the study-abroad students; plus she'd made sure Veronica was tended to and watched over around the clock for the last six days. She'd kept a close eye on Rebecca too, and made sure she was having a good time in spite of everything that had happened with her sister. Diana was reluctant to admit it at first, but she could now see that Rachel's decision not to call Lamont Nilsen had been a good one. Everyone, including Diana, could see how well Veronica was doing.

Diana looked from Rachel back down at the book she'd just given her. The cover was typical Harlequin: an illustration of a man and woman clinched together, the man strong and tall, and the woman beautiful but also satisfied and beatific in her lover's embrace. Diana thought of Rachel again. In a way, she was like the character in this book. Rachel was life-loving, passionate, and full of undeniable guts. She might not have found her Darcy yet, but Rachel was a lot like the romance heroines she herself had described.

That night under the umbrella, Diana wasn't convinced by what Rachel said about the genre. Up until now, romance novels for Diana were merely soft porn for desperate housewives. Moreover, such books were poorly written, littered with adverbs, and recycled trite stories about heroines swooning over *devilishly* handsome men. Portrayals of women within their pages were problematic, and the books themselves were bad for women readers—at least, according to the Diana of old.

But now, as she found herself looking down at the book in front of her, Diana realized she'd been hasty in these assumptions. *Love Everlasting* was a tale of a plucky, passionate woman. a woman in need of love, but only from the kind of lover who would respect and deserve her. She would not settle for second-best, hide her passions, or resign herself to a dull and dreary life with a man who didn't truly love her. She wouldn't choose death over life, like so many heroines in literary classics. As Rachel had argued the other night, romance heroines were not Madame Bovary, Anna Karenina, or Cleopatra.

The more Diana thought about this, the more she realized that *Love Everlasting*'s plucky heroine was the perfect antidote to such tragic women in literature, as well as to those tragic female writers like Sylvia Plath or Virginia Woolf whom Diana always revered so much. No wonder women across the world loved romance novels and bought them in droves. In these books they read stories about strong women, good women, smart women who weren't relegated to the sidelines of the story or killed off at the novel's end.

With a jolt of surprise, it then occurred to Diana that the biggest antidote that *Love Everlasting*'s heroine offered was for Diana's own bruised and battered heart. She had been betrayed by a man who'd clearly never fully respected or appreciated her, a man whom a romance heroine would never, ever settle for. Reading this book about a confident, independent woman who wanted it all—her life, her love, the respect of a good man—was a perfect tonic for the hurt she'd endured in the past week—and the hurt she'd endured for the past five years.

Surprisingly, as Diana realized this, she did not fall into a slump or think any more bitter thoughts about Graham. Instead, without really thinking, she got to her feet and moved in quick and purposeful strides toward Rachel. When she reached her colleague's table, she looked down and asked, "Have you got Thanksgiving plans?"

Rachel looked up, stunned. "No," she said after an awkward pause. "No, I don't."

Diana smiled, probably the first genuine smile she'd ever given Rachel, and said, "Would you like to come for dinner at my parents' home?"

Rachel's eyes widened even further and she seemed unable to speak for a good few seconds. Finally she pushed back a curl, blinked, and said, "Sure. That would be great."

Twenty

Thanksgiving Break

"You've pretty much summed up what my PhD adviser, Tally McGuiness, argues in her book *At the Heart of Harlequin*," Rachel pointed out, as the train she and Diana were riding clattered into another station.

"I have?" Diana responded, her eyebrows raised. "I've never read McGuiness's book, although I know of it, of course. Who doesn't?"

Rachel smiled. "It's a fun read. Basically she argues what you just said. In other words, romance fiction is problematic because it repeats old stereotypes about women needing men and the inevitability of marriage." Rachel paused and then went on: "But Professor McGuiness *also* points out that romance fiction challenges patriarchy and the male-centric literary canon. Thus it cannot be naively dismissed as antifeminist or antiwomen."

As Rachel spoke, a bubble of excitement expanded in her chest. She couldn't help it. However weird it was to be sitting on the train next to Diana on the way to meet Diana's parents, she couldn't help feeling animated by this topic. It was especially exciting that her listener, who'd always seemed so scathing about popular fiction, now appeared engaged and interested.

"It's paradoxically progressive, I agree," Diana said, nodding and smiling. "The message of romance novels is so mixed. On the one hand, it lauds getting Mr. Right over everything else. But at the same time, the genre foregrounds women's stories. And, as you yourself pointed out, the heroine's Mr. Right must really be *Mr. Right*. He must love and respect his woman. He mustn't expect her to change or defer to his will."

Rachel nodded and chuckled. "Exactly."

It had been a curious day, and it just seemed to be getting more curious and surprising by the minute. Seeing Diana reading Harlequins in the bookstore was shocking enough, but when Diana came over and invited her for Thanksgiving dinner, Rachel was floored. So floored, in fact, that she found herself agreeing to come.

Although, of course, that wasn't entirely true. It wasn't just the shock that had made Rachel say yes. The thought of a home-cooked Thanksgiving meal was very appealing. Most of all, though, she said yes because she'd come to a new understanding about Diana—an understanding that made her no longer fearful of her colleague, and an understanding that made her see Diana in a very different light. When Rachel spotted Diana in the café trying so desperately to hide the romance books she was reading, she felt something other than the usual dread and unease. But it was only when she passed by a Virginia Woolf display on the way to the bookstore's bathroom that Rachel had realized what this new feeling was. Her eyes had idly scanned the display and landed on a copy of *A Room of One's Own*, and as she took in the familiar slim paperback that contained Woolf's almost eighty-year-old essay, Rachel experienced a rush of understanding and empathy for Diana.

Rachel had read *A Room of One's Own* many times as a student. She loved how Woolf so eloquently pointed out the struggles women faced throughout the ages: the struggle to be heard or to be creative or even simply to be known. Rachel could almost recite by heart some of the passages where Woolf considered what might have happened to an imaginary sister of Shakespeare's. Thinking about this passage, Rachel leaned over, picked up the small book, and thumbed through to find it. There it was:

Meanwhile his extraordinarily gifted sister, let us suppose, remained at home. She was as adventurous, as imaginative, as agog to see the world as he was. But she was not sent to school. She had no chance of learning grammar and logic, let alone of reading Horace and Virgil. She picked up a book now and then, one of her brother's perhaps, and read a few pages. But then her parents came in and told her to mend the stockings or mind the stew and not moon about with books and papers.

Rachel's eyes flicked over Woolf's words and she found herself thinking about what the retired professor had said earlier about the wind pushing against a woman's sails. Rachel then thought about Diana and all the struggles she must have endured to get where she was today, all the compromises she must have made to be such a successful and commanding professor in an academic world that still favored men. Perhaps her failed marriage, which she'd been so reticent to talk to Rachel about the other night, was one of these compromises. Rachel also realized something about Diana's aloofness—the same aloofness that had always scared and disconcerted Rachel so much. For Diana to carve out a room of her own in this man's world of academe, she had built walls around herself—very lofty and sturdy walls. Her aloofness, her steeliness, her composure and poise, they were her walls.

But as Rachel was now discovering on the rumbling train, these walls did not define Diana. Behind them was a person who smiled and chuckled. Behind them Diana was a person who thought deeply and passionately about things. They hid a woman who clearly experienced life keenly, who'd suffered failed relationships, who lived alone and a long way from her family. In short, the walls she'd built up over the years hid a woman who wasn't all that different from Rachel.

"This is us," Diana was now saying, as she nodded toward the window and stood up.

The train was slowing down at another station. Rachel scrabbled to her feet, gathered up her purse and the flowers she'd insisted on buying for Diana's parents, and followed after Diana along the train car. When they stepped out onto the platform and a stiff November

breeze bit at their cheeks, Rachel realized there were still more sur-
prises to come. Rachel had expected to exit the train into some idyllic
English village. She'd imagined Diana growing up in a place with a
quaint redbrick station, surrounded by trees and neighbored by old
thatched cottages with smoke swirling from their chimneys. Instead,
the station was an ugly modern structure made of concrete and steel.
Looming above it were two slate gray apartment buildings with hundreds of dirty windows. There wasn't a tree in sight, and the only
sound was the roaring of trucks and cars from a nearby street.

As they rode in a cab to Diana's childhood home, Rachel looked
out the window, trying not to gawp at what she saw: row upon row of
tiny terraced houses, graffiti covering the walls, teenagers loitering at
street corners, and grass growing in tufts from uneven sidewalks. This
place was poor and forgotten. It was also a town, Rachel realized, that
would be very hard to escape from. Unless, of course, you steeled
yourself and made yourself impervious, determined, and strong, like
Diana had. Rachel peeked out the corner of her eye at Diana, who sat
to her right, looking out the taxi's other window. Her expression was
unreadable. What was it like to come back here? Rachel wondered,
and as she glanced at her colleague another time, she couldn't help
feeling a pulse of respect and awe. This wasn't new for Rachel. Even
before she started at Manhattan U she was in awe of Diana. But now,
as she saw the place from which Diana had come, this respect took
on a whole new shape and color and depth.

Ten minutes later, they stood in front of Diana's childhood home.
It was a tiny terrace just like all the others Rachel had seen from the
cab. Diana's parents opened the door, their eyes shining with excitement. But there was a glimmer of confusion too, and after introduc-
tions were made and Diana and Rachel had been bustled into the
living room, Rachel heard Diana's mother ask, "Is Graham coming?"

"I'm afraid not, Mum," Diana said in a quiet tone.

Her parents exchanged mystified glances, and her mother finally
said, "Oh, I see."

Rachel silently wondered whether Graham was the ex-husband

Diana had briefly mentioned the other night. She also wondered why this ex-husband had seen Diana off at the airport, and why Diana's parents were expecting to see him here for Thanksgiving dinner. Rachel was confused. Diana just didn't seem the kind of woman who would stay on friendly terms with an ex-husband. Rachel knew, however, that this was no time for questions. Plus, the awkward silence that was now hanging over the room was killing her.

"You have a lovely home, Mr. and Mrs. Monroe," Rachel found herself chiming out.

Diana's father reached over and patted her arm. "Call us John and Ava, love. And thank you," he added, nodding around at the small but cozy living room cluttered with photos of Diana on the mantelpiece and porcelain ornaments of animals and children along the windowsill and shelves.

Diana's father was a small man in his seventies with a shining bald head, ruddy cheeks, and bright, twinkling eyes. Rachel liked him immediately. Diana's mother, with her neat white hair, angular frame, and starched floral dress, had a little more of Diana's frostiness. Although in her case, it seemed that it was shyness that made her a little stiff and reserved. It was clear to Rachel that Ava Monroe felt awkward having a stranger in her home.

Rachel knew how to remedy that. She'd lived in the South long enough to know how to be a gracious and convivial guest.

"Ava," she said, beaming over at Diana's mother, "is that pumpkin pie I smell? It must be. It smells delicious—just like my mother's."

A smile cracked Ava's small, sharp face. "It is." She blushed. "Although it's the first time I've made it, and I'm really not sure if it will be as good as what you're used to." She then blushed an even deeper pink and added, "And I was telling Diana I couldn't find fresh cranberries anywhere. I'm afraid there won't be any cranberry sauce with the turkey."

Rachel waved a hand. "Who cares?" She laughed. "I'm over the moon just to be having some home-cooked turkey and perhaps a slice of that pumpkin pie—if I'm lucky!"

Ava smiled again. "You will have a large slice, dear."

Rachel had done it. She grinned and then replied, "Can I come peek at the pie?"

"Of course." Ava chuckled, looking a little bemused at Rachel's request, but also amused and flattered at the same time.

Rachel and Ava headed toward the kitchen, while Diana and her father sat down together on the overstuffed velour couch in the living room. Rachel had done this on purpose, of course. She knew that Diana probably needed some time alone with her parents, and occupying one of them while leaving the other with Diana was the only way she could think to do it. She hated intruding on their family time, especially because, on the train ride here, Diana had told Rachel she hadn't seen her folks for a good few years. When she'd told Rachel this, her eyes were unsettled and mouth downturned. It was clear to Rachel that Diana was sad and guilty about her long absence, and also anxious about seeing them again after all this time.

"It's perfect, Ava, perfect," Rachel exclaimed, as she peeked inside the small gas stove.

She was telling the truth. The pie and the sizzling turkey on the shelf above looked divine, and for the first time in a week—a week of brooding and sadness and knotted insides—Rachel felt ravenous.

"Thank you, Rachel," came Ava's quiet reply.

Rachel looked up from the stove to see Diana's mother rinsing a large clutch of green beans.

"Can I help you?" she asked.

Ava waved her away with a wet hand. "Don't be silly, love."

But Rachel insisted. "I love to cook," she said. "I'm happiest when I cook. Or when I bake or chop or squeeze or grind, for that matter." She chuckled as she spoke.

Ava looked up. Her eyes had the same bemused but also amused twinkle they'd had earlier. "Here," she said, passing Rachel a knife and the green beans. "You chop these. I'll work on the spuds."

Ava produced a small bag of potatoes from a nearby pantry and began washing them. The two women then worked side by side in a comfortable silence, chopping, washing, and peeling. Only when Ava started filling a saucepan with water and plopping in the peeled potatoes did she finally speak.

"I'm so glad you came, Rachel," she murmured. "It's nice to meet a friend of Diana's. She's was always a little bit of a loner as a girl. I used to worry about her." Ava pushed at her neat white bangs with the back of her hand. "But now she has friends like you, and that makes me happy."

Rachel wasn't going to point out the shakiness of the term "friends" when it came to her and Diana. She certainly wasn't going to point out the near hatred they'd harbored for each other in the very recent past. Instead, she said simply, "I'm glad I came too, Ava. Thank you for having me."

As Rachel filled a smaller saucepan with water for the beans, she realized she *was* really glad she came. In this tiny kitchen with its old eggshell blue cabinets, the aging amber linoleum underfoot, and the steamed-up windows, she felt comfortable, at home, safe. Ava's kitchen wasn't so different from the kitchen where, for many years, Rachel had watched her own mother chop, peel, blanch, and bake— the same kitchen where Rachel had learned, at her mother's feet, the joys of cooking. As the water gushed from the faucet, she smiled a brief, contented smile. She missed her own family, but it felt good to be here with Diana's. In this kitchen she felt happy, and everything that had happened with Carson and Veronica, with work and her life, suddenly seemed a million miles away.

Diana hadn't intended to tell her parents about Graham. Not today, anyway. But, as soon as she was left alone with her father, looking into his familiar bright eyes and remembering how he used to comfort her when she'd scraped her knee as a girl or lost a favorite toy, everything flooded out in one long and unexpected monologue. She told him about the divorce; she told him about Annabelle; she told him how bad she felt about lying to him and her mother, for not telling the truth about what had happened. She even told him about Graham's recent but short-lived return. All the while, her father held her knee and squeezed it gently.

She didn't cry as she spoke, but the tears pricked at her eyes, and when she finally finished and her father sucked in a deep breath, shook his head, and said in a sad, tender voice, "Oh, Diana, I'm so sorry," she began to sob. Quiet, slow sobs. Her father took her in his wiry arms, and she cried some more while he patted and smoothed her hair.

"There, there, love," he whispered from time to time. "Let it all out. You'll feel so much better."

Only when they heard footsteps and chattering coming toward the living room did they finally break apart. Diana dabbed at her eyes, but it was too late, and when her mother and Rachel entered the room they noticed her tear-blotched face, and instantly their eyebrows rose. Without missing a beat, however, Rachel stepped forward and switched her gaze to Diana's father.

"Ava's been telling me about your model ships, John." She smiled. "Could I see them?"

Diana's father looked a little confused, but then, understanding his cue, got to his feet and said, "They're out in the shed. Grab your jacket, love. It can get chilly out there."

Diana gave Rachel a quick nod of thanks as the two of them left, and then she turned to her mother. Ava's face was drawn and concerned, and before Diana even opened her mouth, her mother said, "It's Graham, isn't it?"

Diana's mother had always been a little more spiky and reserved than Diana's father. Her hugs weren't gentle or tender like John's. Instead they felt like an urgent pinch or a brusque grab. Yet Ava understood Diana better than anyone. But only now, after all these years, did Diana remember this about her.

"It is," Diana replied with a small nod, and then, just like it had with her father, it all came tumbling out.

Two hours later, Diana, Rachel, John, and Ava were sitting at the dining table, which was squeezed into a small nook between the kitchen and the living room. The turkey had been eaten and cleared away, half a bottle of cheap fizzy wine had been drunk, and they were now making inroads into her mother's pumpkin pie. Rachel was telling a story about her attempt, as a seven-year-old, to cook a pumpkin pie of her own.

"I thought that if you just placed the whole pumpkin on top of the pastry and threw it in the oven, that would be that." She was laughing.

John, Ava, and Diana laughed too.

"What happened?" Ava asked through her chuckles. "Did you really do it?"

Rachel nodded. "Yep. It made a total mess of the oven and ruined the pumpkin my mom had been saving for Thanksgiving. It also took days to chip the very questionable pastry I'd made from the pie dish."

Everyone laughed again, and as they finished eating and then sat back with their bellies full, Rachel told more stories. Diana watched, listened, and smiled. Everything Diana had ever thought about this young colleague of hers was unraveling by the second. There were depths to Rachel she'd never seen before—or never wanted to see. On the train here, when they had discussed romance novels again, Diana had allowed herself to see how smart and eloquent Rachel was, and how deeply and critically her mind worked. Now, in her parents' home, Diana could also see how intuitive and discerning Rachel was. She knew when to give people privacy or when to make them laugh. She knew how to gauge moods and emotions and act appropriately. Diana envied and respected Rachel for this. Diana had spent so many years shutting down her own emotions that she'd closed herself off to the feelings of people around her too. She realized this now as she watched Rachel.

The doorbell chimed, bringing their laughter and Diana's thoughts to an abrupt halt. Diana's mother scrambled to her feet with a blush rising on her cheeks.

"O-oh, my," she stammered, "I completely forgot." She then turned

to Diana. "I hope you don't mind, love, but I bumped into Tracey
Nicholls on the High Street and she said she saw you up in London,
and I thought . . . well, I thought—"

Ava was cut off by another chime of the doorbell.

"I thought it would be nice to invite them over for a drink, and for
you and Tracey to catch up properly."

Diana felt her stomach roll with guilt. She thought about the card
that Tracey had given her last week and how she'd slipped it into her
pocket, knowing she would probably never call. The card was still
there. She'd idly fingered it earlier while she was on the train.

"Of course it's fine," Diana said finally with a smile. "Quick, let
them in. It's cold out there," she added, getting up and hustling her
mother toward the front door.

With Tracey, her husband, and her daughter in the small house,
it suddenly felt like they were in the midst of a packed and raucous
party. Chatter and laughter and the clinking of glasses rang out
from the living room, and in the kitchen, where Ava and Rachel
had escaped to clean up the dinner things, there was more laughter, as well as the clatter of dishes and the sound of running water.
When her mother had suggested that Diana and Tracey would have
a lot to catch up on, Diana had cringed a little inside. But she was
surprised to find that from the moment Tracey entered the house
there was not one single lull in conversation, and even more surprising was how much Diana enjoyed hearing what had happened
to Tracey in the years since they'd last seen each other. She also
found herself enthralled by tales of local kids they'd both once
known.

"Remember Billy Radford?" Tracey asked, as the two of them sat
on the couch sipping the sherry her father had handed out. " 'E's a
brain surgeon now."

"No, he's not!" Diana laughed aloud.

"I'm not kidding ya," Tracey insisted, "Honestly, Di, it's true."

Diana shook her head, still laughing. "Billy Radford? The kid who used to catch mice and then crucify them to planks of wood with a staple gun?"

"The very same." Tracey giggled. "It's true, though. There was a piece about 'im in the *Gazette* just a few weeks ago. 'E works up at the Middlesex Hospital in London."

"His poor patients." Diana shook her head again. "I hope he doesn't treat them like he treated those mice."

When they were through discussing old friends and shared memories, Diana and Tracey sat back on the couch, sipped their drinks, and watched Tracey's husband and daughter dance goofily to some swing music that Diana's dad had just put on the old stereo. Diana smiled as her eyes followed them around. Brian seemed like such a good man and a loving dad. He joked and teased his daughter, nudged her playfully so she would trip and stumble as they danced, yet all the while he looked at Kelly with twinkling and doting eyes. He looked at Tracey in the same way, Diana had noticed. They'd been married nearly twenty years, according to Tracey, but still he adored his wife; it was so clear. Diana flinched as she realized that Graham had never, ever looked at her in that way, not even at their wedding. His gaze always seemed distracted, edgy, constantly looking for something better and more interesting to settle his eyes upon.

"So where's your 'usband, then, Di?" Tracey asked, as if reading Diana's mind. "Did 'e have to stay in America to work?"

Diana was about to spin some lie in response, but then caught herself. "We're divorced," she murmured, and then with a halfhearted laugh, she added, "Our marriage didn't work out as well as yours and Brian's."

"Gawd, I'm sorry." Tracey gasped, slapping her hand to her cheek. "I didn't know. Yer mum didn't say." She then moved her hand from her cheek and placed it on top of Diana's. "You'll find yourself a good bloke one of these days; I know it, Di. You're too lovely not to. Anyhow"—she nudged Diana—"you wouldn't want to be stuck with one like 'im for twenty years." She nodded at her husband and spoke loudly enough for him to hear.

"What you talkin' about, woman?" Brian boomed, wiggling toward her in time to the music. "You can't get enough of me."

He then pulled Tracey to her feet and spun her around in his arms and kissed her cheek. Meanwhile, Kelly, in all her pubescent embarrassment, blushed bright red and muttered, "Euck. Stop it, you two."

Diana laughed at the whole scene. But then, as she watched Brian give his wife that same adoring gaze he'd given her a couple of times since they'd all arrived, Diana flinched once again. This time, though, she flinched because it occurred to her that she *had* been the subject of such a gaze at one time. Rachel had been right—so right. It was Mikey. Mikey used to look at her in that way. His eyes would sparkle with wonder and love and awe when he looked at her, and even if she hadn't consciously realized it, she'd bathed in the warmth and honesty of his gaze.

As all this occurred to Diana, her stomach somersaulted and a tingling feeling traced up and down her spine. She didn't know whether to sob or to laugh aloud. In the end, she simply sat in a stunned and shocked silence while the music played and Tracey and her family continued to giggle and dance.

It was Rachel's voice that finally woke Diana from her daze.

"Diana," she hissed from the doorway.

Diana looked up and saw Rachel beckoning her with a flustered wave. Her cheeks looked pale and her eyes panicked.

"What is it?" Diana asked, as the two of them bustled out of the room and into the small hallway by the front door.

Rachel shook her head. "I just had a call from Nadini."

"Veronica." Diana sighed. "It's Veronica, isn't it?"

Rachel sighed too. "Yep. Apparently, the tabloids got hold of a picture of her when she was drunk last week, before she passed out. Someone in the pub took the picture on a cell phone."

Diana groaned.

"The *Sun* and the *Mirror* newspapers both ran the picture today. One of the headlines says, 'Where're Your Knickers, Nilsen Sisters?'"

Rachel went on: "The photo is apparently quite revealing. A thong and a lot of flesh, according to Nadini."

Diana groaned and buried her face in her hands.

"That's not all," Rachel said in a frantic whisper. "Lamont Nilsen heard about it and is now on his way to London in his private jet. He'll be here by the morning, and apparently he's mad as hell."

Twenty-one

Visiting Scholars' Return

The train was empty when Rachel and Diana rode back to London. The only sounds in the carriage were the rain now pounding on the window, the whiz and clack of the train wheels moving along the track, and their own voices. While they talked in low, concerned tones, Rachel was kneading her ticket, and it was beginning to wilt and crumble between her fretting hands. The closer they got to London the more panicked she felt.

"We need to be calm," Diana told her for the umpteenth time, as she reached over, rescued Rachel's ticket, and placed it in her purse with her own ticket.

Rachel nodded. "I know, I know, but I can't help worrying. I mean, the man is seriously pissed, and he has every right to be. His daughter was hospitalized and he wasn't told about it. Now there are pictures of her splashed all over the British press," she went on, her frown deepening with every word. "He's going to have us hanged, drawn, and quartered. He's going to have *me* hanged, drawn, and quartered," she corrected herself.

Diana sucked in a breath. "Nonsense. For one, we are in this together, Rachel. I agreed that we shouldn't call Lamont Nilsen. It was a joint decision."

"But . . ."

Diana held up a hand and continued: "Second, Veronica has been doing great, thanks to you. Thanks to all of us. We will explain this to Mr. Nilsen and he will see it for himself."

"But what if she's not okay? What if these pictures have sent her over the edge again?"

"Have we heard anything to that effect?" Diana asked, her eyebrows gathering together.

"No." Rachel shook her head. "Nadini said Veronica and Rebecca had stayed close most of the day. They were in the dorm when she called me, having dinner with some of the other girls."

"And everyone has been keeping up the regular check-ins with Veronica, is that right?"

"As far as I know."

"Well," Diana said, pushing her hair from her face with the back of her hand, just as her mother had done when Rachel was in the kitchen with her earlier, "I'm sure she's doing fine. We would have heard if she'd gone out and tried to get messed up again."

Rachel sighed. "I hope so."

The conductor passed through the carriage and collected their tickets. When he was gone, Diana spoke again. "I will call Peter as soon as we get back to the hotel. I'll let him know what's been happening." She looked at Rachel and saw the fresh panic in her eyes. "Don't worry; Peter will be on our side," she tried to assure Rachel. "He'll understand the decisions we made and why we made them. We'll have him talk to Dr. Goldstein. From now on, we just have to be open and honest with everyone. Including Lamont Nilsen."

Rachel was still thinking about Peter. "You don't think he'll just fire us on the spot?" She half laughed, half groaned.

"He won't." Diana gave a small smile. "Even if he wanted to, a chair of a department hasn't got the power to do that. Moreover, Peter likes us and will understand."

"Likes *you*," Rachel pointed out. "He's your friend."

"He likes you too, Rachel. He's been very supportive of you since you started at Manhattan U." A little color flushed Diana's cheeks. "Actually, there's something he wanted you to know before we left for London," she murmured. "And I, well, I kind of forgot to pass the message on."

Rachel's eyebrows shot up. What did Peter want to tell her? She suddenly and unexpectedly thought of him that night when he came to her house for the disastrous party. She remembered him sitting on her couch next to Mikey, his lean legs sprawled in front of him, smiling and sipping his wine. He'd been so witty and kind that night, so fun to hang out with.

"He wanted you to know that your idea for American Lit 101 was approved."

"It was?"

Diana nodded. "They made a few adjustments. But on the whole, the new syllabus is based on your initial ideas."

Rachel felt a rush of excitement and pride. Strangely, though, she also felt a flash of disappointment. Had she been hoping Peter's message would be something different? Something more personal? It seemed like she had.

"But back to Veronica," Diana was now saying. "We should both get over to the dorm first thing in the morning to see her. Hopefully, we can get there before her father does. I think we need to meet him head-on."

"Okay," Rachel responded, feeling the earlier panic returning.

"We'll explain what happened, and hopefully Veronica will testify to how good she is feeling and how well she's been looked after. Everything will be okay."

As Diana said this, Rachel noticed that she was looking out the window behind Rachel rather than looking at Rachel herself. Her gaze was steady, all the earlier blush had left her cheeks, but Rachel could tell Diana was a little worried. And seeing Diana worried made Rachel fret even more.

Later, as they entered the lobby of their hotel, Rachel's and Diana's steps were tired and slow. They were exhausted from their long day. Nevertheless, they were still strategizing about the morning.

"We should be at the dorm by eight," Diana was saying. "I'll give you a buzz at seven so you have time to get ready."

Rachel agreed. "And we can pick up coffees at that place on the corner. I don't know about you, but I'm going to need a cappuccino grande if I'm going to face Lamont Nilsen so early in the morning."

Rachel was chuckling halfheartedly as she said this. But she noticed she was chuckling alone. She turned to look at Diana and found her colleague staring, openmouthed, straight ahead of her. Rachel turned and followed Diana's gaze. In front of a leather two-seater couch on the opposite side of the lobby stood Carson.

Every pulse, every vein, and every muscle in Rachel's body froze at the sight of him. Of course, he still looked as devilishly handsome as he always did: his hair perfectly mussed, his sleepy eyes dark and enticing. His clothes—Diesel jeans and a navy cashmere sweater—were a little rumpled but perfectly put together. Yet, as her eyes glared at him, she felt no attraction for him, no yearning to be with him again. Instead, anger and humiliation burned and sizzled in her stomach. This fury was beginning to rise up to her chest, and she had an irrepressible desire to run over and slap the sorrowful face that was looking back at her.

But just as she began to move in Carson's direction, an arm looped through hers and pulled her back. It was Diana's.

"He's not worth it, Rachel," Diana then whispered in her ear.

Before she knew what was going on, Diana was frog-marching her across the lobby in the exact opposite direction from Carson toward the elevator. Rachel tried to resist at first, but Diana's grip on her arm was too strong.

"Rachel," Carson's voice shouted out.

Rachel flinched with renewed fury at the sound of Carson's voice, but Diana kept them both walking. When they reached the elevator, Diana jabbed at the button and the door opened straightaway. The two women stepped inside.

"Wait up," Carson called, his voice now close behind them.

"She doesn't want to talk to you," Diana called out before Rachel could say anything. "And quite frankly, Carson, I don't want to talk to you either."

Diana didn't wait for a response. She reached forward and held down the door-close button. Meanwhile, Rachel looked on, stunned and momentarily paralyzed. Was she really going to run from Carson like this? Was it really best to follow Diana's lead and simply ignore Carson? Shut him out? But then Rachel remembered the last time she had practiced such aloofness, such icy calm and indifference. It was just last week, back at the British Library in her argument with Diana about Plath, and it hadn't felt good. It didn't feel true to who she was, and it needled inside of her.

The doors were about to close, and Rachel decided it was time to act. She pulled her arm from Diana's and thrust her other arm between the closing doors. They snapped back open to reveal Carson standing just in front of the elevator, a pitiful look drawn across his handsome face. Rachel held back one of the doors with a shaky hand and pointed straight at Carson.

"You," she growled. "You are a piece of shit."

"Rach—" Carson huffed with laughter.

But Rachel cut him off. "You're supposed to be a smart man—a Harvard man. Yet you run around treating women like objects. Objects!" she repeated in a shout. "Did you never take Feminism 101? Don't you know that women have feelings and don't like to be used as playthings? Sex toys?"

Carson tried to speak again, and Rachel could feel Diana tugging on her arm, but she carried on regardless. "I suppose it is okay, kind of, that you treated me in such a way. I mean, I'm a grown woman, aren't I? I consented to do what I did. But Veronica? A nineteen-year-old girl just out of high school? She's so young, not to mention lonely, immature, and already exploited by the media, which always wants a piece of her. She's in no place to figure out when a guy really loves her or just wants to use her." Rachel jabbed her index finger at Carson again. "That's sick, mister, sick!"

Carson stepped forward and waved a hand. "I think you're over-dramatizing this a little, Rachel," he said with his annoying huffing laugh.

"I wonder if Lamont Nilsen will think I'm overdramatizing."

"You wouldn't." Carson blanched a little.

"No." Rachel shook her head. "I wouldn't. But if you think he won't find out about your little indiscretion with his daughter," she hissed, "you're even dumber than I thought."

With that, Rachel let go of the door she'd been holding. She took a wobbly step back and the doors shuddered to a close.

Alone in the elevator, Diana and Rachel turned to face each other. Rachel's cheeks, Diana noticed, were flushed, and her eyes were wild and panicked. Yet her face also bore an enlivened twinkle too. The two women said nothing for a few seconds, and then Diana did something that, up until today, she'd never thought in a million years she would do: She stepped forward and pulled Rachel into a hug. Rachel flinched in shock at first, but very soon she let out a long, slow breath and willingly returned Diana's hug.

"You were amazing," Diana said as they finally, and a little awkwardly, pulled apart.

"You think?" Rachel asked with a playful smile. "You don't think I just sounded like some hysterical teenager?"

Diana simply smiled and shook her head. The elevator then pinged, announcing their floor, and when the doors opened, Rachel and Diana moved out into the hallway. Rachel froze after a few paces, however, and turned to face Diana. Her smile had disappeared.

"What if he follows me up here?" Rachel asked in an urgent whisper.

Diana halted too. But then she shook her head again and muttered, "No. We won't let that happen." Pointing toward her hotel room, she then added, "Come with me."

Once they were both inside her room, Diana darted around the bed and grabbed the hotel phone. She punched zero to call reception.

The receptionist picked up right away. "Hello?"

"This is Professor Monroe in room four-oh-five," Diana responded. Her tone was cool and authoritative. "I wonder if you can help. A reporter from the *Sun* is currently in your lobby. He's trying to gain information about a high-profile student I'm traveling with. He's proving to be quite a nuisance. I would appreciate it if the gentleman . . ." Diana described Carson down to his shoe color. "I would appreciate it if this reporter would not be allowed up to the fourth floor. . . ."

"Don't worry, Professor Monroe," the receptionist cut in. "I'll talk with security and we'll have them escorted from the building immediately." He then paused and added, "Here at Hotel Islington we like to make sure our guests have a restful and trouble-free stay."

Diana couldn't help grinning at the young receptionist's words. "I would be very grateful," she said, suppressing a chuckle. "Thank you."

Rachel was grinning too when Diana got off the phone. "You're a genius."

Diana shook her head. "The Brits lap up the tabloids. Curiously, though, they also hate journalists. It was an easy call."

A quiet moment followed as the two women stood opposite each other across Diana's bed. There was so much both of them could say at this point. But it seemed Rachel didn't want to go there, and Diana didn't either. The two of them were teetering on the edge of a friendship, but they weren't there yet. They weren't quite ready to dissect together everything that had happened this week, or share the heartaches they'd both endured. Maybe, in time, they would. In fact, Diana hoped one day they might. But for now it was too soon and too raw, and all Diana really wanted to do right at this moment was turn out the lights, crawl under the covers, and sleep.

Finally, Rachel headed toward the door and simply said, "Now all we have to do is save our jobs."

"I'm sure we are capable of doing that, don't you think?" Diana responded with a wink.

"Let's hope so," Rachel said as she opened the door, gave a small wave, and slipped out.

With Rachel gone, Diana slumped back on the bed and closed her eyes. She could have easily drifted off to sleep fully clothed and with her teeth unbrushed, but then she remembered the call she had to make to Peter. She sighed to herself, rolled onto her side, and stared at the phone on the bedside table. She had to do this, she told herself. If they were to stand any chance of saving their jobs, she had to get Peter on their side, and she had to do it now, before the confrontation with Lamont Nilsen in the morning.

Just as Diana reached across to pick up the receiver, however, the phone gave out a violent ring, causing her to blink and start. Before really thinking about what she was doing, she snatched it up and muttered, "Hello," into the receiver.

"Diana?"

It was Graham. Diana almost dropped the phone.

"Diana?" Graham's voice came down the crackling line once again.

Diana still couldn't respond. Her shock was now being replaced by stomach-turning regret that she'd picked up the phone. She'd managed to avoid all Graham's calls this last week, and now she'd blown it; now he'd caught her, trapped her into talking to him. Her regret didn't last long, however, as it was then quickly replaced by disgust and outrage at the mere sound of her ex-husband's voice. How dared he call her? How dared he try to speak to her after all he'd done?

"I know you're there, Diana," Graham tried again. "Please talk to me. We have to talk."

With the phone clutched angrily to her ear, Diana sat up. She wanted to scream into the phone. In fact, she wanted to hurl the phone against the wall. But she knew she must remain calm. Remaining calm and aloof was what she did best. But as Diana thought this, she also thought about Rachel and the lambasting Rachel gave Carson. At first, Diana had wanted to stop her young colleague. Such tirades never did any good, Diana thought. Rachel's heated words would simply bounce off Carson and be forgotten in a few days—more likely in a few hours. But then she watched Carson blanch and squirm under Rachel's attack. Diana also sensed Rachel's tension beginning to wane a little as she continued to rage at the man who'd hurt her. Then she'd seen the invigorated look in Rachel's eyes after she was finished. It was as if the confrontation with Carson helped Rachel and eased some of the pain Carson had caused. Perhaps, Diana thought, still clutching the phone, being stoic and dismissive wasn't always the best solution. Perhaps it was time Graham endured the full force of her anger.

"You think you're so smart," she finally said in a whispery growl into the receiver. "But you're not. What you are is a mean, selfish, egotistical, and abusive man."

"What? Abusive? What are you talking about, Diana?" came Graham's incredulous reply. "I never touched you."

"I don't mean physically abusive, you idiot," she responded, her eyes narrowing into slits and her nostrils flaring. "I mean you abuse emotions. You abuse the love people like me stupidly give you. You abuse trust and devotion and dignity."

"Look, Diana—" Graham tried to cut in.

"Stop right there," she hissed.

Graham persisted. "I made a mistake, Di. I'm sorry."

"With whom—me or Annabelle?" Diana shot back. "Did you mistakenly leave me, or did you mistakenly leave Annabelle last month when you wormed your way back into my life?"

"The mistake was leaving *you*, of course. I made a big mistake, Diana. I've told you that. You must believe me."

"No, Graham, I made the mistake," she said, pulling herself upright on the bed and glaring out the window into London's night sky. "I should never, ever have taken you back. Not for a second. I don't know what you were playing at. You probably had some sordid little plan to get me out of your beloved apartment. I have no idea." She shook her head. "And I have no idea why Annabelle answered your phone last week when she wasn't even supposed to be with you—when you said you were leaving her. But you know what?" she snarled. "I don't care. I don't want to know."

"I am going to leave Annabelle, Diana." Graham's tone had now turned whiny, pitiful, pleading. "Everything I said to you in New York is true. It's just that some things came up, and—"

"Good-bye, Graham," Diana interrupted, as she pulled the receiver from her ear, replaced it in its cradle, and then pulled the phone's wire from the wall.

Twenty-two

Student Evaluation

Rachel woke with a start as the phone next to her bed gave two sharp rings. She'd been in a deep sleep, and her body felt like lead as she rolled over, stuck an arm out from the covers, and picked up the receiver.

"Hello?" she croaked.

"This is your wake-up call, madam," a chipper voice called down the line. "It's seven a.m."

With a click, the voice had gone, and Rachel was left staring at the phone. She was groggy and confused. She hadn't told the reception desk to give her a wake-up call. Diana was going to give her a buzz, wasn't she? Wasn't that what she'd said? Rachel pushed back the sheets with her feet and slowly sat up. She then rubbed her tired eyes and yawned. Perhaps Diana had ordered a wake-up call for both of them, she thought. That would make sense.

As Rachel's eyes began to adjust to the morning light, she looked around the room and spotted her bag on the chair near the door. It was upside down, and the papers and books it had contained had spilled to the floor. Her laptop teetered precariously on the edge of the seat. Rachel had dumped her bag there last night, too tired to care what fell out. She'd wanted nothing but her bed—her wide, soft hotel bed with its crisp white sheets. She'd never felt so exhausted.

Reminded of how tired she'd been last night, Rachel was also reminded of what happened yesterday, as well as what lay ahead of her today. Had she really spent the day with Diana's family? she wondered. Had she really yelled at Carson and called him a piece of shit? And as she slowly moved up from her bed toward the bathroom, she considered whether it was really true that, in just a few hours, she would be facing an infuriated Lamont Nilsen. It all seemed like a surreal and crazy dream.

When Rachel got to the bathroom and caught a glimpse of herself in the mirror, she sighed at the sight of her matted curls, puffy eyes, and pasty skin.

"Good morning, Mr. Nilsen," she whispered at her reflection. Then, after a bitter laugh, she went on: "So nice to meet you. What? Me? Oh, yes, I was the one who decided not to call you when your daughter was admitted to the ER. . . ." She trailed off, buried her face in her hands, and groaned.

But then, realizing there was simply no time for fretting or self-pity, Rachel snapped her head up and stared hard into the mirror. She had to sort herself out. If she was to stand any chance explaining herself to Veronica's father, she had to look better than this. A whole lot better.

"Get a move on," she coaxed herself, before turning toward the shower and flicking on the hot water.

And she did get a move on. Before long, Rachel had showered, dried her hair, dabbed on makeup, picked out clothes, and dressed. She'd also decided her first choice of clothes—black jeans and a thick woolen sweater—wasn't formal enough. She then undressed, found a smarter pair of pants and a cream cashmere cardigan in her suitcase, and threw them on. In spite of the indecisions and the to-and-froing to the bathroom to check herself in the mirror, she was in front of Diana's door by a quarter to eight. As she knocked, she felt a little smug being the first to get ready. In spite of the very recent truce with her colleague, she couldn't help thinking of Diana as one of those disciplined, almost masochistic women who rose with the sun and ran five miles before even looking at a pot of coffee, a bowl of cereal, or the morning paper.

Rachel's knock was met with nothing but silence. She wondered

whether Diana could really still be sleeping, but then she remembered her own wake-up call and decided there was no way Diana
could have slept through that. Rachel rapped on the door again, this
time a little louder, and then stepped back and waited. Sill there was
no answer, and Rachel quickly glanced at her wristwatch to check
whether she'd read the time correctly. Seven forty-eight exactly.

"Come on, Diana," she muttered as she reached forward and
knocked for a third time.

When there was still no answer, she stepped in close and listened
at the door. There wasn't a sound. No running water, no hair dryer,
no voice talking on a phone. The unnerving silence prompted a jolt
of panic and confusion to rise up in Rachel's chest. Where was she?
Surely she hadn't gone to find Lamont Nilsen already. They'd agreed
they would face him together. Why wasn't she here?

"Diana?" Rachel called through the door. "Are you there?"

There was no reply. Rachel frowned, and panic once again flowed
through her chest. She was about to shout another time when there
was a rumble and clank beside her in the hallway. Rachel whirled
around to see a chambermaid pushing a cleaning cart in her direction. She stepped back to let the woman pass, but instead the woman
stopped right beside her and gave Rachel a curious stare.

"Can I help you, love?" she asked from behind the mountain of
sheets and cleaning equipment stacked up on her cart.

Rachel replied, "I'm looking for my colleague." She then nodded
toward Diana's door. "But I think she must have left already."

The cleaning woman's gaze followed Rachel's toward the door.
"Whoever was in there," she said, "they've checked out, love. I'm here
to clean."

Rachel shook her head. "No, that can't be right. She hasn't checked
out. We don't leave for another few days."

The woman peered down at a crumpled piece of paper in her
chubby fist. "Four oh five." She nodded. "Yep, says here four-oh-five
checked out at one this morning."

Rachel still thought there must be a mistake.

"See for yourself," the woman said with a huff.

She then used a card attached to her hip by a small metal chain to unlock the door. She paced into the room and beckoned Rachel to join her. Rachel tiptoed in, still anxious that they might be walking in on a sleeping Diana.

"See," the woman was now saying as she waved about the room. "Checked out."

Rachel couldn't believe her eyes. Diana's suitcase had disappeared. All the books Rachel saw stacked on Diana's bedside table only last night were gone. The bed looked as if it hadn't been slept in. The only thing that proved Diana was once in this room was a flyer for the Globe Theatre left on a nearby desk and an old copy of *The New York Times* on the floor by the bed.

"What the . . . ?" Rachel blurted out.

But she didn't finish, because she was running out the door and toward the elevator. She hammered at the call button. The elevator didn't arrive quickly enough for her, however, so she took the stairs. On her way down four flights, her mind raced as fast as her feet. Why had Diana checked out? Could it really be true? Maybe she'd just moved rooms? As Rachel came to the final flight, her heart was hammering in her chest, and she was now thinking about Lamont Nilsen. If this was true, if Diana had gone, did that mean she had to talk to Veronica's father on her own?

Rachel burst into the hotel lobby, puffing and pink cheeked, and trotted speedily over to the reception desk.

"Excuse me," she said to a small man with lethargic eyes, who was wearing the hotel's red blazer. "Can you tell me if the guest in four-oh-five has checked out?"

The man studied her for a few seconds and then forced his sleepy eyes down to the computer screen in front of him. He then slowly tapped on the keyboard, and Rachel bounced impatiently from foot to foot.

"Yes, four-oh-five checked out last night." He finally nodded, not looking up.

"What? How? Why?" Rachel's questions came out like gunfire.

The doleful eyes slowly lifted back up to meet Rachel's again. "Sorry?"

Rachel had to resist the urge to pick up the man and shake him. He was too slow and laconic for the frantic mood she was in.

"I . . ." she began, but then she shook her head and muttered, "It doesn't matter. . . ."

It was clear she wasn't going to find out anything from this man, and so she started to walk away. Perhaps if she went over to the dorm, Nadini would know something. Nadini would assure her Diana was still here. Somewhere.

"Madam," the receptionist's voice called out across the lobby just as she was about to leave through the hotel's revolving doors. She stopped and turned. "Are you Professor Grey?" he asked.

"Yes," she called back.

"I nearly forgot," the man said in his slow monotone. "The guest in four-oh-five left a message for you."

Rachel bounded back toward him. "A message? Where? What does it say?"

The man puttered about behind his desk, shuffling papers, opening drawers, and saying nothing.

"A message? You said there was a message?" Rachel's voice was strangled and urgent.

"I'm just looking," the man mumbled. Then, under a stack of newspapers, he found a small white envelope. "Aha," he exclaimed, holding it up.

Rachel snatched it from his hands and muttered an unconvincing, "Thank you." She then headed off once again, ripping open the envelope as she went and pulling out the piece of paper inside.

Dear Rachel, Diana's short handwritten note began. *I need to get back to New York—urgently. Peter will be arriving tomorrow (Friday night) to take my place. I am sorry to leave so suddenly, but I have no option.* Before signing off, Diana added, *You are strong, Rachel. Remember that.*

Rachel reread the note ten or fifteen times. Each time her fingers would clench harder on the thick white paper. On the last read-through, she began to feel a little dizzy and so headed for some couches opposite the reception desk. She slumped down onto the leather cushions and dropped her head into her hands. The note crumpled against her hot cheek.

"No," she murmured. "No, no, no."

At first, her mind whirled with questions about what might have taken Diana so "urgently" back to the States. But, realizing she was never going to figure this out without more information, her frantic mind moved on to Lamont Nilsen. She *was* going to have to face him on her own, with no steely and authoritative Diana by her side supporting her. How could Diana have done this to her? she wanted to shriek. How? Lamont Nilsen would take one look at fretting and frantic and way too emotional Rachel and rip her apart. And not only would he bawl her out and belittle her, he'd no doubt get her fired by the end of the day.

Rachel shuddered a little and groaned, but, when she finally raised her head and looked over at the revolving door, a thought bubbled up in her mind. Perhaps she should just run. Perhaps she should just avoid the confrontation with Lamont Nilsen and leave. She could check out just as Diana had done, get on the subway to Heathrow, and take the first flight back to New York. She'd get fired, of course. But did that matter? Only yesterday she'd been thinking about applying for another job. Perhaps this would be a fast-track way out of Manhattan U and back to North Carolina—the place where she could be happy and comfortable and surrounded by friends and family again.

But as quickly as this thought had arisen, it just as quickly receded. Rachel knew she couldn't leave now. She might be impulsive and erratic from time to time, but she'd always been a good girl too. *Rachel is dutiful and responsible*, it had once said on one of her high school report cards. There was no way she would leave the students and the study-abroad program now. And after all that had happened, she couldn't leave Veronica. No doubt Veronica would be fearing her father's arrival as much as Rachel was. He'd want her taken back to the rehab place she hated so much, and without anyone to help or defend her, there was probably little Veronica could do to stop him.

With this thought in mind, Rachel got to her feet. She looked at Diana's note one last time and then pushed it into her purse. After smoothing down her pants and patting at her hair, she took a long, slow breath and began to walk out of the hotel. She had to be strong, like Diana believed she was. She *must* be strong. If not for herself, then for Veronica.

She was still convincing herself of this five minutes later as she approached the student dorm. However, as she rounded a corner and saw the main doors ahead, she could feel her nerve beginning to crumble. She'd only ever seen a few photos of Lamont Nilsen in magazines, and only ever heard rumors about his temper. Nonetheless, Rachel found herself imagining Mr. Nilsen up in his daughters' dorm room, barking out orders, demanding they pack their bags, and shrieking to anyone who'd listen that he wanted to talk to the professors in charge. Rachel's knees felt a little weak, and a burn of nausea rose in her chest as she pulled open one of the heavy glass doors and entered the dorm's lobby.

"Professor Grey!"

Rachel froze at the sound of her name. The voice was female, so not Lamont Nilsen's. Nonetheless, the urgency of the shout made her simmering panic increase to a boil. She turned quickly around to see who'd called and spotted Veronica bustling toward her. Rachel knew who it was right away, but couldn't help doing a small double take at the sight of the usually so glamorous and shimmering Veronica wearing a pair of plain blue jeans, running sneakers, and an unadorned soft pink sweater. Her hair was pulled back into a neat ponytail, and she wore not a shred of makeup.

"Professor Grey?" Veronica said again in a strained and urgent voice, as she moved toward Rachel.

Rachel noticed how tired and gray Veronica's young face looked.

Her eyes were red and her lips were drawn in a sharp, tight line. Her countenance seemed grave. As Rachel took this in, it occurred to her for the first time that perhaps Veronica might turn against her. She'd assumed that Veronica would want her help—that she would need Rachel's help to persuade her father against rehab. But Rachel had forgotten the not so small fact that Veronica still hated her. Rachel, in Veronica's eyes, had stolen Carson, the man Veronica thought she loved. And perhaps this would be the perfect moment for Veronica to enact her revenge on Rachel. She could tell her father it was all Rachel's idea not to call him. She might portray herself as the victim of an incompetent and careless professor.

The thought made Rachel's stomach plummet to the floor.

"Veronica," she finally managed to squeak, "how are you?"

"I was just coming to find you. My father is upstairs," Veronica blurted out. "He wants to see you."

Rachel didn't think her stomach could drop any farther. But it did.

"Okay." She nodded, trying to keep her face composed. "I'll head up there right now." She then waved in the direction of the elevator and began to move.

"Wait," Veronica shouted, as her small hand lunged out and grabbed Rachel's forearm with surprising tenacity.

This is it, thought Rachel. *This is when she tells me she's dropped all the blame and recrimination on me. This is when she informs me her father is having me fired.*

"Carson called me," Veronica said, her grip still firm on Rachel's arm.

Rachel's eyebrows knit in confusion. "Sorry?"

"Last week, the night you came to our hotel room," she replied, dropping her hand from Rachel's arm but keeping her gaze leveled on Rachel's face. "It was Carson who called me."

"Oh, I see." Rachel gave a small nod, unnerved and uncertain about where this might be going.

"He apologized about seeing you to the airport." She frowned.

"He said he was sorry that I had to find out that way about you and him." Veronica waved toward Rachel and then over her shoulder at an imaginary Carson.

"I'm sorry about that too," Rachel murmured.

But Veronica didn't seem to be listening. "He also said that I shouldn't take any of it personally. He said that he doesn't *do* serious relationships. Not with me." She paused and gave a hard stare at Rachel. "Not with you either. Not with anyone."

Rachel's chest bubbled with panic once more. So Veronica *was* out for revenge. There was no mistaking the bitterness in her young voice.

"He said it wasn't serious between you guys," Veronica went on, "just like it wasn't serious between us." As she said these last words, her voice cracked a little. Clearly Veronica had thought and hoped there was more to their relationship, just as Rachel had.

Rachel shook her head. "I think we both had our fingers burned by Carson," she whispered, and then she added with a sigh, "And perhaps our hearts got a little burned too."

Veronica glared at Rachel for a second, and Rachel's heart skipped and tripped as she wondered whether she'd said the right thing. But then Veronica blinked and her eyes dropped to the floor. "I hated you at first," she murmured. "But then I realized we were in the same boat. He used us both." Veronica looked back up again, and her gaze had softened. "What you did for me over the last week," she began, "not calling my dad, not sending me home, calling Dr. Goldstein, and getting everyone to look out for me . . ." She trailed off.

Rachel panicked once more. "I thought it was for the best, but—"

"I'm really grateful," Veronica cut in, her voice awkward but firm. "I ended up having a great week. I made friends. Rebecca and I didn't argue once. Dr. Goldstein's been great, listening to me go on and on about everything." Her eyes began to sparkle with tears. "The best thing, though, was not having to go back to that horrible rehab. Not until now, anyway. My dad says I have to go. He wants me there by

Monday morning. I've tried to tell him I'm better, but he won't listen." Veronica's lips were now quivering.

At first, Rachel didn't respond. Veronica's thanks was so unexpected that Rachel needed a second or two to process it. But after those couple of seconds were up, Rachel reached out and touched Veronica's arm. "Let's go and make him listen, shall we?"

Veronica looked at Rachel, her eyes wide and glassy. In the last few minutes she'd been bitter and resolute, followed by mature and thankful. Now Veronica just seemed like a young girl terrified of her father. "I hope he listens to you," she said as the two of them moved off toward the elevator. "He's very stubborn, Professor Grey. He always gets what he wants. Always."

Fear clutched at Rachel's throat, but she tried hard not to let it show. "Everything will be fine," she assured Veronica, thankful she managed to keep her voice steady.

They rode upstairs without saying anything further. Rachel's mind, however, was a riot of doubts, panicked thoughts, and urgent questions. She'd never taken on someone like Lamont Nilsen before. Could she pull it off? Was she really strong enough? Would she buckle the moment he raised his voice? If only Diana were here with them, she thought. A little of Diana's steel and grit and authority would be damn useful right now. There was no way Diana would let this man get the upper hand. She wouldn't allow him to bawl them out, and she certainly wouldn't allow him to get them fired.

The thought of being fired made Rachel twitch and suck in a breath. In that second, she realized she really didn't want to get fired. She wanted to keep her job. Suddenly it was as clear as day: She wanted her job more than anything else in the world. Just like the retired professor said in the bookstore, Rachel had achieved so much getting the position at Manhattan U. She'd studied hard for years, she'd always dreamed of a life in New York, she'd written a great book that had been reviewed in *The New York Times* and that had gotten her invited onto *Oprah*, and she'd landed herself a job at one of the best schools in the country. She couldn't lose it all now. She couldn't throw it all in because of some bullheaded father.

As the elevator's door swung open and Veronica led the way down the hallway, Rachel pulled her spine straighter and raised her chin a little higher with each step. *This* was the time to employ a little of Diana's poise and composure and steeliness, she told herself. She must not let this man bully or shout. She must be strong and firm. Veronica would not go back to rehab and Rachel would not lose her job. She wouldn't let it happen.

Veronica pushed the door of her dorm room open to reveal her father standing inside, flanked by what looked like two bodyguards. The bodyguards were big men, but Lamont Nilsen was even bigger. He dwarfed the small room with his towering and burly frame. Under a shock of white hair, his deep blue eyes were narrowed and glistening with anger. He said nothing to Veronica and simply glared at Rachel.

"Good morning, Mr. Nilsen," Rachel said, her voice steady and strong and with just the slightest hint of Diana's British accent.

She stepped into the room.

Twenty-three

Support Staff

The cab swung off the highway with a jerk and caused Diana's tired eyes to flick open. She hadn't slept in more than twenty-four hours, and after just ten minutes in the back of the warm, steamed-up taxi, she felt woozy and ready to sleep.

"Could you turn the heat down, please?" she leaned forward and called through the glass to the driver.

He nodded wordlessly and fiddled with a dial on his dashboard. Meanwhile, Diana sat back against the soft leather seat and looked toward the window. Through the foggy glass and the raindrops splattering on the windowpane, she could just about make out the Manhattan skyline in the distance. She blinked her eyes and willed herself to keep awake. She couldn't fall asleep now. In just a short while she'd be at the hospital in New Jersey, and it was better not to sleep at all than to wake up groggy after a few stolen minutes of sleep.

Diana thought she would fall asleep on the seven-hour plane ride back to New York. But it hadn't worked out that way. She was too preoccupied with everything she'd left behind in London and all that lay ahead of her at home. Thoughts about how Rachel was doing with Lamont Nilsen ran through her mind again and again, and each time guilt would ripple through her. Had she done the right thing? Diana asked herself. Would Rachel really hold her own as Diana hoped she would? But then, no sooner had these questions shot through her mind than Diana would remember why she'd left and her thoughts would return to where she was going and what she must do. The phone conversation she'd had with Peter played over and over in her head, and her chest would then clutch with worry and urgency and sadness.

After Rachel had left Diana's hotel room the night before, Diana was so exhausted she'd wanted to turn straight in. But then she remembered she must call Peter and give him the heads-up about what was going on with Veronica Nilsen and her father's arrival the next morning. Rachel and Diana had gone against university protocols, and Diana knew she needed to execute some damage limitation—and fast. Telling the department chair the whole story was the first important step. If Peter was on their side, things might not have to turn out so badly.

Peter was a true friend, of course. When Diana got through to him at his father's place in Oregon, where he'd gone for Thanksgiving, she quickly related all the details, and his first response was, "It sounds like you acted in Veronica's best interests. I'm proud of the two of you." He then paused and added in an apologetic tone, "I will have to tell Dean Washington, though. You know that, don't you, Diana?"

"Of course," Diana replied.

"But I will make sure the dean knows what a great job you did with Veronica, and how much better she's doing, thanks to the care and support you two gave her."

"Thank you, Peter." She sighed.

She knew Peter would argue a good case for Diana and Rachel. But there were no guarantees he could save their jobs. Frances Washington was a fabulous new dean who'd breathed life and enthusiasm into Manhattan U's School of Humanities. She was also a stern woman, however, who was a stickler for the rules and proper practice. She was fair, but she was tough too. Diana and Rachel would be in for a fight.

Peter and Diana had talked some more about Veronica and her father and how to handle the situation. They both agreed to talk again the next day after the meeting with Lamont Nilsen. But as they were about to ring off, Peter cleared his throat and said in an apprehensive whisper, "Diana, before you go, there's something I think you should know."

"What's that?" Diana had replied with a yawn, as she eyed the plump pillows on her hotel bed.

"It's about Mikey."

Diana stiffened at the sound of Mikey's name. "What about Mikey?" she snapped.

"I knew . . . I-I mean, I sort of knew you two were, well, close," Peter stammered. He was clearly embarrassed to mention something that Diana had never talked about and guarded fiercely from everyone, including him. "His daughter's sick."

Diana's heart thudded to a halt. "Sick? What do you mean, sick?"

"She had a very bad asthma attack on Wednesday and was taken to the hospital. Mikey was contacted at work," Peter explained. "I don't know much more than that. I haven't been able to get hold of Mikey since." He paused and then added, "All I know is that she had an attack like this last year and it was serious, very serious. She was in ICU for three days."

Diana sat on the edge of her bed, very still, her face expressionless. Inside, however, she felt as if she were imploding, disintegrating, breaking apart. She couldn't breathe, her chest ached and wrenched, and her eyes pricked with hot, painful tears. She'd never known Mikey's daughter had asthma—bad asthma that had put her in intensive care last year. What kind of woman was she? she wondered as the tears began to slide silently down her cheeks. What kind of woman had an intimate affair with a man like Mikey and didn't even know his daughter had asthma? That she'd been hospitalized only last year?

"Diana? Diana?" Peter called down the line when Diana remained silent.

Finally, she found her voice. "Peter," she said in a shaky whisper, "I want to come home. I need to come home. I need to see Mikey." The words were out of her mouth before she'd thought any of them through.

And before she could take them back, Peter replied very simply,

"Of course." He then said he would get on the next flight to London and take her place for the rest of the Literary London program.

Sitting in the cab—which was currently winding its way through the busy streets of Jersey City—Diana thought about what Peter had done for her and smiled. Peter had been such a great colleague all these years, and now he'd cut short his Thanksgiving break and flown to London just for her. He was a true friend, indeed. Her gratitude was tinged with a little guilt, however, because she knew she'd never been such a true friend in return. Although they'd always had a fun cama- raderie in the department, she'd never let Peter get too close. She was happy to gossip about colleagues or discuss new books or complain about upcoming committee meetings, but she'd never confided in him about the more intimate details of her life. Moreover, she'd never asked about his. She knew he'd been in a relationship with a woman that ended a few years ago, but she had no idea why or what he'd felt about it. She also knew that he wrote a little fiction on the side, but she'd never really asked him about it or offered to read his work.

Diana frowned to herself, but was snapped from these thoughts as the taxi did a final weave and then ground to a shuddering halt.

"This is it," the driver barked out without turning his head.

Diana looked out the window at the building towering above them and then pushed the fare through the gap in the glass. After getting out of the cab, she pulled her luggage from the trunk and moved toward the hospital's main entrance. CHILDREN'S HOSPITAL OF HUD- SON COUNTY, read a sign above the sliding doors, and a small chill traversed Diana's spine as she passed beneath it. The one thing she hadn't thought about on the flight over, the one thing she wouldn't allow herself to think about, was the possibility that something really bad had happened to Mikey's little girl. If Mikey lost Trixie, it would kill him. Diana knew that for certain, and therefore she couldn't bear to think about such an awful outcome.

"She'll be okay," Diana whispered under her breath, as she weaved her way through the visitors and staff milling around in the hospital's lobby toward the main desk.

After finding out where Trixie was in the hospital, Diana moved quickly to the stairs and trotted up to the second floor. She then oriented herself with a few signs and started to walk the long hallway toward room 276. As she grew closer, her heart began to thud in her chest and a stream of doubtful thoughts popped into her mind. Should she even be here? Would Mikey want to see her? She'd so quickly wanted to rush to his side, she hadn't really stopped to think about whether he wanted her there or not. Just over a month ago, Diana had kicked him unceremoniously out of her life, and they'd barely talked to each other since. She might be the last person he wanted to see at this moment.

But then Diana arrived at 276 and all her doubts fizzled away. As she approached, she glanced in through the open door, and although there were four hospital beds in the room and other parents bustling around tending to their kids, Mikey was the first person Diana saw—he was the only person she really saw. He was leaning on the windowsill just beside the farthest bed in the room. His arms were folded in front of his wide chest, and he was staring out the window at the rainy skies beyond. He was wearing a ragged woolen shirt and faded jeans. His kind, familiar face was calm, but she could see the tension in his broad neck even from where she stood by the door. Diana's gaze then darted down to the bed beside him. A little girl lay sleeping against the brilliant white pillows. Her cheeks were pale, but she looked peaceful. There were no tubes or menacing, beeping monitors. It looked like she'd made it through. Diana let out a small, relieved sigh.

When Diana finally looked back up at Mikey, his gaze had turned from the rain-soaked window and was now upon her. At first, he looked shocked and disbelieving, but then as he took her in, a little flicker of what looked like relief darted across his face. Meanwhile, Diana stood frozen. As she studied Mikey from the other side of the room, everything suddenly became clear, and it momentarily paralyzed her. Seeing him like this, in the flesh and beside his young daughter, Diana realized not only how much she'd missed this caring, beautiful

man, but she also realized what a cowardly and snobbish fool she'd
been in giving up on him—giving up on them. It was all so obvious
now. The only reason Diana hadn't wanted their relationship to go on
was because she was ashamed. She was scared of what people might
say when they found out that she, a tenured professor, was dating one
of the department's support staff, just a *lowly* computer tech.

Without even realizing it, Diana had internalized the snobberies
that had always treated her so badly throughout her own life. The
very same snobberies that made her feel alienated and alone when
she was the poor girl at her rich boarding school; that made her feel
ungenerous and penny-pinching when she couldn't afford to "chip in"
for a bottle of champagne at her college graduation party at Oxford;
and that made her feel sad and empty when she stood familyless
at her own wedding amongst Graham's vast and chattering New England clan. Of all people, Diana should have known not to have fallen
prey to these snobberies. But she'd somehow done it anyway.

Still staring over at Mikey, Diana watched as he pushed himself
away from the windowsill. He began to take a step in her direction,
and she finally began to move too. Before she took another breath,
she was in his arms and he was pulling her into a fierce and inescap-
able hug. The familiar smell of Irish Spring soap encased her.

"I'm sorry." She gasped into his warm chest.

"Thank you," he said at exactly the same moment. "Thank you for
coming."

After what felt like hours, their embrace finally broke off, and
although Diana had tears in her eyes, she glanced quickly over at
Trixie's bed.

"How is she?" she asked in a soft voice.

"Better," Mikey responded. "Much, much better."

Diana's eyes were still on the little girl. "She's beautiful."

She then felt Mikey's large hand on her cheek, as he gently turned
her to face him once again.

Before he could say anything, however, she looked up through her
teary eyes and said simply, "I love you, Mikey."

Twenty-four

Summons from the Dean

"Mr. Nilsen has decided not to make an official complaint, as you both know," Dean Washington said, as she eyed Diana and Rachel from across her large mahogany desk.

Behind her sat rows upon rows of books, as well as small paintings and an array of knickknacks propped up here and there on the bookshelves. Rachel was in a state of panic. Nonetheless, she couldn't stop her eyes from drifting from the dean over to these intriguing artifacts, which looked like they'd been brought back from all kinds of interesting and far-flung places. There was a doll made of straw and copper wires, a tiny Ganesh that looked a little like the one in Rachel's own office, a small bust of Martin Luther King Jr., a watercolor of a sun-parched valley. . . .

"Rachel?"

The dean's voice startled Rachel, and her gaze instantly snapped away from the bookshelves. Frances Washington was glaring at Rachel, and under her high and deep brown forehead, the dean's hazel eyes were narrowed into two stern slits. Rachel blushed as she realized her wandering gaze had been spotted and disapproved of.

"It seems you did a good job of placating Veronica's father," the dean went on as she leaned forward, rested her elbows on the desk, and eased her disciplining glare a little.

"Well, I—" Rachel began, her cheeks now burning red.

But the dean clearly wasn't ready to be interrupted. "Apparently, he was pleased with the way you dealt with his daughter. The way

both of you dealt with her," she added, flicking her gaze over to
Diana.

Rachel sneaked a look at Diana herself. She sat very straight in
her chair, her eyes fixed on the dean. Her hands, though, were gripping and releasing ever so slightly in her lap, and her knuckles pulsed
white and then pink and then white again. This small sign of uncharacteristic nerves prompted a fresh wave of panic in Rachel. *Diana
couldn't be nervous,* she thought. It was Diana's job to be cool and
composed. She had to hold it together; otherwise Rachel would completely lose it.

"However," Dean Washington was saying, "I can*not* overlook the
fact that the two of you went against study-abroad and university protocols. 'In the event of hospitalization,'" she read from a paper in front
of her, "'next of kin must be contacted.'" The dean paused and shook
her head. "And no, calling Veronica's nineteen-year-old sister does
not constitute contacting next of kin, as I am sure you are aware."

Rachel's stomach churned and wrenched. She thought she'd never
feel more anxious and scared than when she'd entered that room in
London last week to talk to Lamont Nilsen. But this meeting with
Dean Washington was proving just as terrifying—perhaps even more
so. After all, it was the dean who had the most power. Lamont Nilsen
could threaten to get Rachel fired—which he did at the beginning
of their exchange in London—but it was Frances Washington who
could actually do it.

In the end, confronting Veronica's father hadn't been so bad. He'd
yelled a few times; he'd pointed his large, stubby finger very close to
her face; his bodyguards had stood like terrifying steel statues on either side of him. Yet, despite all this, Rachel had managed to stay calm
and resolute. She explained in a cool, slow tone everything that had
happened. She told him that Veronica had just had her heart broken
(she was careful not to say by whom). She told him how his daughter
was terrified of going back to rehab. And she told him everything that
had happened since: Veronica's full participation in the program, the
friends she'd made, her sessions with Dr. Goldstein, and the Literary

London assignment Veronica had been working so hard on. This last detail finally broke Lamont Nilsen's angry tempest.

"She's writing a paper?" he'd barked out, his tone incredulous.

Rachel nodded. "Yes. She showed my colleague a draft a couple of days ago. It's about the history of London's theater district."

Mr. Nilsen snorted. "I don't believe you. My Ronnie doesn't write papers." He sneered. "Rebecca is the academic one. In fact, Rebecca probably wrote it for her. She's done that in the past."

Rachel raised her chin and replied, "I can assure you, Mr. Nilsen, the paper is all Veronica's own work, and Professor Monroe told me it's shaping up wonderfully. Veronica visited the Theatre Department at the Victoria and Albert Museum to do research. She interviewed a very helpful curator there and I've heard she is planning to visit two theaters in the West End over the weekend."

Lamont Nilsen studied Rachel silently for a few seconds. He wanted to be skeptical, but Rachel's matter-of-fact, tell-it-like-it-is tone was disarming him, it was clear.

"So you're telling me my daughter is writing a decent paper?" he finally said, his voice still booming but now softened a little around the edges.

"I am, Mr. Nilsen." Rachel nodded.

From there on, it was an easy ride. It seemed that as fiery, bossy, and bullheaded as Mr. Nilsen was, he was also a father with old-fashioned concerns about his daughters. Even though he could give them pretty much the world, he could pay for them to enter any career or follow whichever dream they wanted, he still wanted them do well at school. At one point, he even told Rachel that he'd dropped out of college and had always regretted it. It was the last thing he wanted Veronica to do.

"What you did sets a bad precedent. A very bad precedent."

The dean's words brought Rachel back to the present with a start.

"Study-abroad programs rely on trustworthy faculty who will follow protocols—to the letter," Dean Washington went on, tapping the desk with her long, elegant fingers. "These protocols are for the students' safety. We cannot take our students overseas if we cannot guarantee this safety." She glared hard at Rachel and Diana once again. "Don't you agree?"

Rachel couldn't hold back any longer. Panic was bubbling and frothing in her chest, and she couldn't help but blurt out, "We're very sorry. Really sorry." She then shook her head. "No, no, I should say *I'm* really sorry. Dean Washington," she went on, trying to calm her shaky voice, "this is my fault and my fault only. I was the one who made the decision not to call Mr. Nilsen. I persuaded . . . no, I *badgered* Diana into agreeing with me. I really thought it was in Veronica's best interests, which I still believe it was, but I realize I made a big mistake going against protocols. I'll accept it if you must fire me." Rachel's voice trembled again as she said these words. "But please don't fire Diana."

"I—" the dean began.

But now it was Diana's turn to speak. She straightened herself even higher in her seat. "It was a joint decision, Dean Washington," she said, her tone cool as ice. "We made the decision together. If you fire Rachel, you must fire me too."

Rachel's head snapped around and she stared at Diana. She couldn't believe what she'd just heard. Was Diana really putting her job on the line for her? Her tenured position at Manhattan U? Being a professor here was Diana's life; it was everything she was meant to be. The students loved her. The department loved her. No doubt one day Diana would sit where Frances Washington was sitting now. She was most definitely dean material. Diana couldn't jeopardize all that for Rachel.

"No, no," Rachel almost shouted, turning back to look at the dean. "No, it really was my idea. I—"

Dean Washington held up her hands and closed her eyes. Rachel's frantic pleas were brought to an immediate halt.

"I don't care who made the decision initially," she said in a quiet tone, opening her eyes again. "Neither of you followed protocol and that's that."

Rachel sat forward and was about to interject, but the dean held up her palms again.

"I am not planning to fire anyone over this." She looked from Rachel to Diana and back again. "Peter made a good case on your behalf and assured me nothing like this would *ever* happen again."

As the dean sat back in her chair, Rachel could feel relief flooding through every pore and vein in her body. She wasn't going to lose her job, and nor was Diana. Thank God.

"However," the dean added, "I am giving you both a verbal warning that will go in your files. Also, I do not want either of you leading a study-abroad program again. At least, not for the foreseeable future."

Rachel and Diana nodded in silence like scolded children. Meanwhile, the dean's face broke into an unexpected smile, and her eyes twinkled. Rachel and Diana, seeing the dean's altered countenance, exchanged confused glances.

"I have to say, though"—Frances laughed and gave a wink—"great job with Veronica."

A little while later, Diana sat at her own desk. Rachel was lolling in the chair opposite.

"Do you think she didn't fire us because we saved the infamous Lamont Nilsen donation?" Rachel was asking, as she idly pulled at some cotton stuck to her sweater.

"We were the ones who put his donation in jeopardy in the first place, don't forget." Diana gave her eyebrows a playful waggle.

Rachel laughed and replied, "I suppose you're right."

They sat in a comfortable silence for a few seconds. Diana looked around at her office and couldn't help smiling. She was enormously relieved that they had gotten off with just a warning, even if she did hate the thought of a blemish on her otherwise immaculate record. Looking at her bookshelves, the cozy reading nook in the corner of the room, the big sash windows overlooking Broadway, Diana was glad not to be losing it all. But she would have done it for Rachel. There was no way she would have let her young colleague take the rap by herself.

"I don't think I want to go on another study-abroad program ever again." Rachel chuckled, breaking the silence. "The dean did me a favor."

Diana gave a small laugh. "Me too," she agreed.

The Literary London trip had been a roller-coaster ride, and a trip Diana never wanted to repeat. But she'd come out relatively unscathed. Indeed, the roller coaster had dumped her out a whole lot better off. For one, Diana now had a friend. Rachel was no longer Diana's colleague. She certainly was no longer an enemy. She was now a much-needed friend whom Diana had spent a surprising amount of time with since their return from London. Furthermore, the trip had allowed Diana to reconnect with her parents. No longer would she shun them or keep them in the dark about her life, she'd vowed to herself. And only this morning Diana had booked them tickets to come visit at Christmas. London had allowed Diana to get rid of Graham—for good this time. And Mikey? Well, she still had some bridges to fix and many apologies to make. But he was in her life again, and every time she thought about that, warmth would tingle through her belly up to her throat. This glow completely displaced the clutching feeling that she'd carried in her chest for way too long.

The trip had been good for Rachel too, Diana could tell. Since she'd returned to the States a week ago, Diana noticed that something had changed in the way Rachel carried herself. She'd been nervous this morning before their meeting with the dean, but on the whole she radiated a new confidence and assurance. She seemed happy too—much happier than before they left for England. Of course, her perky face and cheery countenance also had something to do with Peter, and as Diana thought of the two of them, she couldn't resist a little teasing.

"I'm not so sure you wouldn't want to go on another study-abroad program." Diana grinned over the desk at Rachel. "A little bird told me you had quite a lot of fun during those last days in London with a certain chair of our department."

Rachel was used to Diana's teasing by now, but her cheeks still colored a little. "I think you and your little birdie friends need to keep your beaks out of it," she retorted with a half smile.

Neither Rachel nor Peter was giving much away. But Diana knew—she just knew—that something was kindling between them. Over the last week, in separate conversations, she'd heard how the two of them had taken a "wonderful" trip to Kew Gardens, and how they'd watched the sun set behind Big Ben, and how they'd found a tiny theater in Shepherd's Bush and saw a fantastic new play. Whenever one of them would talk about the other, their eyes would twinkle and their cheeks would color, just as Rachel's were doing now.

Even though Diana enjoyed the light teasing, she didn't push it further. She knew all too well about wanting to guard something that felt so delicate and hopeful. She wasn't hiding Mikey anymore, but she was protecting what they had, just as Rachel and Peter were clearly doing. New relationships and refound relationships were so fragile, Diana realized. Like a tiny bluebird's egg or an old porcelain vase that had been broken and then painstakingly repaired, these relationships had to be handled with the softest of gloves and the utmost care.

"There's still one thing we have to do," Rachel was now saying, purposely changing the subject.

"What's that?" Diana asked.

Rachel pushed herself up from her seat and moved around the desk. Diana watched her, confused.

"What are you up to?" she asked, spotting the mischievous smile inching across Rachel's face.

"Can I just borrow your computer?" Rachel said, ignoring Diana's question and nodding toward Diana's laptop.

Diana pushed the machine toward Rachel, who was now kneeling on the floor beside her. With a few keystrokes and prods at the mouse, Rachel brought up a site called Rate-My-Professor.com.

Diana leaned in, peered at the screen, and asked, "What *is* this?"

Rachel's eyes snapped up to look at Diana. "You've never seen this?" She was clearly surprised.

Diana shook her head.

"My, oh, my." Rachel laughed. "You're in for a treat." She then pointed at the screen and said, "You really need to look yourself up on here."

"They write about me on this?" Diana asked, appalled.

Rachel laughed again. "Your students love you. Seriously. You get the highest ratings. You even got awarded a chili pepper," she added with a wink.

"What does a chili pepper mean?"

"It means the students think you're hot."

Diana was baffled. "As in, my teaching's hot?"

"No." Rachel giggled and nudged Diana with her elbow. "As in, you're a hot chick!"

"Oh," Diana said, a rare blush rising on her cheeks. "They think I'm hot? My word. Does it say who wrote the reviews?"

"Not usually. Most of the kids post anonymously," Rachel responded. She then waved her hand and said, "But, we're not here to talk about your reviews, Professor Monroe. . . ." She trailed off as she typed "Carson McEvoy" into the Web site's search box.

"What are you doing?" Diana demanded, leaning in even closer to get a better look.

"I think we need to add a few *anonymous* reviews of our own," Rachel whispered, as she gave a chuckle. "We'll work on Carson first. Then I think Graham's page deserves a visit." She looked up at Diana and grinned a Machiavellian grin. "For some reason, the phrases 'small penis,' 'bad breath,' and 'unethical relations with students' keep popping into my head."

"You wouldn't!" Diana said, a similar grin beginning to grow on her own face. She then shook her head. "But isn't Carson being punished enough? I mean, Manhattan U sent him back to Harvard with his tail between his legs, and now Harvard is conducting its own investigation into his rumored antics with students there."

Rachel looked up at Diana, her brow knitted. "I think a little more punishment is *just* what he deserves."

Diana thought for a second and grinned. "You know what, Rachel? I think you're right," she whispered.

She then reached across the desk, took her laptop from Rachel, and began to type.

The MLA Annual Convention

The windowless conference suite on the fourth floor of Manhattan's Sheraton was jammed. It was hot too, and sticky. The ice, snow, and freezing temperatures outside had prompted the hotel to crank up the heating system, and now this heat, combined with the ice and slush on everyone's shoulders, bags, and shoes, was creating hazy swirls of steam that rose up around the room. In this oddly tropical climate, conferencegoers chattered, fidgeted, and waved to old friends they hadn't seen since last year's convention. Some people sat alone, checking their watches, waiting for the session to start. Others flipped through the convention catalog to see which session they would attend next.

Rachel sat at the front of the room on the long table set out for the session's speakers. She sipped her bottle of water with one hand and fiddled with the paper she was about to present with the other. It had been a couple of years since she'd spoken at this convention, and she felt a mix of excitement, nerves, and anticipation. The Modern Language Association's annual convention was a big deal—it was the biggest deal of the year, in fact, if you were a professor of literature or languages. Every year, just after Christmas, the MLA would roll into some big city or other and lure nearly ten thousand professors and grad students from across the country to come hear a myriad of panels, schmooze with their peers, and generally have a good time.

The only people who didn't have a good time at the MLA were those grad students applying for academic jobs. Although job hiring went on all year round, many of the first interviews were done at the convention. The unfortunate applicants had to spend the whole three days of the convention dressed in uncomfortable suits, smiling politely at everyone, and underneath fretting about whether they'd said and done the right things in the interviews they'd just attended. Rachel scanned the room and spotted a few young and anxious faces of those whom she suspected were on the circuit this year. Thank God, she thought, she wasn't among them. If she'd lost her job at Manhattan U she might have been.

"Testing, testing."

Rachel's eyes jumped from the bustling audience over to Diana, who was standing at the nearby lectern speaking into the microphone and tapping its small, foamy head. Rachel still couldn't quite believe that she was sitting here only a few feet from Diana, the two of them on the same MLA panel. Just a few months ago, if someone had told her this would happen, she'd have laughed them out of town. Rachel and Diana giving papers in the same session? Never. But here they were, and not only were they on the same panel, but it was also a panel the two of them had devised and organized together. It had been hastily done, of course. Usually MLA sessions were arranged nearly a year in advance. But a contact of Diana's had said a space had opened up in the convention program, and the next day Diana knocked on Rachel's door and suggested they put together a session. Even though they were now friends—really good friends, in fact—the suggestion had still surprised Rachel. After all, not so long ago Diana didn't even want to touch the books that Rachel wrote about and taught in her classes. Diana certainly would never have entertained the idea that they had enough scholarly interests in common to run an MLA panel together.

Rachel blinked as she realized she was staring over at Diana.
Diana had noticed too.

She turned toward Rachel, smiled, and mouthed the words, *Are
you ready?*

Rachel smiled back and nodded. Diana then looked at the other
two women on their panel, who sat on either side of Rachel at the
long white table.

"Ready?" she asked them.

They both nodded, and so Diana twirled slowly back toward the
lectern, leaned in toward the microphone, and began.

"Good morning, everybody, and welcome." Diana's concise yet
soft tone had the commanding power of a sergeant major's shout, and
the room quieted instantly.

"Just so you know, you're in the correct room," she went on.
"This is session four forty-eight, entitled, 'A Confession of Her Own:
Women Writing In(to) History.'" Diana then paused and scanned the
room. Nobody moved or spoke a word. "Good," she said with a breezy
chuckle. "It seems we are all in the right place."

Rachel looked from Diana back out at the audience. Even though
there were many people in front of them, she had a pretty clear view
of Diana's parents. They sat in the fifth or sixth row, right beside
Mikey. John and Ava Monroe looked minuscule next to Mikey's tall,
wide frame. Also, John's stiff suit and Ava's immaculate dress were in
stark contrast to Mikey's loose and faded Syracuse sweatshirt. Yet, at
the same time, all three were peas in a pod. Each one of them stared
with wide and sparkling eyes up at Diana; all of them were beaming.
Rachel couldn't help smiling herself at the sight of their pride and
their smiles.

"In *A Room of One's Own*, Virginia Woolf's message is simple,"
Diana was now saying, launching into her introductory comments.
"'A woman must have money and a room of her own if she is to
write fiction.' Woolf certainly had a point—not much writing can be
done without a quiet place to hide and some dollars in your pocket.
Take it from me." Diana said this with a grin and a glance around at

the audience. There were a few soft chuckles. "But this simple yet much-needed observation of Woolf's is accompanied in her essay by a brilliant meditation on the struggles women have faced throughout history to write fiction. As Woolf says," Diana continued, holding up a copy of the book in her hands and reading from its pages, "'Fiction is not dropped like a pebble upon the ground. . . . Fiction is like a spider's web, attached ever so lightly,'" Diana looked up again, "'Fiction is something delicate, complex, and hard to achieve, in other words, and not something that can be done easily while caring for children, or searching for the next meal for a family, or working for pennies in a sweatshop. Because of these struggles faced by women throughout the ages, women's words and voices have too often been lost. As Woolf puts it, woman 'pervades poetry from cover to cover; she is all but absent from history.'"

Rachel smiled again as she listened to Diana. Since London, since seeing *A Room of One's Own* in the bookstore that day, Rachel had been thinking a lot about the essay. But, strangely enough, it had been Diana who suggested they use it to introduce their session, and it was Diana who came up with the title, "A Confession of Her Own"—a title that Rachel loved instantly. They had already decided that their panel would consider confessional novels written by women: Diana would talk about *The Bell Jar* and Rachel *The Devil Wears Prada*. But, one early December evening as they sat in Rachel's office brainstorming ideas, it was Diana who pulled out a copy of Woolf's essay and explained to Rachel how they could use it to introduce their session.

"Today, I and my four colleagues will be considering confessional novels by women," Diana was now explaining. "We use the term 'confessional novel' in a loose way to describe novels that are based heavily on the author's own life." She waved toward the women next to her, including Rachel. "Our panel will discuss the cultural and literary importance of these fictionalized confessions. Furthermore, we are going to explore the vital role such novels have played in writing women and women's voices into history." Diana looked straight out at the audience and added with a wink, "I think Ms. Woolf might have enjoyed being with us today to hear about some women writers who did manage to find a room of their own, and who managed to write much-needed confessions of their own."

There were some more soft chuckles, and after they died down Diana introduced the members of the panel. It had already been decided that Rachel would go first, and so, when Diana was finished, Rachel pushed herself back in her chair and moved toward the lectern. Once there, she sorted out her papers and adjusted the microphone. Her hands, she noticed, were trembling just a little. She then looked up and scanned the audience. At exactly that moment, Peter's head popped in through the room's double doors. He spotted her at the lectern and a big smile flashed across his long, handsome face. He'd been conducting interviews all morning and had been scared he might miss her paper. But he'd made it. She beamed back at him, and as she did she noticed that one of his hands was bent behind his back, and although he was trying to hide it, she spotted the tip of a single dark red rose. The sight of Peter, the sight of the rose she knew was for her, made her instantly calm. It also made her sizzle with happiness.

"Thank you all for coming," were her first words into the microphone, and as she pulled her eyes from Peter and over toward her esteemed colleague and new friend, she added, "And thank you, Diana."

Then, with a strong and steady voice, even steadier hands, and a contented glow in her chest, Rachel began her paper.

Photo by Phil Treble

Joanne Rendell was born and raised in the United Kingdom. She has a PhD in literature and is married to a professor at New York University. She currently lives in faculty housing in New York City with her family. Visit her Web site at www.joannerendell.com.

CROSSING
WASHINGTON
SQUARE

Joanne Rendell

This Conversation Guide is intended to enrich the
individual reading experience, as well as encourage us
to explore these topics together—because books,
and life, are meant for sharing.

A CONVERSATION
WITH JOANNE RENDELL

Q. *You have a PhD in English literature. How did this help with writing* Crossing Washington Square?

A. My own academic experiences are everywhere in this book. Like Diana, I once taught Sylvia Plath to undergraduates. Like Rachel, I sometimes struggled to ignite a discussion in a classroom full of tired students! I've also seen firsthand how vicious, snobbish, and competitive academics can be with each other. Yet, at the same time, I have seen what a fascinating and important world academia really is.

While in grad school, I also received a wonderful grounding in literary theory, which really shaped this novel. I know a lot of people come out of literature programs complaining about too much theory and not enough reading of the books themselves. But I really valued the theoretical and philosophical side of my studies. I enjoyed asking questions about how we look at books and why and how politics and culture shape what we read and the books that are written. I particularly loved exploring the debates about "high culture" and "popular culture"—in other words, whether it is more important to study Shakespeare or whether Stephen King and Nora Roberts are worthy of study too.

Q. This "high culture" and "popular culture" debate is very important in the novel. Rachel is a scholar of popular fiction, while Diana is a rigorous Sylvia Plath scholar who thinks that popular fiction is an easy ride for students. Why did you write about this?

A. As I said, I've always found this debate fascinating. I wanted to bring the debate alive in fiction, and in a way that didn't denigrate either side. I agree with Diana that the study of the classics and "high" literature is vital and should not be pushed aside. But I also believe, like Rachel does, that studying popular fiction is important.

Popular fiction—including thrillers, romance, or women's fiction like my own—is often considered fluff, easy reading, or simple escapism. To dismiss it as such, however, is too simplistic, as well as elitist. It overlooks what is positive, fascinating, and important about popular writing. As Rachel says in the book, quoting her mentor, "Popular culture influences who we are, what we think, and what's going to happen in our world and in our lives." How could we *not* deem it important to study what is popular?

I also think popular fiction can be a site of great community. People come together in book groups to talk about such books. Even if readers don't belong to book groups, they often find community within the books themselves. I'm sure there are hundreds, if not thousands of women out there who found solace and companionship in Cannie, Jennifer Weiner's plus-size heroine of *Good in Bed*, for example. Although a reader might find community in the works of Hemingway, Salman Rushdie, or even Shakespeare, they probably wouldn't find this particular kind of companionship.

Q. Do you have a favorite character, Diana or Rachel?

A. That's a tough one! My knee-jerk response is to say Rachel because, out of the two, I identify most with her. As a grad student,

I was always caught in a conundrum. By day I would be reading classical literature and poetry, but at night I loved to read popular fiction. *Bridget Jones's Diary*, I have to say, is one of my all-time favorite books! Rachel is like this too. She's also flawed and emotional, yet good and honest and brave. I like that about her.

Every time I revisit the book, however, I like Diana more too. She has such strength and poise, and even though she is pretty darn mean to Rachel in the early days, she sees the error of her ways and shows great dignity and bravery in the way she changes. She's also frighteningly clever and commanding with her students. She's the kind of über-professor that every academic secretly wants to be.

Q. Are the characters in the novel based on people you know?

A. Rachel and Diana are amalgams, but many of the side characters—for example, the professors in the faculty meeting scene—are based on academics I have known. I'm not going to name names, though! Carson McEvoy is a fabrication, I must admit. Never in my days have I encountered such a handsome, well-dressed, sports-car-driving, and flirtatious professor. Most male academics fit the common stereotype—corduroy jackets, leather elbow patches, smudged spectacles, battered briefcases. As students, we probably all had a crush on some professor or other. But looking back, they were probably no Carson McEvoy. We overlooked their bad dress or questionable looks because we loved their brains!

Q. Crossing Washington Square *makes it seem like university departments are hotbeds for scandal, romance, and gossip. Is this really true?*

A. Professors may look innocent and a little nerdy on the out-side, but I assure you there are all kinds of things going on be-hind closed doors! The university probably isn't much different from other workplaces. Where there are people working side by side, day in, day out, there will always be gossip, romance, and scandal.

Q. *Did any other novels about university life influence you in writing this book?*

A. I always loved the humor of David Lodge's *Changing Places* and Kingsley Amis's *Lucky Jim*. I've also read and enjoyed Michael Chabon's *Wonder Boys*, Richard Russo's *The Straight Man*, Zadie Smith's *On Beauty*, and Francine Prose's *Blue Angel*. But what I noticed about such campus fiction was the lack of female pro-fessors in leading roles. Even Francine Prose's and Zadie Smith's novels focus on male professors. Furthermore, most of these male professors are disillusioned drunks who quite often sleep with their students! I wanted to write a novel with female professors taking the lead, and I wanted these women to be strong and smart and interesting—instead of drunk, disillusioned, and preoccupied with questionable sexual liaisons!

Q. *You chose to leave academia to pursue fiction writing. Did writing this book make you miss the university world?*

A. Not at all! Academia is a tough world these days. There are few jobs and a lot of competition. Plus, if you have young kids like I do, it is hard to juggle teaching, writing, publishing, and committee meetings with the day-to-day demands of being a par-ent. I admire those people who manage to do it. However, my husband is a professor, and together we are faculty in residence in one of NYU's residence halls. This means I still get to keep my toe in the academic waters. I run book groups and events for students in our dorm, and I'm always the first reader of my husband's work.

QUESTIONS FOR DISCUSSION

1. Rachel and Diana are opposites in many ways—one led by the heart, the other by the mind. Yet they are both sympathetic characters with their own strengths. Which character did you relate to more, and why?

2. Which character do you think changes the most during the course of the book?

3. Discuss the epigraph from *Sense and Sensibility*. How are Rachel and Diana like Marianne and Elinor Dashwood in Jane Austen's novel?

4. How does Diana's past shape the kind of woman she has become at the start of the novel?

5. Were you satisfied at the end of the novel with the men Rachel and Diana end up with?

6. Rachel talks about the heroines of romance fiction as feisty and loved by good men because of their strength and independence. Are these the kind of heroines you like to read about or see in movies?

7. Where do you see Rachel and Diana in ten years' time?

8. Women can have complicated work relationships. Why do you think this is so? Have you ever had an acrimonious relationship with a woman at work?

9. Near the end of the novel, Rachel realizes, "For Diana to carve out a room of her own in this man's world of academe, she had built walls around herself—very lofty and sturdy walls." Do you think some women have to "build walls" in order to get ahead in their careers?

10. Do you think Diana is right at the start of the novel: Should popular fiction and modern films like *Clueless* be barred from entering the "doors of learning"? Do you think it constitutes an easy ride for students at a university?

11. And what about snobbery concerning popular fiction? Have you ever experienced it? Have you ever been made fun of for the books you like to read?

12. What did you think of the way Rachel dealt with the Nilsen sister after her drunken episode in London? How might you have dealt with it differently?

13. Did the book make you wonder about the private lives of teachers and professors you might have been taught by?

14. Would you like to be a professor of English? If so, what would you like to study and teach?